"ARE YOU QUITE DONE, THEN?"

The hiss of a whisper floated on darkness through the room and startled Fleur so very much that she stood straight up out of the chair. "Wh-what?" she croaked, her drying tears staining her voice as well as her cheeks. "Who?"

"I asked if you were quite done with crying?"

"Y-yes. Yes I am."

"Good. Once the time of tears passes, the time for action cannot be far off."

"Wh-what? What do you say?" Fleur swiped at her eyes once again, clearing the last of the tears away, and peered into the shadows, turning about in a full circle in search of the owner of the whisper.

"Utterly devoid of brains, Cordelia Wright. Brays like a donkey, looks like a mule and thinks like an ass."

"Oh! How—how dare you?"

"I always dare to speak the truth," replied the whisperer. "Always. Well, most always."

The tiniest of smiles tugged at the corners of Fleur's mouth. "Most always?"

"Sometimes I am faint of heart, but not often."

"Who are you?" Fleur queried, peering about her again. "Where are you? I cannot tell. Your whispering echoes about so and I cannot see you in the shadows."

"Best that you should not see me," answered the whisperer.

THE MYSTERY KISS

Judith A. Lansdowne

ZEBRA BOOKS
Kensington Publishing Corp.
http://www.zebrabooks.com

In memory of Melinda Helfer, who could make me smile no matter what. Thoughts of you linger in my heart and soul. For this I am eternally grateful.

ZEBRA BOOKS are published by

Kensington Publishing Corp.
850 Third Avenue
New York, NY 10022

All Kensington Titles, Imprints, and Distributed Lines are available at special quantity discounts for bulk purchases for sales promotions, premiums, fund-raising, educational, or institutional use.

Special book excerpts or customized printings can also be created to fit specific needs. For details, write or phone the office of the Kensington special sales manager: Kensington Publishing Corp., 850 Third Avenue, New York, NY 10022, attn: Special Sales Department, Phone: 1-800-221-2647.

Zebra and the Z logo Reg. U.S. Pat. & TM Off.

First Printing: April, 2001
10 9 8 7 6 5 4 3 2 1

Printed in the United States of America

One

Fleur awoke screaming, her fists clenched, her eyes stinging with angry, terrified tears. She peered through the darkness of her bedchamber, searching first one way, then the other, fully expecting him to be there. But he was not. No one was there. Nothing. Darkness, silence, the fading glow of coals on the grate, nothing more. She took a deep, shuddering breath. A nightmare. It had been nothing but a nightmare. Marston had not come raging into her room with his demented eyes ablaze, bellowing his obscenities. The dreaded malacca cane had not sliced through the air above her head punctuating his every threat. "You will never enter this chamber again, you devil," she hissed, clutching the counterpane to her breast. "You are dead, Marston. Dead at last."

Yet Fleur continued to shudder. Although her husband had been in his grave for more than a year, the mere thought of him still set her to quaking with rage and horror both. She raised her hand to her cheek and tentatively touched the ragged white line that lingered there. "You won't ruin this for Ally, Marston," she murmured. "I *shall* take her to London. She *will* conquer any number of gentlemen's hearts. She will marry for love as she ought and not for money, because you, you fiend, will have nothing to say about it. Nothing. Your wishes are meaningless. You are gone to Hades where you belong and good riddance to you."

A scratching sounded at Fleur's door and in a moment a

slim young figure in a long flannel nightgown with a ruffled white cap set jauntily upon her curls, entered and crossed the carpet to Fleur's bedside. She set her lamp down on the bedside table and climbed up to sit beside Fleur on the high old bed. "Are you all right, Mama? I heard you cry out."

"No, did I? Loudly enough for you to hear? I'm sorry, Ally. What a goose I am not to be able to wipe it all from my mind and get on with things as I ought. And to wake you tonight of all nights, when you most need your rest."

"I wasn't asleep. I haven't come anywhere near sleep, Mama," Althea admitted with a smile. "You will not believe it, but I have spent the last two hours pacing my bedchamber floor wondering what lies ahead for us. Mary, Dorothea, all of my friends who have had a Season, have told me all about it and yet, I find I cannot imagine what it will be like for me."

Fleur took Althea's hand into her own and gave it a reassuring squeeze. "It will be exciting and enormously entertaining and you will smile from morn till night. What lies ahead for you, my dear, is happiness. I'm certain of it. A very different sort of world is about to open up to you—a most intriguing and delightful sort of world."

"I am not so very confident that I will find it intriguing and delightful."

"Of course you will. You were born to it. You belong in London during the Season with all the other beautiful, elegant young ladies. But I should be much obliged, Ally, if you will remember not to call me mama once we arrive there."

"But you *are* my mama," protested Althea, frowning. "I cannot think why you do not wish me to call you so."

"I am merely your stepmother," Fleur replied quietly. "Your papa never allowed you to call me Mama while he lived and I see, now, that I should not have allowed it after his death. It has become a habit with you. One I hope you will break quickly."

"It is not a habit," Althea protested softly. "It is an appellation I bestow on you with great forethought and determination. I choose to call you Mama."

"Then you must choose not to do it any longer."

"But why?"

"Because I—because you—"

"Just what I thought. There's not one good reason you can think of."

"There is a reason, an excellent reason. I am your stepmother and not your mama at all."

"Bosh! As if I care about that! You are more mother to me than the lady who gave me birth. She could not bear to be bothered with me or Mal for a single moment while she lived and I do not choose to bother with her now she is dead. And Malcolm doesn't either. We will both call you Mama before the entire world. Indeed we will and there's nothing you can do about it. Why you should want either of us to pretend that you mean nothing to us—that you are nothing but our father's second wife—is beyond all understanding."

"There is a very good reason."

"What?"

"I—I—Ally, cannot you simply do as I ask? Please? I can't explain. Not just now. Besides, you will know soon enough. Once we're in London, you will learn everything. And quickly too, I think." Fleur, her fingers playing distractedly with the long, dusky brown braid that lay across her shoulder, gazed up from beneath slightly lowered lids to study her stepdaughter's glorious hazel eyes. "You are so beautiful, Ally. Do you know how beautiful you are? You'll have gentlemen swooning for you all over town."

"You say that as if I ought to look forward to having gentlemen fall down senseless before me," Althea replied, grinning. "Of all things! Just imagine for one moment, Mama, my having to step carefully over gentlemen's seemingly lifeless bodies just to get to my carriage!"

"I can imagine it," laughed Fleur. "Oh, Ally, I can, and I can see you stepping on them instead of over them, too."

* * *

Atticus Charles Howard, the Earl of Hartshire, crossed quietly to the side of the little bed and smiled down at the child nearly hidden beneath the counterpane. With unexpected grace for such a large gentleman, he sat down on the very edge of the bed, smoothed a golden curl from the boy's brow, then leaned forward and placed a whisper of a kiss where the curl had been. "I love you, Will," he said huskily.

"Papa?" queried a small voice as sleep-filled blue eyes blinked open.

"Indeed. It is only Papa come to bid you good-bye, scamp."

"I knew you would come, Papa. I told Mr. Canton so."

"And right you were," agreed Hartshire with a nod. "Do you like this Mr. Canton who has come to be your tutor?"

"Uh-huh."

"I thought you might. He seemed a rather good sort of a gentleman to me."

"He is, Papa. And he's smart."

"Is he?"

"He knows everything in the world."

"Well then, we're lucky he agreed to come, don't you think?"

"Uh-huh." The boy yawned, stretched and sat up in the bed to wrap his arms as far around his father as he could get them. "I love you, Papa."

"I love you, too, Will," Hartshire replied, hugging the child to him, the boy almost disappearing in the circle of his father's arms. "I will miss you exceedingly, scamp."

"No, you will not, Papa, because Mr. Canton and I are going to London with you."

"Yes, well, you are coming to London behind me. That's not quite the same thing. I will not see you for an entire day, I'll wager, as slow as you and Mr. Canton will travel in our lumbering old coach."

"We will just meander along like the little stream, and you will fly like the wind, you and Radical."

"Just so, like a high wind on a stormy day. People will feel our breeze as we pass them by and look to see what caused that sudden draft, but already we will be gone from their sight."

"You won't rescue Uncle Val until I get there, though, will you, Papa? Because I want to help you rescue Uncle Val."

Hartshire grinned. It was a lopsided grin that gave his generally austere face an enticing boyishness. "It's possible, Will, that Uncle Val does not require rescuing, you know. I ain't certain I've read his mama's last letter correctly. He may be fine as fancy fodder for all we know."

"But he may be abducted!" the lad replied enthusiastically, pulling back to stare up into his father's eyes. "He may be got by pirates or snatched by Twelve-String Jack and held to ransom!"

"Or he may be lounging about in some young lady's parlor, quite content with himself and drinking black tea."

"Not Uncle Val," protested Will defensively. "Uncle Val would not be caught dead drinking black tea in some lady's parlor."

"No?"

"Definitely not! Uncle Val wants to be just like you, Papa, and you hate black tea."

Yes, Hartshire thought, the odd silver flecks in his midnight blue eyes glittering eerily. But there was a time I sat in Miriam's parlor and drank the stuff as grateful for it as you please. And look what it brought me. He smiled down at Will and the boy giggled.

"What are you laughing at, Will?"

"You, Papa. You are smiling your silly smile. The one that makes you look like a gudgeon."

"A gudgeon? Me? I should like to see the day when I resemble such an ugly fish as that! I am not sleek like a trout, perhaps. But a gudgeon? Never! Enough now, rascal. Time to go back to sleep, eh?"

"Uh-huh."

"Will, give me a kiss before you do."

"Why, Papa?"

"Because the dawn has come and I leave for London. I need your kiss to keep me safe along the way."

As the sun rose higher in the sky they came through Schrofield Wood at a spanking pace, the enormous grey cutting deftly in and out among the trees, dancing along an unmarked path that existed only in the memory of rider and horse alike. Hartshire reveled in the renewed certainty that despite the enormous alterations in his life, most things in the world did never truly change. The energy and enthusiasm of the horse beneath him, the smell of the burgeoning spring, the lush foliage greening on the trees and blossoming amidst the undergrowth, all testified to an altering world that in most ways altered not. His heart swelled with the sheer joy of being alive and astride Radical on such a glorious day. He slowed the horse, took a deep breath and, in a profound bass, began to sing the first stanza of the marching song from Herbert Van Cleef's *The Innocent Isolda.*

Radical's ears pricked and swiveled nearly backward at the sound. His fine brown eyes widened with a particular devilment. And, as he and Hartshire reached the gradual slope of green between wood and road, this throwback to the warhorses of centuries gone by rose up on his haunches and pawed ardently at the air. He came down with a great thump of his hooves and began to march. He lifted his left foreleg, kicked stiffly out, brought it down. He did the same with the right and then the left again, high-stepping across the verge for all the world as though his master's song bewitched him.

Althea, standing outside the Marston traveling coach with

an arm supportively around Fleur's trembling shoulders, ceased to whisper encouraging words to her retching step-mama the instant she heard Hartshire's bass. Looking up at once to discover what sort of gentleman would be singing so loudly and cheerily among the trees and weeds so early in the day, she stared at Hartshire and Radical, spellbound. "Mama," she gasped, unable to take her eyes from horse or rider. "Mama, only look. It is the most amazing sight."

Lady Marston groaned and straightened slowly, grasping Althea's arm to steady herself. Her head ached abominably and her stomach lurched. "What?" she asked in a breathless voice. "What do you say, Ally?"

"Only look, Mama. There, coming across the verge. Surely it is Mars on the winged horse Pegasus."

"Mars?" queried Fleur, perplexed, attempting to follow Althea's gaze. "Pegasus? Oh, great heavens! Only look at the giant! I am not only dying, but having nightmares as I do! Ally, run to the coach at once," Fleur gasped, as she blinked dazedly at the man and animal who were just then coming to a halt barely ten yards from them. "Your father's pistol lies in the drawer beneath the rear facing seat. We may well have need of it."

Hartshire did not quite know what to make of the traveling coach drawn to a standstill at the side of the road. He ceased his nonsense at once, his fine bass cutting off in mid-chorus. A slight twitch of the reins caused Radical to stop his joyous march as well. "I wonder what the devil's wrong?" Hartshire murmured to the horse, stroking Radical's neck. "Wheels appear all right. Ain't tilting on a broken axle. I say there, Coachman," Hartshire called, setting Radical forward at a more dignified pace. "What the deuce happened to bring you to a halt? May I be of some assistance?"

"Mama, we do not require a pistol. He is not a highway-man. He wishes to be of some assistance."

Lady Marston simply groaned in reply and leaned unsteadily forward to cast up the remainder of her breakfast.

"Ah, not the coach then," Hartshire observed as he dismounted beside the vehicle and peered sympathetically at Fleur. "Your coach is fine, eh? One of your passengers is not."

"Aye," replied the coachman, nodding down at him. "Her ladyship be feelin' poorly, she do."

"Mal de, ah, coach," pronounced Hartshire knowingly.

"Just so. Coach bouncin' about on this thing what they calls a road has turned my lady green," the coachman agreed. "Be better, she will, when we reaches the pike. There ain't a road in all of this part of Kent fit fer a coach ta travel on. Not until ye reaches the pike, there ain't."

"That's so," nodded Hartshire. "Wouldn't ride in a coach to London for all the jewels in the crown. Ain't good in coaches. Obviously, your lady is not either."

"Ye be not thinking ta tell us ta stand and deliver, be ye?" asked the coachman, squinting suspiciously at Hartshire. "My lady ain't up ta that at all, she ain't. Likely send her inta palpitations of the heart. I mean ta say, we ain't alone, ye know. We has got outriders with us."

"You do?"

"Indeed we does."

"Invisible are they?"

"No, they ain't. They has, ah, gone on ahead."

"What a bouncer!" chuckled Hartshire. "You and these ladies are completely alone. Not only no outriders for protection," he said, leaning down and peering in through the coach window. "No one else at all with you."

"I has got a horse pistol," the coachman declared.

"Where? Under your hat? No, no, do not attempt another lie; I intend you not the least harm, Coachman. Do you not recognize a gentleman when you see one?" Hartshire queried.

"Indeed, I does," answered the coachman. "But I has

drived on these roads many a year and I has more than once met with a highwayman dressed all fine and fancy."

"Ah, yes. Jeremy Kidd. You'll not meet with Kidd again, I guarantee you. Hanged him last October at Nonetheless Cross."

Fleur groaned again. The mere thought of a hanging set her stomach to churning.

Hartshire's eyes, brimming with sympathy, flicked instantly from the coachman to the ladies. "Wretched trip, eh?" he asked, stepping toward them. "You're quite green, you know, madam. If I may be permitted to introduce myself."

"No, you m-may not," declared Fleur, lifting her chin with defiance despite her nausea.

"I may not?"

"N-no. It is not in the least p-proper," and then the poor lady clutched Althea's arm, turned dizzily away from Hartshire and attempted to vomit again, though there was nothing left to emerge.

"I don't like to be overly persistent, but I can help her," Hartshire said to the utterly embarrassed Althea.

"You can?"

"Um-hmm."

"Mama, this gentleman says he can help you."

"Tell him to g-go away," pleaded Fleur, attempting to catch her breath.

"But madam—"

"G-go away!" Fleur demanded, standing up as straight as she could manage, wiping at her lips with a lacy scrap of handkerchief. "We d-do not know you."

"No."

"What do you mean, 'no'?"

"Precisely what anyone else would mean, madam, when they say no. I am not going away. I'm Hartshire," he added, his gaze falling on Althea. "Atticus Howard, Earl of Hartshire, and you and your mama are . . . ?"

Althea stared at him, openmouthed. He was not at all what she, in her youthfulness, considered handsome. His face was ordinary; his hair dark, curling beneath his hat; his ears, prominent. But his eyes—his eyes pierced her to her very soul. She had never seen such eyes in all her life. The very power of them made her speechless.

"My dear," Hartshire drawled. "Your mama is so concerned for propriety that she will not let me help her because we are unacquainted. Since I am going to help her regardless, the very least we can do is to manage a sham of an introduction for her sake. 'I am Hartshire,' I say, and you say, 'I am pleased to make your acquaintance, my lord. I am . . .' "

"Gracious," sighed Althea as the sonorous lilt of his voice joined with the mystery of his eyes to send vibrations shuddering up her spine.

Hartshire cocked an eyebrow and a hip at one and the same time. "Gracious?"

"What? No. I do beg your pardon, I was merely—I am pleased to make your acquaintance, my lord. I am Miss Avondale and this is my mama, Lady Marston."

Fleur took the tiny handkerchief from her lips and attempted to glare at the man, but glaring only made her dizzier and she began to wobble.

Hartshire reached out with one hand and seized her elbow. "Always made me dizzy, too," he said quietly.

"Wh-what?"

"Attempting to stare someone out of countenance when I was already violently ill."

"I was n-not attempting to . . ."

"Yes, you were. Now hush like a good girl for a moment. I am correct, am I not, Miss Avondale? You don't actually have any outriders with you? Or anyone else but the coachman?" Hartshire patted at the pockets of his riding coat with one hand as he continued to hold Fleur steady with the other.

"Only John Coachman would agree to come with us," Althea replied softly. "He is fond of Mama."

"Just as I thought," Hartshire acknowledged. He discovered the handkerchief he had been searching for and gave it into Fleur's trembling hands. "Use this and throw that wretched scrap of lace away. I have never understood why ladies' handkerchiefs are purposely made to be of no use whatsoever. There is not so much as a lady's maid with you, Miss Avondale?"

Althea shook her head, setting the pretty white feathers on her blue velvet hat to fluttering.

Hartshire was patting, one-handed, at his pockets again. "Thank heaven. I knew Spencer would not send me off without it," he said enigmatically as his free hand reached the last unexplored coat pocket. "Good man, Spencer. This will do the trick." Without another word, Hartshire swept Fleur up in his arms and strode off with her in the direction of the coach.

"Put me down at—at once!" Fleur demanded, though it was not at all a loud demand, her illness making it a struggle for her to speak.

"In a moment."

"Now!"

"No."

Fleur's perfectly sturdy, though shaky, right hand balled into a fist. The fist rose quickly to the height of Hartshire's chin, then thwacked hard against his jaw.

Hartshire ceased to walk in midstride. "Son of a . . ." he muttered. Abruptly both the lady's fists were pounding at his face, his ears, his shoulders. She muttered words he could not quite catch, and pummeled him again and again.

Hartshire tightened his hold on her to keep her from falling as she assaulted him. He could not dodge the blows without dropping her and he had not the least intention of doing that. From behind him he heard Miss Avondale shout, "Mama, no! His lordship merely wishes to help you!" But it was obvious to him that the woman in his arms did not hear the girl. Whatever sounds she did hear were not emanating from Miss Avondale, or anyone else nearby. This Lady Marston had plunged into some dark, deep crevice all her own. Was she mad as well as ill? The thought occurred to him, but he shuttled it aside as perfectly insignificant at the moment.

Hartshire was so intimately familiar with *'mal de* everything that moved' that he knew perfectly well she could not keep up her attack on him for long. Content in that knowledge, he stood perfectly still and waited until Fleur groaned, ceased to pound at him and began to shrink and shudder herself into a small agonized ball of a woman, just as he had known she must. He adjusted her in his arms. Her cheeks flushed a bright pink and she squeaked as he began to walk again.

He speculated on what place she had entered in her own mind, pondered over what had caused her to struggle so. Then he thought of Celly and he realized that his merely lifting this lady into his arms might have sent her tumbling down into a very deep crevice indeed. Is that it, my dear? Are you and Celly sisters beneath the skin? And where are you now? he wondered as she huddled shaken and silent against him.

Still, nothing this gangly woman in his arms could do would actually matter to him at this precise moment, because he was determined to help her and help he would. He did note that her cheeks were passably pretty now that they were no longer stark white tinged with green, but then he dismissed her cheeks from his mind as well as her earlier protests.

Althea hurried after them, thinking to climb beforehand into the coach and assist the gentleman to get her stepmother inside. She would help Fleur to lie down as comfortably as possible on the front facing seat and then place one of the pillows beneath Fleur's head. And then she would direct John Coachman to drive on very slowly—as slowly as he possibly could. Except, the gentleman did not stop at the coach at all.

Ignoring the vehicle entirely, Hartshire strode past it and directly to his horse. "Hold, Rad," he said and stepped up into the saddle with the lady still firmly in his arms. Then he slid himself off the saddle to the rear and set Fleur on it before him, urging her to rest her reeling head against his chest. With one hand he fished a silver flask from his inside coat pocket. Then, placing both arms around her, he removed the top of the container. "Take a sip of this, madam," he said. "Do you good. You'll feel better in no time at all."

"I loathe b-brandy," Fleur replied in barely a whisper, shoving the flask aside. "B-brandy makes my head hurt more."

"Yes, I'm familiar with that particular effect, which is why this is not brandy," Hartshire said softly. "It's nothing but tea, m'dear. Cold lemon balm tea with honey."

"Tea?"

"Just so. You don't wish to go on feeling as you do?"

"N-no, but—"

"Then do as I say." He felt her tremble and shudder against him again and he softened his voice even more. "I've suffered from this same malady all my life, Lady Marston," he explained. "This particular tea always helps. Always."

Hartshire noted the hesitant manner in which the woman took the flask from him and how suspiciously she sniffed at the liquid. She fought to lift her head from his chest, but she was so dizzy and so weary that she could not manage it. And so, in the deep, rhythmic tone that always worked so well with Will when the boy was ill, Hartshire urged her not to exert herself. "Just rest, my lady," he whispered, adjusting his hold on her so that she leaned more comfortably against him. "If you take just little sips, it will go down just as easily without your sitting up straight."

"It *is* tea."

"Indeed it is. Drink a bit more. Then we will get you to a place where you can lie still for a time."

"I sh-shall simply lie down in the coach."

"It is the jolting of the coach that causes your illness."

"Yes, but we will never reach London do I force John

Coachman to stop every mile and allow me to lie motionless in some glade."

"It's no glade I have in mind, Lady Marston. Merely a—an—inn. A brief pause to allow you to recover fully, eh?"

"Which will do no good at all."

"It will."

"Once I return to the coach, I will—"

"No, you will not, because I intend to give you something to prevent any recurrence of this particular illness."

"There's something that can do that? What?"

"Drive straight up the road," Hartshire ordered the coachman, gathering Radical's reins into one strong hand. "You will come upon an—inn. The Three Legged Rooster it's called. Lady Marston and I will await you there." And before Lady Marston or Althea or even the coachman could protest, Hartshire grasped Fleur more firmly, nudged Radical with one knee and rode up the road at a spanking pace.

Fleur knew perfectly well that she ought to protest Hartshire's audacity in carrying her off in such a manner, but she was not up to doing it. Not at all. Though she did feel a bit more the thing, she realized. The movement of his horse was remarkably smooth—not nearly as discomposing as the motion of the coach had been. The breeze that fluttered around her as they rode, cooled her. And the sheer solidness of the man as he continued to hold her close, had ceased to be threatening and had become soothing instead. She had thought she would scream out when he'd swept her up so unexpectedly into his arms. His very closeness had set her teeth to rattling in her head. But now his arms about her filled her with comfort and she wondered at it.

Hartshire glanced down at the bonneted head that rested against him and smiled the most whimsical smile. He was remembering Miriam whose head had often rested, just so, against him over the years.

Though this Lady Marston is not at all as pretty as Miriam, he decided, studying for a moment the longish nose and slightly jutting chin which were all he could actually see of Fleur because the wide ruffled brim of her bonnet denied him the rest. It's merely the feel of her so close in my arms that brings Miriam back to me. Been an extraordinarily long time since these arms have held a lady. For the past four years, they've held no one but Will.

"Are you feeling better, madam?" he asked quietly.

"Yes."

"Good. A bit of a lie-down and you'll be in fine fettle."

The Three Legged Rooster proved to be a most insignificant sort of place as it came into view. At the rear of a dusty little stable yard, the edifice rose a mere two stories high. Built of stone and thatch with a plank walk surrounding it, it squatted on the land like a lethargic toad.

"Are you certain this is an inn?" Lady Marston queried with a touch of worry in her voice.

"Yes."

"B-because it does not look like an inn. It looks like a—"

"Den for thieves?"

"Possibly."

"Well, it is that, too, but—"

"A den for thieves?" Fleur sat straight up and then groaned as her head began to pound from the suddenness of the movement.

"I ought not to have said that," offered Hartshire apologetically. "I spoke in jest, madam. It is a rather inauspicious inn and nothing more. Are you all right? Here, let me help you down," he added, sliding off the rear of the horse and coming around to lift her from his saddle. "There is no one here will do you harm. I assure you of it. Ah, there is our innkeeper come to greet us himself. Harry," he called, as he set Lady Marston's feet firmly on the ground, keeping one strong arm around her because she wobbled a bit. "Harry Badencock, good morning to you!"

"Devil if it ain't! I knew it were, the very minit I seed yer shadow comin' up the road!" cried a portly man in a stained white shirt, a catskin vest and buckskin breeches as he hobbled across the dusty yard. He combed a hand through hair that existed only in his memory and smiled broadly. "Maddy, it be The Spectre, hisself, jus' like I said!" he called loudly over his shoulder. "Come out an' greet 'im, Maddy, m'love!"

"The spectre?" asked Lady Marston of no one in particular.

"Pay that not the least attention," Hartshire said in her ear—at least where he thought her ear must be beneath the bonnet. "I have been 'The Spectre' to Harry since first I grew too large for my coats. He finds it highly amusing to refer to a gentleman of my size as a mere apparition."

"Hello!" another, higher, voice called happily from the threshold of the building. "Harry, bring his lordship in and his lady, too."

"Can you walk?" Hartshire queried of Fleur as he reached out to take Harry's hand in his and give it a solid shake. "Or would it be best for me to carry you?"

"If you will allow me your arm, I shall do quite well, I think," Fleur replied.

"Good. The lemon balm is working then. Come. Maddy will certainly give you the loan of her sofa for a time—until you are feeling just the thing again. She will offer the use of a bed, but don't accept," he added very quietly. "Fleas."

"Eh? What's that ye say?" Harry Badencock called over his shoulder as he preceded them by a step or two. "What be ye whisperin' about, m'lord? Ye don't be keepin' secrets from me, do ye, m'little ghostie?"

"I cannot believe that he did not remain with you until we arrived," Althea said, settling herself more comfortably against the seatback as the traveling coach lurched forward and they took up the journey once more. "I have never seen a more rundown inn in all my life! And to simply abandon you there!"

"He did not abandon me."

"No?"

"Not precisely. He ate a meat pasty that Mrs. Badencock offered him, downed a glass of ale, tied these beads around my wrists and only then apologized for not being able to remain longer and bid me a fond farewell."

"Did he? A *fond* farewell, Mama?" Althea's eyes sparkled. "I do wish I'd been there to hear him do that. Such a voice he had. And such a manner about him. Despite the fact that he is not precisely handsome, I do think I should have liked to have him bid *me* a fond farewell."

"Althea, of all things. We do not even know the gentleman."

"But I should like to come to know him, Mama, shouldn't you? Only think how he and that fantastical horse came dancing down out of the woods just to make you well—as if some whisper on the wind had summoned him. Perhaps he's magical. He's kind. You must admit that. Kind and possibly magical in a monumental sort of a way."

Fleur, cajoled by her stepdaughter's teasing and the glint in that young lady's eyes could not help but laugh. "What you mean to say, Althea, is that he seemed a very kind monument, rather like Gray's Surgeon's Hospital."

"Mama, he was not as large as that!"

"He's bound for London, he said. If he truly is the Earl of Hartshire, I expect you will be properly introduced to him at one entertainment or another." Fleur's smile departed then and, declining to meet her stepdaughter's gaze any longer, she glanced down and fiddled with the beads Hartshire had placed around both of her wrists. "I thought he was mad to give these to me. I refused them at once, but he tied them 'round my wrists nonetheless. I cannot think how they work."

"I cannot believe he forced the ugly things on you."

"They're simply wooden beads. They should do nothing at all. And yet, the illness has passed and I don't feel it coming on again, which is precisely what he said would happen."

"We haven't traveled far as yet, Mama."

"I realize, but generally, even in so short a time, I begin to feel exceedingly warm and uncomfortable."

"Did he not explain how they work?"

"No. Yes. He said I was not to remove them until I had ceased to ride in the coach. He said they would keep me well. He said he'd learned their efficacy from a pirate."

"A pirate?" Althea sat up quite straight and stared at her stepmama in disbelief. "A pirate? That could not possibly be. A sailor, perhaps."

"No, he said quite plainly, a pirate. An Oriental pirate named Young Cow or some such. I did not quite catch the name. What an odd gentleman, Althea. What did you call him at the first? Mars come down from heaven on the back of Pegasus? And the innkeeper and his wife called him something as well. The Spectre." Fleur smiled again. "Can you imagine dubbing anyone as large as he, a mere spectre?"

Hartshire whistled joyfully as he rode through the dappled sunlight of the late afternoon. The delightfully tuneful sound caused Radical's ears to twitch, his head to nod and shake and his hooves to do a veritable jig. Together, horse and master performed the most amazing frolic across fields and through woods, leaping elegantly over hedgerows, jigging joyfully through streams. It had been four long years since either Hartshire or Radical had actually traveled all the way to London.

"I expect we ought to take to the road again for a bit, Rad," Hartshire declared at last, drawing the grey to a halt. "No telling but that a good deal of the land hereabout has changed hands of late. Farthingale has passed on, I know, and the same with Ditherton. Might well be spotted by some new groundskeeper, you and I, chased down and jailed for trespassing."

The grey snorted in disgust.

"Yes, I know that you believe every path we have ever trod belongs exclusively to us, but it ain't so. Our paths have always been carved from bits of this man's land and pieces of that man's property. Luckily the old gentlemen we imposed upon never did mind. But there is no telling if their heirs will feel likewise.

"She seemed a nice lady, did she not, Rad?" he said then, his mind wandering. "Lady Marston, I mean. She is not precisely pretty, but she's kind, I think. Yes, one can tell from just looking at her that she's kind. And she hits extremely hard when she's a mind to," he added, rubbing at his jaw. "But then, she's timid, too. I thought not to get two words out of her when I bid her farewell. Likely she was overwhelmed by the Badencocks," he added with a chuckle. "Any gently bred lady would be overwhelmed by the Badencocks."

Radical brrred his agreement with this and, noting a slackening of the reins, stepped down into the road.

"She did not appear anywhere near old enough to have a daughter out of the schoolroom," Hartshire murmured as the grey meandered along the road, northwest toward Camberwell. "Of course, that doesn't matter, Rad. Her age is no concern of ours. I hope she reaches London without further incident. The beads should keep her well. Though why I gave her my beads—What the devil am I going to do without them, eh? Well, perhaps we'll see her in London, and I'll ask her if I can borrow them from time to time."

The thought of London filled Hartshire with a distinct uneasiness. He had been too long absent. He had married his beloved Miriam and they had gone off to Wilderhart Hall to enjoy some time alone together. They had enjoyed that time so very much that they had seldom left the place.

Hartshire grinned. "Whoever thought that you and I would become as tame as we did, Rad? We were always used to be right in the midst of things. It was our Miriam domesticated us. Turned The Radical and The Spectre into complacent stay-at-homes, she did. Though we were wild enough at Wilderhart, the lot of us. But if Val has truly gone and opened himself up a regular barrel of bad pork, as Lady Con thinks, we'll be back in the midst of things again shortly, my friend, and that's a fact. Why a lad who was always afraid to say boo to a goose should grow into a gentleman who cannot resist tramping about London getting into every bit of trouble he possibly can—"

Radical interrupted, shaking his head energetically from side to side. He whinnied and brrrred.

"I expect you're right," replied Hartshire, rubbing a hand tenderly along the grey's heavily muscled neck. "If Val truly is in deep trouble, it's likely our fault. Lady Con implied that very thing in her last letter. And I expect I am somewhat responsible. I did tell Val all the Spectre stories and go on and on about the joys and sorrows of attempting to protect Mad Farmer George in my early years. And you, well, I am not certain what you did exactly, but you must have done something to encourage Val in his apparently mad pursuit of trouble, because I ain't going to be the only one to take the blame, old boy. No, I ain't."

Two

"Welcome to London, Mama," Lord Marston greeted, dashing down the staircase of the house in Cavendish Square with a wide grin on his handsome countenance. With unbridled enthusiasm, he swept Lady Marston into an enormous hug and planted a smacking kiss on her cheek despite the interference of the brim of her bonnet. "Are you well? Is she well, Ally?" he asked stepping back to survey his stepmother critically. "You aren't tinged that frightful green color, Mama. I fretted the entire day away thinking of you confined to that confounded coach. You are exhausted, I expect."

"I'm fine, Malcolm," Fleur replied. "Oh, I must call you Marston, now, must I not? All your friends call you Marston, no doubt, and have for an entire year."

"You may call me anything your heart desires," Marston replied with an ingenuous grin designed to set any mother's heart to dancing. "Marston, Malcolm, Rascal, Reprobate—Son."

Joy rippled through Fleur at his response. Son. She placed one hand gently against his smooth cheek, then removed it and proceeded to untie her bonnet and give it into the care of the waiting footman. "Have you no greeting for your sister, Malcolm?" she queried, allowing the footman to aid her in the removal of her traveling cloak.

"Yes, do welcome me properly to London, Mal," Althea urged him, dispensing with her hat.

"Welcome to London, Miss Avondale," Marston intoned solemnly and bowed, then spoiled the formal effect by tugging Althea into his arms and hugging her soundly. "You brought Mama all the way here without incident, did you? However did you manage it? Is she no longer a notoriously bad traveler?"

"She is a wretched traveler," Althea replied, her hazel eyes alive with humor as she gazed up at him. "But the most amazing gentleman came to her aid. He gave her some tea to drink, carried her off to a most despicable inn and then tied beads around her wrists. She has not gotten ill since."

"Is that so? And who was this gentleman? Merlin the Magician escaped from his cave?"

"Merely a gentleman traveling to London on horseback," Fleur answered, repinning several strands of dusky brown hair that had escaped the knot at the top of her head. "The Earl of Hartshire, I believe he said."

"Hartshire?" Marston, assisting his sister from her pelisse, turned to stare at his stepmama. "The Earl of Hartshire, did you say, Mama? Are you certain?"

"That's the name he gave."

"Well, of all things!" exclaimed Marston. "He is just the person I've been wishing to meet!"

"You have?" Althea and Lady Marston responded simultaneously.

"Indeed. He is Conningford's brother-in-law. You remember Connie, Mama. He accompanied me home from Eton the summer that Papa spent in Scotland."

"That quiet little blond-haired boy who read every book in our library and blushed and stuttered each time he was addressed?"

"He didn't read *every* book in our library."

"He made an impressive attempt at it. And every time

your sister entered a room, he left it. Terribly frightened of girls, he was. I thought you called him Hunt?"

"Well, he was Hunt then, but his father died a few years ago so now he is the Earl of Conningford," Marston explained, handing his sister's pelisse to the footman and urging his stepmama and Althea toward the staircase. "Connie is not so timid now. Quite turned about, actually. Well, he is still uneasy with young ladies, but otherwise, he is up to all sorts of mischief. I cannot believe you are both a step ahead of me and have met The Spectre already."

"The Spectre?" queried Althea, pausing at the foot of the staircase to glance at Fleur.

"You have heard Lord Hartshire called The Spectre, Malcolm?" Lady Marston asked. "He implied to me that his being called such was simply a private jest between himself and an innkeeper."

"Well. Well. Of course, he *would* say that," sputtered Marston, momentarily disconcerted. "You will forget that I mentioned it, will you not? I know you dined along the way, but I ordered tea for us the moment I saw the coach turn into the square. A bit of tea, I thought, and then off to bed with you both. I have an appointment to keep, but I wouldn't miss your arrival for the world and I want to have tea with you, especially on your first night here."

"I cannot think why you will walk everywhere when there are perfectly good vehicles to be hired, Atticus," Lady Conningford declared, glaring at her son-in-law from beneath silvered brows while she smothered a smile beneath a determined frown. "This is precisely the sort of thing that happens to people who walk. Really, to be required to remove your shoes and give them over to the footman at my door! To enter my drawing room in your stockings alone!"

"I do beg your pardon, Lady Con," Hartshire replied, standing before the little old lady who scrutinized him intently from her chair. "Have you had word from Val as yet? Has he sent any message? Has anyone contacted you on his behalf?"

"Sit down, Atticus. I always get a crick in my neck when I am forced to look up at you."

Hartshire eased himself down into a high-backed wing chair beside Lady Conningford.

"You need not be so cautious, Atticus. That is the precise chair I bought when it appeared that Miriam had seriously set her heart on having you and she lured you here day in and day out."

"It is? I don't remember it looking quite like this."

"No, I have had the covering changed. But it will not give way under you. You have my word on it."

"About Val—"

"Yes, well, he has returned."

"Not abducted then."

"No. Gone off for a week in the country with a friend. So he said. And now he will have it that I am a hopeless, interfering old woman, because I had the audacity to worry at his absence."

"He never called you a hopeless, interfering old woman? I will comb the scoundrel's hair with a milking stool if he did!"

"No, he did not say that precisely. But apparently I am to realize that he is a fully grown gentleman now. And I am to understand that he will not always confide in his mama where he plans to go and what he means to do."

Hartshire smiled and reached across the space between them to give the back of Lady Con's hand a reassuring pat. "He has reached his majority and thinks himself wise, witty and indestructible, I expect. We all do. Think we are wise to every scheme and quite invincible at that age, we gentlemen. Did you tell him you had written to me about his disappearance?"

"No, I did not. I was so mortified. Atticus, I am so sorry to have brought you dashing to London for nothing."

"Don't think another thing about it," Hartshire declared. "It isn't that I didn't wish to come to London, you know, merely that it hadn't occurred to me that I ought to come until you wrote me about Val. Got your first letter and immediately sent Little and Robes to open the house. Might not have arrived for another few days though, had your last letter not reached me on Tuesday saying that you suspected Val had been abducted. That made me rush a bit, but I would have come regardless."

Hartshire stretched his long legs out before him and contemplated his feet. He wiggled his toes inside his stockings, first one foot and then the other, then all together. "Val is not indestructible or wise to every scheme, regardless of his newly acquired independence. Uncle Pan was right. Lose a guardian, gain an education."

"What does that mean?"

"It means that once a gentleman reaches his independence there will be any number of swindlers out there to teach him that he is not nearly as wise and invincible as he imagines himself to be. It's far better I should come to Town and teach him than that they should do the job."

Lady Conningford studied the gentleman beside her with grateful blue eyes. He could not know how thankful she was that he had married Miriam and come stomping, like some jolly great giant, into her life and into Val's. He had made her smile from the very first and more than that, had managed somehow to make her feel treasured, wanted, needed. And he had taken her timid son and taught him that life was to be lived and enjoyed, not merely to be read about in books. He had given Val a sense of pride, confidence, courage and curiosity.

His shoulders almost as wide as the hearth, his dark curls tumbling wildly over his brow, his white teeth gleaming as he grinned his outrageous lopsided grin at his wiggling toes, all combined to remind Lady Conningford how happy she was to have Hartshire in her family and to be included in his. Her uneasiness over having called him to London fled. Her fears of actually being an interfering old lady vanished. "You look a perfect gudgeon watching your toes jiggle about like that, Atticus."

"You and Will," chuckled Hartshire. "How you both come to be so familiar with how gudgeons look, I cannot think. I will see to Val, Lady Con. You may depend on it."

"I do depend on it. I am most fond of you, Atticus, and I do appreciate all you said about young men reaching their majorities, but I do believe that some blame for the things Val does of late is to be laid directly at your door."

"I know and I hope you're wrong," Hartshire replied with a sigh. "Because if Val is wandering about London attempting to be like me when I was his age, I will be forced to take a knife to him and use his guts for garters."

At that precise moment in Cavendish Square, Fleur bid her stepson good night and made her way wearily up the stairs, shooing Althea before her. She heard Malcolm's footsteps descending the staircase even as she and Althea ascended and she silently wished him a pleasant evening with his friends. Bidding Ally good night at the door of the girl's room, she continued down the corridor to the bedchamber Malcolm had said was to be hers. The master bedchamber was not to be hers any longer. Would never be hers again. Oh, how she thanked heaven for that.

As she opened the door and stepped inside, she paused with lamp in hand to gaze at the room before her. Her deep brown eyes began to itch with approaching tears of joy. This was just the thing—a cheery room with soft blue walls and creamy white trim. A bright, flowered quilt covered a slender sleigh bed. Matching flowered curtains were drawn across the windows. The fireplace surround was decorated with blue tiles etched in white and the fireplace mantel was white, etched in blue. Orange-red flames hissed and sputtered energetically on the hearth. "Oh, how lovely," Fleur whispered, swiping at the happy tears as they began to fall. "How perfectly lovely. He has not only refurbished the public rooms, but he has created this wonderful, safe chamber for me as well."

All was due to Malcolm's thoughtfulness, of course. Fleur had never said a word to him when he'd departed a full ten months earlier to open Marston House and prepare it for his sister's first Season except to request that he take charge of hiring a competent staff.

"And look what he's done," she murmured in disbelief. "He's fashioned a lovely home for us all from a cold, ancient tomb."

Lady Marston took a deep, shuddering breath. All of the ghosts she had expected to meet on her arrival in Marston House had disappeared beneath the onslaught of her stepson's thoughtfulness. "I don't know what I've done to deserve such consideration as this at Mal's hands, or at Ally's either," she whispered to herself as she turned about in a small circle, attempting to absorb the pure gaiety of the chamber all at once. "I only loved them, nothing more than that. And how could I not love them? How could I not?"

A soft scratching at her door drew her attention. "Come in," she called, and smiled as the lady's maid Marston had selected for her entered the chamber. "It is Davis, is it not?"

"Yes, madam," the abigail responded with a token of a curtsy. She was an older woman, in her late thirties, perhaps, tall and thin with reddish hair, green eyes and a nervous, darting glance. "I have come to ask if you require any assistance, your ladyship."

"Yes, you may lay out my nightrail, Davis, if you will, and undo the fastenings of my dress."

"Certainly, my lady."

"You are a Londoner by birth, Davis?"

"Yes, your ladyship," the maid replied, crossing to an elegant white armoire trimmed in gold and fetching Fleur's nightrail, unfolding it and laying it across the foot of the sleigh bed. "I didn't know precisely where you'd like your things," she said softly, "and so when I unpacked, I put them where my other lady was used to keep hers."

"Have you been in service long, Davis?" Fleur queried, turning so that the abigail might undo the fastenings of her plain grey striped traveling dress.

"Indeed, madam. I have been in service my entire life. I began as a scullery maid in Lady Blessing's kitchen when I was a mere dab of a girl."

"Lady Blessing?"

"Yes, madam. And on my fifteenth birthday, I became an upstairs maid, and then a year later, one of the parlor maids was—she was got in the family way, if you know what I mean, my lady. Well, she was discharged, of course, and I was allowed to ascend to that position. And then Lady Blessing's niece came on to need an abigail and I was privileged to be trained for it. The Countess of Dashfield, she was, and a more birdwitted lady I did never know, if you will pardon my saying so, your ladyship. I know I ought not say it, but—"

"And what happened to bring you to us, Davis?"

"Why, the Countess of Dashfield cocked up her toes, madam."

"Cocked up her . . . ?"

"Died, madam. Barely eight months ago. It was in all the newspapers. And, as she had no further use of me, I was at loose ends so to speak until I discovered that Lord Marston was seeking an abigail. He is a very kind sort of a gentleman, your son," said Davis as she helped Fleur to slip out of her shift and then assisted her into her nightrail. "Hired me without a recommendation from my old employer, he did. Well, but then I couldn't get one, could I? Lady Dashfield was dead, after all, and Lord Dashfield so overcome that he could not be bothered. If you will be seated, my lady, I will be pleased to take the pins from your hair and brush and braid it for you."

"No need, Davis. I shall do that myself. My traveling dress had best be taken down to be cleaned, however. It has had a most trying time of it today. Oh, and Davis . . ."

"Yes, your ladyship?"

"I do not generally gossip with the servants, you understand."

"Oh, yes, madam."

"But I have been gone from Town for a number of years and I merely wonder—The Countess of Dashfield was but newly married when last I lived here. She cannot have been much more than twenty at that time."

"Indeed, your ladyship. Twenty she was when she married his lordship."

"So she would have been—"

"Twenty-six when she snuffed it, your ladyship."

"So young. Do you happen to know what she died from, Davis?"

"Boredom. One moment her ladyship was alive and despairing of the scarcity of acceptable company in Town and the next she was lying cold and dead on the floor of the sewing room with a scissor through her heart. Could not abide the dullness of summer in London no longer."

Fleur gasped.

"Well, but my lady," Davis added, gathering the traveling dress from the floor and laying it across her arm, "it *is* dreadful dull in London once all the best people have gone off for the summer."

Hartshire, his shoes restored to him clean and shining, was about to take his leave of Lady Conningford when he queried, rather offhandedly, if Lady Con knew a Lady Marston.

"I know Lord Marston, Atticus. He's an intimate of Val's."

"He is?"

"Indeed. They went to Eton together, and then on to university."

"Lord Marston is as young as that?" Hartshire frowned.

"As young as what? He is Val's age, I believe. Perhaps a year or two older."

"And he has married a woman with a fully grown daughter? Well, he must have done. Miss Avondale cannot be *his* daughter, not if he is Val's age. But Lady Marston cannot possibly be so old as to have a—"

"What *are* you jabbering about?" Lady Conningford took his arm as they strolled toward the staircase. "You are not making a bit of sense, Atticus. The trip to Town took a greater toll on you than you realize. You aren't as young as you once were. You ought to go directly home and straight to bed, I think."

"I ain't a doddering old man," Hartshire protested.

"No, of course not."

"It is merely that I met a lady on the road. Lady Marston she was called. And—"

"Oh! That will be the shipbuilder's daughter. She's Lord Marston's stepmama, Atticus, and now that I think of it, the family name *is* Avondale. Miss Avondale will be Marston's younger sister then."

Hartshire took hold of the gargoyle that decorated the top of the newel post at the first floor landing and paused, gazing down into the vestibule below. "The shipbuilder's daughter?"

"Yes, precisely. The Shipbuilder's Daughter, Atticus. The Drab Dab of Piers and Planks."

"What?"

"Oh, you never did pay the least attention to Society. You pretended to, but you never did. I am amazed that you and Miriam ever came to meet each other, much less marry. It is a minor bit of ancient nonsense, nothing more. The late

Lord Marston," she explained in a most tutorial tone, "married a younger woman who was the daughter of a shipbuilder. It is ten years, at least, since he did. I believe it was a marriage of considerable convenience—the father got a titled son-in-law and Marston considerable wealth. The girl got nothing, of course, but that is generally the case. Though when her father died, I believe he did leave Lady Marston his entire fortune and in her own name. Do you mean to tell me why you wish to know about Lady Marston, Atticus?"

"No. I mean, I don't wish to know all that much about her. I met her along the road from Kent is all. And I wondered, you know, if you might be known to each other."

"Well, we are not. She is in London, you say?"

"She ought to have arrived late this evening if she paid strict attention and did as I said."

"Paid strict attention? Did as you said? Atticus, if you know this woman so well that you may instruct her and lay down rules for her in one thing or another, why do you ask me anything at all about her?" Lady Con reached up, playfully seized one of Hartshire's ears in each hand and tugged him gently down to where she could bestow a kiss upon his cheek. "Thank you for coming," she said softly as she released him. "I feel quite confident Val will be safe now that you're here." She freed him and watched as he descended the staircase, collected his hat and gloves and waved her good-bye.

The Shipbuilder's Daughter? The Drab Dab of Piers and Planks? Hartshire frowned as he descended to the pavement. "Damnable nicknames were not intended in a complimentary fashion, I'll wager," he muttered to himself as his heels clicked along Brook Street. "So, she is the stepmother of the present Marston. And Marston is an intimate of Val's. Will make it less awkward for me to inquire how the lady goes on at least."

Hartshire's heels had clicked no farther than a block west along Brook Street when he noted a shadow glide into a small alley on his right. Mere seconds later another shadow flowed after it. There was something distinctly familiar about that second shadow. At least, Hartshire thought there was. Drawn by an instinct long dormant and a worrisome recollection of a particularly thin set of shoulders and a rather neglectful manner of setting one's hat upon one's head, and urged on by his own curiosity, Hartshire's heels ceased to click and he proceeded along the pavement to the alley with a stealth extraordinary and unexpected in so large a gentleman.

He pressed himself against a damp wall and all but disappeared into the bricks of the house which sided on the alley and then he peered around the corner of the building to glimpse one of the shadows providing the other with a leg up to a window ledge. Slowly, carefully, Hartshire floated down the alleyway toward them. His eyes easily adjustable to the darkness, his breath so slow and steady as to be quite inaudible and his footsteps soundless, he came to a halt a mere cat's whisker away from the pair. He blinked his midnight eyes once, twice, and then in a whisper that hissed through the silence of the night like a razor through paper he said, "Val, what the devil do you think you're doing?"

The shadow who stooped stood up abruptly. The other shadow was thus sent flying into the air where it soared past the window ledge, then fell swiftly downward to land with a thump and a groan in the middle of the alleyway.

Before either of the two could gather their wits about them and run off, Hartshire stepped away from the building. In the faint light of the moon, he caught Lord Conningford by the shoulder with one enormous hand. Then he reached down and seized the other gentleman by the collar of his coat, tugging him, wiggling, to his feet.

"Ohmigawd!" Conningford exclaimed breathlessly. "Ohmigawd! Atticus, is it you? Where the deuce did you come from? You have frightened ten years off my life."

"Have I?" drawled the earl. "How very appropriate since my intention is to pummel another ten years off of it if you don't provide me at once with an adequate explanation. Why the devil do I discover you attempting to break into someone's establishment?"

"Atticus?" queried the shadow dangling just above the cobbles. "Do you mean to say, Connie, that this is The Spectre?"

"Just so," Conningford responded. "Atticus, do let Marston down. His feet are dangling."

"Are they?"

"Yes, and we do have a perfectly good explanation, but we can't explain here. Someone may come."

"Ah, you noticed that, did you? A wonder you did not think of it before you came slithering in here and attempted to break into this house."

"We did not slither," protested Conningford. "We, we, ah, sneaked."

"Didn't sneak well enough. I saw you."

"Atticus, do set Marston's feet back on the ground so that I may introduce him to you properly."

Hartshire released his hold on both of them so suddenly that Conningford and his mate stumbled before they found solid footing. "Come with me. Now!" hissed Hartshire, stalking straight up the middle of the tiny alleyway and back into Brook Street without once turning his head to see if they did follow as he had commanded. His long legs carried him angrily but silently all the way to Grosvenor Square and Hartshire House with the two young men huffing and puffing five steps behind the entire way. Hartshire lifted the knocker and let it fall, growled a greeting at Little as that worthy opened the door, and kept on going straight back along the corridor into his study. Behind him, Conningford and Marston whispered to one another, nervously handed their hats and gloves to the butler and then followed hurriedly in the path Hartshire had set.

"Come in, Val, and don't act so deucedly timid about it.

You're not hoaxing me one bit. I *know* you are brave when you wish to be," grumbled Hartshire, turning at the sound of their arrival on his study threshold, a decanter of brandy in his hand. "And close the door behind you. Somehow, I don't think that what you're about to tell me is anything I wish Little or the staff to hear. You do drink brandy now, do you not?"

"Y-yes, of c-course," nodded Conningford, shoving his friend ahead of him into the room and pulling the door closed behind him. "We truly do have a perfectly good explanation for what you saw, Atticus. We were not doing at all what you think we were doing," he said.

"Devil, you say! And here I stand ready to wager a duck to a duchess that you were about to do precisely what I was thinking. Will wonders never cease?" With a bit of an angry flourish, Hartshire poured the contents of the decanter into three glasses.

The young man standing wide-eyed beside Conningford, nudged Val in the side with his elbow. "You said you'd introduce me," he whispered eagerly.

"Oh, yes! Atticus, I wish to make known to you my good friend, Lord Marston. Marston, my brother-in-law, Hartshire."

"You're The Spectre," breathed Marston in awe. "Connie has told me everything about you!"

"Marston." Hartshire passed each of them a glass and pointed them to chairs. He took his own glass in hand and, lowering himself into a chair before the fire, took the most amazing gulp. It seared down his windpipe, through his gullet, burning a regular cavern within him. It brought the sting of tears briefly to his eyes. "Marston," he said when he could speak again. "Don't tell me that you're Lady Marston's stepson."

"Yes, sir."

"I said, *don't* tell me. I don't wish to think of it. That poor woman has suffered enough this day just getting into Town and now I must seek her out and confide in her that her stepson has gone into the honorable profession of burglary? And at the instigation of my very own brother-in-law?"

"No, no, we weren't going to burgle anything, Atticus," Conningford protested. "At least, just one particular thing, if we could find it."

It took the younger gentlemen almost ten minutes to explain, quite satisfactorily they thought, precisely why they had been attempting to enter another gentleman's house by means of an open window. Hartshire sat the whole while drumming his fingers on the arm of his chair and sipping his brandy. "Are you quite certain that this Dashfield has it?" he asked at last. "I realize you've seen him with a malacca cane any number of times, but perhaps that cane merely resembles your father's, Marston."

"No, it's Papa's cane all right. It looks precisely like it. Even the top is the same. And no one has seen Papa's since the night he died."

"Yes, but the fact that it has gone missing does not necessarily mean that Dashfield stole the thing. Your father's cane may have been misplaced. He died suddenly you said. Who would take note of where his cane was put after such a disturbing accident?"

"No one. I expect Dashfield thought the same and took advantage of that fact," replied Conningford knowingly. "I told Marston so and he agrees with me."

"Yes, Val, but why would this Dashfield even wish to possess someone else's cane? And wish it enough to steal the thing? And if he did steal it, why would he walk around London with it, bold as you please? It don't make a bit of sense."

"Nonetheless, it's so," Marston declared. "Papa's cane has gone missing, Dashfield has it, and I will have it back."

Hartshire sighed. "Very well, perhaps you're both correct. Perhaps Dashfield has stolen the cane. Even so, what the devil makes the two of you think, for one moment, that it is perfectly acceptable for you to climb into his house through a window in the dead of night and steal the cane back?"

"You have climbed in through any number of windows, Atticus, any number of times, and stolen things when you did, too," Conningford pointed out with what he imagined to be perfectly acceptable reasoning.

"Yes? And?"

"And what, sir?" asked Marston, his blatantly admiring gaze fastened upon the earl.

"And if I had once thrown myself under the wheels of a passing carriage, would the two of you do that as well?"

"That ain't the same," Conningford protested.

"No, it ain't," Marston agreed. "Connie has got you there, sir. One thing don't rationally follow the other. Fellow would be a fool to throw himself beneath the wheels of a moving carriage."

"What if the Watch had seen you at that window?" asked Hartshire in a slow drawl designed to conceal the bit of fear for the boys that had begun to flourish in his stomach.

"But the Watch didn't see us," Marston replied, stubbornly.

"No, *I* saw you. Had I been a watchman you would both be giving your names up to John Stafford at Bow Street this minute instead of sitting here in my study sipping brandy."

"Well, no, not actually," Conningford said, turning his glass around and around in his hands, watching the splendidly glowing liquid slosh against the sides. "In the first place, Atticus, there is not a Charley in all London can run fast enough to catch us. And we would have run, wouldn't we, Marston? And then again, even if a Charley could catch us, Stafford is perfectly aware of the whole thing."

"Stafford is what?" Hartshire bellowed. He banged his brandy glass down on the side table and rose to his feet. With a mutter, he tugged the elegantly tied neckcloth from around his neck and let it flutter to the floor. He shed, with some effort, his coat, unbuttoned his waistcoat, and in an attempt to regain a cooler demeanor, stuffed his hands into his breeches' pockets and began to pace. "Your mama will run a sabre through my heart, Val!"

"Really?" Conningford asked in sincere wonder. "Why?"

"Why? Why? Because you have got yourself connected to Bow Street. Worse, you have got yourself connected to John Stafford at Bow Street, and that villain has got you to go spying about London for him. Like as not he will get you killed!"

"John Stafford?" exclaimed Marston. "Got us to go spying for him? Spying? He is nothing but a clerk."

"Precisely. Told you to say that, didn't he? Damnation, if Stafford's neck were within my reach this very minute!"

"He's something besides a clerk?" Marston asked, his eyebrows rising. "Well, I'll be deviled! I should never have guessed it. Connie only intended to imply, sir, that John Stafford at Bow Street knows m'father's malacca cane is missing and that I have seen it in Dashfield's possession. That's all. Truly. Connie didn't intend to make you think that we worked for Stafford or anything. He only meant that Stafford would realize at once we were only attempting to retrieve the cane and nothing more."

"Why do the Bow Street Runners not retrieve it, if they know it's yours and know that Dashfield has it?"

"Well, because Dashfield is a peer and they don't wish to accuse him without the least proof. I cannot actually *prove* that Dashfield's cane is my father's and not a copy," Marston added in an apologetic tone. "I know it is, but I cannot prove it. I cannot prove he stole it either, because—because—"

"Because Val's father might have lost the thing to Dashfield on a wager," Conningford provided. "Of course, he didn't."

Hartshire ceased pacing and rested one arm along the mantel. His long fingers seized a glass statuette of a hound that rested there and turned it 'round and 'round. He studied Marston in perfect silence. No matter how hard he tried, however, he could not bring to mind a likeness of the lad's father. The Marston title had been gnawing at him since first he'd met Lady Marston that very morning. And now it gnawed the more. There was something about the previous Lord Marston he ought to remember and it troubled him that he did not.

"You don't resemble your father, eh? Neither you nor your sister, Marston?"

"He don't what?" asked Conningford in wonder. "What have Marston's looks got to do with the malacca cane, Atticus?"

"My mind has wandered for a moment and the two of you ought to give thanks for it. You will hear more of what I have to say on the matter of the cane soon enough. But for the moment—Marston, do you resemble your father or not?"

"No, sir. Not a bit. Nor does Ally."

"Ally?"

"My sister, Althea. You met her and my mama along the road this morning. Mama said as much. Oh, you will know Ally as Miss Avondale. I keep forgetting she ain't a babe anymore."

"You met Lady Marston and Miss Avondale on the road, Atticus?" asked Conningford. "Well, of all things. Why didn't you say so?"

"And Lady Marston is your stepmother?" Hartshire asked, ignoring Conningford's query. "She is The Shipbuilder's Daughter?"

"Do not call her that!" Marston exclaimed, popping up out of his chair. "As much as I have come to respect you, sir, after all Connie has told me about you, I will still be forced to call you out for it, do I hear you call her that again."

"She isn't a shipbuilder's daughter, your stepmother?"

"No. Yes. Well, she is but—"

"Never mind, Marston. I can guess the tale. My fellow members of the illustrious upper ten thousand thought her an encroaching mushroom when she married your father, eh? They resented her attempt to force her way into our ranks and referred to her by that particular appellation in the most derogatory fashion, no?"

"She did not attempt to force her way into your ranks or anywhere else," Marston replied, stamping across the Aubusson carpet to stand with hands on hips before Hartshire. "And if you say one more derogatory word about her, sir, I will—"

"You will what, Mal?" Conningford queried innocently from his chair. "You ain't about to call Atticus out? He is a great deal better with pistols and swords and even fisticuffs than you. And besides, he won't go. Atticus ain't said nothing derogatory about your stepmama. He was merely asking who she was, is all."

"Just so," nodded Hartshire. "I merely wish to set it straight in my mind, Marston, precisely what I will be forced to deal with."

"What you will be forced to deal with?"

"Well, yes. Now that I find Lady Marston is your stepmother and you are Val's dearest friend and fellow burglar, I cannot simply ignore her should we happen to meet, can I? No, of course I can't. And we are likely to meet. Unless she does not intend to chaperone your sister about Town?"

"Oh. Oh! I had not thought of that," Marston replied, shoving his hands into his pockets. "Ought I to hire a chaperon for Ally do you think?"

"You had best ask your stepmother about that," Hartshire replied. "Apparently she didn't have the best of all times here in London. Perhaps she'll wish to avoid Society altogether. No, don't glare at me like that, Marston. I intend her no slight by the observation."

"Of course he doesn't," Conningford agreed. "Even if all the very best people insulted your stepmother at every turn and took immense joy in it, too, Atticus would not."

"Indeed not," Hartshire responded. "I don't make it a point to do things simply because I know others have done the same."

"Of course not," Conningford agreed again, heartily.

"Which brings us back full circle to climbing in people's windows," Hartshire pointed out with a distinct chill in his tone. "Do return to your chair, Marston. Val, cease staring at me like a wounded deer. I should like to discuss this bit of burglary you attempted more thoroughly."

Three

Fleur, in a walking dress of pale lilac poplin beneath a pelisse of a darker lavender color, descended from her coach before Madame Annette's in Bond Street and gazed uncertainly about her. She had, of course, known perfectly well that Althea would require an entirely new wardrobe for her come-out. Had been prepared to accept the enormous expenditure as a decidedly worthy investment in her stepdaughter's future. Had, for goodness' sake, even allowed herself to entertain the notion of having a gown or two made up for her own use, but she had not once expected that now, just as the coachman drove off to discover a suitable place to wait for her, Althea and Davis, that her feet would oppose her, hesitating to enter the establishment of this particularly successful London dressmaker.

"What is it, Mama?" Althea asked, stepping to Fleur's side. "Is this not the correct shop?"

"Yes, it is. That is to say, it's the shop Malcolm said all the young ladies are wild about. Pay me not the least attention, my dear. It's only that I am a bit shy of entering a shop so filled with ladies of Quality. Nothing more. There, I have gotten over it already," Fleur said, forcing herself to smile grandly. "In we all go."

Althea opened the shop door only to step back as two ladies emerged. "I do beg your pardon," said the younger of them as she brushed against Ally's arm. And then, "Oh!" she exclaimed, looking Althea up and down with considerable surprise. "You're Lord Marston's sister! You are, aren't you?"

"Yes," Althea replied, "but I do not think I—"

"No, you don't," interrupted the smiling brunette, "know me, I mean. But I must know you, you look so like your brother. You're Miss Avondale. Miss Althea Avondale. Lord Marston was so very excited about your coming. I have never seen him jollier than when he confirmed to me that you were to make your come-out this very Season. I'm Miss Tate," she announced, extending her hand to Ally. "Of course, you must call me Julia, because I am determined we shall become bosom bows."

"Then you must call me Althea," said Ally, smiling. Truly, she thought, Miss Tate's own smile was quite contagious. "And this is my mama, Lady Marston," she added, turning to include Fleur in her introduction.

"Lady Marston, I am so very pleased to make your acquaintance."

"Julia," hissed a voice. "Come away at once."

Miss Tate peered back over her shoulder.

"Do you hear me, at once!"

"But Mama, it is Miss Avondale, Lord Marston's sister."

"Good day to you, Miss Avondale," Miss Tate's mother said stiffly, from behind her daughter with a regal nod. "Welcome to London. We are pleased to have you with us. Come now, Julia."

"And this is Lady—"

"You need not introduce us. I know perfectly well who *she* is," sniffed Lady Tate, her nose rising to an extraordinary height. "We are late to the hosier's. To the coach at once," commanded Lady Tate, turning her back on Fleur with great significance.

"Well, I never!" exclaimed Althea. "Of all the rude things to do. Mama, what is it? Are you all right? You're trembling."

"No, no," breathed Fleur. "I'm not trembling. I am—There was a chill breeze and I—" Lady Marston's voice faded as another mother and daughter exited the shop. Two extravagantly bonneted heads nodded pleasantly to Althea but the eyes beneath the bonnets' brims, excessively cold grey eyes, passed over Fleur as though she were not there.

Althea's mouth opened at the insolence of it and a tiny squeak emerged.

"You must go inside without me, Ally," Fleur said as determinedly as she could. Her fine brown eyes glistened with tears, but she refused to let them fall. "You cannot possibly want me with you. No, you can't, for it will be simply more of the same in there and you'll feel absolutely degraded. At this moment I am nothing to you but a detriment. Davis will accompany you. You must choose whatever you like. Be levelheaded. Choose material of the best quality. Select styles that will suit you to perfection. We have discussed precisely the sort of dresses and gowns you ought to have. And don't bother about the cost, Ally. Order only the finest of what you find; the price is of no consequence."

"Well, of all things! No, Mama, I'm not going inside without you," protested Althea. "What on earth was wrong with those women? Why did they stare past you as though you were invisible? And why should Lady Tate have spoken in such a fashion? Are all Londoners possessed of such wretched manners?"

Directly across Bond Street, his broad shoulders resting against the window of Grisham's Tobacco Shop, Hartshire stood watching the ladies. His attention had been claimed at once by the Marston coach which had departed just as he had exited the tobacconist's. With a particular degree of interest, he had settled back to see whether Lady Marston truly intended to enter the doors of the most popular dressmaker in London, or if she would prove faint of heart. Though the brief conversations among the ladies escaped him at such a distance, for he could not quite read their lips, the considerable height to which one woman's nose rose and the affronted dignity with which she tugged her daughter away from Lady Marston and Miss Avondale, left him in little doubt of what had been said. Nor did he misinterpret the direct cut bestowed on the shipbuilder's daughter by the other two ladies departing the shop.

His considerable imagination was even now providing him with words quite amazingly close to the words that were traveling back and forth between Lady Marston and Miss Avondale, though he was not quite as confident of what the girl might be saying, because one never knew what sort of relationship to expect between a stepmother and a stepdaughter.

Memories of Miriam gathered about him unbidden. She would have known at once what must be done to alleviate the situation. And she would have done it, too, had she taken a liking to Lady Marston. "You definitely would have taken a liking to her, Mir," he murmured. "You were always one to harbor odd ducks under your wing." Hartshire abandoned his languid posture, adjusted his coat into precise position and crossed the street.

"There are other dressmakers in London. You cannot convince me that this is the only one. We shall both go elsewhere, Mama," he heard Miss Avondale say, and he was amazed at how fine it made him feel to hear her say it.

"Quite right," he replied, startling both ladies, who had been so engrossed in their conversation that they had not noticed his arrival at all. "Any number of dressmakers in London. I expect my mother-in-law would be more than willing to direct you to any or all of them. Good morning, Lady Marston, Miss Avondale. I planned to call on you this afternoon to assure myself of your safe arrival, but here you are and here I am."

"Good day, Lord Hartshire," Fleur replied, her slightly

jutting chin set stubbornly, the moisture of unshed tears evident in her eyes. "Thank you for your concern, but we've no need of any other dressmaker. Marston assures me that Madame Annette is all the thing among the younger ladies."

"Yes, and among the older ladies," offered Althea, her blue eyes sparking at Fleur. "If you won't go in with me, Mama, then I assure you, I won't go in either."

"You won't go inside?" asked Hartshire quietly, his remarkable eyes focused intently on Fleur.

"No. You can't possibly understand, but it appears obvious that for me to do so would likely cause Ally the greatest embarrassment and I'd not embarrass her for the world."

"Balderdash!" Althea exclaimed. "As if anything you could possibly do would embarrass me!"

Just then the door to the shop opened again and a pair of elderly ladies appeared. Both paused on the threshold. Both glanced and nodded at Althea, then Hartshire, but they positively glared at Fleur. "It is this dastardly damp London air!" said the eldest of the ladies at last in a most piercing voice. "Mushrooms sprouting everywhere one looks!"

"Not to mention the ugly old toads hopping about," Hartshire drawled, concentrating the most insolent, withering gaze on the two.

Althea smothered a giggle behind her gloved hand as the women's faces registered profound shock and they huffed away up the street. Only then did she take note of Davis standing respectfully a few feet from them. The abigail's eyes were alight with laughter.

"That was perfectly wretched of you, Lord Hartshire," mumbled Fleur, nibbling anxiously at her lower lip.

"I thought it was just the thing," Hartshire replied, glancing down into those sad brown eyes. "They *are* ugly old toads."

"They are ladies of the ton. Now, rather than merely feeling superior, they are heartily offended as well and will spread it about that not only am I an encroaching mushroom but I have—I have—"

"You have a gentleman friend the size of Mount Olympus, with ears vaguely the size of a jacka—ah." He ceased to speak, the most ingratiating grin slipping across his face.

"That is not what I intended to say at all."

"No, you are much too gracious to point out that I am the size of Mount Olympus and my ears are—"

"I was not going to point out any such thing," interrupted Fleur. "Do cease grinning at me in that particular way, Lord Hartshire, or I shall—"

"Laugh?" queried Hartshire.

Fleur did laugh. She did not understand why, because she was very upset with him and with Althea, but still, a bubble of laughter gurgled out from between her lips.

"Miss Avondale, I have just had a thought."

"A thought?" asked Althea, puzzled.

"Yes indeed, even mountains think."

"I did not mean that."

"No, I realize you didn't. I'm making a jest of myself, is all. I've a tendency to do it first—before anyone else can, you know. Do I understand correctly that you have no intention of patronizing this shop if your mama does not, Miss Avondale? You're quite certain?"

"Quite."

"Althea!"

"Don't argue, please, Mama. I have quite set my mind against this Madame Annette."

"But it is not she, Althea, who causes the—the—" Fleur could not finish the sentence. Every semblance of laughter deserted her. "Madame Annette is the most fashionable dressmaker in all of London."

"Perhaps, but she's patronized by the rudest people in all of London as well."

"No, they are—It's not them. It's me, Ally. It is all my fault."

"How can any of their words and actions be your fault, Mama? All you did was descend from the coach to the pavement."

"Well, she did one thing more," offered Hartshire, rubbing a hand against the back of his neck and staring off up the street for a moment. "You've not explained to her?" he asked, returning his gaze to Fleur.

"No. That is, I will, but—"

"It's a matter of class," he interrupted ruthlessly, his midnight eyes gazing directly into Ally's. "All of those ladies were born and bred into the highest society, you know. Your stepmother, on the other hand, is but a shipbuilder's daughter."

"How dare you tell that!" Fleur exclaimed.

"I dare because you did not, madam."

"I would have done."

"I have no doubt of it. Eventually you would have done, but Miss Avondale needs to know now. You," he continued, the silver flecks in his eyes catching the sunlight as his gaze returned to Althea, "are born to the blood, Miss Avondale. Your stepmama is not. Thus, the difference between your welcome and hers."

"Well, of all things! Mama is a titled lady now."

"Now is not what counts," whispered Fleur. "My roots are among the merchant class and I cannot change the fact."

"No, but you *can* change dressmakers. Both of you. If only I can convince her," added Hartshire in barely a whisper. "Wait here for your coachman to return and when he does, meet me in Oxford Street, near the Tenterden corner. There's a dressmaker there who will be perfect for you, if only she's not—that is to say—if she's still in the business."

With all the polish of a town dandy, albeit a rather large town dandy, Hartshire lowered the coach steps for them when they arrived at the corner of Oxford and Tenterden. He ably assisted the ladies and Davis down. "Do I not know you?" he asked quietly as the abigail descended.

"No, my lord, certainly not."

Hartshire studied her a moment. He had the oddest feeling about the woman. "Davis is your name?"

"Yes, my lord."

"I do know you. I shall remember presently who you are, I warn you of it." And then he simply turned away, offered one arm to Fleur and the other to Ally and escorted them two doors down to a tiny shop above which hung a barely legible sign proclaiming it to be the premises of Madame Celeste. A tiny silver bell jingled as Hartshire opened the door and urged them inside.

It was a rather ragged little shop. Discarded bolts of cloth lay everywhere—on tables, chairs, the floor—with years old fashion magazines strewn beneath, atop and among them. High in the corners, covering the cornices, cobwebs glistened in the muted sunlight from the filthy front window. The bits of floor that could be seen through the material strewn about were covered in lint and dust. Overall hung a musty, unused smell that caused Althea to wrinkle her nose in distaste.

"No, no, go away, Hartshire. I have changed my mind," declared a chubby little woman, rushing from a back room and waving her hands frantically at them as if they were vermin she would shoo back into the street. Extremely short black hair streaked with gray sprouted atop her head in the most bizarre fashion. Faded blue eyes blinked at them from beneath black lashes. And when they did not shoo on command, she stamped a large foot attached to a chubby little leg. "Do you not hear me? You must go. All of you. I have changed my mind."

"Devil you have!" exclaimed Hartshire as the ladies beside him moved uneasily back toward the door. "We've just five minutes ago settled it between us. Cease behaving like a Bedlamite, Celeste, and allow me to present Lady Marston and Miss Avondale. You said you would take them on. I hold you to it."

"Lord Hartshire, I think perhaps—" ventured Fleur.

"Don't let her frighten you," urged Hartshire. "I know how she looks, but she is actually not a mad elfin fishwife about to attack you with a wet flounder. Stick out that chin, Lady Marston, and show the courage I know you have."

"You have not the least idea whether I am possessed of courage or not," Fleur replied, studying the short, sturdy dressmaker whose remarkable hair stood straight up from her head in places. The woman's dress was askew and her hands continued to wave quite uselessly. She was as stout as she was tall. Sturdily built. Heavy but compact. "Good morning, Madame Celeste," Fleur said most politely. "I fear there has been some mistake. It is clear to me that Lord Hartshire thought—"

"I know what he thought," interrupted the dressmaker. "It is clear to me as well what he thought. I know better what he thinks than he knows himself. Four years he has not come to see me here in London and now, suddenly, he must have all my time and I must hire girls and buy new materials. Bah! Men!"

"Bah! Women!" echoed Hartshire with what Fleur noticed in amazement was considerable glee. "Never know what they want," he continued. "Always changing their minds. You are done with dressmaking, eh? And if it were Miriam standing here, you would shoo her out in just such a fashion?"

"Ah, Miriam," said Celeste softly. "If it were only she."

"Well, it can't be she, Celly. She's dead."

"Poor, poor Hartshire," sighed the dressmaker, and in a moment she had crossed to him and was putting her arms as far around him as she could, resting her head against his midsection. "You were so devastated. We were all of us so devastated. To lose our lovely Miriam so soon."

Althea knew it to be a sad moment. They were discussing

a lady who had passed on, the two of them. Certainly it was a moment of considerable feeling for them both. Yet, it took all of Ally's considerable self-control to keep from bursting into laughter at the sight of the chubby dressmaker attempting to comfort the leviathan that was Hartshire. A leviathan who stared down at Celeste, his arms sticking out from his sides as though he feared to touch her. Althea gazed at Fleur and discovered that her stepmother's countenance flickered between puzzlement and laughter itself.

"Tell me when you've finished with this maudlin nonsense, will you, Celly?" Hartshire said. "I've plans to meet Uncle Pan at White's at two o'clock."

"Unfeeling wretch!" exclaimed the dressmaker. She released her hold on him, backed away the merest bit and stomped down on his toe. "And don't make faces, Hartshire. That didn't hurt you in the least. I did it merely for the principle of the thing. So," she added, advancing on Fleur and Althea, "you do not think highly of Madame Annette, eh? You require the services of a superior dressmaker. Well, and about time someone saw through that woman, too. Not even French, she isn't. I will do it!" she exclaimed with such excitement and unexpectedness that Fleur and Ally both jumped. "Do you hear me, Hartshire? I've changed my mind again. Go! Go to your club! No, wait! Give me some money first, you fiend. I have goods to purchase and girls to hire."

"I—we—" gasped Lady Marston as Hartshire pulled a considerable number of gold coins from his pocket and placed them in Celeste's waiting hand. "We have money to pay for your services, madame. It is not Lord Hartshire's responsibility."

"Yes, it *is* Hartshire's responsibility. It is all his idea for you to come here, is it not? Just so. But don't you worry, my dear, I will allow you to pay your share as well," Celeste responded with great good will. "I will charge you the most exorbitant fees. I promise you. These, these paltry coins, are merely to begin my work. Now go, you great lump," she said, giving Hartshire a mighty shove toward the door. "I have work to do. Goodness, yes. Only look at what they're wearing!"

It was nearing two as Hartshire stared up at the great columns and glistening windows of White's Club. He smiled at the thought of Celeste and the look on Lady Marston's face when he had abandoned her to deal with the eccentric little woman alone, but the smile did not quite reach his eyes. In a moment, it disappeared completely.

"Regular beetleheads Val and Marston are," Hartshire mumbled to himself. "Reporting a cane stolen, actually attempting to break into a man's home to recover it! It'll prove in the end that Marston's father lost the cane to Dashfield on a wager, I expect. Nothing havey-cavey about it. No reason for one man to steal another's cane. Too much imagination, no common sense, those lads. Playing at being me."

Damnation, how I hate to admit it, but Lady Con's correct, he conceded silently. I've filled Val's head so full of criminals, subversives, radicals and conspiracies that he sees one or another of them around every corner. And now he has got young Marston seeing them as well. Must learn to keep my tongue from wagging quite so freely when Val is around.

With a guilty and despairing sigh for having catapulted his brother-in-law's imagination in the particular direction it had taken, Hartshire crossed St. James's Street, mounted the stairs and handed his hat and gloves to the footman in charge of the door. "Ingles, is it not?" he asked.

"Yes, sir," agreed Ingles with a grin. "I'm amazed, my lord, you should remember. It's been a considerably long time since we have had the pleasure of your company."

"A considerably long time," Hartshire agreed. "Is Lord Panington about, Ingles? I was to meet him here at two."

"Indeed, he is, sir. In the front parlor, I believe."

Hartshire nodded, stuffed his hands into his breeches pockets and strolled through the vestibule into the parlor. He gazed around him to discover any number of elderly gentlemen ensconced in comfortable chairs, their noses buried in newspapers. "Hartshire!" a gravelly voice called, annoying everyone in the room enough to start myriad papers rattling. "Here, m'boy. Here I am. Come and make your bow to your godfather like you ought."

Hartshire grinned and directed his feet toward the grey-haired gentleman pleasantly at ease in an armchair near the fire. "Uncle Pan, a pleasure to see you again, sir," he said, bowing much like a ten-year-old boy before the ancient. "How have you been? Not had a note from you since Christmas."

"Been much the same. Much the same," grumbled the gentleman. "Bored to the top and then some. Don't ever grow old, boy. Ain't no good in it."

"No, sir. Intend to cease aging any time now. And how does Lady Panington go on?"

"Worse and worse," grumbled the old lord. "Never saw such a one for being in charge. Better we should call Wellesley home and give over command of our forces to your aunt Alicia. That would teach those Frenchies. Sit down, boy, and stay awhile. Never knew a better cure for boredom than you. M'day brightened considerably the moment I got your message. What have you been up to, eh?"

Hartshire lowered himself cautiously into the matching armchair beside his uncle. He sat slowly, gingerly. He placed his shoulders gently against the chair back and only then stretched his long legs out before him.

"Ain't got over it yet, have you?" chuckled Panington, watching with gleeful eyes each of Hartshire's movements.

"I beg your pardon, Uncle Pan?"

"That old chair of Alicia's falling apart under you. Lingers in your memory to this day."

"Indeed." Embarrassing adventures with other chairs crossed Hartshire's mind as well and brought a wide smile to his austere countenance. This smile did reach his eyes.

"So, what brings you to London, boy?" Panington queried, an eyebrow rising the merest bit. "Trouble in the offing, is there?"

"No, sir. What makes you think—"

"Come, come, be honest with me, Atticus. My heart is not so very ancient that it cannot bear a bit of vicarious excitement. You have not been in London for years. You have grown comfortable at Wilderhart Hall. And who's to blame you? Miriam touched you and Will tamed you. You would not have left the place unless the Home Office spies have mucked up royally, or unless there is something havey-cavey going on amidst the byways and the back rooms. Who are they who rise against the Crown this time?"

"Shhhh," hissed Hartshire, moving in the chair to look around and see who might have overheard. "Uncle Pan, you know perfectly well that I do not now or have I ever—"

"Boy," the old lord interrupted, "I was not your guardian for five seemingly endless years without knowing precisely the things you did. I was always well aware of the danger you tossed yourself into, though I did not think it proper to distract you at the time. No, don't scowl at me. I ain't about to let things slip. But I intend to know what you're up to now, eh? Just a bit of it. Things are dull as dust here and I need perking up."

Hartshire sighed and ran his fingers through his dark curls, disrupting them considerably. "I should like to provide you considerable entertainment, Uncle Pan, but I truly am not involved in anything at all exciting. At least, I don't expect it to prove exciting. It's merely that Lady Con has requested I take Val in hand. Give him sound advice, you know. Quash a number of silly notions he's acquired. Nothing more than that. In fact, that's precisely the reason I sought you out at once. Because one of the things he's become involved with concerns a Lord Dashfield. I wondered if you knew the fellow and might provide me with an introduction to him."

"Dashfield? You are after Dashfield?"

"No, Uncle Pan. I ain't after anyone. I simply wish to make that particular gentleman's acquaintance."

"By Jupiter, I knew he murdered her!" exclaimed Lord Panington jubilantly. "The scoundrel!"

"Shhhh! Uncle Pan, what the deuce are you going on about?"

"That poor murdered woman. Though why they have brought you in on it, I cannot guess. She wasn't royalty, after all. No, and she is already dead. Birdwitted sort of a woman, but already dead. That ain't your general area of expertise. Stop 'em *before* someone's killed, that's what you're accustomed to do."

Hartshire had the greatest wish to sink down into his chair until he was completely out of sight—an impossibility to be sure. He'd not guessed once that his uncle Pan had known about the things he'd done before he'd married and settled down and grown older. Nor had he ever expected the old gentleman to go discussing them at the top of his lungs in the middle of White's. Well, perhaps he wasn't speaking at the top of his lungs, but—

"I haven't the vaguest idea to what you refer, Uncle Pan," Hartshire said at what he hoped was a volume loud enough to carry to whoever had overheard his uncle, but still not loud enough to sound as if he were attempting to reach those particular ears. "You're imagining the oddest things of late."

"I refer to all the deviltry in which you've been involved for years now, you rascal, and I ain't grown into a doddering old fool yet. I am just as quick as I always was. Though I can't think why they should call you to London to set things right by Lady Dashfield. That I cannot grasp. No, wait! The lady's death was but a part of a conspiracy to do away with Prinny! That will be it! You are back in London to protect old Farmer George's heir! Did good by the Farmer, you did. Likely the Home Office expects you'll do just as well by the Regent, eh? Who is it out to kill our Florizel? You can trust me with the names, boy. I'll not let on."

Hartshire could not think whether to laugh or cringe. He did neither. He prayed instead that no one in the parlor had overheard that last bit about conspiracies, Farmer George and the Prince Regent. Please God, he prayed silently. Please let no one be paying us the least bit of attention.

It was fast approaching four o'clock as Fleur stepped up into the coach and settled back. "What a very odd woman," she murmured, gazing out at the nondescript little shop. "What an amazing woman."

"I do wish we knew her story," Althea added wistfully, settling herself on the rear-facing seat beside Davis as the coach pulled away from the curb.

"Indeed," agreed Fleur. "To think that she lives above that dreadful little shop when she might live anywhere she chooses."

"Did you believe that part, Mama? About her independence?"

"Oh, yes. Did not you take note of the paintings on her walls, Althea? And the china she used for tea? And the what-nots standing all about? Celeste is possessed of a good deal of money. The proof is all about her in those rooms."

"And yet, she required monies of Lord Hartshire to begin work on our dresses."

"Yes, well, perhaps it was not so much the money she required of him."

"What do you mean, Mama?"

"Only that between them, perhaps, his money was a symbol of something."

"Of what?"

"I have no idea. But I know she is neither poor, nor French, nor a true shopkeeper. And I know as well that we ought to be most grateful to Lord Hartshire for taking us to her because I have never seen such beautiful designs as she sketched for us. You will be the belle of every ball, Althea, in such dresses as she will make for you. Oh, how I wish you could take the floor at Almack's in one of her gowns."

"No, thank you very much. I do not care to go to Almack's. Ever," Althea replied with a frown.

"You have never been. How do you know?"

"I know all about it. I have heard any number of young ladies in the country tout its importance and I find I do not have the slightest wish to enter its sacred portals. Sacred portals! Of all things! As though to enter a veritable marriage mart disguised as an assembly were to enter the gates of heaven."

"Well, perhaps not quite the gates of heaven," Fleur replied with a winsome smile, "but you need not protest against the place so very strongly, Ally. The truth is that did I know of a way to gain you entreé, I would most certainly do so. Perhaps your aunt Helen? I will send her a note when we get home. If she agrees to speak for you and to chaperone you, just on Wednesday nights—"

"Aunt Helen? Accompany me to Almack's? Mama! Aunt Helen is the most spiteful, horrid woman who ever wore evening slippers!"

"Yes, but I think she can gain you entrance, dear heart, and I know I cannot."

"If Aunt Helen can obtain vouchers to Almack's for me," Althea replied with a defiant tilt of her pert little nose, "she can obtain them for you as well. Then *you* can accompany me to the Gates of Hades every Wednesday evening."

"Ally!"

"Oh, very well, perhaps I ought not have said the Gates of Hades, but I will not go there with Aunt Helen, nor will I go without you."

"They will not— I cannot—A woman must be of impeccable lineage to gain admittance to that particular place, and more, she must make an excellent impression on one or another of the patronesses when they come to pay her a call."

"So I have been informed over and over again by Miss Sarah Parks."

"Oh. Well, it's true. And I—"

"You have never been there," stated Althea, her hazel eyes flashing. "Is that not so?"

"But your aunt Helen has been and would not have any difficulty securing you vouchers. I am positive of it. You are, after all, of the most impeccable and ancient lineage."

"I will not go anywhere without you," Althea declared warmly. "Especially I will not go to Almack's. I will wager those rudesbys who accosted us outside Madame Annette's attend Almack's every single Wednesday. And you wish me to associate with *them?*"

"They are your peers, Ally. You must accustom yourself to associating with them. And you must learn to ignore the manner in which they choose to treat me. I think it likely Malcolm was correct at breakfast. I think we ought to hire a companion to accompany you into Society. Things would prove so much easier for you. You would be invited to so many more entertainments were the ladies all certain that I would not accompany you."

"Now it is not merely Almack's at which you intend to abandon me? You intend to send me out into London with a perfect stranger? Mama, you cannot! The very first time you attempt to do so, I shall faint dead away from the devastation of it."

"You, Ally?" asked Fleur, her brown eyes abruptly bubbling with laughter. "Faint away?"

"What a sight I should be. So very pitiful, all pale and still, stretched out, gracefully to be sure, on the drawing room carpet. You will not wish to see it, I promise you."

"But there are so many people who will not have me anywhere near them and therefore not invite you, Ally, to their balls and parties."

"Then that will be their loss," Althea replied, gazing regally down her nose. "With the help of Madame Celeste, I will be all the rage. I am quite decided upon it. And if the rudesbys do not invite me to their little entertainments because of you, then it is they who will be the poorer for it."

"They would not dare be rude to you. They were not rude to you this morning. They all addressed you or nodded to you. A good many of those women, you know, have marriageable daughters, and your brother—heaven forbid Mal should hear me say it—your brother must be considered a good catch. He'll be eagerly sought after now that he holds the title. All of those particular ladies and their daughters will be sweet as honey to you and Mal."

"Good!" exclaimed Althea. "Excellent! They will have me no matter what? Nothing better! And I shall be certain to remind them all that—"

Fleur's eyes opened wide in amazement as in midsentence her stepdaughter stuck her lovely head, hat and all, out through the carriage window.

"—I am the daughter of a shipbuilder's daughter!" Althea shouted as their coach turned into Brook Street.

"Jupiter! What is that female shrieking about?" queried Conningford as both he and Hartshire, having discovered each other at White's, paused to stare at the passing vehicle. "The coach ain't being robbed or anything."

"I'll be deviled," murmured Hartshire, noting the coat of arms on the door. "Now what?" He waved imperiously at the coachman, stepped off the curb and onto the cobbles, and strode directly toward the vehicle as the driver brought the horses to a standstill in the middle of the street.

"What the deuce are you doing, Atticus?" Conningford called, racing after him.

"Good day to you, again, Lady Marston, Miss Avondale," Hartshire said most politely. "You do not require any assistance, eh? I mean to say, we heard an exclamation of sorts and I thought perhaps—"

"Lord Hartshire. Oh, my goodness. I had no idea you were out there," Althea replied, her cheeks turning an enchanting shade of pink. "I was, well, quite carried away by passion, I suppose one might say. No, we don't require assistance, but it is so very sweet of you to inquire."

"Shrieking like some heathen in the middle of Brook Street. Sounded like a rabbit dying," mumbled Conningford as he reached the coach. "And what the deuce has a ship-builder to do with anything? Ain't no ships being built in Brook Street."

Althea looked away from Hartshire and at the gentleman who had just spoken. "What sounded like a rabbit dying?"

"That insufferable shriek." Conningford looked up and noted for the first time the very pretty young lady who had just addressed him. He took a quick step back at the sight of her.

Althea lifted her chin and gazed down her nose at him in the most imperious manner. "Obviously, sir, your ears deceive you. There are no rabbits in this coach, dying or otherwise."

"Was it you sh-shrieked?" Conningford stuttered, the particular ears Althea referred to slowly turning a bright red. "Well, of all th-things! Let us go, Atticus. I cannot th-think why you hailed the driver to stop in the first place. Anyone can plainly see they are just f-fine."

"We'll go in a moment, Val. After I have introduced you, eh? Cannot think of a more opportune moment. I will introduce you to the ladies and in return, you will introduce me."

"B-but how can you introduce me if you don't know them?" sputtered Conningford.

"It is not a case of not knowing them," Hartshire replied. "It is merely a case of never having been properly introduced. Had to introduce myself first, then the next time I did not even bother. But this time, I have you to do it. Lady Marston, Miss Avondale, may I present my brother-in-law, Lord Conningford. Say good day, Val."

"G-good day," Conningford replied brushing a blond curl back from his brow as he doffed his hat and bowed.

"Very nicely done. Now introduce me."

Lady Marston giggled. She did not know why, precisely. In all her life she had never been prone to giggle. Perhaps it was a reaction to Ally's shout, or the manner in which Lord Conningford's ears had turned so red. Perhaps it was the perfectly innocent and bewildered gaze Lord Conningford had turned on Hartshire, or even the abrupt dropping of Althea's nose to a proper angle as the younger gentleman had bowed so charmingly before them. But she rather thought it might just be Hartshire's insistence upon being introduced to them in a more proper fashion that caused it.

"You find something amusing?" Hartshire asked, his midnight eyes fixed on Fleur, a distinct twinkle in their depths.

"You do this because of what I said to you on the road to London, Lord Hartshire, about propriety, but you do realize that this is not a proper introduction either, do you not?"

"I do. But it is the best I can manage at the moment. I will try again later, I assure you. Are you just now coming from Celly's? You've decided to make use of her then?"

"Indeed. Her ideas and designs are fascinating."

"Just so. She is a rather daunting sort of woman, Celly, but I thought you would not dismiss her out of hand. I'm pleased you did not. She will not fail you, you know. You and Miss Avondale will rapidly become the two most fashionably dressed ladies in London. And by the way, I should be proud if I were you," he added softly.

"Proud, my lord?"

"Yes. To share your coach with such a spirited daughter of a shipbuilder's daughter," Hartshire replied, his fingers playing with the brim of the hat he held in his hands. "Well, it is my pleasure to see you again, Lady Marston, Miss Avondale," he added more loudly. He then bowed quite as nicely as had Lord Conningford. "Carry on," he called up to the coachman. And in another moment the coach was on its way and the gentlemen were back on the pavement and strolling toward home.

"That was Marston's s-s-s-sister," gasped Conningford, his cheeks quite as red as his ears.

"Um-hmmm. And his stepmother."

"She is positively beautiful, Atticus! I don't remember her ever looking beautiful. I wouldn't have known her even if I did spend an entire summer in her house when I was a schoolboy. Did you take note of her eyes, Atticus? How wonderfully changeable they were? Those eyes did not remain the same color from one moment to the next."

"They did not actually change color at all, Val. They merely grew warmer and more—enticing. I didn't notice that this morning. Of course, she was decidedly perturbed with me this morning.

"And her hair, Atticus, it shone like bright gold guineas where it peeked out from under that outrageous hat."

"Gold guineas? Her hair is brown. A dusky brown as though someone has shot it through with moonglow. And her hat was not outrageous. It was a perfectly genteel hat for a perfectly genteel lady. And she was wearing the beads. Put them on in precisely the right manner too."

Conningford ceased to walk in midstride. "Beads? What beads?"

"You know very well what beads. The ones I use whenever I must climb into a coach or set foot on a ship."

"You gave Lady Marston your *beads?* When? Why? What the devil has got into you to give away your beads? You'll be walking or riding horseback the rest of your life, Atticus. You'll never be able to climb into a coach or set foot aboard a ship again! Rad'll have to swim to France with you on his back if you wish to get there once the war has ended."

"What?" asked Hartshire, who had continued walking and now found himself required to take four steps back. "What is it you're babbling about, Val?"

"Oh, nothing," Conningford responded, noting the bemused yet frustrated look on his brother-in-law's rough-hewn countenance and wondering if he ought to mention this particular encounter to his mama. Lady Con had been wishing aloud for Hartshire to come to Town since they had visited him for Christmas. "Needs a bit of romance to set those remarkable eyes of his alight again," she had said innumerable times since then. "Never find love holed up in Kent, he won't." Conningford pondered the thing seriously. Perhaps he ought to mention Lady Marston's name in his mama's presence. Lady Marston's name and the fact that Atticus had given that lady his treasured beads.

Four

Throughout the next week, the shipbuilder's daughter built a small cottage for herself in Hartshire's heart. He could not quite understand it, but it was true nonetheless. Those warm brown eyes, that shimmering dusky hair, even the longish nose, the slightly jutting chin and the husky, hesitant sound of her voice never left him. Wherever he wandered in London, Lady Marston followed, though when he glanced up to see her, she was never truly there. When his uncle Pan introduced him to Dashfield in a box at Drury Lane, he heard Lady Marston's voice comment on the play from the adjoining box and paused right in the midst of accepting Dashfield's proffered hand to look for her, only to discover the box occupied by complete strangers.

He saw her driving through Grosvenor Square in an open carriage just as Will arrived from Kent. Swinging the laughing, protesting boy up into his arms, he gazed intently at the vehicle, only to find it actually contained no one but his neighbor, Lady Browne, her abigail and a considerable number of packages.

As the days passed, Lady Marston appeared to him everywhere. He caught glimpses of her at Gunter's, Madame Tussaud's and the Tower of London, at Week's Mechanical Museum, Westminster Abbey and Whitehall. And yet, he actually saw her not at all.

"Who is it you're always looking for, Papa?" Will asked at last, stuffing his hands into his pockets in imitation of Hartshire as they strolled through Green Park late on a sunny afternoon.

"What, Will?"

"I asked who you are always looking for."

"No one. Not precisely. It is merely that I keep seeing someone out of the corner of my eye but when I turn to look, well, I don't see her. Poof! She's gone!"

"Who?"

"Just a lady."

"What lady?"

"You have never met her, Will."

"Why?"

"Well, because I have never introduced her to you. But I will, should she happen to come by."

"Good, because I should like to meet a real ghost."

"I didn't say she was a ghost."

"Uh-huh," Will replied with an enthusiastic nod of his head. "You said you saw her and then she poofed and you did not see her. I should like to know who else can do that but a ghost. Papa! Look!"

"Where? At what?"

"There, Papa! There in that tree. Right under those leaves." Will freed his hands from his pockets and dashed to the bottom of a gnarled oak. He stared upward for a moment, hands on hips, then gathered himself and made a leap for the lowest branch.

"Whoa, there, Bucko," Hartshire drawled, putting his arms around the boy. "You can't possibly jump high enough to reach that limb, Will."

"I'm a good jumper."

"Yes, but not as good as that. What is it you're after?"

"It's right up there, Papa. Right in those leaves on the very first branch. Can't you see it?"

"No," admitted Hartshire, squinting up at the spot described. "All I see are leaves, Will."

"It's right in there under that bunch of them. Lift me up, Papa. If you lift me up, I can get it."

"Not until I know what *it* is, my boy."

"It's a dormouse. I think it's a dormouse. It looks just like the drawing in Mr. Canton's book. It ought not to be out now, Papa. It ought to be sleeping yet, somewhere safe. I expect something terrible has happened to it."

Hartshire's hands gripped his son's slim shoulders firmly. He squinted once more up into the newly greening tree, then down at Will. Visions of a frightened, injured dormouse sinking its teeth into his son's hand flashed through his mind, rapidly followed by visions of Will discovering a dead dormouse lying beneath the oak on their next walk and the boy turning to glare accusingly up at him.

"It may bite, Will, if it's injured. I'll fetch it down to you, eh? Not likely it will bite through my gloves. Here, hold my hat. No, better yet, take my hat and fill it with some of that dried grass over there and a few old leaves and a flower or two. Make a nest of sorts for him, eh? That's m'boy."

"It's the most beautiful dress I have ever seen!" exclaimed Althea, turning first one way and then another before the looking glass. She stepped forward; she stepped back; she twirled in a full circle. The sweetly embroidered hem of the pale blue jaconet flared around her ankles, the deep blue, embroidered half-boots peeked from beneath her skirt as she spun.

"And now the pelisse, Miss Avondale," urged Madame Celeste, assisting Althea into the most exquisite three quarter length coat fashioned of velveteen, the same deep blue as her half-boots.

"And your bonnet and gloves," added a smiling Fleur, setting a confection of pale blue silk with deep blue ostrich plumes on Althea's guinea gold curls and handing her the

matching gloves. "How lovely you look. Malcolm will be
overwhelmed. He awaits you out front in his curricle this
very moment. We will be extremely lucky if he does not fall
right off the seat and onto the cobbles from the shock of
how splendid you look."

"Oh, Mama. Mal? Overwhelmed by me? I should like to
see the day."

"This," declared Madame Celeste confidently, "is the day.
And once he climbs back onto his seat, he will drive you
through Hyde Park and cause all the other gentlemen to go
falling from their carriages and their horses as well."

"What a sight that will be," Fleur said with a grin. "Oh,
how I wish I could be there to see it! All the gentlemen of
the ton dropping like flies beneath an invisible swatter!"

"Why do you not come with us, Mama?" Althea queried,
securing the blue silk ribbons of her hat in a rakishly tilted
bow. "Mal and I should like it extremely."

"No, no, there is no room in a curricle for three, Ally."

"We will take the barouche."

"Your brother wishes to drive in style, dear heart. A con-
servative old barouche will not please him in the least."

"But—"

"Your mama cannot go with you now, Miss Avondale,"
Madame Celeste said quite loudly in what Althea had come
to define as her usual abstracted way. "I have it in mind to
design a number of dresses for your mama and we must confer, she and I. You wish your mama to be stylish, do you not?"

"Oh, yes," Althea replied enthusiastically. "Very well,
Mama, we shall go without you this once. But do not think
that we shall always be leaving you home alone, for we
shan't." With a smile and a swish, Althea departed the room,
waving a farewell with one elegantly gloved little hand.

"She looks positively ravishing, Celeste," Fleur said with
a sigh. "I cannot thank you enough."

"No, you can't," declared the dressmaker. "The dress did

turn out quite well, did it not? But it is not me you have to thank for it."

"Who then?"

"Hartshire, of course. I don't make dresses for just anyone. But for Hartshire, yes. Always. Do not tell him so," she added with a shake of one chubby finger.

"Do not tell him?"

"He came to me thinking he must convince me to do this thing for him. To bribe me to do this thing."

"He did?"

"Just so. I would have made the dresses for you and Miss Avondale simply because he requested it of me, but to offer money—Well, it requires that I demand the money, no? And give him something extra into the bargain."

"The extra was your professing to have changed your mind and demanding we leave your shop?" asked Fleur, a smile flickering across her face and then lingering softly on her lips. "And addressing him as simply Hartshire?"

"Changing my mind, yes, that is the extra I gave him. Hartshire, I have always called him, from the day he inherited the title." Celeste ran her fingers through her hair, much as any gentleman might, and set it to standing on end.

"You've known Lord Hartshire a very long time, Celeste?"

"An eternity. I dressed his sweet Miriam, you know. He brought her to me much as he did you. She was *such* an imp!"

"An imp? Truly?"

"Indeed," grinned Celeste, her eyes aglow with fond memories. "A veritable sprite with hair so pale gold as to be almost silver and eyes the color of a summer sky, and a mouth—oh, such a mouth!"

"Lips like a Cupid's bow?" asked Fleur, attempting to imagine the woman who had won Lord Hartshire's heart.

"No, no, not her lips, her mouth—A mouth like a sergeant-major, I vow it. There was nothing sweet Miriam would not

say. Oh, such a girl was Miriam! Frightened the wits right out
of Hartshire at first. Chased him all over London. Took hold
of him by the ears and forced him to propose to her at the
last, I think. Such an imp! Nothing was beyond her once she
met him. She *would* have him. 'I will follow him to Hades
and back' she told me once, 'if that is what it takes to get him
to marry me!' So in love with him, she was. And then, when
they married, she went with him to Kent and to the surprise
of every one of us, they both grew quiet and comfortable
together. At least, they seemed to do so, though I do not doubt
for one minute that she rode with him astride and fished and
hunted with him, and stamped on his foot from time to time
with great authority."

"You stamped on his foot."

"Yes. It's a matter of principle to do so."

"That's precisely what you said when you did it, but I do
not understand what principle it could possibly—"

"You will come to know him well, I think. Yes, do not
deny it, for you will. I promise you this. And when you do,
you will stamp on his foot, too, just for the principle of the
thing. Then you won't need to ask what principle it is. One
day, *voilà,* it will come to you. Enough of Hartshire! The
day is glorious. I am thinking to go for a wander through
Green Park. Will you join me or not? We shall discuss precisely the gowns I have in mind to make for you. Particularly
for you. There is something about you calls to my very soul.
Most extraordinary, you are. I see it as clearly as I see the
sun shining through that window."

"Indeed, I should like to wander aimlessly with you
through the park," grinned Fleur.

They traveled to Green Park in style, with John Coachman
driving them in the barouche and Davis in attendance, the
abigail prepared to walk along the paths, trailing but a few
steps behind them, for as long as they desired.

"What a wonderful idea," Fleur declared as she descended
from the vehicle, slipped her arm companionably through

Celeste's and strolled off along one of the footpaths. "I am so very pleased you thought of it. Now, before we discuss dresses, may we discuss you? For a short time merely? I am not so gullible that I take you for an ordinary shopkeeper, my dear Celeste. You are of the Quality, are you not?"

"I am."

"But where are you from? What brought you to London? Why do you make dresses and only for particular people?"

"Because I can," declared Celeste succinctly. "With very hearty thanks to Hartshire, I can do what I please when I please, and never again be told to act this way or dress that way or made to follow everyone else's rules. I am free as the proverbial bird and rich as well and I take full advantage of it."

"And it was Lord Hartshire set you free? But how?"

"Ah, that is a tale to be told very late at night before a dwindling fire with thunder crashing and the wind whistling down the chimney. It cannot be told here, in the midst of a fine afternoon."

"I do beg your pardon. I ought not have pried."

"You beg my pardon? No, no, you need not. You are merely curious. I am not opposed to satisfying that curiosity and telling you the whole of it, but not here and not yet. Some night, as I say. Some stormy night, perhaps I will tell you all, for by then you'll have become my very good friend. Perhaps more than a good friend. Perhaps we will discover that we are sisters of a sort. Yes, the tall, gangly you and the short stubby me, I think we are sisters beneath the skin. We shall see if I'm proved correct." Without the least hesitation, Celeste halted on the path and with one short, stubby finger, traced the thin, jagged line on Fleur's cheek, the scar that stood out so starkly in sunlight.

A shudder made its way swiftly up Fleur's spine. Though the breeze was warm and the sun bright, she shivered as they approached the flower garden. She cannot possibly mean what I think she means, Fleur thought. Marston could not have reached out so very far as to ruin this woman's life as well as mine, could he? No, I am imagining things. Celeste refers to something else entirely. It can't have anything to do with Marston. The blasted scar merely caught her attention for a moment. Nothing more.

Fleur raised her glance toward the heavens. God, give me the strength to deal with whatever Marston has done that I don't so much as know about yet, she prayed silently. Give me strength for Ally's sake and for Malcolm's! If there are secrets to be yet revealed about that beast who was their father, let me be the one to face them and wipe them out on behalf of his children. "Oh, great heavens!" she cried aloud.

"What is it, Little Flower?" asked Celeste at once.

"Madam?" called Davis, rushing to her mistress's side. "What has happened? What can I do?"

"You frightened me half to death!" declared Fleur roundly, hearing neither of the women, still gazing upward.

"I do beg your pardon," answered a sonorous, bodiless voice, nearly sending both Celeste and Davis into palpitations. "I didn't notice anyone near when I climbed up here, and I thought, if I just remained silent—"

"Climb down at once," ordered Fleur. "You will fall and break your neck."

"No. I won't do that," replied Hartshire, smiling down at her, his face dappled by the leaves. "Won't fall and break my neck, I mean. Ah, there's my boy," he added as he caught sight of Will hurrying back across the green.

"I have got lots and lots, Papa," Will called running as fast as he could while clutching his father's hat carefully in both hands. He came to a halt beneath the oak facing Lady Marston, Celeste and Davis, his eyes growing large at the sight of so many women gathered beneath the tree.

"Will, say a proper 'how do you do' to Lady Marston and Celeste and hold up my hat. Lady Marston, my son, Viscount Howard."

"How do you do, ma'am," Will managed, bowing as best

he could without losing his grip on the hat. "How do you do, Celeste. It is very nice to see you again. Who is the other lady, Papa?"

"She is Lady Marston's abigail."

"Good afternoon to you, Abigail," nodded Will politely.

"All right, Will, enough of introductions. Hold the hat as high as you can. That's m'boy."

One long and very well-muscled arm reached down from the branch and set something into the hat. Fleur could not see what, but she noted that the earl was quite gentle with it. Then the leaves rustled, the branch swayed and the Earl of Hartshire was swinging most gracefully to the ground. How he managed to look perfectly elegant doing so, as large as he was and swinging down out of an oak, Fleur could not imagine. But he did.

"Ladies," he said as he stood before them. "Davis. I must apologize, I fear. Had I known anyone was about I would not have—Well, yes, I would have climbed up regardless, but I should have given you some warning of my presence."

"Are gentlemen not to be expected to appear in the trees in Green Park?" asked Celeste with a twinkle in her eyes. "Do you mean to say you were doing something exceptional again, Hartshire?"

"No. I mean to say that it was an emergency is all, and I couldn't refuse to do it. I really could not."

"An emergency?" asked Fleur, her lips twitching upward. "In a tree?"

"Papa! He *is* injured!" cried Will, abruptly.

"Yes, so I discovered, but I think we can fix him up all right and tight, Will."

"Who is injured?" asked Celeste and Fleur together.

"Well, I don't think he has a name as yet," Hartshire replied. "Though I doubt not that he'll have one by tomorrow morning. He's broken a leg. I dare say we shall be forced to make a splint for him, Will. Bring the hat closer, m'boy, and allow the ladies to see our wounded warrior."

"A dormouse!" exclaimed Fleur softly, looking down into eyes as brown and appealing as her own. "Celeste, only see how perfectly adorable he is. And just look at those ears!" she chuckled. "I don't believe I have ever seen such enormous ears in all my life."

"Just so," Celeste agreed. "The little fellow has ears almost as large as Hartshire's."

Hartshire found he could not be still. He had taken Will and the dormouse home, most competently splinted the dormouse's leg and then eaten his dinner in the schoolroom with his son and Mr. Canton. He had made Will laugh by offering the dormouse a forkful of flounder and had made Mr. Canton laugh by offering the same forkful to him. Proposing, after dinner, that the boy and the tutor discover what dormice actually did eat and where they preferred to sleep, he left them and wandered off down the stairs. The truth was, Hartshire had had quite enough of the dormouse. It was the oddest thing, really, and not at all the little fellow's fault, but each time Hartshire looked at the dormouse and it gazed innocently and trustingly back at him with those melting brown eyes, he saw Lady Marston's eyes instead of the creature's. And if that were not bad enough, the dormouse's ears would then remind him how big his own ears were, and how Lady Marston had laughed at the sight of them.

Sans coat, his hands stuffed into his pockets, his dark curls in disreputable disarray, he proceeded by the most meandering path to his chambers where he called for Robes and changed from his morning coat, buckskin breeches and boots into a rig more acceptable for an evening in London.

"You are deplorably out of fashion, my lord," Robes said as he assisted the earl to don a coat of deep burgundy velvet. "Four years and more out of fashion. Your coats should be tighter, your collars higher and your hair shorter."

"Oh?"

"Indeed, my lord. And your coat should be black or dark blue for evening. I've been taking notes and asking about Town since Little and I came to open the house. Everyone agrees that you ought to seek out a tailor by the name of Weston, my lord. That is the name the valets of all the best gentlemen give me. Mr. Brummell swears by him, I understand."

"Is that so?" asked Hartshire with a rather grim smile. He studied himself seriously in the looking glass and his smile faded completely. "This Weston, does he work miracles, Robes?"

"I beg your pardon, my lord?"

"Miracles. He's a tailor, eh? But is he a tailor of such great talent that he can fashion clothes to make me appear less than I am?"

"Less than you are, my lord?"

"Yes, a good deal less than I am."

"His fashions are all the crack, my lord, and doubtless, he could outfit you to perfection, but to make you less than you are? I am afraid I do not take your meaning."

"No, of course you don't."

"I am sorry, my lord."

"Do not persist in 'my lording' me, Robes."

"No, my lord."

"I realize that you have a significant amount of professional pride involved in my appearance. And I am well aware that when I walk out of this establishment, I am by no means a gentleman of whom you're proud."

"I did not say any such thing!" exclaimed the valet in amazement. "I would never—"

"All the 'my lording' in the world cannot change what I am, Robes, nor can a fashionable tailor," the earl interrupted gruffly. "I would gladly fork over the money for a new wardrobe simply to gain you esteem among your peers. I would do it gladly. Because I like you and I should hate to lose your services."

"I have not said a word about you losing my services,"

protested the valet, stunned. "Not a word. And it is you blathering on about my prestige and my esteem, not me."

"Lord knows you could do much better for yourself with any other gentleman in Britain, Robes. The Lord knows it and I know it, too."

"Balderdash! Whatever freakish temper you're in, I wish you will sail your way out of it and quickly. I would not choose to work for any other gentleman in Britain did he come crawling to me on his knees with bags of golden guineas in his hands."

"I'm in a freakish temper," muttered Hartshire, readjusting his neckcloth the merest bit. "Possibly because I'm a freak."

"My lord!" gasped Robes.

"Only look at me, Robes. I tower over everyone I know. My shoulders are wide enough to make me turn sideways simply to squeeze through some doorways. If people still believed in giants, they would run into their houses the moment they glimpsed me walking down the street. Yes, they would. Run into their houses, hide their sons and lock up their daughters."

Robes stared perfectly dumbfounded at the earl. He tugged on his right earlobe. He shuffled his feet.

"And were I to wear my coats any tighter, Robes," Hartshire continued, "my collars any higher or my hair any shorter, I would look more freakish still. I would look like a lion stuffed into a barn cat's skin."

Robes ceased to fidget and fairly bristled up at that. "Complete balderdash!" he responded heartily. "Tripe! You are the very essence of true British manhood, that's what you are. There is no gentleman in all of Britain who does not secretly envy every inch of you! I have ever been proud to be your valet!"

Hartshire's remarkable eyes blinked into the mirror at his valet's reflection and then his own, and his heart sank. "I apologize, Robes," he said in a much gentler tone. "I cannot think why I should toss such a tantrum. Anyone would think I was no older than three. I expect it was having it pointed out to me this afternoon how large the dormouse's ears were."

"The—the—dormouse, my lord? Ears, my lord?"

"Yes. I expect she didn't mean it as an insult. Well, I know she did not. But Lady Marston laughed up at me, and I remembered on the spot exactly how large my ears are. And then I remembered how large the rest of me is, too. In comparison, you know. At any rate, I do beg your pardon. You were quite correct to point out that my clothes are considerably behind the times. Quite right. It is fundamental to your position, after all, to make me aware of such things. It is just that I cannot imagine that I will ever do anything about it, Robes. The present fashion would not prove kind to me, I fear."

Thoroughly embarrassed by his outburst *and* his attempt to explain it, Hartshire departed his chambers leaving a much perplexed Robes behind to wonder what had prompted such outrageous words to burst forth from his employer. "He has not bemoaned his size since the day Lady Miriam was introduced to him all those years ago," murmured Robes, folding his lordship's buckskin breeches over his arm. "Oh, how he did go on then, I do recall. Named himself all sorts of vile names. Intimated he might well be larger than the London bridge. Great heavens! It cannot be that he has met another lady for whom—Could he have done?" pondered Robes in a whisper. "I shall have to speak with Little about it. Yes, indeed I shall. We will be forced to keep our eyes and ears open if it's so, in order to discover who she is, this Lady Marston person."

Even as Robes pondered, Hartshire, with a sigh and a shake of his head at his own foolishness, descended to the ground floor and stepped into his study. Finding himself with nothing on his desk that actually required his attention, he wandered aimlessly to the library, then into the front parlor, where he peered out the windows into the square.

* * *

Lady Marston lifted the card from the silver salver in the vestibule and stared at it. "When did it arrive?" she asked the butler quietly. "It is Wickens, is it not? Yes, of course it is. Do forgive me, Wickens. I shall have everyone's name straight in a matter of days. It is so very daunting to have an entire house filled with new servants. Was it you opened the door when this invitation was delivered?"

"Indeed, madam," Wickens responded. "A footman delivered it shortly before dinner."

"A footman?"

"Yes, my lady."

"Very well. Thank you, Wickens." Fleur wandered off toward the drawing room where Ally and Marston awaited her.

"Ally," she announced, as she entered the room. "Already you've received an invitation. And to think, you have only just stepped out into Society this very afternoon."

"I should think she stepped out into Society," teased Marston. "Had every unmarried gentleman on the strut racing across the park to be introduced to her, she did. Never saw such a bumblebath. Stepping on each other, they were. Edging each other's mounts to one side. All speaking at the same time. A regular riot of beaux. And all for Ally. I thought I would fall off the box laughing at them."

"Untrue!" declared Althea. "I threatened to throw you off the box for laughing and for continuing to encourage even more of them to gather 'round. Who is the invitation from, Mama? It is not from Aunt Helen?" she added with an abrupt frown.

"No, not Helen. It is from Lady Conningford."

"Lady Con? Jupiter!" Marston exclaimed. "I expect it's Connie's doing then. But he wasn't at the park to see you, Ally."

"Perhaps not," smiled Fleur. "Ally and Lord Conningford did meet, however, as we were entering Brook Street some days ago. Lord Hartshire was kind enough to present him to us. He has not altered so very much from when he was a lad," Fleur added. "He is still as slim and delicate, though he has grown taller, of course."

"Did he stutter, Mama, when he was presented to Ally? He's still fairly shy around the ladies and it comes out in his speech."

"He stuttered abominably," declared Ally. "And he said I sounded like a dying rabbit."

"He said what? Connie? I can't believe it!"

"Well, apparently he's fond of young ladies who sound like dying rabbits, for he has got his mother to invite us to a musical evening," Fleur said. "The invitation is addressed to you, Malcolm, but on the bottom is a handwritten note including Ally and myself by name." Fleur could feel the butterflies flitting about in her stomach as she said the words. She had held out some hope, for a moment, that Ally and Malcolm would not wish to attend. That, of course, had been delusional. Certainly they wished to attend. And rightly so. And she must attend as well because not only had Althea's aunt Helen refused to intercede for the girl with the patronesses of Almack's, Helen had declared loudly and clearly that she would not be cajoled into chaperoning her brother's daughter anywhere.

"What did Marston ever do for me?" she had asked Fleur in the most freezing tones during their brief and very private conversation several days earlier. "He teased me, taunted me, attempted to prevent my marriage. And then he went out and married a shipbuilder's daughter! It has taken me years to live your marriage down, you encroaching little mushroom, and now you return to London to put me to the blush again. I cannot have you expelled from London, but I shall not welcome you to it, or accept any responsibility for Althea. Do not expect it of me!"

"Mama? Is there something wrong?" asked Althea, noticing Fleur's countenance pale quite suddenly as she sat down upon the embroidered silk loveseat. "Are you not feeling well?"

"Shall I fetch your vinaigrette?" Marston offered.

"No, no, I'm fine, children. Mal, did you not say you had agreed to meet Lord Conningford this evening? Yes, you did. Go, then. Off with you. You don't wish to waste your evening lolling about the house with your sister and me."

"But if you are not feeling just the thing—"

"I'm fine. Truly. Go and meet Lord Conningford and say that we will be pleased to attend his mother's musical evening. He is likely on tenterhooks wondering whether Ally will be there or not. Assure him that I shall send his mother an acceptance note first thing in the morning."

Hartshire ceased staring out into the square, turned on his heel and paced back and forth across the parlor. Twice. But that was all he could bear of it. The third time across, his feet led him out into the corridor and down it as far as the kitchen and the butler's pantry. He stepped in, discovered a small silver pitcher on one of the counters and took it up into his hands. He turned it over and over again, then set it down and took up a remarkably beautiful plate instead. He stared curiously at it, set it down, and reached behind Little's back to snatch up a silver spoon.

"Is there something you require, my lord?" asked Little, thoroughly discomposed by what he recognized to be his employer's restlessness. The butler set aside his polishing cloth. "May I fetch you some brandy and a volume to read perhaps? In your study?"

"No, thank you, Little. Setting your teeth on edge, am I? Never mind. You needn't answer that. I know I am. To have someone fidgeting about in your pantry always sets your teeth on edge. Besides, I can see it in your eyes."

"You cannot see it in my eyes," Little objected adamantly, setting the silver bowl he held down with a considerable thwack. "You cannot see anything in my eyes. Do not say that you can. I have been practicing before the looking glass for hours on end ever since Robes and I came to open the house. I am a stoic. My eyes reflect stoicism and nothing more. I have determined to become the perfect, inscrutable butler and I am doing a damnably fine job of it, too."

"Are you?" Hartshire grinned. "I wish you will not."

"May I ask why not, my lord?"

"Because I would not relish a change in that direction."

"My lord, a proper butler does never let on, not even by the merest blink of an eye—"

"Little, you are the best butler I've ever had," the earl interrupted, shoving his hands into his breeches pockets and tapping the heel of one Hessian boot against the wood trim along the very bottom of the cupboard.

"Me, sir?"

"Indeed. No matter how hard you strive for the requisite bland expression, your biases are always observable. Your nose twitches or your lip quivers or a certain light in your eyes betrays your emotions. It's enjoyable, actually, the combination of strict butler etiquette and the opinions constantly flickering across your face. I don't wish you to become the perfect inscrutable butler. I don't wish you to change one thing about yourself. It may not be clear to you, but it is to me. You were born specifically to be *my* butler and I cannot think why we did not discover one another sooner."

"Perhaps because butling for you did never occur to me, my lord," Little replied, folding his polishing cloth carefully, avoiding Hartshire's gaze. "An infant is not born into the world hoping he will grow to be a butler. Butlerhood is conferred upon one."

"Yes, well, it was conferred upon *you,* at any rate. Never thought to aspire to it, eh?"

"Never, my lord."

"Aspired to various other things, though, didn't you?"

"Ah, yes, my lord."

"You have not had a, ah, a relapse in that direction recently, have you, Little?"

"A relapse, my lord? Well, there is always a tiny twitch at the back of my mind. Rather an itch of sorts." Little placed the polishing cloth tidily into a drawer, turned to face his employer, clasped his hands behind his back and stared with blatant interest straight into Hartshire's eyes. "I have managed to twitch the itch away for a goodly number of years now, my lord," he said with a hint of suspicion. "However, I do believe that I am perfectly capable of discovering a tendency to backslide if you should require it of me."

Hartshire nodded. "Still, I don't like to ask you to do it, Little. It could prove dangerous, you know. And I would be on tenterhooks worrying about you. Besides, it likely will not prove necessary. No, I shouldn't think it will prove necessary at all."

"If you should change your mind, my lord," Little replied with a bit of a smile. "If you should at any time change your mind, you need merely give me the nod, you know. It would not be at all difficult for me to revert to—my old instincts."

"You'd relish a bit of excitement, eh, Little?"

"I should not be opposed to some, my lord, if it should happen to become unavoidable."

"Just so."

"I do not expect for a moment that Robes would be opposed to a bit of an adventure either, now that I think on it," Little added. "Quite dull, the two of us have been, for a goodly long time. Are you aware that the Duchess of Darlington has had another child, my lord? It's all the talk at the Silver Swan."

"The Duchess of Darlington? A child? Why should that be all the talk, Little?"

"Well, because the duke has been shut away at his estate in the Cotswolds for over a year now, my lord. And because the Regent has been a frequent visitor at Her Grace's residence here in town."

"No, I hadn't heard a word about that. But then, I've not been out and about with any of the gentlemen much. Mostly showing Will the sights, you know. And Will don't know a duchess from a dowel. Besides, I doubt I shall so much as get a glimpse of either the Duchess of Darlington or the Prince Regent. Unless, of course, I decide to attend some party where Prinny deigns to appear. Regular social butterfly, our Regent, eh? Fond of older ladies still. Well, at least I'm not obliged to keep him from becoming fodder for the gossip mill. I'd hate to be forced to attempt that impossible task. Don't doubt for a minute that Prinny's escapades helped to drive King George mad."

"Just so, sir."

"I shall cease driving *you* quite mad now, Little, with my wandering and my fidgeting and my spewing forth of stupid ideas. I'm going out. Conningford was to arrive here an hour ago. I cannot think what has made him so very late, but I can wait no longer. Patience is not one of my virtues at the moment. If he should turn up at our door, tell him I have gone 'round to White's, will you? And tell Robes he need not wait up for me. You need not wait up either. Leave a lamp burning on the table in the vestibule. That will suffice."

Five

"Is that it?" Hartshire asked quietly as he took Marston's arm and tugged the young man closer to his side. "It's not the one Dashfield carried when I made his acquaintance. More ornate, this."

Marston studied the malacca cane as Dashfield, dressed in the very height of fashion, leaned it negligently against the edge of the card table and sat down to a game of whist. "Yes. That's m'father's all right."

"What makes you so certain?"

"The handle. The significance of that particular handle has puzzled me for years now. He designed it himself, m'father. Had it fashioned at Rundell and Bridges, he told me. At any rate, he then hired a workman to fasten the handle onto a particularly fine length of malacca. Tossed out all of his other sticks shortly after my mother died and carried only the malacca from then on."

Hartshire's gaze lingered on the handle of Dashfield's cane for a very long moment. "Definitely distinctive, but there might well be more than one cane with the head of a falcon fashioned in silver as a handle."

"I know. I did think of that, Hartshire. Anyone might make a cane like my father's. But if you look closely, the falcon has one ruby eye and one emerald. And at the very base, where it attaches to the stick there is a large sapphire."

Hartshire glanced again at the cane. An emerald eye and then a ruby one winked at him in the glare of the lamps. At the base of the handle, a sapphire gleamed. "Still, it's unlikely he stole it, Marston. Way too audacious to bring it with him here to White's where anyone who knew your father might recognize it, if he actually stole the thing. He does know you're a member here, does he not?"

"Yes, sir, he does."

"Makes it even more unlikely, then. You wouldn't happen to know where Val is, by the way?" Hartshire added, turning from the table and making his way through the room crowded with whist players and spectators toward the doorway.

"We're leaving? But I thought we were going to retrieve m'father's cane," Marston whispered as he followed Hartshire.

"We will in time. Dashfield ain't likely to pick up the cane and go trotting out the front door until the game is over. He'll stay until the last hand is finished."

They stepped out into the corridor, turned right and strolled together along the hallway, passing and nodding to innumerable gentlemen along the way.

"Terribly crowded tonight," Marston observed.

"Quite. About Val, Marston. He was to meet me at Hartshire House well over an hour ago. I left word for him that I had come on here. Where the deuce can he be? You never did answer me."

"I—I—cannot imagine where he is."

Hartshire slowed his pace and gazed steadily at the young man. He cocked one eyebrow in the most haughty manner. "You cannot?" he asked quietly, and then turned into the last of the rooms at the very rear of the corridor. "Ah, a place of solitude and silence at last. Close the door behind us, Marston. We might yet gain some privacy if we're lucky. Val knew we planned on finding Dashfield tonight and requesting a look at the cane, did he not? Yes, he did," Hartshire answered his own query as he crossed the carpeting in four long strides, studied a brocade wing chair before the fire, nodded silently to himself and sat down cautiously in it. "I remember distinctly that we all agreed tonight would be the night."

"Yes, and we've found Dashfield, but we haven't requested to see the cane yet," Marston pointed out, flopping down into the chair beside Hartshire's. "I don't see what good it will do to request to see it anyway. I have already seen it. I know it's Father's."

"Um-hmmm. And what do you think we ought to do, Marston?"

"I think you ought to walk right back in there and pinch the thing, sir."

"Me? Pinch a fellow's cane?"

"You can. You have stolen things before, right out from under people's noses. I know you've done it. Connie told me."

"Val has an extremely large mouth," mused Hartshire. "And his lips flap like the wings on a wren in mating season."

"It is not Connie's fault."

"No, it ain't, because my mouth is at least three times as large, my lips flap even more and I am the one who told him all the stories to begin with."

"Just so," nodded Marston. "And all he did was tell them to me. And I positively knew the very moment you turned up that you would be the one to—"

"There is something else going on, ain't there?"

"I beg your pardon, Hartshire?"

"All this business about the cane, wanting me to go back and pinch it, it's nothing but a sham," murmured Hartshire. "Val is up to something and you and he have devised this bit of nonsense to distract me."

"What? No, sir. That ain't the case at all. Dashfield has stolen m'father's cane and I do want it back."

"Um-hmmm."

"It's true. I give you my word on it."

"And do you give me your word that Val is not somewhere

he ought not to be even as we speak? Doing something he does not wish me to find out about?"

"I—I—"

"No, you cannot give me your word on that, can you? Devil take it, what has that scoundrel gotten himself into? What has he gotten you into?"

"Connie has gotten me into nothing," Marston drawled with as much sophistication as he could manage. "I have a perfectly good mind of my own and—"

"Yes, yes, never mind that, Marston. I comprehend. He did not force you into it. You joined in of your own free will."

"Exactly."

"What did you join him in?"

"Sir?"

"Must we go through all this roundaboutation again? Do you forget already, Marston, who I am?"

"N-no, sir."

"Good. You would be well advised never to forget it. Now, once again, where is my soon to be infamous brother-in-law?"

"I don't know."

"Marston!"

"No, sir. I truly don't. He ought to have been here by now. I cannot think why he isn't. I ought to have accompanied him. I said as much, but he would not hear of it. He said it was more important for me to—ah—"

"Direct my mind toward other things."

"Yes. Well, not exactly. I mean the cane is damnably important to me, Hartshire."

"From where, Marston, has Val not returned?"

"From The Nag's Head."

"The Nag's Head? What in Hades is The Nag's Head?"

"It is a—a public house in Carnaby Market."

"Oh, joy," Hartshire sighed. "Just the place Val belongs. He'll fit right in with the general run of patrons, eh? Stand out like a swan's egg in a sparrow's nest."

"You are fair and far off there, sir. Connie fits in perfectly. And I do as well."

"Oh, gads!" sighed Hartshire, the exclamation rumbling from deep in his throat. "How do you *fit in?* Or need I ask?"

"Well, we each have a special set of clothes, you see. Keep them in Connie's stables. Not even our valets know about them. You never know, Connie says, a valet can be a radical, too. Ain't that right, Hartshire? I mean to say, anyone can be a radical. At any rate, we've practiced over and over with our speech as well and I'll wager when we are suitably dressed and in one of the public houses even you could not tell us from a pair of regular ruffians."

Hartshire stared at the young man, took a very deep breath, released it slowly. "Tell me precisely what goes forth."

"I have told you."

"No, you have been dancing all around it with great delicacy. If you make me guess, Marston, both you and Val will be much the worse off for it. What I imagine the two of you to be involved in is likely much worse than what you actually have become involved in. At least, I hope it is."

Marston's eyes, as changeable as his sister's, turned a deep amber as they caught the firelight. His hair shone like polished gold, curling low over his brow and whispering around his ears. The very sight of the young man nibbling at his lower lip and tapping his fingers uneasily on the arm of the chair brought Miss Avondale to Hartshire's mind at once. The thought of Miss Avondale produced at once a thought of Lady Marston. And the thought of Lady Marston sent an unexpected flash of heat down into Hartshire's belly.

"Back to The Nag's Head," he said at once, attempting to ignore that particular flash of heat. "Explain to me, Marston, what goes forth. All of it."

"I don't know all of it. That is to say, Connie began the thing on his own. I only joined in a few months back, but he has been involved in it a good deal longer than that. We go to public houses all fitted out, as I said, like regular ruffians. We leave from Connie's stables and go out through the mews so no one will take note of us. Well, we couldn't possibly stroll out the front door of the house dressed as ruffians."

"And you go to The Nag's Head in Carnaby Market."

"Not always. That is merely where Connie went tonight. We go to any number of places. Wherever the meetings are held."

"What meetings?"

"The meetings of what Connie calls the Spancersomethings."

"Spancersomethings?" Hartshire leaned his head against the high back of the chair. His hand went to cover his eyes. For a long moment he moved not at all, nor did he make a sound. Then, "SpancersomethingsSpancersomethingsSpancersomethings," he muttered, making the word sound much like a growl. "You do not mean Spencean somethings?" he asked abruptly.

"Yes, that's more like it! Spencean! The Spencean Philosophers I think Connie calls them." Marston felt the greatest relief at having discovered the correct words. "Though I think it rather uppity of them to call themselves philosophers. And they are certainly the most eccentric philosophers I have ever listened to."

"Damnation!" Hartshire bellowed and slammed a fist down on the arm of his chair, startling Marston no end. "You will get yourselves killed!"

"Not a chance," declared Marston confidently. "Connie says we are doing everything precisely as you would. We are going to save the Crown—or the Prince Regent or the members of Lords or somebody—from certain doom. That's what Connie says. Though I don't see it myself. I think it's all a sham. Surely philosophers don't go about threatening the Crown and killing princes and other people. Although, these particular philosophers do talk a lot about revolts and equal suffrage for all men and pandemonium in the streets and things."

Hartshire groaned, lowered his hand from before his eyes and blinked three times, very determinedly, at the fire. Then he leaned forward in the chair until he could stare directly into Marston's eyes. "I have, over an extended number of years, come to call them the Spencean Philanthropists, Marston, not the Spencean Philosophers. I named them that. Someday they may take the name for themselves. Who knows? It certainly suits the followers of Thomas Spence. They're a group of men spurred on by his teachings and writings. He's just got released from debtor's prison of late, I believe. A complete zealot, Spence. Completely mad and takes his own notions from the works of people like Joseph Priestley, Mary Wollstonecraft and Thomas Paine."

"Yes, well, but any number of people—"

"Yes, any number of people, including myself, can see a benefit in some of the radical ideas floating about. These particular people, however," Hartshire frowned, "are notorious for spawning violent revolutionaries."

"Well, but I don't see where chalking words on brick walls is actually revolutionary," grumbled Marston.

"Not that, no. But it was Thomas Spence and his followers instigated the bread riots in 1801, though it was not proved. And they've stirred up any number of violent protests since then, too. Get carried away at times, do the followers of Thomas Spence. And they put the foulest ideas in the minds of madmen. Men like Hadley and Despard are bred among them, find supporters and encouragement amongst that crowd. Always there is some Spencean to urge them on."

"J-John Hadley?" asked Marston, wide-eyed.

"Exactly. John Hadley. The gentleman who so kindly forced me to squeeze into the pit at Drury Lane and act like an utter fool simply to ruin his aim when he began shooting at the King. Yes. And Colonel Edward Despard who also had it in mind to do away with old Farmer George. He and three dozen men found support from Spence and his followers. So you see, Val is correct to a point. They are a danger to the Crown. But they're more than that. They're flat-out radicals, Marston, bent on a violent revolution and the overthrow of the entire government, not merely the King or the Regent or a lord here and there."

"No!"

"Yes, and you and Val are out there playing games among them and have been for—How long? Do you know? Gawd, Lady Con *will* have my guts for garters if she finds out about this, as will your stepmother. Where the devil is this Nag's Head? I know you said in Carnaby Market, but where? Has it a sign or is it simply some hole in the wall?" Hartshire asked, gaining his feet and crossing hurriedly toward the door.

"You are not going there now?"

"Of course I am going there now. Val ain't here, is he? Then likely he is still there. Even more likely they have found him out for a peer and are circling around him like a pack of wild dogs ready for dinner even as we speak. Of course I am going down there!"

"Down where, Atticus?" asked Conningford as he opened the door and stepped into the room. "I hope it ain't far, because I have been rushing about all over London the whole night and I'm truly exhausted, let me tell you. Honestly, I don't know how much more gadding about from place to place I can handle."

"Val?"

"What? Did you not expect me? Little said you was here and I was to come and find you. Dashfield is playing whist just down the corridor. I was looking for you and saw him as I peered in. He has got the cane with him. Are we going to pinch it?"

"I have no idea what you and Marston are going to do, Val," drawled Hartshire in a low, gentle tone. "But I will tell you what I have in mind. I am going back up the corridor into that very room. I am going to excuse myself to Dashfield.

Then, I am going to pick up that malacca cane, bring it right back here to this chamber and BEAT YOU SEVERELY ABOUT THE HEAD WITH IT!!!"

Fleur was just at that moment gazing out into the night. Standing at the drawing room window with a cup of tea in hand she stared down into the tiny yard at the rear of the establishment. The yard itself was surrounded by a high stone wall. Moonlight flickered over a newly planted herb garden just beyond the kitchen door, tremulously illuminated the privy midway between the garden and back wall and then quivered onward along a cobbled walk to the heavy wooden gate that led into the mews. "I cannot think who she might be," she said softly. "But she is someone of significance. I am certain of it."

"Who, Mama?" asked Althea sipping daintily at her tea and staring into the fire on the hearth.

"Madame Celeste."

"Is she not wonderful? I have never had such extraordinarily beautiful dresses in all my life. Certainly Madame Annette cannot outdo her for a moment. Madame Celeste has such talent, such flair."

"And she is such an imposter," murmured Fleur.

"An imposter? What on earth can you mean by that? You do not believe she made the dresses herself?"

"Of course I believe she made the dresses, Ally. Did I not see her draw them and measure for them and fit them along the way? No, what I mean to say is that she is not what she claims to be. Not a mere dressmaker. Not merely a very rich dressmaker. No. Someone else entirely. She is of the Quality. She admitted that much to me this very afternoon."

"Madame Celeste?"

"Indeed. And she is beholden to Lord Hartshire. No, more than beholden, she absolutely adores him, I think. She agreed to make our gowns, Ally, only because Lord Hartshire requested that she do so."

"How very odd."

"Yes. And she called me her sister. Well, not exactly, but she did intimate that we were both members of some sort of sisterhood. I cannot think what she meant by that. I thought at first that perhaps your father. . . ."

"Perhaps Father what? You need not be careful what you say before me, Mama. You know you need not. Oh! You don't think that Father harmed her in some way as he did you? But how could he?"

"Your father came here to London often. He remained here for weeks at a time. We have neither of us the least idea what he may have done during those times."

"No. That's true enough. But I cannot think that he would have had anything at all to do with such a woman as Madame Celeste, Mama. Only think how she looks. Papa might well have sneered and made some dreadful remark at the sight of her, but to actually approach her or develop an acquaintanceship with her? I think not."

"Perhaps, when he knew her, she did not look as she does now. Perhaps it was long ago. It need not have happened after your father married me, you know."

"You ought to just ask her," Althea said as she looked away from the fire and up at Fleur.

"Yes, I expect so."

"And ask her why she adores Lord Hartshire as well. I should like to know that."

"She has promised to tell me that story already, but only on a moonless and stormy night."

"Truly?" laughed Althea. "Oh, I do so like Madame Celeste, Mama! She is more elf than human. That's what I think."

"Elf? You think of her as an elf?"

"Yes. A very well-fed elf to be sure. But elves may be chubby. There is no one says particularly that they must all be small and slender. You do not suppose, Mama, that at one time there was a—an—*affaire de coeur* of sorts between the elf and the giant?"

Fleur stared into Ally's eyes for the longest time, and then she burst into laughter. "Oh, Ally, for shame!"

"I know," chuckled Althea. "I didn't intend to be unkind, but I could not resist attempting to make you laugh. I rather like the giant. He makes you giggle. I never heard you giggle before he came along."

"You must not call Lord Hartshire the giant."

"But whyever not? He *is* a giant, surely."

"He is tall and large, yes, but he is far from a giant. There are any number of gentlemen as tall—somewhere. And it might well hurt him to know that you think of him as such."

"Hurt him?"

"His feelings, Ally. There are gentlemen in the world who are possessed of sensibilities, you know."

"And you believe Lord Hartshire to be one of them? Most interesting."

"What is most interesting?"

"Oh, nothing. I was merely thinking how I should like to marry a gentleman possessed of sensibilities. Should not you, Mama?"

"Marry a gentleman possessed of . . . ? No. No. I do not wish to be married ever again, whether the gentleman be possessed of sensibilities or not. I have been married, Althea, and I find I do not like it overly much."

"What an understatement! But don't forget, Mama, what you told me. All gentlemen are not like Papa. Some gentlemen are fine and thoughtful and loving. You were not telling me a bouncer, were you, when you said that?"

"No. It is truth. You need only look with wide open eyes at your own brother or—or—"

"Lord Hartshire?"

"Yes. Lord Hartshire. I do believe Lord Hartshire is quite kind and thoughtful and was a most loving husband to his wife. You can always discern the good gentlemen from the bad, Ally, if only you don't let yourself become blinded by a title or riches or a handsome face or—some sham of love. Love is a marvelous thing. To love and be loved by a particular gentleman is the grandest thing in all the world. My grandmama was loved in just such a way by my grandpapa. I remember how it was with them even in their ancient years. I wish the same for you, Ally, with all my heart—a marriage built on a union of hearts not an arrangement made for titles or money or the pride of having a handsome gentleman to escort one about town."

"I will have a true and loving husband," Althea declared with conviction, "or no husband at all. Mama, I have it!"

"Have what?"

"Madame Celeste was imprisoned by an evil dragon and Lord Hartshire came to rescue her. He slayed the dragon and set her free. That is precisely what happened to make her adore him."

Fleur sighed and turned her gaze back out into the night. "You are being just plain silly now. Lord Hartshire, a dragon-slayer. Of all things."

"Perhaps he isn't, Mama, but he certainly strikes me as a gentleman *capable* of slaying a dragon."

"Now who can that be?" Fleur asked quietly. "My goodness, is it Davis?"

"Where?" asked Althea, abandoning her teacup and her place before the fire and crossing to the window to look down into the garden just as Fleur was doing.

"There, entering through the back gate from the mews. It is Davis! I can tell by the way she lopes along. Like a wild creature, wary, yet determined. I don't recall her seeking permission to leave the house this evening. Not at all."

"Perhaps she went on an errand for François."

"Our chef send our abigail on an errand? Our abigail? And at this hour of the night? I think not. How dare Davis take it upon herself to go out roaming about in the darkness?

Why, anything might happen to a woman alone on the streets of nighttime London."

"Perhaps she was not alone, Mama," whispered Althea with a touch of glee. "Perhaps our Davis has a secret beau."

Dashfield, having just won five hundred pounds, was in extremely good humor as he rose from the gaming table to discover Hartshire approaching him followed closely by Conningford and Marston. "Not one to play too deeply," he said with a wide smile. He was a fine looking gentleman, a gentleman in his prime, with dark auburn hair, expressive eyes the color of emeralds, and a handsome countenance.

"Might I have a word with you, Dashfield, before you depart?" Hartshire queried, smiling his own particularly friendly smile. "It will take no longer than the shake of a lamb's tail."

"Certainly, Hartshire. What is it? Like me to teach you my technique, eh?"

"I shouldn't mind if you did, actually. I'm a complete incompetent at whist. Cannot seem to keep my mind from wandering. You know these two rapscallions, do you not? Marston and Conningford?"

"Conningford and I have met in passing," nodded Dashfield. "And Marston, of course. Knew your father a bit, Marston. Good evening to you both. Now, if it isn't whist, what is it that you wish to speak with me about, Hartshire?" he added as he led them out into the corridor and in the direction of the main staircase. "I've promised myself to Skeffington for a late supper at Grillon's."

"It's about your cane actually."

"Atticus!" hissed Conningford.

"Well, it *is* about his cane. I cannot think why we should use any roundaboutation. Where did you get it, is what I wish to know, Dashfield."

Marston gasped. That Hartshire would ask the fellow

straight out like that! The gasp set Marston to coughing. Hartshire reached over and thwacked him soundly on the back.

"Is he all right?" asked Dashfield, coming to a halt and gazing at Marston.

"Fine," mumbled Conningford. "He's fine."

"It seems Marston's father once had a malacca cane like yours," Hartshire continued, starting for the staircase once again. "Knew him, you said. Might remember the cane, eh?"

"Afraid not. Not one to go about scrutinizing gentlemen's canes. Brummell, now, might remember what sort of cane Marston favored, but not I."

"No. Well, apparently the late Lord Marston's cane looked exactly like the one you carry tonight."

"Did it?"

"Yes, and it has gone missing since his death. You don't mind my asking, eh, Dashfield, where you got your cane?"

"This one?"

"Yes."

"I, ah, purchased it from a, ah, pamphlet seller in Oxford Street. Don't know where he got it but he was most eager to be rid of it and took a mere pittance for the thing. A guinea is all it cost me. Seemed anxious for the money, don't you know?"

"A guinea?" asked Conningford from behind the two older men as they began to descend the stairs. "For a stick such as that? Merely a guinea?"

"I expect he hadn't the vaguest idea that the stones were real. They are real, you know, the jewels in the eyes and at the base. I thought them mere paste as well when I purchased it, but I have since taken it to Rundell and Bridges and they assured me that the falcon's head is truly silver and the stones a ruby, an emerald and a sapphire. Quite a bargain it was, for a guinea."

"I should think so," mumbled Marston. "And a bargain for the pamphlet seller as well, since he paid not one cent for it."

"Stole the thing from Marston," grumbled Conningford.

"Should like to get my hands around that fellow's neck," Marston said angrily. "Pamphlet seller, indeed. A petty thief is what he is."

"Perhaps," offered Dashfield thoughtfully, "the man didn't steal it at all. Well, not actually. Your father tripped and fell into the way of the Manchester *Defiance* and was trampled to death, Marston. I have not misremembered that?"

The silver specks in Hartshire's eyes sparkled on the instant. That was why the Marston title had seemed so very familiar to him. It had been in all the papers and the very happening itself had aroused Hartshire's suspicions for a time. But then Will had come down with the measles and the entire incident had slipped his mind. "Outside the Post Office, just as the coaches were being loaded, was it not?" he asked softly.

"Just so," young Marston acknowledged. "Street was clogged with mail coaches all pulling out at eight, the way they do. M'father went down to watch them. Well, everyone does at one time or another. Fascinating sight. All the coaches, throngs of people."

"Just so," drawled Dashfield. "And that will be where the fellow got the cane, I should think. Picked it right up out of the street after they took your father off, most like. Thought no one would notice. Did not steal it exactly, you see. Though now I comprehend why he seemed so anxious to get rid of it."

They had, all four of them, reached the bottom of the staircase and turned in the direction of the front vestibule.

"Quite likely the case," Hartshire nodded. "Might well have happened exactly that way. The lad would like to have the cane back, Dashfield," he added. "Belonged to his father and he would like to have it, ain't that so, Marston?"

"Y-yes," Marston replied, again appalled at Hartshire's forthright manner. He had expected something entirely different. Some plan, some devious action. Well, Hartshire was The Spectre, after all, and he had actually believed The Spectre would steal the thing back for him.

"I don't see why he shouldn't have it," Dashfield said as he stopped to collect his hat and gloves. "I've got any number of other sticks at home. Have you got a guinea on you, Marston?"

"Yes, sir."

"Give it to me, then, and the cane is yours. Had I known it belonged to your father, I would have brought the thing to you straightaway. Ah, that's the ticket." He smiled a perfectly satisfied smile as Marston placed a gold coin into his hand. "And here's your cane. Take it and good fortune to you. Good night, gentlemen." And with a nod of his head and a slight bow, Dashfield turned his back on them, tipped the doorman and started down the steps into St. James's Street.

"And I'm bound for home," Hartshire said, collecting his own hat and gloves.

"We'll share a hackney with you, Atticus," Conningford offered. "I am only up Brook Street, you know, and Marston is in Cavendish Square."

"I think not."

"Oh, your beads. I forgot. You don't have them anymore."

"No. Not anymore. You two go on. I'll walk home. You ought to be pleased to have me do it, too, Val, because I haven't finished with you about this Spencean Philanthropist nonsense."

"It ain't nonsense."

"No, you're quite right there. Not nonsense at all. And we will discuss it thoroughly, the three of us. But not tonight. I cannot think why, but I am plain exhausted tonight."

Cavendish Square, Hartshire thought as he bid the two young men good-bye and stepped down into St. James's Street. Not such a long stroll from Grosvenor to Cavendish. A man might cover that distance in a considerably short amount of time. "Except that I have not the least reason to do so," he muttered to himself as he eased his way past a group of gentlemen holding a rather loud discussion on the pavement. "No reason but to see how Lady Marston goes on, and I cannot do that at this hour of the night. She'll think me as queer as Dick's hatband do I just pop in at this hour. Probably thinks me a Bedlamite already having discovered me up that tree. Confounded luck that."

Hartshire could not think what it was that urged him to take an interest in the shipbuilder's daughter but an interest he had taken. He was quite aware of it and it puzzled him.

Not had a woman jumping into my mind with such frequency since Miriam, he mused as he took a northerly direction at the next corner. Of course, Lady Marston does keep popping up in the most unpredictable places. Who would've thought her to be walking beneath that tree at precisely the time I was up in it? I expect I ought to have made a noise or called to her or something before she gazed upward. But then, who on earth thought she would gaze upward, and just then, too?

And she is brave. And I do like a brave woman, he thought. He noted the sound of footsteps on the pavement behind him and paused to turn and see if it was anyone he knew. There was no one there. Hearing things, he told himself and continued onward. Yes, she is brave, Lady Marston. Took Miss Avondale to the most patronized dressmaker in town, he thought, his mind continuing onward as well. Brave as any soldier. Ready to place herself right in the enemies' stronghold for Miss Avondale's sake.

The sound of boot heels clicking on the pavement behind him drew his attention once more. He spun around quickly this time and caught a glimpse of a large object descending toward his head. "Be deviled if you do!" Hartshire exclaimed, one arm going up to block the descending cudgel, the other flashing out at the man who wielded it. Hartshire's fist coaxed an immediate ooph! from the villain as it pounded into the dastard's stomach. "What the deuce is wrong with you? Have you not a brain in your head?" asked Hartshire, taking the cudgel away from his attacker with one tug and tossing it out into the street. "Are you blind?" he continued, grasping the man by the front of his shirt, lifting the fellow's feet clear off the pavement. "Or are you so desperate you think it nothing to attack a fellow as large as me? You don't mind being killed yourself, eh?"

"Don' be a throwin' me inta the street, Yer Highness! I'll crack m'head open, I will, an' then I'll be dead," pleaded the ruffian.

"Didn't think a thing about cracking my head open," Hartshire responded.

"No, I dinit, but I be thinkin' about it now, Yer Grace. An' I be thinkin' as 'ow I were very wrong not ta think about it afore. But yer was contemplatin' so deep about somethin' that I couldn't not help m'self. I seed how big ye was, but yer looked like sich a easy mark as deep as yer was in whatever yer were thinkin'. Ye done presented me wif the sweetest temptation!"

Hartshire lowered the man enough so that his feet touched the pavement but he did not let go the fellow's shirt front. "So, this little toss-about is my fault, is it? I forced you to sneak up behind me and attempt to cudgel my brains out?"

"Uh-huh."

Hartshire could not help himself. He grinned. "Uh-huh? It *is* all my fault?"

"Well, p'rhaps not all o' it. But ye did tempt me so great, Yer Majesty. An' I do be so 'ungry. An' yer do look like what ye gots coins jus' jinglin' away doin' nothin' in yer pocket."

"Hungry, are you?" mused Hartshire, easing his grasp on the man's shirt. "I expect you've a wife and a houseful of kiddies at home who are hungry too, eh?"

"I could 'ave, Yer Highness, did it make yer think ta let me go. Would it make yer think ta let me go?"

"Not for a second. If you don't have a wife and kiddies,

however, I might have a proposition to offer you. A way to actually earn some money."

"Ain't never married no gel. Not never. Ain't got one kiddie I knows about. Ain't even gots me a 'ome. Free as a bird be Tom Landy. What is it ye be thinkin' fer me ta do?"

Fleur heard Malcolm enter the house and make his way up the staircase and into his chambers. She set aside the volume of poems she'd been reading, lowered the lamp wick and settled down to pursue sleep once again. He's home safe, she thought. If it's worry over Mal keeps me awake, then I shall be in dreams shortly. She nestled between the sheets and rested her head comfortably upon a pillow. She yawned and stretched and relaxed again. She had been attempting to fall asleep for hours now, and had at last reached the conclusion that it was worry over Malcolm kept sleep at bay.

At first she had thought her wakefulness due to her curiosity about Celeste. But surely something as simple as curiosity would not force one's eyes to blink open time and time again.

Then she had guessed it was concern over the invitation to Lady Conningford's musical evening. That was, of itself, daunting and might be expected to cause her a sleepless night or two. Yet, she had rather doubted it could be blamed, for her mind did not seem to be nibbling and scratching at the invitation in particular.

She had even guessed that Davis's unauthorized meandering to who knew where for who knew what reason might be the cause, though that did not seem at all likely, because she did not actually care that Davis had gone off without so much as asking her permission. She was most unaccustomed to wielding any authority over her servants at all. For all of her married life, Marston had controlled the servants. They had been his and his alone. There was not a one of them had ever desired to please her, except for John Coachman. John

Coachman had developed the most remarkable fondness for her. And though he had not dared to stand up against the others, he had always gone out of his way to offer her his assistance where he could.

And why should Marston's staff have given me the least loyalty, Fleur thought, when he made it perfectly clear to all of them that my needs and wants were of no consideration whatsoever, especially not to him?

In the end, she had decided that, reasonable or not, she was simply waiting to hear Malcolm return safely home and once he did, she would fall directly asleep, content that her stepchildren were both accounted for.

Now the silence of the night settled around her. She breathed softly, evenly, thinking of nothing, floating at last into that twilight world between sleep and waking.

And then her husband's face rose up before her. A handsome face with wide-set green eyes beneath gently sloping brows, a finely shaped nose and lips distinctly and uncompromisingly masculine, firm, tempting. Even in slumber, Fleur's breath caught in her throat. Her eyes popped open. She sat up in her bed and tugged the counterpane up around her.

"HeisdeadHeisdeadHeisdeaddeaddead," she recited over and over again in a terrified whisper until the very monotony of the words leveled her ragged breathing and calmed the heart which had been jolted into rapid, agonizing beats within her breast. It very much amazed her that just as she felt her composure return, thoughts of Lord Hartshire began to flutter about her brain.

"Of all things," she murmured with a tentative smile. "Why should I think of him now?"

Even so, she did think of him and her lips parted the tiniest bit and turned upward at both corners. "What an odd gentleman he is," she said softly. "So large, yet so graceful; so fierce-looking, yet so gentle; so overwhelming, yet so humbly kind." With the smile lingering, Fleur lay back down and tugged the counterpane up under her chin. Sleep once again approached and she welcomed it hopefully, inviting it in. And just as she reached that twilight world between slumber and waking, while her heart beat steadily and sturdily within her breast and the last threads of tension left her, a face again appeared upon the horizon of her dreams. Oh, how persistent it was! A plain, gentle face, distinguished only by eyes like midnight filled with silver stars winking and blinking across their heavens. A face with lips not uncompromisingly masculine, but soft, inviting and formed into the most boyish of grins—a lopsided, engaging grin designed specifically by God to gentle a woman's very soul.

Six

Hartshire took the dormouse into the palm of his hand and studied it most seriously. "Yes, I do believe you're correct, Mr. Canton," he drawled. "Looks like a Socrates to me."

"Uh-uh, Papa," protested Will, climbing up onto one of the schoolroom chairs and peering down at the dormouse. "His name is Henry."

"No, do you think? Does not look at all like a Henry."

"His name is Henry nevertheless, Papa. I will show you. Here, Henry. Come here to me."

Hartshire was surprised to see the lazy little creature wiggle its nose and then its left ear. It turned its head the slightest bit to peer up at Hartshire, then turned back, scrambled over the edge of Hartshire's hand and lowered itself into Will's waiting palm. "Well, I'll be hanged for a poacher. Did you see that, Canton?"

"I have seen it for the past five days, my lord," the tutor replied, a smile creasing his boyishly handsome face. "The lazy little fellow sleeps the day through, but once Will and I have had our dinner, he is up and scrambling about and hobbles to Will every time the lad calls him Henry."

"I see," nodded Hartshire. "A Henry in Socrates clothing. Of all things. That splint can come off soon, I should think.

You have been taking excellent care of him, Will, have you not?"

"Yes, Papa. You'd know if you were here more often."

"I'm here all the time, scoundrel."

"Uh-uh. You are hardly ever here at all."

"How very odd. And I thought I shared a nuncheon with you every day."

"Yes, but that ain't often. You aren't ever home after dinner anymore. No, you are not, Papa. You even left before dinner last night and didn't come home until morning. You have not come home until morning for nine whole times in a row."

"I beg your pardon?"

"I've been getting up to peek out my window after you come and kiss me good night, Papa. And for nine whole days in a row it has already been light outside."

"I see. And you wish me to come and wake you up right in the middle of the night when it is very dark outside. Well, I shall try to manage that sometime soon, though I doubt it will be tonight. Tonight is your grandmama's party. Little spoke to you, did he not, Canton? You will not mind taking charge of the house tonight?" Hartshire added, watching as the dormouse climbed up on Will's shoulder and wiggled its whiskers in the boy's ear.

"Shan't mind at all, my lord. I shall keep my eyes open and my ears as well."

"And you will keep all the doors and windows locked," added Hartshire.

"Certainly. Have Mr. Little and Mr. Robes keys to the kitchen door, my lord?"

"They have, and I shall let myself in at the front. You need not come to the door for any of us. Do make use of the library, Canton. I think I have told you as much before. And do not answer to anyone's knock, eh? I expect no one."

The tutor blinked a bit oddly at this, but he merely nodded and said nothing further.

"It's because Papa is working," Will announced two seconds after his father had given Henry a one-fingered pat, Will a hug, and departed for his own chambers to dress for the evening. "That's why he don't want us to answer any knocks. We have to be most careful in London when Papa is working."

Canton shook his head in puzzlement. "I can't think that's the reason, Will. Giving speeches in the House of Lords is not a particularly dangerous job, you know. No reason someone should come knocking on our door with evil intentions, simply because of something your father said in a speech. But Parliament cannot possibly be working as late into the night as your Papa makes it seem. There is nothing spectacular reported in any of the papers as regards the House of Lords. Not even a mention of extended sessions."

"He isn't speaking in Parliament. I don't think he is. Well, I expect he could be because he is an earl. But not at night. At night he is working at his old job. The one he was used to work at before he married Mama and found me."

"Your Papa found you?"

"Uh-huh. In the kitchen garden at Wilderhart Hall. Under a cabbage leaf."

"Ah, just so. I ought to have known."

"Uh-huh. Papa found me under a cabbage leaf and I found Henry under an oak leaf."

"And how fortunate you and your papa and Henry are. What is your papa's other job?" Canton added, curious.

"It's splendid."

"It is?"

"Positively. He is a protector of the King. It's his job to go about and listen in on all the radicals and keep the King and his family from getting killed by them."

Mr. Canton stared at the boy confounded. He cleared his throat. He reached in his coat pocket, pulled out a flower seed and offered it to Henry. Then he sat down on one of the schoolroom chairs. Then he stood up again.

"Your father is a spy for the Home Office?"

"No."

"But, if his job is to spy on radicals—"

"He don't spy exactly. He just listens. And he won't do it for the Home Office. Papa does not like the men in the Home Office. He says they cause more trouble than they stop. He says they're insti-instig—"

"Instigators?"

"Are those the people who say stuff to make things happen that wouldn't happen otherwise?"

"Um-hmmm."

"Well, that's what Papa says they are then, instigators."

"And your father is not one of them?"

"No. Papa just listens, and when he comes across someone planning to harm the King or the King's family, it's his job to stop them any way he can. He said he wasn't ever going to do it anymore now the King is ill, but I think he is. Just doing it a little. Maybe he's teaching Uncle Val to do it right, because that is what Uncle Val wants more than anything."

"What?"

"To be just like The Spectre."

"The Spectre is a veritable legend!" gasped Canton, his heart beginning to thrum with excitement. "Your father was The Spectre, Will?"

"Uh-huh. He still is."

Little set a chair immediately beside his own stool for Robes and studied the valet with a keen eye. They were in the butler's pantry with the door closed and the pass-through closed as well. The rest of the staff, dinner having been dispensed with, were gathered in the servants' quarters.

"Saw our lordship on his way but moments ago, Mr. Robes," Little said, settling down on his stool. "You have outdone yourself tonight, I think. He looked magnificent."

"And so I told him, Mr. Little. But would he believe me?

No, he would not. Peered at himself in the looking glass, grunted and made the most awful face."

"Did he?"

"Yes, he did and has done ever since he arrived in London. I have not seen him so very hard on himself, Mr. Little, since he first met our dear departed ladyship."

"Ah, that's it, is it? Imagining himself a veritable leviathan again. And his ears? Has he mentioned the size of his ears? Well, he has to me. And there's no sense to any of it. Though how anyone is to convince him, I cannot think. He is perfectly irrational when he gets to thinking of himself in such a way."

"Just so. And it does break my heart to hear the words that spew forth from between those lips when he thinks I am not paying the least attention. He is not so large and not so odd looking and his ears are not any bigger than yours or mine—comparatively speaking of course."

"Well, I expect he imagines himself freakish because he was teased forever about his size when he was a boy."

"He was?"

"I expect so. I have no reason to know it for a fact, but having been a lad in my time, I expect I could not have resisted teasing him from one day to the next. He was the size he is now at fifteen he told me once. Only think how large he must have been at ten. But that is neither here nor there, Mr. Robes. I have not asked you here to discuss our lordship's propensity for imagining himself odd and ugly."

"No. Why did you ask me here?"

"I rather thought that since our lordship has arranged for Mr. Canton to look after the household tonight and given us this evening to ourselves, Mr. Robes, I rather thought you would like to join me in a glass of ale at The Silver Swan."

"I should like that indeed, Mr. Little," responded Robes cordially.

"Indeed. A bit of ale, a bit of conversation with a number

of our compatriots. Likely quite a number of them with some time free tonight. We will treat them all to ale."

"Treat them? You and me? All of them?"

Little smiled the fondest smile. His salt-and-pepper eyebrows rose the tiniest bit. His fine grey eyes glowed with good humor. "Tonight, my dear Robes, you and I shall pretend we are rich as Croesus. Lay our coins right out on the table top where they may wink the night away."

Robes grinned crookedly. "Something is up, is it not, Mr. Little?"

"Aye, Mr. Robes. Something that requires our peeping into it. So says our lordship apologetically as he presented me with these not an hour ago." Little took a small leather pouch from his pocket, untied the thong that fastened it and poured a goodly number of coins out onto the countertop.

"What is it our lordship wishes to know?" asked Robes, tugging nervously at his right earlobe.

"Anything. Anything and everything. Did you not hear the dustup in the parlor between Lord Conningford and our lordship on Saturday last, Robes?"

"No."

"Bellowed at the poor lad, our lordship did."

"Bellowed? Our lordship?"

"Yes, well, I expect it was enough to make him bellow, hearing how Lord Conningford has got himself mixed up with those followers of Thomas Spence."

"By Jove!" Robes exclaimed, one carroty red eyebrow leaping upward, followed a bit more slowly by the other. "By Jove, Mr. Little, are you certain?"

"As certain as I am that you and I have been called upon to lend our aid, Mr. Robes. As certain as I am that these coins here are intended to be spent in an effort to learn what we can of Thomas Spence and his lads and what they may be doing these days. And we are to begin this evening at The Silver Swan."

"From whom in particular, Mr. Little, are we to learn these things? Did our lordship say?"

"That he did not. Has not a notion, as yet, where to start. Except, a goodly number of ladies and gents will be going off to Lady Con's musical evening this evening, and others to a soiree given by the Countess of Bowlingreen and still others to a card party in Holland Circle. He reckons as how a goodly number of butlers and valets might well find themselves with time to visit The Swan once all the ladies and gents have left."

"Knows we will," smiled Robes.

"Knows we certainly will tonight, Mr. Robes. I did say to him, you know, at one point, that I might not be opposed to a bit of adventure again and that you might well feel the same. We have been so extraordinarily reserved, you and I, Mr. Robes, for the longest time."

"You had best be correct, Val," Lady Conningford said as she descended the staircase to the first floor. "I shall suffer nobly for the cause, but if the cause is nonexistent, I will certainly box your ears for what you put me through this evening."

"You cannot know, Mama, that anything out of the ordinary will happen just because you invited Marston's stepmother," Conningford replied.

"I can know it. And I do."

"Oh. Well, but the cause is existent. You didn't see him, Mama, or hear him. Atticus likes her immensely, this Lady Marston."

"After one meeting? Is she so very beautiful then?"

"No, not beautiful at all. Plain, I should say. Not her looks that draw him on. Something else. But it was not simply one meeting. Atticus mentioned having met her at least twice before. He is plainly taken with her. Do you know the look in his eyes? The one you are always saying you should like to see gone? Well, it was gone for a time. I vow it was. Even I noticed. And what's more," Conningford added with a note of triumph, "she apparently suffers from the same malady as Atticus when she rides in a coach."

"You think he is interested in this woman because she gets *mal de mer?* Valerian, of all things!"

"No, no, not because she gets it. Because he gave her his beads, Máma. Gave them to her. Has not so much as requested their return or thought to do so."

"That's why he walked here from Grosvenor Square! He gave her his beads! Well, whatever happens tonight, it is worth it then," replied Lady Conningford with a determined nod. "I would go through Hades to see Atticus cease grieving for Miriam and find someone to truly, deeply love again, someone to put that special light back in his eyes."

Conningford was about to point out to his mama as they reached the head of the stairs that Atticus was not a gentleman to grieve, that the lack of light she noted in the earl's eyes was likely due to boredom. But just as he began to do so, the first of the evening's guests arrived and the entire discussion was forsaken.

Two, three, four at a time they came, illustrious members of the upper ten thousand, proudly ascending the staircase to be greeted by their host and hostess. Young and old, male and female, all in glorious good humor, all eager to enjoy the evening. Lady Conningford was especially impressed with the number of younger gentlemen who appeared. Friends and acquaintances of her son, some of whom she had not seen since Conningford's school days. "I cannot believe it," she whispered to him at a break in the line. "How did you know these young gentlemen would come, Val? I thought you had lost your mind to request me to invite the lot of them. These gentlemen? To a musical evening?"

"They were in the park when Marston drove his sister, Mama. I simply put it about that Miss Avondale would be in attendance, and *voilà!*"

"Voilà what?" asked Hartshire, striding up before Lady Conningford, taking her hand into his own and placing a kiss upon the back of it as he bowed. "Good evening, Lady Con. Your gown is marvelous. Val, you're looking quite up to snuff."

"I should hope he does," laughed Lady Conningford. "Set him back a pretty penny that particular coat."

"I have it from Weston," Conningford declared with pride. "Ordered it especially for tonight."

"Ah," Hartshire responded. "Need I guess why?"

"N-no," said Conningford with a surreptitious glance at his parent which Hartshire did not miss.

"So, I expect it will prove a delightful evening," Hartshire drawled. "Has Marston's party arrived as yet, Lady Con? Val mentioned they might attend."

"Did he? No, they are not here as yet, Atticus. But I'm sure they'll appear shortly. Everyone is gathering in the Ovid Saloon. We shall adjourn to the music room when all the performers are ready for us. I don't know why you refuse to sing for us, Atticus. You have such a delightful voice, and it is all in good fun. Merely an evening for us amateurs. It is not as though there are to be actual artistes present."

"Here she is," hissed Conningford, and three heads turned to watch as the Marston party ascended the staircase.

Althea led the way, gowned in a robe of white satin with an underdress of gold silk that shimmered and glowed much like the golden curls that framed her face. The robe, with its white satin bishop's sleeves, and a collar that stood stiffly, yet softly erect, revealed the underdress not merely in an upside-down V from the high waistline, but in a decidedly tempting group of small spaces between bosom and collarbone. Conningford inhaled raggedly to see it. Hartshire chuckled lowly in his throat at the sound.

Directly behind her came Marston, dressed to the nines in a dark blue superfine evening coat, blazingly white waistcoat, and neckcloth tied to perfection. On his arm, Fleur trembled the least bit, caught her lower lip between her teeth for a moment, then lifted her chin a bit higher. Just high enough to see Hartshire standing before host and hostess, his hands on his hips, his head tilted just so, his extraordinary eyes alight with approval. She smiled a bit. Truly, it was such a relief to see him here.

Lady Con, realizing at once which of the ladies must be the shipbuilder's daughter, noted when Fleur smiled and peeked to see if it had been the sight of Hartshire that had caused it. Oh, most certainly, she thought. How could anyone not smile at such an impish look of admiration as he bestows on her now? No matter what happens tonight, I will stand beside this woman, she thought then. Does she continue to put such sparkle as that in Atticus's eyes, I do not care if she is a shipbuilder's daughter or a pirate's former mistress.

The Silver Swan stood near the corner of Charles and Manchester Streets, which was precisely where the hackney hired by Mr. Little and Mr. Robes came to a halt. A perfectly plain building, huddled among other perfectly plain buildings, the door to this establishment stood open wide in invitation to any and all upper servants of the Quality. Not that others would be turned away. No. Never. But The Silver Swan had over the past few years become the place for majordomos, butlers and valets who resided in the area to gather. This evening, they had gathered in force, just as Hartshire had thought they might.

Mr. Little and Mr. Robes were welcomed heartily into their midst as they made their way toward one of the few remaining tables. "So, your lordship has at last come to Town, eh, Little?" asked Mr. Wickens, leaving his own table to join them. "Thought he was a figment of your imagination, took him so long to appear."

"Arrived just before your ladyship, I believe."

"Just so. Just so. But I have had his lordship in residence

since autumn. I expect your free time has been severely curtailed now that Lord Hartshire is here, eh, Little? Eh, Robes?"

The Marston butler winked. He was a perfectly ordinary man. Neither short nor tall, handsome nor plain, young nor old. He stood an unastounding five foot six and weighed just enough to keep from being either fat or thin. His hair was a bland sort of brown and there was neither too much nor too little of it. A more nondescript butler had never wandered into The Silver Swan.

"I expect you are no longer bored, Robes," offered another voice, and Mr. Rupert, Lord Tate's valet joined them as well. "Have a glass of ale, my lads. On me."

"No, no, it is all on us tonight," protested Little, taking the leather pouch from his pocket and clanking it down on the table top.

"Lord!" exclaimed Rupert. "What did you do, Little? Find buried treasure?"

"Only a bit of a bonus for opening up the house in such fine fashion. Our lordship was most pleased. He can be a generous gentleman when he's pleased."

"Yes, but I should dread to displease him," Wickens replied. "Such an intimidating personage. Caught a glimpse of him in St. James's Street the other day and had to ask if anyone knew who he might be. Everyone did. Hartshire, they told me. Lord Hartshire of Wilderhart Hall."

"Which reminds me," said Little. "You never did say why you left Lord Dashfield's employ and went to Marston, Wickens. I cannot think you ever displeased Dashfield."

"Because of her ladyship's death, of course. I could not bear to remain in that house. Murdered she was."

"Surely not."

"Oh, no one will say as much. No, they will not. But she did not stick those scissors into her own breast; I am positive of it. Well, but there will be none of that at Marston House. Perfectly nice sort of family the Marstons."

"Is that not Travis Dean?" asked Robes abruptly. "Wave him over, do, Little. I have not had a word with Dean since first we arrived."

"Nor I since we arrived," agreed Rupert. "Fine fellow, Dean. Tell me, Robes, does your gentleman not intend to refurbish his wardrobe? I did notice him strolling down Oxford Street the other day. He is decidedly behind the times."

"Yes, and so I told him straightaway."

"You didn't?" asked Rupert aghast.

"But I did. Not one to fear, my lordship. Willing to listen to what a man has to say, he is. Though I doubt he will ever be in style as long as the style remains as it is. Dean, come and sit with us," Robes added, as the Duke of Diddenmoor's valet strode, smiling, up to the table in conjunction with the delivery of the requested ale.

"Don't mind if I do," replied Dean cheerily. "Have a considerable amount of time tonight for tending to my own needs. Have not seen The Swan so crowded in ages."

"Little and Robes are paying for the ale," Wickens offered with another wink. "Courtesy of their lordship."

"Well, we will need to invite a few more people over, no, Wickens?" queried Dean. "Spread the bounty around a bit."

Mr. Little and Mr. Robes exchanged triumphant glances.

Hartshire's heart went out to her. Marston having been convinced to escort his sister, Lady Marston had entered the Ovid Saloon on Hartshire's arm. All eyes had fastened on the four of them. Conversations had ceased in midsentence. Heads had turned. An ominous silence had suffused the room. It had seemed for a long moment as though all were holding their breath and staring. And then, a veritable army of eligible gentlemen had galloped from all corners of the room to make their bows to Miss Avondale, and people began to breathe again. But with the breaths had come a series of nose raisings among the ladies that would have sent Hartshire into chuckles if he had not been perfectly aware that they were intended to snub the lady whom he escorted.

Nonetheless, he had led her about the room with the best of intentions. He had introduced her to his uncle Panington, who had welcomed her heartily and then to his aunt Amelia, who had droned a quite proper "How do you do, Lady Marston. We did never expect to see you in London again," in the most frigid voice and had walked off at once. He had inserted her expertly, amidst smiles and flirting eyes, into a group of ladies busily discussing the newest fashions, only to see her completely ignored by the lot of them the moment he departed to join in a conversation with some of the gentlemen.

His ire rising, his heart truly aching for her, he stood now with arms folded across his chest, leaning against the elegantly carved mantel near the bust of Ovid for whom this particular room had been named, as a group of gentlemen discussed the war on all sides of him. Lady Marston, he noted, stood alone and silent near the curtained windows, her gaze fastened intently on her stepdaughter, her hands playing uneasily with her reticule.

I will go over there and rescue her, he thought angrily. If the ladies will not have her, I will bring her over here with the gentlemen. Most of them will not give a fig who her father was.

Some of them, of course, would. Teweksbury had asked him, aghast, if he knew whom he had escorted into the room, and Larksbury had pointed out to him that he would not have come had he known The Shipbuilder's Daughter had been invited. "Of course," Larksbury had added, his piggy little eyes gleaming lecherously, "I expect Lady Marston will become an inevitable guest now that she chaperones Miss Avondale. If our ladies wish for these younger gentlemen to appear at their entertainments so that their own daughters can take a shot at them, I expect Miss Avondale must necessarily be invited everywhere. Only look at the gel, Hartshire. Should a man come upon her unaware in such a dress as that, his heart would stop. If blood flows through a fellow's veins, he will follow that gel wherever she goes."

Just as Hartshire nodded in reply and was about to excuse himself from the group of gentlemen around him, Lady Conningford appeared to advise her guests that all the young ladies and gentlemen who had agreed to perform this evening were quite prepared. "We must now adjourn to the music room," she said, smiling.

Hartshire took three steps in Lady Marston's direction, intending to escort her there, but was then seized upon by Mrs. Snyder-Joylnes who, clinging possessively to his arm, announced with great significance that her eldest daughter, Jane, had quite managed to make her way through the marriage mart for the last three years without having found even one of the eligible younger gentlemen desirable. "She prefers older, sensible gentlemen," Mrs. Snyder-Joylnes said, with the most audacious look in her eye. "I know, my lord, how much she would like to meet you. You have not been properly introduced, I think?"

"No, I think not," Hartshire responded, gazing back over his shoulder to see naught but a noisy crowd of guests meandering along behind him.

"Oh, you need not attempt to spy her, Lord Hartshire. She is not present this evening. And she will be so disappointed that she did not come once I tell her of your presence."

"She will?" asked Hartshire. "Are you certain of that?"

"Indeed."

Girl must be utterly desperate, thought Hartshire, to be disappointed not to meet me. Likely Mrs. Snyder-Joylnes is telling an enormous bouncer. One look at me and this daughter of hers will climb willingly up onto the shelf and twiddle her thumbs happily away into spinsterhood.

He attempted to free himself from the woman all the way along the corridor. He tried to shake her off his arm by knocking against the doorjamb as they entered the music room. He went so far as to have a coughing fit right in the middle of the room, but he could not detach himself from her and was consequently led into one of the little rows of gilded chairs to sit beside her.

With the most convincing twitch and shudder, he began to cough again. This time most raggedly as though something had stuck in his windpipe. His eyes watered convincingly. He rose from his chair, quickly excused himself with a wave of his hand and exited the row to discover a place for himself beside Lady Marston. He saw her enter just then, after everyone else was seated. He set out after her as she took a seat in the second to the last row beside Mrs. Cordelia Wright. And, ceasing his coughing, he heard Mrs. Cordelia Wright exclaim loudly, "I am so very sorry, Lady Marston, but you cannot sit here. I have such a weak stomach, you know. I cannot bear to have the stink of the shop so close beside me."

Fleur could not bear it, not any of it, any longer. With tears threatening to stream from her eyes, her bottom lip quivering, her fingers picking in agitation at her pretty gold-beaded reticule, she rose from the chair and made her way with as much dignity as she could manage out into the corridor and down that long hallway to the first empty room she could find. It was the library. Its door stood open and the darkness within beckoned to her. A perfect hidey-hole. A safe, quiet, dark place in which to hide away for a time.

"Just until I am calm again," she whispered, as she stepped across the threshold and closed the door quietly behind her. "Merely until I have regained my composure and my determination. I will not cry like an infant. I will not!"

The curtains had not been drawn across the library windows and so a sliver of moonlight slithered in, pleased to reflect itself in winks and blinks and bursts of sparkle from the vases and busts and statuettes that Lady Conningford had distributed throughout the nooks and crannies. With seeming glee, the moonlight struck a cut glass decanter here and a crystal glass there along its way. And with each flickering reflection of itself it cast other bits of the library into deeper shadow.

There was a large chair near the cold, empty hearth. Fleur made her way to it and sat, opened her reticule and pulled from it a fine lawn handkerchief. A quite large, fine lawn handkerchief. "Oh," she whispered, dropping the reticule to the carpet and taking the handkerchief into both hands, twisting it first one way and then the other, her tears more insistent, stinging at the back of her eyes. "Oh, dear. I brought it along partic-cu-larly to return to L-Lord Hartshire. And I com-com-pletely for-for-for-got. Damnation! Damndamndamn!" she cried softly as she burst into sobs and her tears flowed. "I can-can-not even d-do that prop-er-ly."

From the music room, barely audible, came the sweet song of a violin, a cello and a harp in lilting conversation, but Lady Marston noticed it not at all. Nor did she notice the slight sound of the latch lifting on the library door as it opened or the snickering of it as it fell back into place. She was sobbing much too hard to hear anything but her own stertorous breathing and the soft wails she could not control no matter how hard she tried. And it did not help that she had fairly buried herself in the enormous chair. The very depth of that piece of furniture muffled all sound even more. At last, her sobs became gasps for breath, her shoulders heaved and she strove with all her might for self-control. She blew her nose heartily into the handkerchief, scrubbed with an edge of it at her tear-stained cheeks, shuddered visibly and willed herself into quiet.

"Are you quite done, then?" The hiss of a whisper floated on darkness through the room and startled Fleur so very much that she stood straight up out of the chair. "Wh-what?" she croaked, her drying tears staining her voice as well as her cheeks. "Who?"

"I asked if you were quite done with crying?"

"Y-yes. Yes I am."

"Good. Once the time of tears passes, the time for action cannot be far off."

"Wh-what? What do you say?" Fleur swiped at her eyes once again, clearing the last of the tears away, and peered into the shadows turning about in a circle in search of the owner of the whisper.

"Utterly devoid of brains, Cordelia Wright. Brays like a donkey, looks like a mule and thinks like an ass."

"Oh! How—how dare you?"

"I always dare to speak the truth," replied the whisperer. "Always. Well, most always."

The tiniest of smiles tugged at the corners of Fleur's mouth. "Most always?"

"Sometimes I am faint of heart, but not often."

"Who are you?" Fleur queried, peering about her again. "Where are you? I cannot tell. Your whispering echoes about so and I cannot see you in the shadows."

"Best that you should not see me," answered the whisperer. "You might run screaming from the room."

"I would not."

"You are brave, are you, m'girl?"

"I know it does not seem so at the moment, but I am. I attempt to grow braver day by day."

"Excellent. Then you will not fear to stroll back into Lady Conningford's music room and take possession of the chair you vacated, the one directly beside Cordelia Wright. It remains vacant still."

"How do you know?" asked Fleur, moving with tiny steps toward the place she thought the voice to originate.

"I know."

"Mrs. Cordelia Wright sent me running in here."

"I know that as well. You are very far off."

"I am what?"

"Very far off. I am nowhere near the bust of Nero."

"Oh! But how can you—?"

"I can see what you're doing very well. Go to the room

reserved for the ladies, put some water on your face, fix your hair, straighten your skirt and hurry back to the music room."

"Mrs. Wright will stand the moment I sit down and strut off in the most imperious manner with her nose so high in the air that she will likely trip on the carpet. She has been telling everyone the entire evening that I am naught but a shipbuilder's daughter no matter how well I dress and were it not for everyone's duty to welcome Marston and Miss Avondale into their fold, I should not have been let through the door this evening."

"And if she does rise like the tide and overflow into another row, you will say to her, loudly enough for those around you to hear but not so loudly as to seem bold, 'Please, you need not depart on my account, dear Mrs. Wright. I am not put off by that parfum you wear, as are all the others. Truly, you must not think it. It makes me smile, in fact, for it much reminds me of the steaming tar that was used in my father's shipyards.' "

"I could not!" exclaimed Fleur.

"No? Why not?"

"Well, because—because—only think how it would make her feel."

"Ah, yes. But there are times when we must be cruel in order to gain someone's attention. Think of it as striking a donkey to get it moving out of a burning barn."

"But Mrs. Wright's barn is not burning."

The whisperer chuckled. "So, you do not argue against her being a donkey, eh?"

"Well, well, she is acting like a perfect—" Fleur swallowed the word she wished to say and sighed. "I expect you are correct."

"I am. Now, off with you, first to the ladies' room to straighten yourself up and then to the music room. And should Cordelia Wright rise and strut off as you expect, say exactly what I've told you to say. And say it calmly and with a smile on your face, too. You don't wish for anyone who hears to think you the least bit upset by her."

"They will know I am."

"Perhaps, but they will wonder at your audacity and the exquisite manner of your thrust. Especially when you refer to your father's shipyards. Enough of this hiding. You hope to put off the inevitable. You cannot do that forever. Soonest done, soonest done with, I say."

The violin, the cello and the harp had been replaced by a young lady at the pianoforte by the time Fleur returned to the music room. She paused on the threshold. Her gaze wandered over the attentive audience. Althea was seated safely between her brother and young Lord Conningford. Lady Conningford was busy behind the velvet curtain that formed the back of the little stage upon which the musicians performed. Fleur could see the very edge of Lady Conningford's puce gown as she fiddled about, most likely helping to prepare for the next performer. Lord Hartshire, she discovered, was leaning nonchalantly against the wall, several feet from where she stood, looking tall and broad and extremely bored.

With a lift of her chin and a swish of the skirt of the apple green gown that Celeste had designed for her—a wickedly beautiful gown, to be sure, for all eyes had been drawn to it rather than to its wearer when first she entered—Fleur made her way to the second to the last row, where remained one empty seat, right beside Mrs. Cordelia Wright.

Seven

By two o'clock the following afternoon, the entire vestibule of Marston House was festooned with flowers. Gentlemen's calling cards spilled from the silver salver on the hall table. Wickens had replaced the first footman who was generally in attendance at the door, that poor man having been worn to a frazzle by the constant banging of the knocker and the jingle of the bell. Even now, the second footman rushed back and forth between the vestibule and the kitchen, carrying the tokens of gentlemanly esteem into the hands of the housekeeper and the downstairs maid who searched eagerly for enough vases and places to distribute the offerings. "I never," declared Mrs. Belding, her keys jingling as she hurried back into the butler's pantry. "So many of them and all at once."

"Our ladies must be the most sought after ladies in all the whole of London," observed the downstairs maid, with extraordinary pride. "Just think you, Mrs. Belding, what a fine piece of fortune it be for us to be employed in the household of two such belles."

"Aye," agreed Mrs. Belding from the pantry. "But where are we going to put all these flowers, Milly? That's what I want to know. I have placed vases in every room in the house and still they keep coming!"

As if to prove her correct, the front doorbell jingled again and Mrs. Belding sighed.

Wickens, juggling a bouquet of pink roses in one hand and a most extraordinary rhododendron plant in the other, gazed about him for a spot to set one or the other down. Finding none, he did his best to steady both offerings in one arm and open the door with the other. "I do beg your pardon," he began, expecting another perfectly unknown young gentleman with yet another offering for his ladies.

"As well you might, Wickens," laughed Marston. "Great heavens, what is all this?" he added, stepping into the vestibule. "Looks like a greenhouse in here."

"We are attempting to keep up, my lord," announced Wickens with as much dignity as he could muster, "but James is worn to pieces, so there are only Roberts and I. A person can run only so fast and so far, my lord."

"Just so," nodded Marston, peering at the salver overflowing with calling cards. "My sister has proved quite successful in her first outing, has she not?"

"Oh, yes, my lord. Thank you, my lord," added Wickens as Marston condescended to take the rhododendron from him. "They are not all for Miss Avondale, however."

"They are not? For whom, then, Wickens?"

"A goodly number of them, my lord, are for Lady Marston."

"For my mama? How perfectly marvelous! Where are they, Wickens, the ladies?"

"Out, my lord. Off to a fitting at Madame Celeste's, they said. Took the barouche. Davis accompanied them."

"Just so," nodded Marston. "I shall be in my study, Wickens, after I have carried as many of these as I can balance to the—"

"Kitchen, my lord. Mrs. Belding is in charge. I do thank you, my lord."

"Not at all, Wickens. Cannot have the vestibule filled to overflowing with flowers. People will mistake us for a greenhouse, eh? I expect Lord Conningford to arrive shortly, by the way. You may send him directly to me. He knows the way."

* * *

"But I know you ride. You are fond of horses. You have told me tales about the horses you kept as a girl over and over again. You *love* horses and know as much about them as any gentleman I have ever met. Of course you ride," stated Celeste with great authority.

"Yes, Celeste. And when I return home, I thoroughly intend to purchase at least two horses from Carey Farm in Ireland. That's where my Bonny Brooks came from. Carey Farm. I thought I would die when Marston wouldn't allow me to keep Brooks once we married," acknowledged Lady Marston. "But I have no intention of riding while in London, Celeste. I am sorry that you went to such trouble on my account, but I did never request that you—"

"Enough," interrupted the little dressmaker. "You will wear it in the country then. You admit you will ride in the country."

"Yes, but I—"

"You are going to tell me that you have no need of anything at all elegant for the country. And you are not going to tell me that you prefer to ride astride when no one can see you, eh?"

"Celeste! Whatever gave the idea that I—"

"I am correct, am I not?"

"Y-yes," Fleur admitted, her cheeks flushing with embarrassment. "Now that I need not please my husband any longer, nor anyone else, I intend to enjoy riding the way I always wished to do. I intend to alter a pair of Marston's old breeches and one of his hunting jackets and ride like the wind without anyone beside me to scowl at me and think ill of such unladylike behavior."

"Oh, Mama!" exclaimed Althea. "I never dreamed you wished to do that! What fun it sounds!"

"Indeed," Celeste agreed. "You are just as much a horse-woman as I imagined, which is why you will at the very least try on this wonderful habit I've made for you. After I and my girls have stitched our fingers to the very bone, you would not be so cruel as to decline it out of hand."

"Do try it on, Mama," urged Althea. "Please?"

"But it is pointless. I have not the least use for a riding habit now and if you had only asked, Celeste, I should have told you so directly. Perhaps it can be altered to fit Althea."

"It is not for Miss Avondale. It is for you. It is a gift. Will you tell me now that you don't wish to accept a gift from me? What have I done to make you despise me, eh?"

"You know perfectly well I don't despise you," smiled Lady Marston. "Of all the wheedling things to say."

"Yes. Did it work?" asked Celeste. "If it worked, I do not care a pittance whether it is wheedling or not."

"But why should you give me a gift at all? And a riding habit of all things? Celeste, it is too much."

"It is nothing. I thought of it—the design for it—and I thought to myself that there is one woman in all of London who could wear it to perfection."

"Me?"

"Mama?"

"Indeed. Now do as I say, Little Flower, and try it on."

Fleur could not imagine what had possessed the dressmaker to fashion her a riding costume. She most definitely was not going to ride anywhere. Not here. Not in London. Not she. But as she stepped into the dressing room and Celeste helped her to don the intriguingly designed habit, she began to smile. "Oh, Celeste, it is so—so—"

"Perfect?"

"No. That is to say, that is not what I was going to say. I was going to say it is so—"

"Magnificent?"

"Odd, Celeste. I was going to say, it is so very odd."

Celeste chuckled and her pale blue eyes glowed with delight. "Exceptionally. Exceptionally odd," she acknowledged as she fastened the skirt at Fleur's waist and then held open the coat for her to slip into it. "Ah, but I was so correct! It is perfect for you! Come. Come see if the lovely Miss Avondale does not think I am correct as well."

"Oh, Mama!" Althea exclaimed as Fleur entered the room and went to stand before the looking glass. "It is so—so—positively intriguing! You must have it. And you must ride, too. How can you resist to go for a ride when you possess such a habit as that?"

"The hat!" Celeste cried, her hands fluttering excitedly. "I have forgotten the hat! Just a moment. Do not dare to move. It must have its hat!"

Fleur studied herself in the looking glass and inhaled softly. "I cannot guess what possessed her, Ally. Only look. It is quite the most extraordinary riding habit I have ever seen."

It was, in fact, one of a kind, as were all of Celeste's designs. From the deep green velvet skirt which was not a skirt at all, but actually extremely wide-legged trousers designed to fall exactly like a skirt, to the white ruffled shirt front, to the austerely cut, masculine-style forest green jacket with its deep collar and braid trim, it was precisely the sort of riding costume Fleur would have liked to have worn as a girl. Of course, young ladies did not wear such things. Not even these days, they did not. But, oh, it was wonderful. Fleur's fingers went to play with the brass buttons that closed the jacket and then caressed the wide lapels. She smiled wistfully.

"And thus," proclaimed Celeste, setting a matching slouch hat on Fleur's head, "it is finished! Now you will tell me that you do not wish this gift, my Little Flower? No, you will not. You wish to have this very habit with all your heart. I see the answer in your eyes."

"Oh, Celeste, it's exquisite. Truly it is. And I do want it, but I cannot think I will ever have an occasion to wear it until I am in the country once again."

"Then it is yours. Not every lady can wear such a style as this. Perhaps no other lady. You shall take it with you today and whether you ride or not in London this Season, you will always have it. And when you do ride, you will think of Celeste. Yes, this pleases me exceedingly well, that when you ride, you will think of Celeste. And now, we proceed to the ball gowns for Miss Avondale. Come, Miss Avondale and we shall begin."

Davis sat, in silence, in the chair farthest from the looking glass. She watched. She listened. She noted everything that occurred and her countenance glowed with a subtle satisfaction as she gazed at Lady Marston's delighted face while Althea donned one gown after another.

"Most extraordinary thing I've ever seen or heard," declared Lord Panington. "Bless the gel, I say! Did precisely what needed to be done. Sent her flowers for the doing of it, too, I did. A bouquet of wildflowers. M'wife would have a fit did she know, but she don't know, nor I ain't going to tell her."

"Yes," Viscount Dunn agreed with a grin. "I sent the lady a bouquet, myself. Entertainment was well worth the price. Never did like that Wright woman. About time someone set her down a bit. Enjoyed it so much, Panington, sent roses. Pink roses."

"No, did ye?"

"Just so. Vastly entertaining, the way in which she handled the episode, I thought. And tasteful, as well. Not your general run of cat fight, it weren't. Ended almost as soon as it began. Roses to the victor, I say."

"You do realize the victor is a shipbuilder's daughter, Dunn?" offered Mr. Hayden, adjusting his hat at a more rakish angle as the three strolled along the walk.

"How could anyone not realize that? Cordelia Wright and the rest of the hens seize upon every opportunity to point it out. I say Lady Marston did just the thing and more power to her."

"To whom?" asked a rather rotund, middle-aged man who met them at that precise moment on the path that skirted the flower gardens in Hyde Park. "Panington, Dunn, Hayden— Well met. More power to whom, Dunn?"

"The Shipbuilder's Daughter," Dunn replied. "Attended a musical evening last night at Conningford's, she did. Gave Cordelia Wright the most exquisite setdown. You ought to have been there, Sir Ethan. I cannot remember when I enjoyed an evening more."

"Ah," nodded Sir Ethan. "I did hear about that. Yes, indeed. My niece and her mother attended. You will remember that wretched sister of mine, eh, Panington? Elizabeth? Yes, well, she and Tate are visiting me again. Forced Tate to come to London to give Julia another Season. Fine gel, Julia. Not a thing like her mama. Deserving of another opportunity, I think. So delighted was Julia with Lady Marston's setdown, she could not wait to tell me. Came running down to the breakfast room first thing this morning with the tale. Sent Lady Marston a rhododendron, I did. Never did like Cordelia Wright. Time someone had the gumption to take her down a peg or two. Julia said Arlington was there. Said his ears perked up like a regular terrier's. Thinks Teweksbury took an immediate interest in her as well, the moment he heard her remark."

"Teweksbury?" asked Dunn, as they passed beneath the line of oaks bordering Rotten Row, where but a few riders had yet appeared. "Now, that would be a coup. Teweksbury ain't taken an interest in any lady for years now. The Marquess of Teweksbury and The Shipbuilder's Daughter! That would set the ton on its collective ear, would it not?"

"Won't happen," Panington protested. "Teweksbury despises the woman. Made that clear enough when she was married to Marston. As particular about the smell of the shop as that Wright woman, he is. Never had a kind word to say about Lady Marston before. Won't have now. Ain't easily caught, Teweksbury. Certainly won't be caught by her."

"Still, if she proves witty and droll enough, she might hold his interest," offered Hayden. "Known Teweksbury for years. Finds every gel he meets insipid. That's why he ain't married one."

"Yes, but witty and droll for one moment won't do it," Panington said. "Must prove witty and droll on a continuing basis. And she's got to be horse mad as well. Teweksbury's got no use for a woman who ain't interested in horses. M'boy likes her."

"Who? Hartshire?" Sir Ethan queried with a chuckle.

"Don't laugh at m'godson. Got himself hitched to the loveliest gel ever to come out last time he went looking," protested Panington. "Finest lad ever born, my Atticus."

"Largest lad ever born," Sir Ethan responded, his eyes aglow, and all the gentlemen grinned at that, even Panington.

Conningford paced Marston's study restlessly. "You're certain she ain't here, eh, Marston?"

"She ain't here, Connie. I have told you over and over. She and Mama have gone shopping or some such."

"Yes, but it's past three."

"So?" Marston was playing with his father's cane, practicing twirling it and leaning nonchalantly on it, walking from one side of the study to the other, tapping it rhythmically as he did. Then he would take a step, catch the bottom of the cane on the tip of his shoe and kick it up into the air with a flourish.

"Will you cease and desist with that stick," demanded Conningford. "I am attempting to speak to you seriously, Marston."

"And I'm listening, Connie," Marston replied as they paced past each other across the middle of the room. "Ally ain't going to drive with you in the park this afternoon."

"I never said I—"

"No, but that is just what you're thinking. Why else would you arrive in your curricle, all spiffed up like you are?"

"I ain't spiffed up!"

"Yes, you are. You have even gone and pasted down a curl in the middle of your forehead."

"That curl's always been there."

"Not pasted down like that, it has not. You've gone flat-out lunatic over Ally. And you cannot even speak to her without stuttering," Marston added, tossing the cane into the air and catching it with one hand. "First you tell her that she sounds like a dying rabbit and then you stutter at her, and last night when you sat beside her, all you did was scowl at the poor girl."

"Shows how much you know," protested Conningford, ceasing to pace and slumping down into the chair behind the desk. "I wasn't scowling at all. I was gazing seductively at her from beneath partially lowered lids."

"You were what?"

"Women find gentlemen who do that romantic. Yes, they do, Marston! Don't laugh! I have read it in any number of novels!"

"Well, I'll be deviled," Marston murmured.

"You ought to read more. You would know these things."

"What? Oh. No, I ain't speaking about you scowling, Connie. Look here," Marston added, crossing the carpeting to set the cane atop the desk almost beneath Conningford's nose. "The handle is loose."

"I should think so, the way you've been plaguing the thing to death for the past three quarters of an hour."

"It wiggles," continued Marston, sitting on the desktop before Conningford and taking the cane back into his hands. "Look at this." With minor effort, Marston moved the falcon head backward and forward, then side to side.

"Is there a fastening of some sort?" asked Conningford. "Below the sapphire? Perhaps something we can tighten?"

Marston wiggled the falcon again, his fingers fumbling

over and around the brilliant jewel. With a soft click the falcon head detached itself from the malacca stick.

"By Jove!" Conningford exclaimed. "It ain't just a cane, Marston. It's a swordstick."

"Very short sword," Marston observed as he held the handle up before him. The bejeweled falcon head was attached to a twelve inch blade that glittered before their eyes in the sunlight streaming in the window. "No wonder m'father never left the house without this thing. Depended on it for protection. Fine looking blade. Short, but sharp. Connie, what the deuce are you doing peering into that stick? I have already got the sword out."

"Yes, but, there is something else in here as well, Marston." Conningford stood up with the malacca cane in his hands and shook it violently. "Won't come out."

"What? What is it? Let me see."

"Looks like paper to me."

"Jupiter, it does!"

Fleur stepped into Hatchards with chin high and eyes wary beneath an exquisite little straw hat with a wide brim pushed up at the front and held there with pink and yellow silk flowers. It was already nearing four and she had given in to Ally's pleading, hoping the booksellers would be quite empty of patrons. After all, the weather was fine and the promenade of the ton through Hyde Park ought to be just under way. She was not up to confronting any of *them* today. Truly, she wasn't. She had had quite enough confrontations last evening. Several people were peering through the books and magazines displayed on the tables. More browsed nonchalantly among the freestanding shelves.

Not empty then, Fleur thought. But not overflowing with people either. If we simply step up to the clerk and request him to fetch us the volume, we shall most likely not even be noticed.

"Oh, Mama, only look!" exclaimed Althea quietly. "Every book ever written must be on these shelves!"

"Perhaps," smiled Fleur, "but you gave me your word that we shall take just one of them home with us."

"Yes, and you will love it, too. Julia Tate was going on and on about it in Lady Conningford's Ovid Saloon last evening before the entertainment. It sounded precisely like the kind of thing you would enjoy. I mentioned it to Mal only this morning, and he said you must have it."

"He did, did he?"

"Indeed. It is called *Waverley,* and is very new. Julia says it's exquisite."

"Ask the clerk to fetch it to us, then, Ally, and we will be on our way."

"May I not look around a bit first, Mama? Oh! Over there! Do you see that line of volumes in marbled bindings? Those will be the books from Minerva Press. Julia says they publish the most outrageous novels she has ever read." And before Fleur could so much as utter a protest, a joyous Ally was off to inspect the shelves.

With a well-disguised sigh, Fleur took a seat at one of the tables and picked up a magazine lying there. She did not take note of its title. She only wanted it to hide behind in case one of *them*—Mrs. Cordelia Wright, for instance— should actually be in this shop and not promenading in Hyde Park at all. Really, last night had truly taken a toll on her nerves and she did not wish to be noticed by anyone at all today. Not one single person. She required a bit of time to recover before she took them on again.

"Davis," she hissed from behind the magazine. "Davis, come and sit beside me."

With her distinctive lope, the abigail who had been standing patiently just inside the entrance to the booksellers, crossed to the table and stood behind Lady Marston's chair.

"No, no, do sit down, Davis. You will call everyone's attention to me directly standing there like a waiting footman."

"But my lady, it is most improper. I am merely—"

"Oh, pooh! I don't want to hear lectures from you about propriety, Davis. I merely wish to be obeyed."

"Yes, my lady," Davis replied and slipped into the chair beside Lady Marston at once.

"Pick up a magazine, do. Then no one will pay either of us the least attention."

Davis did precisely as she was told.

The ruse proved most successful. No one seemed the least suspicious once Fleur reminded herself that it would be an excellent idea to turn a page now and then. She could not imagine what Ally found to keep her so long among the volumes, but she was rather proud that her plan was working so very well. The little bell over the shop door jingled; people came and went; and each time she thought it appropriate, Lady Marston nudged her abigail in the ribs with an elbow and they both turned a page. As long as we are quiet and continue to pretend interest in these magazines, no one will so much as bestow an inquisitive glance upon us, Fleur told herself confidently. Davis and I will just melt into the woodwork so to speak.

"I have never seen the like," declared a gentleman in dove-colored breeches, softly.

"No, neither have I, Farmingdale. Almost like watching a dance ain't it, the way they turn the pages at the same moment like that?"

"I expect they're Irish," offered Lord Larksbury as he and the Marquess of Teweksbury, in a splendid raspberry waist-coat, joined the group gathering before the first of the book-shelves on the north side of the store to observe the two women as they turned the pages of their magazines in unison.

"Irish? Why would you think them Irish, Lark?"

"Well, only look at what the one in the flowered hat is reading."

"Just so," sighed Teweksbury, peering at the cover of the magazine. "What woman who ain't Irish would know the first thing about horses, much less wish to read about the breeding of them. I've been waiting for that copy of _The Avid Horseman_ to come in for a week. I wish she will hurry and finish with it."

"Likely married to McDaniel or Carey or Kelly," offered Farmingdale. "All three of 'em have come to London. Offering beasts for auction at Tattersall's tomorrow."

"Why the devil do the Irishmen have all the decent luck when it comes to women?" Teweksbury grumbled. "Why can't an English woman take a sincere interest in horses?"

"Some do," grinned Farmingdale. "You just ain't had the good fortune to meet one as yet, Teweksbury."

"Oh, well, Lettie Lade and another one or two of them. But they're all married. I am sick to death of young women who pose atop horses that are nothing but flash and who think it most adorable of themselves to be always simpering up at me, pretending to require my assistance with a beast that ain't got a bit of go anywhere in its body. Could I find but one woman who actually knew a well-bred bit of blood and bone when she saw one and loved to ride it above a walk, one who knew the difference between a stable hack, a plough horse and a thoroughbred, I'd marry her straightaway."

"What the deuce are you all staring at?" asked Hartshire, strolling up to the little congregation of gentlemen, a parcel of wrapped volumes under his arm.

He was duly informed and turned, grinning, to watch the page-dancing Irishwomen. And then he saw the beads on Lady Marston's wrists, just peeping above the tops of her gloves, and the most interesting idea descended upon him. "Quite a sight, indeed," he commented. "But you will excuse me if I don't continue to share it with you. Forgotten a book Lady Con specifically requested me to pick up for her."

Hartshire left them on the instant and walked quietly along the aisles of the shop until he found the girl. He was right, then. Lady Marston _was_ waiting for her stepdaughter.

Stealthily he moved down the opposite side of the shelves Althea was just then inspecting.

Althea, her cheeks flushed, her eyes alive with excitement, posed in the most delicious manner at the end of the table with *Waverly* clutched to her bosom and a fond smile for Fleur and Davis wreathing her lovely face. She held the pose until she felt all the gentlemen's eyes turn away from the two readers to study her, and then she moved with grace and elegance around the table and leaned down to whisper in Fleur's ear.

"Oh!" Fleur gasped, but Althea shushed her and continued to whisper.

"Oh, I couldn't," Fleur protested.

"Yes, Mama, you can. You are the most courageous person I know. I shall take this to the clerk and have it wrapped and Davis and I will await you at the door."

Fleur nibbled at her lower lip, considering. Then, with merely a bit of a sigh, she lowered the magazine, closed it and stood up with it in her hand. She gazed at the gentlemen gathered along the shelves, who were just then pretending that they had not been observing her at all. Lord Teweksbury was the one in the raspberry colored waistcoat Althea had said. With considerable fear but grim determination, Fleur set a pleasant smile on her face, stepped around the table and made her way directly to Teweksbury.

"I do beg your pardon," she said softly. "You are Lord Teweksbury, are you not?"

Teweksbury gazed at her, appalled. She could see he knew precisely who she was and that he was gathering himself to give her a distinct setdown. She did not allow him the time to do so.

"You must forgive me, my lord, for allowing my interest in horses to deprive you of this marvelous magazine for such a lengthy period. Had I known you were in the shop, I certainly would not have read each and every word, but would have rushed through it instead so that you might have it for your own. You are the particular person for whom it was ordered, are you not?" she added with a shy lowering of her gaze. Then she raised it again. "How stupid of me to ask. Of course you are. You are one of the most illustrious horsemen in all of Britain."

"I—I—" stammered Teweksbury.

She handed him *The Avid Horseman* with a smile and a bit of a curtsy. The pink and yellow flowers on her hat brim nodded delightfully. "You need not reply, my lord," she said softly. "A mere shipbuilder's daughter ought not expect a reply from such as you. Nor ought I aspire to speak of horses with such an expert as yourself. It is merely that they are—a passion with me. Again, my lord, I do beg your pardon." And with that, she turned from him, walked with back straight and chin up to where Althea and Davis awaited her, and together the three of them exited Hatchards and entered their waiting coach.

"Did you see, Mama, when you left him? No, of course, you did not, for your back was turned that whole time. He clutched that magazine as though his life depended on it and his eyes followed you all the way to the door. They were positively glowing and never left you. I vow it. And his smile was as wide as his face. He will defend your honor for the rest of his life. I just know it. Lord Teweksbury has become your slave!"

"Pooh! My slave. As if he has not detested the very thought of me since first I appeared in Society."

"Well, he may have done, but he does not detest you now. I knew the moment he whispered it to me that he was quite right."

"Who? Who whispered to you, Ally? Certainly not Lord Teweksbury."

"No. Certainly not."

"Who then?"

"I cannot say."

"Why not?"

"Well, because I don't know, Mama. The gentleman did not precisely whisper in my ear. The whisper came from between the books on the shelves and begged me to relay the message to you exactly as I did."

"And the voice was not at all familiar to you?"

"No, not at all. But it seemed such an excellent idea, and totally to your good. You are fond of horses, after all, and have always been one to read about them. So I listened intently and then did precisely as he asked."

"Davis? You did not see anyone whispering to Miss Avondale?" asked Fleur abruptly.

"Me? Oh, no, my lady. I was hiding behind the magazine and turning the pages just as you told me," replied the abigail. "I didn't see anyone at all."

Hartshire reached home to discover Conningford and Marston eagerly awaiting him in the back parlor. "About time you was here, Atticus," Conningford offered in greeting. "Marston and I have been kicking our heels for near an hour."

"Just so," agreed Marston. "Except I should not say we were merely kicking our heels with nothing to do. We've played blindman's buff in the garden, enjoyed a rousing game of hare and hounds and learned everything there is to know about dormice, I should think. Rather intriguing creature, your dormouse."

"Oh, no. Not my dormouse. Henry belongs solely to Will."

"You don't know then," grinned Conningford.

"Don't know what?"

"That Henry has developed a preference for sleeping in your armoire. Sneaks in at every opportunity, Canton says. Suspects Will of aiding and abetting the little fellow, but Will says he don't. I knew you would laugh at that, Atticus. You always were a jolly good fellow."

"Um-hmmm. And what else am I to prove jolly good about, Val?" Hartshire asked, eyeing the two gentlemen suspiciously. "I see you're already making use of your father's cane, Marston."

"Indeed, sir. That is to say, not exactly making use of it. I was planning to do so and then we discovered . . ."

"Discovered what?"

"This!" exclaimed Conningford, freeing the swordstick from the malacca cane.

"And more," joined in Marston. "We found this stuffed down inside the stick as well."

Hartshire took the rolled up paper that Marston offered him, sat down on a flowered sofa directly across from the two young men, and unrolled the thing. "You found this inside the cane?"

"Yes!" they answered simultaneously.

"Can you read it, Atticus? We made the attempt, but it makes not the least bit of sense. It is English, of course, but totally absurd."

"So absurd," added Marston, "that we thought it might be some sort of code."

"Uhmmmm," Hartshire responded, glancing over the handwritten message.

"You don't think Marston's father was a spy, do you, Atticus?" asked Conningford excitedly.

"If he was, he will have spied for the Frenchies," grumbled Marston. "Contrary old man, m'father."

"Marston!" Conningford exclaimed, brushing at the blond curl on his forehead. "No matter how you despised him, even *you* cannot suspect your father of spying for the French. That would have been high treason. Had he been caught, he would have been hanged."

"I should have gone to see that," growled Marston, "and brought along my lunch in a basket."

Hartshire looked up. "Why?"

"Why? Because I should have enjoyed seeing m'father hanged for the way he treated m'stepmother, but a man can't get hanged in England for that. She still don't sleep good at night, Ally says. Plagued by nightmares. I ought to have been there," Marston added, his eyes clouding with guilt. "I ought to have been there, instead of frittering away my time at university. Beat her, he did, and more. Made her life a misery. But she would not say nothing to me when I came down for holiday. No, and she would not let Ally say nothing either. Found out just before he died, I did. Ally couldn't keep it a secret no longer. Would have pushed him under those horses m'self had I discovered the opportunity."

Hartshire and Conningford both stared at him in silence.

"Beg pardon," Marston murmured. "Ought not to have mentioned it. Not any of it your concern. About that paper, sir. *Is* it some sort of code?"

Hartshire nodded. "In a way. Rhyming cant."

"He never did touch your sister?" asked Conningford, earnestly. "He never did hurt Ally?"

"Oh, now she is Ally?" The cloud of guilt departed Marston's eyes and he grinned. "Does m'sister know you think of her as Ally, Connie?"

"No, she don't. I expect she don't believe I think of her at all. And she never will because she is never at home when I call."

"You have only come to call on her once. Today."

"Yes, but—"

"Did he ever harm your sister?" interrupted Hartshire very quietly.

"No. Ally says not. Says she heard Mama tell him once that if he so much as raised his hand to either of us, she would shoot him dead on the spot. About that paper, sir. Is it something important? Ought I to give it to someone at the Home Office or something?"

"What you ought to do, Marston," Hartshire replied, rolling the paper back into a tube shape, "is put it right back inside that cane."

"Put it back? But Atticus!" Conningford exclaimed.

"Hush, Val. Let me finish. As much as I wish you both to cease all your larking about and adventuring, I rather think that now is not the time for you to do it."

"It's a letter from one of Spence's followers?" asked Marston.

"Well, a rather Spencean-sounding letter let us say. What Thomas Spence had to do with your father or your father with him, I cannot imagine, Marston. But you have tumbled into something here that could prove dire."

"And you are not going to forbid us to be involved in it, Atticus?" asked Conningford eagerly.

"Not at the moment, no. Put this back in the cane, Marston."

"And then what, sir?"

"Then we wait."

"Wait?"

"Quite possibly that message was intended for your father on the day he died. In which case, it's old news and all was foiled because of his accident. Or . . ."

"Or what?" asked Conningford and Marston together.

"Or else it is newly written and intended to convey a message to someone in Marston House."

"In my own house?"

"Um-hmmm."

"But how could anyone know that this cane would come to be in my possession? You must be mistaken, sir. Perhaps it's a message intended for someone in Dashfield's household. It was he who carried the thing about with him of an evening. I've just come by it, you know."

"Just so," nodded Hartshire. "Perhaps you're right, Marston. Or perhaps, as I said, it's a year or more old and was intended for your father. We have no way of knowing at the moment. That's what we're going to find out. I want you to leave the cane lying about during the day, Marston. Don't take it from wherever it is generally kept except when you go out of an evening. And every morning, sometime when you can manage to be completely alone, I want you to remove the swordstick and check to see if this paper is still in the cane."

"Yes, sir. I can do that easily enough."

"I want you to take the paper out each time, Marston. Check to see that it is this very message. If it proves to be a different message or if it's missing completely, you must send me word at once. At once, Marston. It's immensely important."

"Y-yes, sir. I will."

"Ain't you going to tell us what it actually says, Atticus, this rhyming cant?"

"No, I ain't. Likely what it refers to all came to nothing a long time ago with Marston's father's death and we are doing this for no reason. Or, as Marston suggested, it was intended for someone in Dashfield's household and whoever it is will not get the message at all. That will put a definite kink in their—in what the writer of the message plans to do. It's best to be certain, is all. If you need to know what it actually says, Val, if it does turn out to be a plot just in the hatching and we learn more, I'll tell you what you need to know. There is something else I wish you will do for me, Marston," he added, standing and beginning to pace the room.

"Anything, sir."

"I wish you will take home with you a particular horse I bought from an old friend earlier today and pretend to your mama that you bought it for her."

"A horse, sir?"

"Yes. I cannot give it to her myself. It would not only be highly improper for me to do it, but she would not accept it. Her dressmaker has presented her with a new riding costume and—"

"Mama will not ride in London, sir. She has said as much time and time again. She will not so much as allow me to drive her in the promenade through Hyde Park in the barouche."

"The day may come when she'll change her mind," Hartshire said, a smile playing across his face. "I have every confidence that it will, and Gaily Lad is the sort of horse she will long for then. Take him with you when you go. My grooms know he's intended for you. And I had best go and play with Will for a time and take a quick peek into my armoire to see if Henry's there. You'll excuse me, scoundrels, will you not?"

Eight

"I presented her with the riding habit today. Did you purchase the horse as you said you would, Hartshire?" Celeste looked down from her window above the shop into Oxford Street, her back to Hartshire where he sat gingerly on the edge of a Louis XIV chair.

"Yes, I did. And there is more reason for her to ride in Hyde Park now than the new riding habit, Celly. If she did as I said—and I am almost positive she did—Teweksbury will call on her soon and invite her to ride beside him in Rotten Row."

"Teweksbury? You wish our Little Flower to ride with the Marquess of Teweksbury?"

"I certainly do. To be seen in his company will do her a world of good. He is one of those who have been against her from the start. But he'll be in the process of altering his opinion even as we speak. Horse mad, he is, and she, well, he knows she's an avid horsewoman by now. He couldn't help but think otherwise. Not if she did as I said. It was damnably lucky she picked up that particular magazine to hide behind. I can't help but think that the gods are smiling down on her."

Celeste turned from the window. Her hands fluttered the merest bit and she quickly clasped them together to keep them still. "But not on you, Hartshire. I assumed you would ask her to ride with you, and you do not."

"I will."

"When?"

"After she rides with Teweksbury."

"Hartshire!"

"No, don't begin scolding me, Celeste. Teweksbury is an influential gentleman, a town dandy and handsome to boot. She will like to ride with him. Were I to rush over to Cavendish Square and request her to accompany me, she would think it merely done out of pity. And she would know straightaway that you had told me about the habit, too, and then start to wondering where the horse really came from."

"But you love our Little Flower, Hartshire!"

"I what?"

"You love her."

"I do not."

"Yes, you do. Do not be playing the fool with me. You may have convinced sweet Miriam that you did not so much as realize you loved her until she took you aside and told you so, but I know better. You are unsure of yourself now just as you were then. You think our little flower cannot possibly return your love, just as you thought sweet Miriam could not. But you're wrong, Hartshire. Wrong, wrong, wrong. She is a fine, intelligent lady, our Fleur. If you can only bring yourself to grant her the opportunity, she will see beyond your large size and your plain face and your—ears. Give her a chance, Hartshire. Admit that you love her and then let her prove that she is as intelligent as I believe her to be."

Hartshire sighed. He stood up and stuffed his hands into the pockets of his buckskin breeches. He took them out again and clasped them behind his back. Then he began to pace. He paced diagonally, from one corner of the room to the other. Then he switched and paced the length. Then he paced the width of the chamber. In no time at all, he was pacing in a neat square around the room.

Celeste set her fingers free to roam through her hair, sending the shortest pieces of it skyward. She settled into her favorite chair and waited patiently. She had known Hartshire forever and she knew that now was not the time to speak more to him. She had said what must be said. Now was the time for her to wait and then to listen.

At long last Hartshire came to a halt before her chair and stared down at her. "I cannot just walk up to her and say I love her, Celly. There are things—things in the way. I—she— Her husband beat her, Celly," he said quietly. "He treated her shamefully. She still cries out in the night in fear of him, Marston says. No wonder she struggled so when I swept her up into my arms that afternoon. It was more than mere protest at my audacity. It was panic."

"You swept her up into your arms?"

"Yes. Well, she was quite ill. I only intended to help her. I did help her, too. But before I did, she pummeled me excessively."

"I once pummeled you excessively."

"Yes, you did," murmured Hartshire, his countenance darkening. "I remember it well. You thought me to be Drake that night in the garden when I came to surprise you and instead was so gravely surprised myself. I thought you would kill me before you realized who I was."

"And for a moment I expect Lady Marston imagined you to be Marston, eh? When you swept her into your arms? You have picked a little flower that has grown in a garden quite like the garden from which you rescued me, Hartshire. Not at all like Miriam. Not a fresh innocent blossom, free from fear. But at least our little flower is already free of her evil gardener. Yes, indeed she is. You need not rescue her from the teeth of the dragon. You need merely rescue her from memories of him."

"I will, Celly. I will make the attempt at least. You do not seem at all surprised that she was beaten. Did she tell you?"

"Not a word. But then, she would not, our Fleur. She

would think herself weak to complain of it to anyone, especially now that the man is dead."

"I wish you will cease to call her 'our Fleur' and 'our Little Flower,' Celly. She doesn't belong to either one of us. How did you know about the beatings then? If she did not confide in you? It was her stepson told me."

"I didn't know for a certainty, Hartshire. I suspected, eh? And so I am not surprised to learn that my suspicions are correct. There is something in her I noticed at the very first. It called out to me as a sister calls to a sister. I cannot explain why I suspected it any clearer than that. Why do you say you don't love her, Hartshire? Tell me. Am I right? Is it because you're afraid?"

"I ain't afraid of anything, Celly, and well you know it, too," protested the earl, stuffing his hands back into his pockets and staring intently down at Celeste's lemon yellow kid slippers. "I expect I do c-care about her. But I barely know her. A man cannot love a woman he barely knows. It takes time."

"It takes time. It takes time. It takes time." Hartshire's own words echoed at him over and over in rhythm with the clicking of Radical's hooves on the cobbles and the jingle of Hartshire's spurs as the horse and rider made their way through the thickening night toward home. Spent too long with Celeste, he thought. Ought to have departed the very moment she mentioned the word love. What a fool I was to remain and hear her out. Well, but the way I feel about Lady Marston is my own fault. It ain't Celly's. All she did was take note of it and dare me to say otherwise. And I did say otherwise, too. I said it over and over again. Still, she didn't believe me, that wretched gnome.

He pushed his hat farther back on his head and sighed. "I didn't believe me either," he muttered. "I *am* in love with the lady." But Teweksbury would be so much more acceptable. And she deserves someone like Teweksbury. And I will get over her, he thought, frowning. I will. And if I don't—

He could not bear to think what would happen to him if he didn't. Quite likely his heart would break. Not that he would let on, because he wouldn't. No, never, not The Spectre. And yet, his heart was betraying him this very moment, stirring up the most awful waves in his stomach, making his head pound, closing up his throat with a great lump.

"P-perhaps I'm mistaken, Rad," he managed softly, around the lump. "Perhaps Robes is right. Perhaps my face is not so plain and my ears are not so large and funny looking. Perhaps I ain't as gigantic as I think or so very ugly that Miriam was the only woman in all of England who could ever love me."

Radical picked that precise moment to snort a most derisive snort, and Hartshire's heart sank. "You're correct, of course," Hartshire mumbled. "I look like a gudgeon. An extremely large gudgeon. An extremely large, excessively ugly gudgeon with dormouse ears. What woman would not run screeching from the room the moment the words 'I love you' fell from my lips?"

I shall simply go on as I have, he decided, riding straight past Grosvenor Square without giving it a thought. I will help her all I can to become accepted. Yes, and I will do more of it as The Spectre, from dark corners and behind bookshelves, and less of it as just plain me, because then she will not be bothered thinking that she owes me something for whatever help I can give her. No, and she won't think I do it out of pity either. Likely she will not think of me at all once Teweksbury truly gets to know her. He will keep her so busy with his courting, she won't have a minute to spare for me. "And she will be a good deal better off to be loved by some handsome gent with a deal of spit and polish about him like Teweksbury," he added with a decisive nod. "Much better off."

It was just at that moment Radical halted and pawed with his right hoof at the cobbles.

"Rad, what the devil are you doing? I didn't tell you to stop, you old reprobate." And then Hartshire looked about him and realized, quite to his dismay, that he had ridden right past Hartshire House. "By Jove, Rad, where the deuce are we?"

Radical, with an energetic shake of his head, declined to answer, though he did cease clicking his hoof against the cobbles.

"Blast," murmured Hartshire, peering through the darkness and the flimsy layers of fog. "It's a square, but it ain't our square. Wait. Yes, I think it is." He dismounted and looped Radical's reins once through the circle of the nearest hitching post. "Stay right there, Rad. I'll be back in a moment. I am fairly certain that's Denbigh House, just there."

There was a time I would have known whether it was Denbigh's or not straight off, he thought. Been gone too long. Way too long. He moved softly toward the residence so as not to call attention to himself. His boot heels made not one click on the pavement, nor did his spurs dare to jingle as he approached the front door. A lion's head knocker emerged from the darkness before him and, though he had to squint to see it, he could make out a bronze mermaid balanced on the tip of the lion's nose. Correct, he thought. Denbigh's. Cavendish Square.

Cavendish, he thought, stepping back and staring into the darkness around him. A few lights flickered in the windows of the houses up and down the square, but most of the residences were dark and locked up tight for the night. "Cavendish Square," he whispered to himself. "Marston House. Right between Denbigh's and Allencort's, Celly said." His gaze followed his thoughts, taking in the tall, narrow residence to his right. Visions of Lady Marston safely and soundly asleep inside stirred his heart. "Her stepchildren love her," he murmured. "Marston will keep her safe and

Miss Avondale will rush to her if she should wake crying in the night." Still he lingered, imagining her in some chamber above him, tucked into bed, a ruffled nightcap set on that dusky brown hair. In the street, Radical snorted. Hartshire gave himself a mental shake and went to the horse.

With a weary sigh, he mounted and turned Rad toward the east end of the square. Then he tugged on the reins and brought the horse to a halt. "If we simply go between Denbigh's and Marston's, Rad, through the double mews and around Parson's stables into Brook Street we will be at our own stables in a matter of a few minutes.

Fleur had been so restless that she had given up her attempt at sleep, had slipped into an old round gown, seized the nearest shawl and gone to prowl about the walled garden. Now, she wrapped the shawl closer around her and stared upward, searching for stars through the clouds, the fog. Just one star, she thought. Let just one star shine through. I should so like to wish on it.

Gracious, wishing on a star, she thought then. Have I lost all common sense? I'm being silly beyond belief. But still, I should like to know who he is, this gentleman who gave me such good advice in the Conningfords' library and who whispered to Ally in Hatchards. I cannot think why he should bother, but even in so short a time as the past two days, he has changed my life for the better. Indeed, he has. And I should like to thank him. To *see* him and to thank him.

The truth was that Fleur had not at all expected to return home and find the silver salver on the table in the vestibule overflowing with gentlemen's calling cards. She had expected a few from the bravest of the young men who had made Ally's acquaintance in the park and at the Conningfords'. But to discover nearly fifty cards, together with numerous invitations to balls, soirees, at-homes, had surprised her utterly. Likewise, she'd been flabbergasted to discover the house filled to overflowing with floral offerings, and even more speechless to discover that a number of the floral offerings were for herself alone. Her cheeks had flushed like a schoolgirl's. Her eyes had sparkled with happiness. The flowers sent to her had come from the old guard—from Lord Panington, Viscount Dunn, Mr. Hayden, Sir Ethan Darlington—the very gentlemen whose wives and daughters and sisters despised her. Perhaps the ladies never would accept her, but her hopes had begun to grow then and there. Now that the husbands, brothers, fathers, had chosen to take note of her, she began to think that the ladies' hearts might soften toward her as well.

"And it is all his doing," she whispered. "With one well-turned phrase, he provided me an opportunity to make things better for myself last evening and so make this Season in Town more delightful for Ally. I cannot think what will happen because of what he told me to do and say at Hatchards, but I am certain it will be proven quite as magical."

It did seem to Fleur that the result of her brief and quiet confrontation with Mrs. Cordelia Wright had been magic. And it seemed to her that this gentleman who had persuaded her to do it must be somewhat magical as well. Who on earth was he? Where had he come from? Why had he been hiding away in the dark in Lady Conningford's library? And why had he said nothing at all when she had entered and disturbed him?

"And then for him to appear at Hatchards and whisper to Ally and send her to whisper to me! To think I was making a laughingstock of myself and did not so much as realize, and then for him to be suddenly there and come to my rescue!" I *will* discover who he is, she decided, and I will give him my dearest thanks for what he's done. He has proved so very kind. As kind as Lord Hartshire has proved to be.

The thought struck her at once. Lord Hartshire. Perhaps he—but no, that could not possibly be. Lord Hartshire had been in Lady Conningford's music room when she'd departed it, and he had been there when she'd returned. And certainly he hadn't been in Hatchards. She would have noticed immediately had he been in Hatchards and Ally would have noticed as well. He was so large, after all, they could not possibly have overlooked him. Well, of course, he might have hidden behind the shelves when he saw them enter, but why would he have done that? He could not have known that she was about to make an utter fool of herself. "No, not Lord Hartshire," she said quietly. And then she smiled a most wistful smile.

He turned as he heard her speak. He had been so thoroughly engrossed in getting Radical and himself quietly through the narrow passage between the houses, that he'd not once gazed over the Marstons' wall into their garden— not until he'd heard "No, not Lord Hartshire," in that oh, so familiar voice.

With a tug on the reins, he brought Radical to a halt. He leaned forward and whispered directly into the horse's right ear, "Invisible, Rad."

Radical knew that word. He'd not heard it for years, but he knew at once what was expected of him—to stand, like a statue, without so much as a twitch or a shudder, and to remain as silent as death.

The wall rose merely to the height of Hartshire's waist as he sat astride the horse. He peered over the rock formation into the darkness beyond, searching for her. And then, for a moment, the breeze that had been tattering the fog about rose higher into the sky and puffed a cloud away from the evening star. He heard Lady Marston give a tiny gasp as it did and following the hint his ears had given him, discovered her standing alone in Venus's faint glow. He watched her as she stared up at the star, her back straight and proud, her head thrown back as though she could not get enough of staring at the sky. His heart swelled in his chest and his lips parted in wonder. And then he recalled her words and the lump returned to his throat. "No, not Lord Hartshire," she'd said. What had she meant by it?

He cursed himself in silence. If she was doing what ladies did—what Miriam had confided to him she had done often before they'd met and married—wishing for love in the starlight, then he knew perfectly well what the lady had meant by "No, not Lord Hartshire." Of course she would not choose to love him. What rational woman would? No, not Lord Hartshire. Anyone but Hartshire, he thought to himself gravely. Still his heart persisted in longing for her. She looked so very fragile and yet so very brave with that straight little back to him, with her face raised so innocently to the skies. For the first time in years, his feelings overwhelmed him and before he could think what a stupid thing it was to do, he was off Radical and over the wall. Like The Spectre they named him, he glided through silence and shadow until he was near enough behind her to smell the lavender that drifted from her gown and touch the long braid that trailed down her back. At that precise moment, as if it were a devoted compatriot, the breeze blew the clouds around again, covering the evening star and abandoning Fleur and Hartshire both to the darkness of the night.

Fleur lowered her head, her wish made. "How odd that it should show itself just when I was most longing to see it," she murmured. "Is my life to change so much that even the wishing star appears when I desire it to do so? No, I can never believe that."

"Believe it. Do."

Fleur gasped aloud and began to turn toward him, but Hartshire seized her by the shoulders and kept her from doing so. "Don't be afraid, my lady," he whispered in the voice that was peculiarly The Spectre's and not his own at all. "I saw you standing here in the starlight like the angel you are and I had to come to you. I did you no harm at Conningford's or at Hatchards. I will do you no harm now. You have my word on it."

I have his word on it, Fleur thought, amazed that she had not called out for help the moment his hands had touched her. But his touch was not at all like Marston's. It was gentle, somehow reassuring. This is a gentleman to be trusted, she thought. She could not think why or how she knew, but she did know, deep in her heart. "Who are you?" she asked, his touch sending shivers through her. "What do you want of me? I ought to scream, you know. My son and daughter are just inside as are my servants."

"No, are they? And fast asleep, I think. Don't scream. Don't wake them. I merely wish to—to—"

"To what?"

Hartshire's hands left her shoulders. His arms slipped gently around her from behind and drew her back against him until he cradled her against his chest. "Trust me," he whispered, his breath tickling at her ear. How the very feel of her set his pulses racing. He leaned closer, his lips parted the slightest bit, and he kissed her softly, tenderly on the cheek.

Fleur's hands found his and rested easily on them as he did. He's kissing me, she thought in amazement. And I'm allowing him to do it too. Not merely kissing me, but kissing me so very gently on the very scar that Marston's signet ring made, as if he could make it disappear, did his lips linger long enough.

"Why did you do that?" she asked quietly when his kiss ended.

"Because I find you beautiful."

"Me?"

"Indeed. Beautiful and beguiling."

Fleur smiled, though she knew he could not see. "How you can find me anything of the sort, sir, when we have never come face-to-face, not even in the darkness."

"Have we not come face-to-face? Are you certain of that?"

"No," she admitted, "I'm not. Perhaps we have. But surely you have never spoken to me. Never before last evening at the Conningfords'. I would have recognized your voice else. Will you not tell me who you are?"

"I am the wind that whistles down Little Bridge Street late in the afternoon and the starshine that glitters through the night when all God's children are asleep. I am the fog, too, wisping through the darkness and the footsteps that hesitate just beyond hearing."

"And will you give me no name at all? I cannot call you wind or starshine or fog or footstep."

"Montague," whispered Hartshire, his heart near breaking for wanting her that very moment. "You may call me Montague."

"And am I then a Capulet?"

"Just so." He leaned down and kissed her again. "I cannot stay longer. I did not plan to come at all. You must do me one favor, my lady."

"And what is that?"

"You must give me your word that you will not turn around, not attempt to catch a glimpse of me. Promise that you will stand here and count to twenty before you make your way back inside your house."

"My word?"

"Your word of honor."

"You think a woman has a word of honor like a man?"

"Indeed. Exactly like a man, and bound to keep her word like a man or lose her honor completely."

"I give it to you then," Fleur replied. She felt his hands move beneath hers, and then they were gone, his hands, his arms, his chest, all gone, though not a sound did she hear as he melted away into the night. She stood alone in the garden, as if in the midst of a dream, and counted slowly to twenty.

* * *

Davis watched from beside the privy as Lady Marston entered the kitchen door and closed it tightly behind her. Davis shivered a bit as the breeze kicked up again. Truly, that gent's a wonder, she thought. To think I believed all the tales about him to be exaggerated, and they were just the opposite. Just the opposite. If he is anything, he is more than they give him credit for. I will need to be more careful from now on. Already he thinks he knows me. I shall need to be exceptional careful, or he will remember where he knows me from and then he'll be drawn into this thing will he, nil he.

She waited for a good five minutes before she loped—in her peculiarly wild, wary fashion—toward the house, giving Lady Marston time enough to mount the staircase and make her way to her bedchamber. Davis opened the kitchen door with the key she'd stolen on her first day in the house when Mrs. Belding, the housekeeper, had so conveniently dropped her keyring while leading her through the garden, bragging about the excellent establishment of which Davis had just become a member. A smile wreathed Davis's face as she closed and locked the door behind her. I am good at what I do, too, Spectre, she thought. Got that key off that ring in the bare moment between my picking the ring from the ground and handing it to the Belding woman.

Yes, and I am almost as invisible as you, too, she thought with pride as she lit a candle and entered the servants' staircase. I go all about town with my lady and Miss Avondale. I ride with them in their coach, trail them through the shops, patter along behind them on the pavement and through the park and no one takes the least notice of me. I am merely the abigail, after all, and it is quite accepted that I am meant to be invisible.

Davis reached the third story, stepped quietly into the small room she had to herself because the house was large and the female servants few, and went to draw the curtains aside from the little window. Candle in hand, she stared down into the space between Marston House and Denbigh House and whistled a low, soft whistle. "Just imagine him making his way through there on horseback," she murmured. "And not so much as a clip or clop or clunk to betray his passage. What a wonder he is. Yes, and what a wonder his horse must be, too. Not a sound from either of them. Not one sound. I was that stunned when he appeared behind her ladyship and took her by the shoulders. Thank gawd it was him. Thank gawd for that."

"We thought you were never coming home at all, my lord," said Little, surprising Hartshire no end as he jerked open the front door just as the earl set his key in the lock. "Robes and I have been waiting forever."

"You have? For me?" Hartshire put his hat down on the hall table. "Why?"

"To speak with you about our night at The Swan."

"Oh? But we've spoken about it already, Little. You said that several of the men knew of Spence but none, apparently, were in support of his cause."

"Yes, but we have been discussing it between us, my lord, and Robes and I—Robes and I—think we remember something that might prove useful to you. We are in your library, my lord," the butler added, preceding Hartshire down the corridor.

Hartshire, his mind still bewildered—though joyously so—by his impulsive leap over Lady Marston's garden wall and its result, followed dutifully as a lad in Little's footsteps. He grinned distractedly at the sight of Robes popping up from one of the leather chairs, wineglass in hand, and nodded him back down as Little and he joined the valet. The feel of Lady Marston's cheek beneath his lips and the warmth of her in his arms muffled Hartshire's mind, compelling him to take note of all around him as if peering at the world through wet muslin.

"Will you have a glass of port, my lord?" asked Little.

"What? Port? Yes, certainly. Drinking my port are we?"

"We did not think you would mind, my lord," offered Robes as Little went to fill a glass for their employer. "Not after what we have to tell you."

"I don't mind anyway," murmured Hartshire with a vagueness that caused both Mr. Little and Mr. Robes to raise their eyebrows. "Don't mind if you indulge yourselves and empty out the entire wine cellar."

"Are you not feeling quite the thing, my lord?" Robes queried worriedly.

"I'm fine, Robes. Just fine."

"Perhaps you have had enough wine for tonight, my lord," suggested Little, placing the glass of port into Hartshire's hand and settling down in a chair directly across from him.

"Why do you say that?"

"Well because you do sound, ah, a bit other-worldly, my lord."

"Other-worldly?" Hartshire grinned at that. "No, do I? How very odd. But never mind. It ain't wine what's done it. What is it the two of you have recalled?"

"A female, my lord," declared Little.

"A female?"

"Indeed, my lord," nodded Robes. "It didn't strike us as odd, you know, at the time."

"Being as we were all a bit fuddled," Little inserted, "from all that ale, my lord."

"Everyone had left The Swan but the two of us and Mr. Wickens, Lord Marston's butler," Robes continued. "And we were just saying our good-byes outside the door. The door is always let open at The Swan, my lord, until the last of the patrons depart."

"Yes? And you were the last of the patrons and departing? Have I got that down correctly, Robes?"

"Just so, my lord. And as we were saying our good-byes to Mr. Wickens, why I spied a—a—female person, my lord, clinging to a gent like her dress were stitched to the very front of his jacket. That close they were, my lord. And I did think to myself what a jade she must be to be standing there right in a public street, kissing a fellow."

"I thought the same, my lord," interjected Mr. Little righteously. "Even Mr. Wickens commented on the impropriety of it."

Hartshire stared at the two, puzzled. "This is why you waited up for me? To tell me that you recall seeing a woman kissing a man in the public street? What the deuce can that have to do with Thomas Spence and his followers?"

"That is just the thing, my lord!" exclaimed Mr. Little.

"Precisely the thing, my lord!" exclaimed Mr. Robes.

"What is the thing?" Hartshire asked, his eyebrows drawing close together in a puzzled frown.

"We didn't see how it could have anything to do with the Spenceans either, m'lord, and so we dismissed it from our minds," Little explained.

"Yes," agreed Robes, his voice rising with a tinge of excitement. "Dismissed it completely until after we dined this very evening when we began to discuss the evening at The Swan again, to be certain we had not missed anything."

"And, by gawd, if we had not missed that female!" Little cried triumphantly. "But we have got her now!"

Hartshire gazed into his port, attempting to collect his wits, which he began to suspect had gone wandering far afield. "Am I just plain stupid, or is there something I don't know?" he asked with an aggravated shake of his head.

"There is something you don't know, my lord," replied Little. "What you don't know is that she was clinging to this gent just off to the side of the door, in the shadows. And the very moment Wickens bid us a good night and strolled off, the very moment his heels could be heard clicking off down the pavement in the direction of Cavendish Square, she ceased to kiss the fellow, turned on her heel and loped off in the exact direction Wickens had taken."

"And the gent walked off the other way, m'lord, without so much as uttering a fare-thee-well. Left the female to walk off alone, he did. At night. On the streets of London. And she, not so much as looking back at the bloke."

"Yes, but, perhaps he—she—" Hartshire faltered, attempting to think of a way to put the thing that would not assault Mr. Robes's sensibilities, only to be interrupted with enthusiasm by the prudish little valet himself.

"So we thought, when we were not actually thinking about it, you know, my lord, that she was a—a—lady of the evening so to speak, and he simply one of her—patrons." Robes, his face reddening, took a large sip of his wine. "And then, when we began thinking about it, we began to think that if that were the case, she would not have been clinging to him as she was, nor kissing him so."

"Not at all," inserted Little. "Such methods she would have used to lure him into her clutches, my lord, not to bid him good-bye."

"You've got a point there," nodded Hartshire. "If they seemed that close one moment and that distant the next. Well, she likely wouldn't have so much as seen him to her door once he paid her price."

"Just so," nodded Robes. "Precisely so. That's what led us to our conclusion!"

"What we concluded they were doing, my lord, what we believe now that they were doing, was hiding in plain sight!" exclaimed Mr. Little.

A smile wreathed Hartshire's face. "Go on," he urged, his pride in them apparent. "I admit it did not occur to me until you said as much just now. Go on with it."

"Well, my lord, who were they hiding from is the question," said Mr. Little.

"And why," added Mr. Robes.

"Exactly, who and why," nodded Hartshire.

"Mr. Wickens!" exclaimed the two simultaneously.

"Well, Robes and I knew it couldn't be us, after all," Little said, leaning comfortably back in his chair. "And since we were the last to leave the place—with Mr. Wickens—"

"And since the female person followed after Mr. Wickens," Robes put in.

"We have concluded not only that it was Mr. Wickens they were hiding from," declared Little joyously, "but that the female person was bent on learning where Wickens resides."

"Of course she was!" Mr. Robes exclaimed. "Why else would she follow him but to learn where he resides?"

"And why would she wish to know that?" Hartshire queried, perfectly enthralled by the joy and pride bursting out all over his butler and his valet.

"Because Mr. Wickens saw who killed Lady Dashfield, my lord, though he didn't say a word about it. Likely it was that very gent who the female was kissing did the vile deed, which is why he couldn't follow Wickens himself. Couldn't chance being recognized," Mr. Little explained, twirling his wineglass around by the stem. "Sent the female instead. It's a definite known thing, my lord, that Lady Dashfield supported the suffrage movement. Lord Dashfield admitted as much to the Bow Street Runners who were looking into the thing. And they did find a copy of Thomas Paine's *The Rights of Man* in her little writing desk, my lord."

"Yes, and a copy of Spence's own *Pig's Meat*," Robes added.

"So," said Hartshire thoughtfully, "you think Lady Dashfield was a supporter of Spence."

"Indeed, and when she discovered what a radical group they really are, my lord, likely she threatened to go to Bow Street and betray them to the Runners," Little replied.

"And the Spenceans got word of it before she could and one of them killed her," added Robes. "And now, like as not, they are out to murder poor Mr. Wickens, and him not the least aware of it."

Hartshire sat back and pondered. Dashfield again. Dashfield's wife murdered; Dashfield in possession of Marston's cane. *The Rights of Man* and *Pig's Meat* found in Dashfield's house. And some female person trailing Dashfield's former butler home from the public house in the middle of the night. Hartshire drained his wineglass and set it down on the table beside his chair. "What did she look like, this female person?" he asked. "Did you get any kind of a look at her at all?"

"Oh, yes, my lord," responded Little.

"Indeed, my lord," nodded Robes. "She walked right past us, right through the light from the open doorway. She was about so high." Robes demonstrated by the use of his hand. "And she had carroty hair and greenishlike eyes. Sneaky eyes. And she was thin as thin could be."

"Yes," Little agreed. "And she did not walk. She loped along, my lord, like one of the street hounds on the prowl. Oh, but she was a sight to see, though we did almost neither one of us take note of her, not expecting her, you know, to be of the least importance."

Fleur peered up from between partly lowered lashes at the young woman seated beside her on the bed. "Do not tell me that I woke you with a cry or a scream, Ally," she said softly, "for I know I didn't."

"No, Mama, you didn't. But you were talking, and quite loudly, too."

"Talking? In my sleep?"

"Uh-huh. You have never done that before—actually held an entire conversation with someone."

"What did I say?"

"Oh, the oddest things. You spoke of loving the wind that blows down Little Bridge Street of an afternoon, and having a passion for the glitter of starshine. You said that the fog was possessed of some most extraordinary qualities and that you were pleased to listen for the whisper of footsteps the rest of your life. I cannot think who you were speaking to, but you were quite passionate about it all, as though you were obliged to convince the person of the truth of it."

"Oh, Ally!" Fleur sat up in the bed and buried her face in her hands. Her shoulders shook; her breath came in little gasps.

"Mama? Don't cry, Mama. Devil it, but I shouldn't have told you a thing of what you said! What a dunderhead I am."

Fleur shook her head in protest. "N-no," she managed. "No, Ally. D-do not casti-castigate yourself on my be-behalf." She lowered her hands from her face, reached out and took Althea's hands into her own.

"You aren't crying," Ally whispered in surprise. "Mama, you're laughing."

"Only a bit. I ought to cry, Ally. Truly I ought. I was such a fool tonight. I placed myself in the most imprudent position and such horror could have come from it."

"Horror, Mama?"

"Oh, yes. But it did not, you see. Apparently, since I have declared that I love the wind, am passionate about starshine, find genuinely good qualities in fog, and am willing to listen for the whisper of footsteps the rest of my life—apparently what came of my foolishness was a distinct softening of my heart toward a particular gentleman."

"A particular gentleman? Mama, what are you talking about? No gentleman came to call on us tonight."

"Well, no. Not on us. And I don't think what he did actually qualifies as paying a call. But Ally, I have had the most amazing experience, like something out of a faery tale, and I do not regret a moment of it. Not one moment."

Nine

Althea paused on the threshold to the morning room and frowned in puzzlement. Her brother and Lord Conningford were huddled together before the windows in the most conspiratorial manner, backs to the doorway, shoulders touching, whispering excitedly. She thought for a moment to sneak up behind them and say "Boo!" to see how high the two might jump, but her vision of herself as a sophisticated young woman overruled the child who lingered in her heart and she decided instead to step back into the corridor and make a bit of noise before stepping to the threshold again. With barely a sound she left them, halted a good three feet from the threshold and coughed loudly, several times. When she reached the threshold again, Malcolm and Conningford were seated side by side on the chintz-covered sofa, both pretending to be extremely at ease and both looking as guilty as little boys caught with their fingers in the cream.

Ally grinned. "Good morning, Mal, Lord Conningford," she said as she strolled into the room. "What a pleasant surprise, Lord Conningford, to find you here so early in the day."

"Y-yes," replied Conningford beginning to rise at her entrance as did Malcolm. And then they both froze midway between standing and sitting, looked at each other and, wariness and consternation dawning on both their faces, they flopped back down again.

"Too late by far, Mal," Althea announced with sisterly superiority. "I have already seen it."

"Seen it? Seen what, Ally?"

"The cane the two of you are hiding behind you."

"The c-cane?" asked Conningford, his blue eyes striving for innocence.

"Have you lost your senses, Ally?" asked Marston. "Why would we be sitting on the sofa with a cane behind us?"

"Precisely what I should like to know. And you are going to tell me, are you not?"

"N-no," Conningford replied, his glance darting around the room, seeking somewhere to settle his gaze besides on the lovely young lady who stood before them.

"Yes, you are, Connie," said Althea sweetly.

"Ally!" Marston exclaimed. "You can't call him Connie. It ain't at all the thing."

"Bosh, *you* call him Connie."

"Yes, but I ain't a—a—an eligible young lady. It's beyond anything fast for you to be calling him Connie. He'll think you're a regular hoyden."

"Do you think me a regular hoyden, Connie?" asked Althea, taking a most unreasonable delight in watching the young earl's gaze dart more anxiously about the room and his ears begin to tinge with red. "I am no more than Mal's little sister, after all, just as I was when you came to visit us one summer."

"I—I—" stuttered Conningford.

"You see, Malcolm. He does not mind at all. Why he is at this house or you at his every day of the week. We are practically family. Connie is fast becoming like a brother to me."

"Fa-fa-family?" Conningford managed, appalled. "A b-brother to you?"

"Ally, do cease teasing," Marston ordered. "Can't you see how nervous you're making him? She is merely having fun with you, Connie. She don't think of you as family. No, she don't. She knows that you're a perfectly eligible bachelor and you have got as much a chance with her as anyone else."

This little declaration, meant to boost Conningford's spirits, sent him sinking farther down into the sofa, hoping to disappear completely into the chintz.

"Don't, Lord Conningford," said Althea, noting his response and abruptly feeling sorry for him. "You can't actually disappear, you know. I shan't call you Connie if you don't wish me to do so."

"I—I—d-don't."

"There, you see," declared Marston. "He don't wish you to call him Connie. I knew he didn't."

"N-no. Wish you to—to—call me Val."

Marston shifted to stare straight at his friend. "You do?"

"Uh-huh. B-but I don't w-wish her to think of me as a b-brother, though. Th-that I don't wish at—at all."

"Connie! Well, I'll be jiggled! That's practically a declaration that you have feelings for the girl."

"It is not!"

"Yes, it is. By gawd, you've never said anything like it to any girl I've ever seen you with. You ain't actually thinking to court Ally?"

"Now who's teasing him?" asked Althea. "Stop at once, Malcolm, or you will have him running out of here as though the house has burst into flames behind him, and that will ruin everything for you, because then I will definitely see one end of the cane and you won't be able to deny it's there at all."

"It—it is a c-cane," Conningford admitted, swiping at his brow with the back of his hand.

"Connie!"

"Well, she already knows it is, Marston. It's your father's cane. The one with the s-silver fal-con." Conningford sat forward and tugged the cane out from behind them.

"I hate that cane," Althea said with a frown as she sat down on the footstool close before the gentlemen's knees. "I have not seen it for over a year. I thought you'd lost it, Mal."

"No. It was stolen," Conningford replied, shifting both his knees to the right, as far from Althea's knees as he could get them. "Why do you hate this cane, Miss Avondale?"

"Because Father used to threaten Mama with it. Yes, he did, Mal," she added as her brother frowned. "I saw them once in the parlor, him waving it wildly about and slamming it down on things and her flinching, but refusing to give ground. I would have rushed in and pulled it from his grasp if I had been braver. I ought to have been braver."

"No, you ought not," declared Marston. "Do you think he wouldn't have hit you with it did you attempt to wrest it away from him? He would have done, Ally. Now that you tell me, I am amazed he did never hit Mama with it."

"I don't know that he didn't," sighed Ally. "I only saw him wielding it that once. He was bellowing about you, Mal. Which is why she stood up to him so bravely, you know. She did never back down when it was something to do with you or with me."

Silence enveloped the three of them at the thought of kind, quiet Fleur standing stubbornly and alone against a raging Lord Marston.

"You ought to have told me, that time I was there," Conningford said at last, softly.

"Told *you?* Why?" asked Ally, looking up at him. "You were merely a lad, and a shy, quiet one at that. What could you have done? Besides, Papa was away in Scotland that entire summer. It was the only peace we ever had, when he was away."

"M'sister was already married to Atticus," Conningford confided with some pride. "I would have written to him and told him. He would have put an end to all of it. Indeed he would."

"No, how could he?" asked Ally.

"He could have done," Conningford replied with a nod. "He did it before, for someone else. He could have done it for your mama. If only I had known to tell him."

Marston and Ally stared at the young man.

"I can't tell you about it. I promised never to tell anyone about that particular thing. It was my sister who told me and made me give my word."

"Oh," Ally replied, taking a deep breath. "Well, but I don't know why we are talking so seriously about Papa anyway. Papa is dead a year and more."

"Because you saw the cane," offered Conningford.

"Connie! She almost forgot about the cane!"

"No, I didn't. How can I forget it when it is right here before me. Why were you hiding it? And why were you discussing it so earnestly before the windows? It was the cane you were discussing, no? Because that's what you hid when I came in."

"How did you—when did you—?"

"Never mind, Malcolm. Just tell me what's going on. I intend to know and I will pester you until I do. You know I can."

The two gentlemen gazed despairingly at each other. "She will," sighed Marston. "And eventually she will wear me down and get it out of me, now she knows it's a secret of sorts."

"Well, but," Conningford began and then he sighed as well, gave a shake of his blond head and shrugged his shoulders.

Althea listened as Marston and Conningford between them, with a hesitation here and a stutter there, divulged to her the story of the cane.

"And when we looked again this morning, just before you came in, the paper inside had disappeared," Marston finished the tale. "Someone in this household knew there was a message inside there and took it."

"But what did the message say, Malcolm?"

"We don't know," pouted Conningford, his stutter lost in consideration of the seriousness of the conversation. "Atticus wouldn't tell us. He hoped it was an old message and long past any meaning at all. But it ain't. Someone took it. Someone was waiting for it and took it."

"Well, we shall have to discover who," Althea declared with some enthusiasm. "You left it in the stand in the vestibule, you said, Mal. Anyone could have taken it from there. Though why anyone should pass a message to someone in this household by way of Papa's cane at this late date, I can't think. How would they know that you would even get the cane back? You said Lord Dashfield had it. How would they know he would not continue to have it? Perhaps the message was intended for someone in his household and—"

"He did it on purpose!" Conningford exclaimed, abruptly.

"Who?" asked Marston and Althea simultaneously.

"Dashfield. Dashfield carried that cane about on purpose so that you would see it, Mal! He wished to send that message to someone in this house and he made certain that it would reach them by carrying that cane every place he knew you would be. No wonder he gave it back to you for a mere guinea. He wanted you to have it and carry it home with you. We will have to tell Atticus as soon as possible."

"Right now," suggested Marston eagerly.

"No, not right now. He ain't home. Taken Will on an outing. He won't be back until late this evening."

Fleur gazed at the gelding, her eyes wide with wonder. "But where did he come from, John?" she asked the coachman.

"His lordship come leadin' him home yestaday af'ernoon, m'lady. 'I has boughted a 'orse fer m'mama,' he tells Beasley, pretty as ye please."

"Aye, that he done, m'lady" replied Marston's head groom. "Proud as a peacock 'e was, too."

Fleur, who had come trailing restlessly into the mews with the thought of inspecting the old barouche and deciding if it might be made more presentable, or if, perhaps, they ought to look about them for a new one, reached up to pat the chestnut's nose. "What a fine fellow you are," she told the horse quietly. "Yes, a fine, handsome gentleman to be sure. What is his name, Beasley? Did his lordship say?"

"Gaily Lad, m'lady. Comed from Carey Farm in Ireland, he did."

"He did? Well, just think of that. Some of the very best horses in the world are bred at Carey Farm."

"Yes, m'lady." Beasley's eyebrows rose considerably. Most ladies, in his experience, had not the least idea that where or by whom a horse was bred could make the least difference.

"I have had a horse or two in my lifetime from Carey Farm," Lady Marston said, grinning at the groom's ill-hidden amazement. "And I have recently read in a magazine what marvelous beasts they breed there. I do think he is adequate proof of it, don't you? Only see how bright his eyes are and how interested he is in every word we say. Not only are you handsome, my lad, but you are obviously intelligent as well, are you not?"

Gaily Lad snorted and shook his head with great goodwill.

"How I should love to ride you. You have spirit and heart and a brain as well, not like the old cob I was made to settle for at home."

"He be broke to the saddle, m'lady," John Coachman offered at once.

"Just so," nodded Beasley. "Broke to both, his lordship said. Will carry a lady or a gen'leman. If ye should be wishin' ta take him out an' try 'is paces, m'lady, I should be pleased ta accompany ye."

"No, no, I could not, Beasley."

Beasely and John Coachman looked at each other with great consideration. They had come to be friends, the new head groom and the one old servant who had stuck by Lady Marston. The story of her ladyship's unfortunate birth to a shipbuilder, and her unfortunate marriage because of it, had filled many a night between them.

"Ye needn't be ridin' in Hyde Park, m'lady," John offered.

"No, no, ye need not," agreed Beasely. "That be ta say, Ladyship, if ye were wishin' ta truly ride an' not hold sich a fine lad ta little more than a trot, why there be places where it can be done. An' they be nearly empty always. Mos' of the grand ladies an' gents goes ridin' jus' ta be seen, ye know, not ta enjoy the ride."

A look of pure longing arose on Fleur's face as the playful gelding poked her shoulder with his nose.

"Beasely be tellin' the truth, m'lady," John Coachman prodded. "There be bits of woods an' fields about what stan' empty mos' of the time. Ye could get to 'em wifout bein' noticed and back again the same way. An' once ye was there, why ye could put this pretty lad 'ere through his paces an' not a soul ta take note o' ye."

"I am sorely tempted," smiled Fleur. "You cannot either of you imagine how tempted I am. Perhaps early tomorrow morning."

"Anytime, m'lady," Beasley replied with a grin and a bow. "I should be pleased ta accompany you and the Lad at any hour, day or night."

Fleur thanked them both, and deciding that the barouche was not worth discussing—she would send Malcolm to purchase a new, more modish one—she wandered from the stables back toward the garden and the main house.

"Now that were kind of ye, Beasley," John Coachman said as they watched her ladyship depart. "Right kind of ye."

"No more'n my job, John. Accompany the ladies of the house ridin'. Keep a close watch over 'em."

"Even so, there was them what worked fer the old lord in Kent wouldn't never do it. She didn't never ride but an old cob in Kent and that she did alone unless Miss Avondale was free ta join 'er."

* * *

Teweksbury straightened his shoulders, extended a hand encased in an elegant dove grey glove, seized upon the knocker, pulled it outward and let it fall. He was not at all sure he should be doing this thing. Not at all. His mind had nibbled away at his resolution all through the previous afternoon and evening. But even a night of whist and wine had not driven her from his thoughts. She was The Shipbuilder's Daughter, an encroaching mushroom who had bought her way into his class by adding significantly to Marston's coffers. She deserved neither his interest nor his consideration. She was beneath him.

She is beneath me, he thought as he stared at the front door of Marston House. Quite. I am mad to be here. I shall just turn around and go to the club. But she was reading *The Avid Horseman,* he reminded himself. She called it a marvelous magazine and read each and every word of it. Yes, and she knew I was the one among all the fellows who had the best claim to it, too. Called me one of the most illustrious horsemen in all of Britain. He reached out, took the knocker in hand and let it fall once more.

It can't hurt simply to pay her a call, he told himself. Who will know, after all? Even does someone drive by and see me standing here, they will only think I've come to pay my respects to Miss Avondale. They cannot possibly fault me for doing that. She is decidedly of the blood, even if her stepmother is not. They'll all be calling on Miss Avondale sooner or later, even the ladies. "Yes, they will," he murmured with a decided nod. "I'll wager in a week or two, that particular young lady will be all the rage."

The door opened. The first footman, a tall, lean fellow in livery and a powdered wig requested Teweksbury's business just as he ought. He took Teweksbury's card, bent the corner significantly, and placed it on a silver salver. He then took his lordship's hat, gloves and cane, stowed them safely away and invited Teweksbury to wait in the front parlor while he determined whether Lady Marston and Miss Avondale were at home. It was all quite proper and impressive, so why it amazed Teweksbury, he couldn't say. It just did.

Perhaps I didn't expect propriety in a household headed by a shipbuilder's daughter, he thought. No, that's nonsense. Ain't headed by her, anyway. Headed by Marston.

The footman returned straightaway and escorted Teweksbury up the staircase and down a long corridor to a room at the very back of the house.

"Lord Teweksbury, do come in," greeted Althea with a smile. "How kind of you to pay us a call. Mama has stepped down to the kitchen to confer with Cook about dinner. She will return in a moment. You know my brother, I believe. And Lord Conningford?"

"Indeed. Afternoon Marston, Conningford."

"And, of course, you are familiar with Lord Carruthers and Mr. Haley, Sir Edmund and Captain Gale. And this is Miss Tate, Lady Tate, Miss Gonnering, Lady Gonnering."

Teweksbury bowed in the direction of the other ladies and gentlemen, his mind awhirl. Ought not to have come. Word will get out at once. Not one of them who won't blab all over London that I've compromised my good breeding by paying a call on Lady Marston. Who'd have thought they'd all be here? Who'd have thought any of them would be here? His face grew a bit pale as he imagined an item in the gossip column of the *Times* wondering in bold, black print what illustrious horseman had climbed off his steed and placed himself within reach of a shipbuilder's daughter. Perspiration broke out on his brow. He reached for his handkerchief and wiped it away. Leave. I'll leave. "You are extremely busy," he said haltingly. "I ought not bother you."

"No, we are not busy at all. We are simply sitting about having a nice little chat," offered Althea, her smile widening.

"Speaking of taking a barge on the Thames as far as the Tower," offered Captain Gale, reaching out to shake Teweksbury's hand. "I'm the only one you don't know, I expect. Frederick Gale, Barrington's fourth son."

Teweksbury shook the proffered hand, his own perspiring badly. "Y'r servant, Captain," he mumbled uneasily. That's it, he thought, his eyes darting around the room. I'll pretend to be paying a call upon Miss Avondale just like the rest of them. Nothing to be ashamed of in that. That will do the trick. And I'll leave in a quarter hour just as I always do when I call on a lady.

"Come to speak to Mama, have you, Teweksbury?" Marston asked from across the room.

Teweksbury cringed.

"Well, I should hope so," said Althea with a happy clap of her hands. "Mama was so overcome yesterday in Hatchards, my lord, when she realized that you were there—and waiting for your magazine. She was so thrilled to make your acquaintance, she nearly fainted dead away when she reached the coach."

"No, she did not," declared Marston. "Mama don't faint over anything. She ain't a bit delicate."

"I should think not," Conningford agreed, "or you would never have bought her Gaily Lad. Bought her a steady old mare instead. Or encouraged her to ride forever in the barouche."

"Gaily Lad?" asked Teweksbury.

Althea could barely keep from laughing at the way Teweksbury's ears seemed to perk up as his voice lowered. She, Malcolm and Conningford had shared all they knew about the riding habit, the horse and Hatchards and all three of them were delighted to see Teweksbury standing here before them. They had not the least intention of allowing him to leave before he and Fleur had had an opportunity to get to know each other. This was just the man to take Lady Marston riding through Hyde Park. The perfect man. Hartshire would be glad for it; the man who had told Ally what to tell her Mama would likely be glad for it, and Celeste's wonderful riding habit would not go to waste in the back of Lady Marston's armoire.

* * *

Hartshire had spent the morning with Will at Tattersall's negotiating the purchase of a pony. They had then lunched at Grillon's Hotel, gone to the Exeter 'Change to see the animals, and were finishing two lemon ices at Gunter's when the earl's serious attempt at self-control gave way at last. "How would you like to pay a call on a lady, Will," he asked, "just like a young gentleman down from university?"

"Ugh!" grunted Will around a mouthful of lemon ice.

"No, really, it'll be fun."

"Ladies ain't fun," Will declared with a frown. "Ladies are proper and nice and smell good, and they're good enough to have about on Christmas, but they ain't fun."

"Well, this particular lady is different from the rest."

"How?"

"She ain't young and missish for one thing."

"Is she old like Grandmama?"

"No, not quite that old I shouldn't think."

"Don't you know, Papa?" Will stared up at him in disbelief.

"I don't know everything about everyone, Will."

"Uh-huh."

"No, it only seems that way," grinned Hartshire. "We'll just step in for a minute, eh? Just to say 'good day' to her."

Will pushed the glass that had held his treat away from him. He was just high enough to place his elbows on the high table. This he did in the most deliberate manner. Then he rested his chin on his fists and studied his father intently.

"What?" asked Hartshire.

"I am thinking."

"Ah, that's the grinding sound I hear."

"No, Papa, the grinding sound is coming from the street. I don't make noise when I think."

"Are you certain?"

Will blinked up at him and began to smile. "Who is the lady, Papa, that you want to go and see?"

"Lady Marston. You met her the day we found Henry in Green Park. She was with Celeste."

"Oh. The Screecher."

"She is not a screecher."

"Uh-huh. She is, Papa. I heard her screech at you all the way over where I was getting grass to make a nest for Henry."

"Well, perhaps she did yell a bit. But you would have yelled in surprise, too, Will, to look all unsuspecting up into a tree and see my face staring down at you."

"Is that what happened, Papa?"

"Exactly."

"Well then, I expect she ought to have screeched."

Hartshire moved uneasily on the chair. "Really? Would you have done, Will? Is my face that frightening?"

"No, Papa, but it's a big face and it probably looked scary up there among the leaves. It'd be like looking up and seeing God looking back at you if you weren't expecting it. I s'pose we could go and just say 'good day' to her," Will agreed with great consideration. "Did you go and say 'good day' to Mama, when she was a lady in London?"

Hartshire met Will's steady gaze across the table. It was the first time the boy had asked about Miriam in a long time. A very long time.

"Most certainly, I did. Did it a number of times."

"And did Mama say 'good day' back?"

"Yes."

"How many times did you say 'good day' and how many times did Mama 'good day' you back before you married her, Papa?"

"Oh, I should think ninety at the very least," Hartshire replied, innocently, "before I married her."

"That's an enormous lot of 'good days'."

"Yes, well, it didn't seem like very many at the time, Will.

And then, of course, there was a 'good evening' I muttered now and then and a few 'good afternoons' as well, I think."

Fleur smiled affectionately when the first footman bent to whisper in her ear. When they appeared on the threshold, she excused herself to Teweksbury, rose from her seat beside him on the flowered settee, and went to greet them.

Hartshire bowed over her hand, going so far as to raise it to his lips and kiss the back of it. Whereupon Will made the most awful face and asked loudly if he had to do the same.

"Good gracious, no," Fleur answered immediately. "I would think you a positive dandy and you are too young to wish to be thought a dandy, yet. You must just bow and say 'good day' and I will curtsy most properly and reply."

"Good day to you then, Lady Marston," Will said, bowing.

"And good day to you, Lord Howard," Fleur replied. "May I inquire as to the health of your charming dormouse? I don't believe he had a name when last we met."

"His name is Henry," Will replied, thoroughly impressed that this lady should think to ask after the little creature. "And he is very well, thank you. He's the best dormouse in all the world and he likes to sleep in my Papa's pockets."

"In my pockets?" asked Hartshire, thoroughly surprised. "I thought it was my armoire the beast was enamored of."

"No, Papa, it's your coat pockets. He only sneaks in your armoire so he can climb inside one of your pockets. His leg is healed exceptional well," Will added. "Papa took his splint off yesterday and he doesn't even limp."

"How marvelous. I'm so very happy for him," Fleur replied. "Not only has he found a loving home, but he doesn't limp either."

"Precisely. Henry's lucky, ain't he?"

"Oh, my yes. Extremely lucky," agreed Fleur. "Most likely the luckiest dormouse in all of Britain."

Hartshire, one hand resting on Will's shoulder, stared at

Fleur like one bewitched as she centered her attention on his son. The silver specks in his eyes sparkled not only with love but with admiration and respect as well. No wonder Marston and his sister would do anything for her, he thought, listening to the conversation going forward between the two. I expect did she have the care of Will for any length of time, he would lay down his life for the woman as well. She even remembered to ask after Henry.

"You will stay for a while, won't you?" Fleur asked. She looked from Will to Hartshire, and the unexpected glow in his eyes startled her. Her heart seemed to miss a beat in her breast. She struggled abruptly for breath. "W-we are in the midst of tea," she managed, unable, unwilling to look away from him. "James has gone to fetch a fresh pot, another cup, and a glass of lemonade for Lord Howard."

"You may call me Will," announced the properly addressed Lord Howard enthusiastically. "Are there tarts?"

"Indeed," Fleur replied, struggling to turn her gaze from Hartshire and back to his son but discovering herself unable to do so. "Strawberry tarts."

"Will's mad after strawberry tarts of late," murmured Hartshire, the need to wrap his arms around her and hold her tight against his chest as he had last night coming near to overwhelming him. "I find myself craving—strawberry tarts—as well."

"How fortunate you came then," Fleur responded in not much above a whisper.

They stood silently together in the doorway lost in each other's eyes while Will stared up at them and a room filled with people gazed on curiously. Then Will tugged impatiently at the hem of his father's coat.

"You didn't say it yet, Papa," he announced loudly.

"What? What, Will?"

"You didn't say it."

"Oh? Oh! I do beg your pardon. I forgot."

"When we walked all the way here from Gunter's just so you could?" asked Will in astonishment.

"Um-hmmmm. I bowed properly, did the dandy, and then the other just slipped right out my ear. Good day to you, Lady Marston," Hartshire said so gently, so softly, so seductively that Fleur imagined she could feel each word caress her cheek.

"That's one," announced Will.

When at last all the company had departed Marston House and Malcolm and Althea had gone for a drive in Mal's curricle, Fleur climbed the stairs to her chamber, opened her armoire and took out the riding habit Celeste had made for her. She placed the oddly feminine slouch hat on her head and gave the brim a tug. She held the deep green jacket before her and stared at herself in the looking glass. She had agreed to ride with Teweksbury in Hyde Park. She could not believe she'd agreed to it, but she had. Malcolm and Ally, Lord Conningford and even Julia Tate had talked her into it. "Well, and how could I say no," she whispered to her reflection, "when even Lady Tate and Lord Hartshire said that I should?"

Lady Tate had come to call. Of course, her daughter had brought her. Forced her more likely. Because anyone could see that Miss Julia Tate had developed a definite passion for Malcolm. "Apparently one may associate with a ship-builder's daughter when one's own daughter makes it necessary," she murmured. "No, that's not fair at all. Lady Tate was most gracious this afternoon. Perhaps her mind has altered a bit concerning me. It could be so. I begin to think that even the most improbable things can be so."

She set the riding habit aside, her thoughts drifting to Lord Hartshire. What had he meant by it, that look in his eyes, that infinitely caressing tone in his voice? Had he realized how deeply he'd stirred her, how profoundly he'd spoken to her, body and soul, by simply saying 'good day' and murmuring something about strawberry tarts? She wondered what it would feel like to be enclosed in Hartshire's arms in the dark of night in the garden. Would his breath whisper as enticingly against her ear? Would his lips caress her cheek as softly, as tenderly as the man who named himself Montague?

"I'm being perfectly absurd," she declared, stuffing her habit back into the armoire. "Of all things, to think of Lord Hartshire in such a way. He cannot help how his eyes sparkle or how his voice sounds. Likely he was merely exhausted from tramping around town with Will all morning. He said nothing at all out of the ordinary. He was most polite and kind—as he has been from the very first."

What a fool I am, she thought, sitting down on the bed. What a perfect fool to think that not only am I loved by a stranger who will not so much as let me see his face, but also by a purely kind gentleman who wishes nothing more than to be my friend. Am I so desperate to be loved that I will see it everywhere? In every word? In every glance? Next I will come to believe that Lord Teweksbury has developed a passion for me merely because he takes me riding in the park. And I do not even wish to go riding in the park!

Still, she could not divest herself of the feelings swirling through her. She knew, beyond a doubt, that she was fatally drawn to the gentleman who had kissed her with such tenderness in the garden last night. And she knew as well that her heart had stuttered and seemed to stop at the very look in Lord Hartshire's eyes. "Am I falling in love?" she asked the walls that surrounded her. "Is this what it's like to fall in love? But how can I possibly do so with two gentlemen at one and the same time? And both of them beyond my touch," she added in a scolding tone intended to shake herself out of the faery tale feeling that surrounded her. Certainly the Earl of Hartshire, though he has been kind as he can be, cannot be thinking to stoop so low as to court a shipbuilder's daughter, she thought. He is not at all like Marston. He has no need of my father's money—my money, now. And what else is there to draw such a gentleman as Lord Hartshire to my side?

"And as for you, Montague," she said. "You made it clear enough that any hope of an alliance between us would prove disastrous. To name yourself a Montague and to allow me to be a Capulet. How much more clearly could you have stated it? What became of those lovers? Dead. Romeo and Juliet, dead and gone. But then what do you want of me, Montague? If it is not love, why have you taken up my cause? Why did you tell me what to say and what to do when most I needed to know it? And why did you steal into my garden like the darkness and the fog and kiss me so? Why?"

Hartshire stared at the three of them. "No," he said after the longest pause. "Oh, no."

"But Atticus—" Conningford pleaded.

"Absolutely not. You are all of you moonstruck if you think for one minute that I am going to allow the three of you to be involved in this thing."

"But I am already involved," Marston declared, sitting on the arm of the chair in which his sister had eagerly settled.

"Yes, he is," Althea agreed, "and so am I. The message was delivered in our house, after all, and by means of my father's cane, which makes us, in a way, responsible to foil whatever vile plot these people intend."

"No, it does not," Hartshire replied, pacing across his study to close the door tightly and then leaning against it. "You are no more responsible for whatever goes forward, Miss Avondale, than is some mouse running about in your walls."

"The very least you could do, Atticus," Conningford sighed in seeming surrender, "is to tell us what the message said. The one that's missing now. You did say you would, you know, if Marston discovered it gone."

"Did I?"

"Yes, you did," declared Marston. "I remember distinctly."

"And did I say that I would tell Miss Avondale, as well?"

"I wish you would call me Ally," protested Althea abruptly. "I am not Miss Avondale to Val any longer and I don't wish to be Miss Avondale to you either."

"You aren't?" asked Hartshire, an eyebrow cocking. "Not Miss Avondale to Val?"

"No, she ain't," Conningford said. "I am to call her Ally and she is to call me Val."

"Since when?"

"Since this morning," Marston enlightened him, "when Ally demanded to know what was going on and Connie told her everything."

"Everything I knew at least," Conningford conceded. "She knows you are The Spectre, too, and all you told us about Spence and his followers."

"Don't tell me," grumbled Hartshire. "Now you are planning to take Ally to The Nag's Head with you to introduce her into the society of the Great Unwashed."

"I am not!"

"What's The Nag's Head? Oh! Is that the public house you told me about, Val, where they meet sometimes?"

"Good Lord, you did tell her everything," groaned Hartshire.

"Yes, he did," Marston confirmed with a nod. "And now we are stuck with her, because she will not give in, you know. She is the stubbornest girl alive."

"And possibly the bravest," Conningford added with the most adoring look on his face as he gazed at Althea.

"No, not the bravest. Her stepmother is the bravest," Hartshire said before he so much as thought what he was saying.

The three young people stared at him—Conningford with joy, Marston with surprise, Althea with considerable suspicion.

"Well, she is. You may not think it extremely brave of her

to come to London and face the ton once again, but you're wrong. It takes a great deal more courage to do that than most people have. And to agree to ride with Teweksbury in Hyde Park, in front of the entire world, leaving herself open to whatever scorn or ridicule the illustrious ladies and gentlemen of the ton deign to throw at her—and to do it for someone else's benefit, to attempt to become somewhat acceptable for you, Ally, to insure you a joyous Season and every opportunity to discover a husband you can love—well that is something only the bravest heart in all of Britain would dare."

"Quite right!" exclaimed Marston, totally enthralled by Hartshire's description of his mama's particular brand of courage.

"Hear! Hear!" Conningford cheered. "You have got the right of it, Atticus."

"You know her so well," said Althea quietly. "I wonder that you do. You see right down into her soul. I vow it. And you can see down into my soul, too, if you but make the attempt."

"He can wh-what?" asked Conningford, rising from the chair before Hartshire's desk and stuffing his hands into his pockets.

"Do not you begin to stutter again and stare at your shoes, and let your ears turn red, Valerian Hunt," Althea ordered in the most authoritative tone. "I did not intend anything romantic by it. Not in the least. It is simply fact. Lord Hartshire sees more deeply into people than any gentleman I have ever met. Now, Lord Hartshire," she added, leaning forward to confront him from beside her brother. "You will please tell us what that message Malcolm brought you said. Because we are all of us determined to be concerned with it whether you approve or not. And there is no telling but what we may be of more help than hindrance if only you will allow us to be."

"Ally, hush," Marston pleaded.

"No, I will not hush. You aren't as young as you used to be, you know, Lord Hartshire. You may discover that it's more difficult for you to be everywhere at once. Three more sets of eyes and three more pairs of ears could prove most useful to you."

Ten

It was quite late that same evening when Hartshire found himself standing silently outside Fleur's garden wall. He knew he ought not to do it. It was foolish beyond all measure. But he could not help himself. He scaled the wall soundlessly and dropped without so much as a shush of the earth beneath his feet into Marston's garden. *She is not here wishing on stars tonight,* he noted. *No sign of a precious Little Flower blooming in the darkness and longing to be picked. Well, and she should not be here,* he thought, angry with himself. *She is most likely upstairs in her bed where she belongs.*

And he knew precisely where that bed was. He had convinced Marston and Ally to draw him a floor plan of the house. "In case there should be some emergency," he'd told them. "Just in case my help should be required, or I should need to reach one or the other of you directly. Because whoever took that message from the cane is likely a very dangerous sort."

He'd not told any of the younger set precisely what the message that had been in the cane had said. No, he'd given them a roundabout sort of interpretation. They'd been horrified enough with that. Ally's eyes had grown so very wide that he'd thought they would pop right out of her very pretty head. Val and Marston had grown still, pensive, and then a grim smile had creased Val's face. "I expect Marston and I are to have our adventure now," he'd murmured.

Hartshire moved smoothly, lithely through the garden shadows, making no more sound than the wind that ruffled the leaves of the oak tree at the west side of the house. When he reached that particular tree, which stood just inside the garden wall, he jumped upward and snagged the lowest branch. He grinned as he swung himself up onto it. Not as young as I used to be, am I? he thought. Should like to see Val or Marston snag that branch on the first attempt.

Like some wild creature of the night, he made his silent way upward through the leaves, pausing once to count the windows across the second story of the house. Hers were the third and fourth from the left, and they were dark, the curtains drawn. He altered his path through the branches a bit and then climbed higher, above the second story and the window he wanted. Then, testing the strength of the branch before each step, he walked outward from the trunk and with as little fuss as if he were stepping from a carriage, stepped down onto Lady Marston's window sill.

They were tall, narrow windows, but not nearly as tall as he. He stood, holding to the bricks of the house with one hand and listened, stooping to press his ear against the glass. Nothing. Not a sound. She *was* asleep then. Good. He would simply slip inside, leave the note somewhere she would be certain to find it and be safely away before the cat could twitch its tail.

He tugged his knife from the inside of his boot and slipped the thin, narrow blade behind the window frame, where he knew the latch would be. He gave the blade a quick, sharp twist and the latch sprang open.

Cautiously he stepped onto the sill of the adjoining window and opened the window he'd unlocked. He slipped in behind the closed curtains and paused to listen once more. He could hear the soft, steady sound of her breathing as she slept. For a moment he imagined her there, in her bed, tucked safely between sheets scented with lavender. His heart thundered in his ears. He shook his head to clear it, located the center of the curtains, drew them aside and stepped into the chamber.

A faint glow from the dying coals in the hearth showed him the room. He gazed about, attempting to decide. Where would she see it? Where would it be safe from the prying eyes of an abigail and yet apparent to her on the instant? The washstand? The bedside table? The top of the chest of drawers? Just inside the clothes press? He hesitated, drawing in a long breath and attempting to remember what it was Miriam did in the morning when she woke. In what order. What her lady's maid had helped her to do and what she had not.

The washstand, he decided at last. If I put it beneath the pitcher on the washstand, surely she will see it when she pours the water into the bowl. He floated, a shadow amidst shadows to the far side of the chamber and lifted the filled pitcher carefully, placing the folded paper beneath it. He turned away with the most exquisite grace. And Lady Marston sat straight up in bed, her arms thrust out before her. "No," she cried. "No, do not! No, Marston, no!"

Hartshire exhaled the air he had suddenly gulped. A dream. She is dreaming, he realized. And a damned rotten one it must be, too, from the sound of it. He started to cross to her, then stopped. What am I doing? I can't wake her. She will scream even louder to discover a man in her bedchamber. Someone will hear her and come running. Ally is probably on her way even now. I had best leave the way I came and quickly, too. He stepped toward the window, hesitated, stepped back. She had ceased to cry out, but she was thrashing about among the covers, tearing at them, gasping as though she would strangle in their grasp. And no one beyond her chamber door seemed to have heard her. He listened, thankful this once for the size of his ears. They had always allowed him to hear the least hint of a sound. And there was not the least hint of a sound coming from any direction, not so much as the whisper of a slipper across a carpet. Fleur was breathing wildly now, caught in the web of sheets and coverlet.

He stepped toward the window again. He would have helped her, longed to help her, but he had broken into her chamber and—"And what?" he muttered then. "What will she do? She don't know it's me. Won't know either do I stay with my back to the coals." Thus having decided, with four long strides he was around the bed, the dim glow of the fading fire behind him, his face deep in shadow. He eased himself down beside her on the edge of the mattress, put his arms around her and began to rock her gently, whispering in her ear. "Hush, m'dear one," he whispered. " 'Tis a dream and nothing more. Hush now. You're safe, my little flower. No one will hurt you anymore. I promise you. Never again. Not ever." He took one arm from around her and began to untangle the bedclothes, gently, easily, with movements as delicate as the touch of butterflies.

Fleur had ceased to struggle against the bedclothes the moment his arms had encompassed her. Now her gasping ceased as well. Her head in ruffled nightcap resting against him, she began to murmur softly. He could not understand the words, but he knew from the very feel of her that the nightmare had ended and a more pleasant dream had taken its place. His heart cried out to him to remain, to hold her through the night into the dawn, to keep her safe from the memories that hurt her so, but he laid her back down on the pillows and covered her instead, tucking in the sides of the bedclothes as he had always done for Will until they had come to London. As he would do again when they returned to Kent. Then he leaned down and placed a whisper of a kiss on Fleur's brow.

Fleur woke the following morning to a cup of hot chocolate on her bedside table, Davis opening wide the curtains, and sunlight dancing through the windowpanes.

She sat back against the pillows and smiled. "I had the

most wonderful dream, Davis," she said. "I don't remember what it was about precisely, but I don't think I've felt so warm and safe since my mama died. Truly, I wish I could remember what I dreamed about. Davis?" she asked, reaching for her chocolate and stopping abruptly. "What's wrong with the coverlet? It feels as though someone has—"

"Oh, my lady, you have been tucked right in, just like my own mama used to do when I was a little girl."

"Well, of all things! It must have been Ally. But why on earth would she do such a thing? I will wear the rose morning dress, Davis, but you need not lay it out as yet. I intend to be most indulgent and just sit and drink my chocolate without doing another thing."

"Just so, my lady," nodded Davis, her green-eyed gaze darting about the room as though in search of something. "When shall I return?"

"Oh, I should think in a quarter hour, Davis, will be soon enough. And I should like some toast and another cup of chocolate when you come."

"Yes, my lady," Davis replied and exited the chamber rather haltingly, her gaze meeting the mantelpiece and the little white ladder-backed chair and the table that held the sewing box before she finally closed the door behind her.

It was locked last night, that window, Davis thought to herself as she loped down the corridor. Locked it last night myself before I pulled the curtains closed. So why was it off the latch this morning? She opened the door to the servants' staircase, made her way down to the kitchen and asked Cook to prepare some toast and another cup of chocolate for Lady Marston, to be ready in a quarter hour, and then she let herself out the kitchen door and into the garden.

Walking along the cobbled path, she swung her head one way and then the other, looking quite like a hound seeking a particular scent on the air. But it wasn't a scent she was seeking. It was some evidence of an intruder, some sign of a stranger having entered the garden. She reached the little gate at the rear only to discover that it was locked up tight. Came over the wall then, she decided. She left the footpath and wandered along the edge of the wall, staring down, studying the ground. If anyone had seen her, they would have thought she'd lost her senses, but she hadn't. No, not by the farthest stretch of the imagination. She was doing now what she did best, and just between two of the rose bushes, she found it. A footprint in the newly turned soil. Just one, the other foot having landed, she supposed, on the grass. But one was enough. Quite enough. She was certain it wasn't The Spectre's from the night before last, because she had smoothed out the soil herself where he had landed. No, this was a fresh footprint. Someone else had discovered a purpose for which to scale the garden wall.

Her nose fairly twitching with excitement, Davis loped through the rest of the garden to the old oak where it stood with ancient dignity between the last bit of garden wall and the house. She gazed upward, knowing what had happened, realizing, with a shiver that traveled along the entire length of her spine, that someone had climbed the tree to Lady Marston's window, opened the latch from the outside and—

"And what?" Davis whispered to herself, staring up through the leaves. "What did he do? Why go to so much trouble and then depart having done—nothing?"

Well, but perhaps something had been stolen, though the room had looked quite as it ought. Not so much as a statuette missing from the mantel or a painting from the wall. Perhaps he had gone off with her ladyship's jewelry case then. She would check on that when she went back to help Lady Marston dress.

"But why the devil would someone break into a window on the second story when they might more easily do so on the ground floor?" she asked herself. "To take such a risk as to climb that old tree—Why?" She thought she knew why, but she shoved the thought away from her as though it were a meat pie filled with poison, and after gazing once more up into the tree, she turned on her heel and loped back toward the kitchen door.

In her bedchamber, Fleur arose just as Davis's hand touched the kitchen door latch. She stretched luxuriously and dangled her bare feet over the end of the bed. "I cannot remember when I've had a better night's sleep," she said happily to herself. "Perhaps it was because Ally tucked me in so sweetly. But when did she do that? I thought she was fast asleep when I retired. Well, obviously not. I shall have to thank her for it first thing."

Feeling for the first time since childhood like dancing in the sunbeams, Fleur stood and twirled her way across the room to the washstand. "Perhaps I dreamed of him, of Montague," she said. "Perhaps I dreamed he kissed me. I seem to recall a kiss in my dreams somewhere." She lifted the pitcher to fill the bowl, stopped abruptly and stared at the piece of paper that it had been covering. "What in the world? Did Martha set this down here while she was cleaning and simply forget about it? No, it couldn't have been Martha. Martha can't read or write. Perhaps it is something belongs to Davis?"

Her curiosity piqued, Fleur unfolded the paper.

Little Flower of My Heart, it began.

> *I cannot think of another way to reach you before you ride with Teweksbury, so I must write this down and hope it can be safely delivered. You will not like what I say, but I have not failed you yet, I think. Ride astride this afternoon in Rotten Row. Keep your chin high and a smile on that brave little face. Handle the reins lightly, dear one, and treat Teweksbury with a light hand as well.*
>
> > *Montague*

Montague? Fleur read the note again. Ride astride? I cannot possibly, she thought. And however did this get beneath my pitcher? Which of my servants did he pay to deliver this for him? I will find out as soon as I am dressed. Yes, indeed, I will. And then I will ask straight out what the gentleman looked like.

Fleur welcomed Davis heartily and hurried into her morning dress. "You did not, by any chance, Davis, agree to deliver me a note this morning?"

"A note, my lady?"

"Um-hmmm."

"No, my lady. Are you expecting a note from someone?"

Fleur wondered whether to confide in Davis that she had found Montague's message beneath the water pitcher, but decided against it. It was not Davis's business, after all, to be concerned with such things. If she knew nothing of a note to be delivered, she had certainly not delivered it.

Surely, then, it was Martha who left it for me, Fleur decided. Or perhaps Cook sent it up by way of the pot boy—if it came to the house by way of the kitchen door. Well, it could not have come by the front door, or one of the footmen would have left it on the salver on the vestibule table.

"I am thinking, Davis, that I should like to wear my hair differently," she thoroughly surprised herself by saying then. "I have been wearing it in a plain knot on the top of my head for so very long. But I cannot think of any other way. Have you any ideas?"

Davis, her own carroty hair piled high on her head, studied Lady Marston as she took a seat before the little vanity. "There are any number of ways, my lady," she said. "The thing is to know which will look the best. I have seen hair kept braided and caught here and here with silver clips." Davis demonstrated with her ladyship's night braid and stared at Lady Marston's reflection in the looking glass.

"The thing is, Davis, that I should like it to look a bit—a bit—untamed."

"Untamed, my lady?"

"Perhaps not that precisely, but, freer. I ride this afternoon with Lord Tewexsbury and I should like it to—oh, I don't know—look different somehow beneath my hat."

The hat! Davis had seen the hat, indeed, the entire riding costume and, regardless that she would never in her life possess such an ensemble, she had fallen in love with it at once. She had thought it would be wasted on the plain Lady Marston, but now, as she began to unbraid her ladyship's hair, a regular spurt of images galloped joyfully through her mind. "I know just the thing!" she exclaimed, reaching for the silver-backed hair brush. "We shall need a scissors."

"No! I don't want it cut short, Davis."

"No, my lady, certainly not all of it, but here, at your brow and just before your ears. We will curl it with the iron, just so and—" Davis demonstrated as best she could, then left the room to fetch the scissors. On her return she brought the hat from the armoire as well. "You'll see, my lady. It will be exquisite."

"I don't know," murmured Fleur, "about cutting it." And then she thought about riding beside the handsome Lord Tewexsbury on Gaily Lad who was definitely the most beautiful horse she'd ever seen. And then it occurred to her to hope that perhaps the invisible Montague would be present, somewhere nearby, to see her as well. She thought of riding astride in Celeste's perfect costume for it, and she sighed. Well, I cannot possibly ride astride. Everyone would wonder at my audacity. But I can—"Cut it," she declared with barely a nibble at her lower lip. "Go on, Davis. Chop away."

Davis smiled as the lady on the seat before her closed her eyes tightly and clutched the sides of the little bench. Then she lifted a hank of hair and sheared through it. "Will you look at that!" she exclaimed. "Curls all by itself, it does. Won't need no curling iron at all."

"It did used to curl," murmured Fleur, her eyes still shut, "before it grew so very long and heavy."

* * *

Lord Panington caused his driver to stop the barouche in the very middle of Hyde Park, stepped down from the carriage, and strolled over to peer beneath a willow tree. "I thought that was you, boy," he said. "And Celeste! Your servant, m'dear. Haven't seen you in centuries."

"No, do not say centuries, sweetest. It has not been centuries."

"Where the deuce have you been hiding, gel? Been gone so long I thought you was dead."

Hartshire chuckled.

"Nothing funny in that, m'boy. Death is a damnable serious business when you get to be my age."

"Yes, sir."

"Having yourselves a reg'lar picnic, are you? All alone here beneath the willow, just the two of you and that basket. Have to marry the gel, Atticus. Can't be having a picnic just the two of you and no one to play propriety. Ruin her reputation if she had one."

"Me? Marry Cousin Celly? I think not," protested Hartshire with pretend indignation. "Throw myself off a cliff first."

"Not before I threw myself over," offered Celeste. "Of all things to suggest, Uncle Pan! That Hartshire and I make a match of it! Besides, he can't. He's in love with someone else and so am I."

"You are, Celly?" Hartshire asked hopefully. "Who?"

"Yes, gel, who?" added Panington, his eyes alight with glee. "Tell me and I'll catch you the fellow in the lick of a cat's whisker."

"His name is Arthur. That's all I'll tell you," Celeste replied primly. "Uncle Pan, dearest heart, your vehicle is blocking the road. There's a string of carriages lined up behind your barouche all the way back to the Grosvenor Gate. Don't you think you ought to get back to the Promenade?"

"No. Came to ask Atticus when Dashfield's to be arrested. Soon, eh, boy? Dastardly villain! Always knew he was.

Killed his wife and now he's planning to kill the Regent, Celly. Did you know?"

Celeste's jaw dropped. Her eyes widened. "Lord Dashfield killed his wife? He's planning to kill the Regent? Hartshire!" she cried, taking her closed apricot parasol into her hand. "You knew all this, Hartshire, and you didn't tell me!" and she gave him a whack on top of his head.

"Ow! Celly, that hurt!"

"Bosh! It did not. I couldn't hurt you if I whacked you over the head with a newel post. You are the most aggravating human being, Hartshire."

"Me? I ain't doing anything but sitting here."

"You knew about Dashfield and told me nothing."

"Ah-ha! Told her nothing!" exclaimed Lord Panington. "For shame, Hartshire. After all our sweet Celeste has done for you? Whack him once again, Celeste, for good measure."

"Do not dare," growled Hartshire. "And Uncle Pan, you go right back to your barouche before your coachman starts to cry. The poor fellow is staring behind him as though he'll panic any minute. And do not," Hartshire added, staring up at the old gentleman, "say one more word to anyone about Dashfield. I have not come to London to save Prinny from Dashfield—or from anyone else for that matter."

"No?" asked Lord Panington. And then he smiled. "Oh, I got it, m'boy. It's a secret, eh? Even from Celeste. Well, well, I'll say no more about it then. Not a word."

He left them together beneath the willow and returned to his coach wondering what could possibly cause his niece and nephew to linger together under a tree in the park. "Something's up," he muttered to himself as he climbed back into his carriage and waved at the coachman to be on his way. "Be deviled if I ain't correct. Something's up."

Celeste and Hartshire watched over their shoulders as the vehicle continued on its way. "And you said no one would so much as take note of us," Celeste said. " 'We'll hide under that willow close by the fence and be overlooked,' you said.

Honestly, Hartshire, I don't know why I listen to you. Here, have an egg," she added, taking a hard-boiled one from the basket, peeling the shell from it and handing it to him.

"I was not actually thinking of Uncle Pan when I said that, Celly."

"You were not thinking at all. Lost your mind. Love does that to you. I've seen it before."

"I am not in love."

"Oh, Hartshire, cease and desist. You *are* in love and you know it as well as I. We would not be sitting here else—with an excellent view of Rotten Row—waiting for our Little Flower to make her appearance."

Conningford turned up on Marston's doorstep at precisely three o'clock and spent a half-hour kicking his heels in the morning room, waiting for Althea to appear. When she did at last, she fairly stole his breath away. In a riding habit of sky blue that matched her eyes to perfection, with a tall blue hat that sported three white plumes and a trailing veil, he found her absolutely delicious. So very appealing, in fact, that he stuttered over his greeting to her and his ears began to burn.

"Valerian Hunt," she said, taking both his hands into hers, "you have got to throw off this timidity in the presence of young ladies. We are none of us going to bite you, you know."

"I know."

"And you aren't the least bit timid really. You have grown up to be the most engaging and adventurous gentleman. You're as brave as you can stare. No, do not deny it. You are. Only think of your going to those dreadful public houses to spy on radicals and save the Crown from certain doom, and placing yourself in danger on behalf of me and Marston, helping to discover who stole the message from Father's cane. And yet, when a young lady says 'good day' to you, you fall all to pieces."

"N-not just any young lady," Conningford protested. "Only—only—beautiful young ladies."

Althea smiled so very sweetly that Conningford's head filled up with the glow of it and it sparked back out at her through his most admiring eyes.

"Come sit down again," she said softly, wondering why she had not noticed what an adorable and very handsome young man Conningford was before Malcolm and he had included her in their adventure. "Mal's gone to pick up Julia and they are to ride back here and meet us and Mama and Lord Teweksbury and then we will all ride to Hyde Park together." She led him by the hand to the small settee, sat and tugged him down beside her.

Conningford's head began to spin from the mere nearness of her. She smelled of warm sunlight, lilacs and burgeoning spring.

Fleur stood before the largest looking glass and surveyed herself with tremendous disbelief. Silvery brown curls framed her face beneath the wide, soft brim of the deep green slouch hat. Davis had pinned the rest of her hair up in a long, oddly comfortable line that began at the very top of her head and ended in loose, dusky brown waves that lay easily against her neck between the brim of the hat and the high collar of her riding coat. Amazed enough that morning to see how she looked in the rose-colored morning dress once Davis had got finished with her, this afternoon Fleur felt a surge of joy rising from deep within her. "Oh, Davis," she said, as the abigail turned to hang up the morning dress. "Oh, Davis, you're a wonder."

Davis grinned. She peered back over her shoulder as she hung the dress away and for the first time in years, her gaze did not dart warily about, but remained proudly on Lady Marston.

"You are, Davis. A regular wonder. You and Celeste.

Whyever did you say nothing of your talents? If you had not taken those scissors into your hands and begun to snip away, I would never have known how very talented you are."

"It is nothing to cut hair and arrange it attractively, my lady," Davis demurred. "Especially when the hair is on someone else's head." But a particular pride swelled within Davis's breast even as she said the words. She had done wonders for Lady Marston and she'd been pleased to do it. Nothing, of course, could rid the lady of her plain face, longish nose and slightly jutting chin, but the curls softened the harsh angles, lowered the imposing height of her brow, and drew a person's gaze to the lovely, innocent brown of her eyes instantly. And that little elf of a dressmaker is to be thoroughly commended, thought Davis. I could not believe that riding costume when first I saw it. So outrageous! But it is perfect for her ladyship. Only see how intriguing and cosmopolitan it makes her seem.

It was the oddest thing. Davis had sensed it growing in her over the passing weeks and thought it so very odd that she had feared to probe at it more deeply. I am becoming enormously fond of Lady Marston, she thought now, her gaze fastened on that lady. So enamoured of her that I might easily be persuaded to remain her abigail for the remainder of my life. How can that be? Why should that be? Me, who has always despised to be in service.

"Davis," Fleur said, turning from her reflection. "Will you do me the smallest favor? Run down and tell Wickens to send a footman to the stables?"

"To the stables, my lady?"

"Yes. I—I—No. Never mind."

"You what, my lady?" asked Davis, knowing the question to be beyond her station, but curious nonetheless.

"I merely thought to tell Beasley not to put a side saddle on Gaily Lad. That I should like to ride astride."

Davis's jaw dropped.

"Yes. Just so. Not at all acceptable. I know it isn't. But

this costume would look so—so—extraordinary if I did do it. It is made expressly so that I may, you know. But I cannot think Celeste intended I do so in the middle of Rotten Row with all the ton looking on. And certainly Lord Teweksbury would be embarrassed beyond all measure. Likely he would refuse to accompany me."

"Did you ride without any saddle at all, my lady," Davis replied, "Lord Teweksbury would still accompany you."

"Do you think so, Davis?"

"Oh, yes, madam. Lady Dashfield was used to have Lord Teweksbury about the house often. He is a paragon of propriety—except when it comes to horses. He will throw over all his beliefs in 'the proper thing' to enjoy a fine horse well ridden and watch it and its rider sporting about before his eyes."

"He will? Davis, what makes you think so? How do you know these things? Certainly you were not sitting in Lady Dashfield's parlor when she entertained his lordship?"

"No, my lady, but servants go in and out, you know, and word gets about among us."

Davis actually blushed and Fleur was amazed to see it. Great goodness, she thought, why should speaking of gossip among servants bring a blush to Davis's cheeks? She cannot believe I don't know that servants talk among themselves.

"Should you like me to tell Mr. Wickens to send word to the stable, my lady?" asked Davis, attempting to bury visions of herself with her ear pressed against Lady Dashfield's parlor door beneath other thoughts and thus rid herself of the pink she felt suffusing her cheeks.

"I—I—don't know." Fleur thought back to Montague's note. Her inquiries had not produced one servant who admitted to passing along his message. Not one servant who would acknowledge that they had seen the gentleman and taken a paper from him and placed it in her room. And yet, the message had arrived. He had thought it important enough, it seemed, to pay some member of her household most handsomely to deliver it and then deny that they had done so. "Must have paid them handsomely indeed," she murmured.

"Pardon, my lady?"

"What? Oh, nothing Davis. I was merely thinking aloud. You don't think it would be thoroughly audacious of me to ride Gaily Lad astride in Hyde Park?"

"Oh, yes, madam, thoroughly audacious and—and—"

"And what, Davis?"

"And delicious as well, my lady."

"Delicious, Davis?"

"Oh, yes, my lady. Only think of it! For you to oppose the restraints placed upon us women by this world of men! It would be so wonderful!"

"The restraints placed on us by men, Davis?"

"Oh, yes, madam. It is the men, you know, who force us women to comply with the most insignificant rules. It is they, for instance, who say you must endanger yourself on one of those dreadful side saddles just so that you will meet their standard of proper womanhood. Well, who are they, I ask you, to say what a proper woman may do and what she may not? We aren't all the same. No, and we don't all wish to please men before ourselves. Some of us, my lady, have minds of our own, with our own ideas and our own needs!"

Fleur stared at Davis wide-eyed. She opened her mouth, closed it again. She cleared her throat. She smoothed her hands over the svelte, split skirt of her costume. She cleared her throat again. And all the while Davis visibly squirmed beneath her stare.

"It is not merely ladies of the upper classes who suffer to meet gentlemen's expectations, Davis?" she asked at last. "It is the same for the serving class? I didn't think it was so. I thought that perhaps—well—you are so—so much your-selves, you see, in certain ways."

"Not so much ourselves as we yearn to be, my lady," Davis replied quietly.

* * *

" 'Ere yer is!" exclaimed a gruff voice with the sound of swishing willow leaves and crackling branches gathered around it. "I has been ta eighteen willow trees so far this af'ernoon, I has, Yer Majesty!"

Celeste started, but Hartshire placed a hand on her arm and she settled back down immediately as a short, thin man with lank black hair made his way out from behind them and plopped flat on the ground before Hartshire.

"There ain't eighteen willow trees in the whole park," grinned Hartshire. "Celeste, may I present Mr. Thomas Landy."

"No," Celeste responded, her gaze roaming over the dirty little man in his yellowed shirt and catskin vest. "I'd rather you didn't."

"Oh. Never mind then. What've you learned, Tom?"

"That I be one o' the disinherited seeds o' Adam," recited Landy with a grin. "An' I done has larned ta spell a word what ta chalk on walls, too, Yer Graceness. I does enjoy that bit. Sneakin' about of a evenin', chalkin' that word up on walls."

"What word?" asked Hartshire.

"Universalsuffrage," Landy replied proudly. "Gits all the letters right, too, I does. 'Stremely good at it I be."

"That's two words," observed Celeste, attempting to avoid the smell of the man by keeping her nose pointed in the opposite direction though her ears remained tuned to every word he spoke.

"Yer funnin' me," Landy replied. "Two words?"

"Indeed," nodded Hartshire. "Universal is one and suffrage is another."

"Well, I'll be damned."

"Without doubt," murmured Celeste.

"What else Tom?" Hartshire queried. "Any talk going about concerning, ah, an evening at Vauxhall, for instance?"

"Not what come ta m'ears as yet, Yer Majesty. An' I has been ta three o' the meetin's I has. Las' one were jus' las' night at the Carlisle in Shoreditch."

"Well, keep your ears open, Tom, and your eyes as well."

"Aye. Fer sure an' certain. I ain't fixin' fer ta have no blade pryin' in atween m'shoulder blades fer bein' no traitor, I ain't. I's bein' careful as a one-eyed cat."

Hartshire reached into his pocket and produced a small leather pouch which he passed to Landy. "That ought to make your nights safer, Tom. At least safe from the likes of me. Don't forget to keep in touch with Mr. Little. He will tell you where to meet me next time just as he did today. And should there be something you think I must know at once, you will just come to my kitchen door and ask for Little, eh?"

"Indeedy-do," agreed Landy, happily tossing the pouch of coins into the air. "I likes yer Mr. Little. He be a reg'lar peach. I be seein' him onc't a week at least. I'll be orf now, Yer Lordship, if ye don't got nothin' more ta discuss."

"Nothing. Go. But do go in a rather roundabout manner, will you, Tom, so no one notices precisely where you started from?"

Celeste turned to watch the man make his way out from under the willow tree behind them. "Do you mean to say you actually pay that person to spy for you, Hartshire?" she asked, turning back.

"Yes."

"You were accustomed to spy things out for yourself in years past."

"Yes. But Tom was—and I was—and it seemed like a fairly good idea at the time. Never mind, Celeste. He is merely helping me out a bit. It ain't as though I'm actually depending on him."

"No. It sounds to me as though you are depending upon Mr. Little."

"Well, I am that. And Robes as well."

"Oh, Hartshire!"

"They wished to become involved, Celly! And besides, I'm not certain we are actually involved in anything, really."

"After the two of them were nearly hanged right along with Colonel Despard, you've allowed them to join in some adventure that you admit you know little or nothing about?"

"Just so. Because Little said he was growing bored and might enjoy a bit of an adventure. Said Robes would as well."

"Before or after they discovered you were involved in something nefarious again and required assistance?"

"Well—well—sort of in the middle. It was after I laid down the law to Val but before we knew about the—Never mind, Celly. It ain't your business."

"It is my business. Do not you place those two gentlemen in any real danger, Hartshire," Celeste ordered imperiously. "Do not you dare. They may play games and gather information if they like, but do you allow them to go as far as they did with Despard, I will never speak to you again. Never, for as long as we live!"

Hartshire stared at Celeste, a puzzled frown encompassing his face. His mind raced back to the year of Despard's disastrous assassination attempt on the King. Then it raced forward again to today. In thoughtful silence he took an apple from Celeste's basket, fished his blade from his boot and sliced the fruit into quarters. He handed two of the quarters to Celeste. She thanked him and he grunted in return, his mind continuing to flit backward and forward in time. As he bit into the second of his quarters, his frown finally disappeared to be replaced by a look of sheer astonishment. He stared at Celeste; he muttered; he looked away; he muttered again.

"What? What are you grumbling about under your breath like that?" Celeste asked, biting into the last of her apple as well.

"Little," Hartshire replied, after swallowing a bite.

"What about Mr. Little?"

"I have recalled something, Celly. Something quite interesting."

"You have?"

"Yes, indeed."

"What?"

"That before we all agreed to call him something else, Little's name was Thoroughgood."

"Well, and what is that to put such a look on your face and send you to muttering under your breath? Really, Hartshire, you are the oddest person I have ever known."

"His name was Thoroughgood, Celly. *Arthur* Thoroughgood."

Eleven

Carriages came to a halt along the path while their occupants peered across the green. Pedestrians gathered along the rail and riders inside the rail brought their horses to a standstill as the party from Marston House passed by. Teweksbury took note of it and straightened his shoulders. He strove to sit taller in the saddle, lifted his chin a smidgen higher than he generally did, and angled his own horse in closer beside Lady Marston's. Behind him, Marston and Conningford did the same. They were united in their support of Lady Marston on this expedition and they attempted to make it clear to all. And evident it was, too, to those who watched. The sense that any disparaging remark on the lady's choice of habit or manner of riding would prove dangerous was lost on none of them, nor was the sense of pride that emanated from Teweksbury as his bright, handsome smile rested on his stunning riding partner.

"I cannot think when I have felt more excited or more exquisite," Lady Julia announced with enthusiasm from her position directly behind Lady Marston and Gaily Lad. "I would ride every day in Rotten Row if your stepmama rode with me, my lord. I vow I would."

Marston gave her the most splendid look. It was so filled with admiration that Julia thought she might shout in triumph to the skies. So this was what it took to gain his admiration—

outright approval of his stepmama. Well, Julia thought, I can do that. I am coming to think her the most amazing woman I have ever met. And I do like her. I truly do, regardless of what Mama says about her being beneath us.

"Do you mean it?" Marston asked. "You aren't ashamed to be seen with her in public?"

"Good heavens, no!"

"Not even at this very moment when she wears a perfectly radical riding habit and rides astride?"

"I think she looks positively elegant in that habit. And if I were more courageous, I would ride astride myself. My own mama would never have the audacity to dress so and to ride so. My mama is very old-fashioned, Malcolm. May I call you Malcolm? I should so like us to be good friends."

"I expect you may," nodded Marston, feeling in excessively good humor with the young lady. "You call Ally, Ally, after all."

"Yes, and it is very kind of her to allow me to do it since the very first time we met, my mama stuck her nose up into the air so high she nearly tripped over her own feet."

"She did? Your mother? Stuck her nose up at Ally?"

"Oh, no, not at Ally, at your stepmama. She won't do it again, I promise you."

"How can you promise that?"

"Because that's my papa," Julia replied, waving at a gentleman in the crowd near the rail. "The one with his hat pushed back on his head, his neckcloth all askew and his arms folded on the top rail. Apparently he's thoroughly bewitched by your stepmama. Only see how he stares after her. He'll not hear one word out of Mama's mouth against her now."

Conningford, paying not the least attention to the conversation going forward between Marston and Lady Julia, stood up in his stirrups in an attempt to get a clearer look at the riders ahead of them.

"Can you see her better from up there, Val?" asked Althea with a grin.

"Indeed. Her chin is up, her back straight and Gaily Lad prances as proudly as if he carries a veritable princess on his back. Whatever possessed your stepmother to ride astride?"

"You don't approve?" Althea queried.

Conningford brought his horse closer to hers. "I must approve, I expect, or you won't have another kind word for me, will you?"

"Then you don't approve!" Althea exclaimed.

"Well, it's just that it ain't the thing, Ally. I've no doubt at all that nearly everyone will consider your stepmother eccentric from this day forward."

"Eccentric? Mama? But she is not the least—what if I were to order a habit made in the same fashion and ride astride in Rotten Row myself? What then?"

"Then you'd be considered eccentric, too."

"*You* would consider me eccentric, Val? Well! I expect then you'd have no more to do with me either, would you?"

"Of course I would."

"But my reputation would be in ruins, my lord. I would be that eccentric Miss Avondale from then on. You would be thoroughly embarrassed to be seen with me."

Conningford gulped a tiny gulp. His hand tightened for an instant on the reins. He'd known the moment the words had left his mouth that he ought not to have said them, but once they'd escaped, he couldn't call them back, could he?

Well, well, perhaps he could. The least he could do would be to make the attempt. "Being thought eccentric ain't always a bad thing, Ally," he said, tugging at a neckcloth that had abruptly grown tighter than it had been when he'd tied it that morning. "I mean to say, for your stepmother to gather her courage about her and appear as she does this minute— the mere fact that she has done so—will be the making of her reputation, not the ruining of it. She won't be The Shipbuilder's Daughter any longer. Not after this."

"And pray tell me, sir, what will she be?"

Conningford gazed at the stubborn little face confronting him, thought as rapidly as he could, and then smiled. "Why, she'll be The Indomitable Lady Marston or the One and Only, possibly even the Paragon, because she's perfect, you know, at the moment. As perfect as a painting. She was made to ride so here and everywhere, regardless of whether it's the thing to do or not."

"First you don't approve and now you do approve?" asked Althea, suspiciously.

"Well—well—I expect it is just as Atticus always says."

"Yes? What does Atticus always say?"

"That all of us are created to be unique individuals, but very few of us have courage enough to do it. Now that I have thought more about it, I expect that's what it is. Your stepmother is one of those with courage enough to be unique."

From beneath the dappling of the willow, Hartshire watched Fleur make her way along the Row. His heart soared with pride and gratitude. She did it, he thought. She trusted in Montague's advice again. And only look at the stir she's causing!

"Just take a look at Teweksbury," Celeste said, tearing his attention away from his own thoughts by poking him in the ribs with her elbow. "You were right to let our Little Flower ride out first with Teweksbury, Hartshire. Though how you managed to persuade him to invite her, I cannot think. Oh! Yes, I can. It's that horse, isn't it? He's horse mad and you bought her the finest horse in all of England."

"I wouldn't go quite that far," Hartshire replied. "He is not the finest horse in all of England, Celly. Actually, Gaily Lad comes from Ireland, from Carey Farm."

"Fleur mentioned Carey Farm. Is that significant?"

"Well, yes. Carey Farm is—Never mind, Celly. What you know about horses would fit in a thimble. I shouldn't think it advisable to stuff your brain with any more of it."

"Do look at Teweksbury, Hartshire," Celeste said excitedly, pointedly ignoring his final remark. "He may have begun by lusting after the horse, but now it is our Little Flower he finds desirable. Teweksbury's fairly caught in Fleur's web for all the world to see. There'll be no more harsh words spoken against our girl now. At least not in public there won't be. Not now that the Marquess of Teweksbury has thrown his support her way. And set your gaze on some of those ladies, Hartshire! They are quite in awe of her."

"It appears so. But why, Celly? I knew the gentlemen would not be able to take their eyes from her, especially mounted on Gaily Lad with Teweksbury up beside her, but the ladies—"

"The ladies are all wishing they had the nerve to do it themselves. Well, not all of them, but a highly significant number, I assure you. And the rest may mumble and grumble about her audacity, but they won't say anything aloud in public, for which we may be thankful. Our sweet Lady Marston is free, Hartshire. She is proclaiming right here and now, to all the world, that she is who she is and does not care a fig what anyone else has to say about it."

"Are you certain? You don't think she does it to—just to—to—please someone?"

Celeste eyed him speculatively. "To please whom?"

"Just—just—someone who told her he thought it would be a good thing for her to do."

"Hartshire!"

"Well, it *is* a good thing for her to do, Celly. Just look at her. She's filled with such triumph that the feel of it flows from her right into Gaily Lad. The deuced horse is prancing and posing as though he's Pegasus come down from Mount Olympus to receive the adulation of the pagans."

"Hartshire, you *told* her to ride astride? She did not think of it on her own? My riding costume did not—did not—lure her to it?"

"I expect the riding costume had a great deal to do with it," Hartshire responded as his gaze followed Fleur along the Row. "She couldn't possibly do it, you know, in a regular old habit. Not and look as perfectly beautiful as she does at the moment. You're the best cousin in all the world, Celly, to have made that thing up for me—for her, I mean."

"You think she looks perfectly beautiful, Hartshire?"

"Like a goddess."

Celeste nodded. "Love," she whispered to herself, turning from him and grinning. "My dearest giant has toppled into the pit once again. If only the flower will have him. If only he will *ask* her to have him."

Lady Conningford was thinking the exact same thing as she stood watching Teweksbury and Lady Marston make their way along the Row. She had abandoned Mrs. Haley and Lady Stowe who had chosen to remain in the Haleys' coach and stare at the woman from there, and now she strolled across the green in the company of Lady Tate for a closer look at the bevy of riders. "Your Julia looks lovely," Lady Conningford said. "Lord Marston and she are a veritable vision together." Lady Conningford knew, of course, that Julia was determined to have Marston for a husband and that the girl had told Lady Tate so in no uncertain terms. Val had given his mama the word to that effect as much as two months ago. And Lady Conningford had told any number of her acquaintances. But no one had told Lord Marston as yet.

"Yes," Lady Tate replied. "They do look quite lovely riding one beside the other. And your son, my dear, is most definitely smitten, I think, with Lord Marston's sister."

Lady Con smiled. That was very true. Valerian had never actually wished to go anywhere near a husband-hunting young woman before in all of his short life. But Miss Avondale had decidedly altered his determination in that regard. Altered it quite drastically and in so short a time, too. "I cannot think it would be a bad thing for Val to fall in love with Miss Avondale," she confided in Lady Tate. "She seems a delightful young woman. I must say, I never expected it, having known her mother."

"The Shipbuilder's Daughter," sighed Lady Tate, glowering.

"No, my dear. Lila Grey. Her mother, not her stepmother. I should have thought that any daughter of Lila Grey's would grow up to be a smug, selfish, spiteful little witch. Of course, I did imagine that young Lord Marston would grow up to be a domineering, self-important bag of wind, too. I find I was mistaken about them both."

Lady Tate turned from watching the riders to cock an eyebrow at Lady Conningford.

"Well you may be skeptical, Marisa, but you did never actually know Lila Grey. I did. And I knew this Marston's father as well. Thank God The Shipbuilder's Daughter came into the elder Marston's life when she did, I say. Absolutely saved the children. Influenced them extraordinarily for the time she had them."

"How do you know?"

"I know. Malcolm confided his profound thanks for her in Val over and over again when yet the boys were in school together."

Lady Tate's face took on a most thoughtful look. "You like her?" she asked. "This Lady Marston?"

"Indeed. And I hope I shall learn to like her even more in the future. Only look at her, Marisa. Have you ever seen such an intriguing, independent young woman before in all your life? Not one of the sheep, Lady Marston. Born to be a leader, that one. Will be one day or I miss my guess. Just look at Teweksbury's face. He would follow her anywhere."

Which, Lady Conningford thought to herself, is going to

prove vexatious to say the least. How Atticus is ever to have a chance with the woman when Teweksbury has decided that he will have her, I cannot imagine. Such a face and figure as Teweksbury has! Such power and address and fortune as he possesses! And he wants her. Anyone with eyes in their head can see that. Why, he's so entirely hooked that all he requires is a bit of reeling in on her part.

I will be forced to speak quite plainly to Atticus about this happenstance, she thought, pondering how to go about it. He is the most courageous of gentlemen when it comes to adventures and danger, but he will be thoroughly intimidated by Teweksbury when it comes to courting Lady Marston. Likely he'll give up all thought of her without so much as making an attempt. I vow, he would never have come within a mile of marrying Miriam if she had not sat him down and explained to him that *he* was the gentleman she preferred. Yes, indeed, I shall be forced to take Atticus aside and—No, I will get Val to speak to Atticus. That's what I'll do. That will prove a deal better than my doing the thing. Encouragement in these matters always seems to do better when it travels from man to man. I will just take Valerian aside and tell him what he must say and then send him straight to Atticus.

Unlike Lady Conningford and Lady Tate, who had remained on the green, Lord Dashfield had taken up a position right at the fence rails. He'd been curious to see what all the hubbub was about. Now he stared at Fleur, entranced, as she passed him by. "Marston's stepmama," he murmured. "Must be. He and his sister ride right behind her."

This is the second wife? The one Marston despised? he wondered, his gaze following Fleur as she and Teweksbury continued down the line. Blazes! Always knew Marston was completely mad. How could anyone despise such a woman as that? But he was smart to keep her in Kent. That he was.

A woman as intriguing as she might well have gotten us all hanged.

"We'd have not gone unnoticed in anything we did, that's a surety," he whispered with a disbelieving shake of his head. But my gawd, had I seen her first I would never have married Lydia. I would have jumped at the chance to—Well, devil it, I did see her first, he remembered abruptly. And what did I do but turn my nose up at her like everyone else. Damnation, but she could not have been as striking then as she is now, or I wouldn't have done, not for a moment. Unless I turned my nose up so high and so fast that I missed seeing her completely? Lord, there is something about the gel that's almost mystical. No wonder all eyes are on her.

"We will have to think things over now," he muttered, turning to follow Fleur with a most studious gaze. "Have to give a second thought to every one of our plans." Because when a woman possesses such charisma, such magnetism as that, he thought, fiddling with his cane, it's best to stay as far away from her as we can get. No telling what sort of mind lies beneath that intriguing slouch hat. She is not a featherbrain like Lydia, that's certain, and only look at all the time and trouble Lydia caused us. Damned Runners nosed about forever before I actually got them to believe that she took her own life.

"Yes," sighed Dashfield, moving back from the rail, "we'll certainly have to take that lady's presence in Marston House under consideration. What slips past young Marston may very well not slip past her."

Fleur had not noticed Dashfield as she passed him by, nor had she taken note of anyone else in particular. She was really much too busy attempting to take stock of herself. Never had she felt so very exhilarated—or so very confused. She'd set out this afternoon to knowingly and willfully defy the social rules and to defy as well the gentlemen who made them. On behalf of Davis and all the other Davises in the world, on behalf of all women as a matter of fact, she had taken it upon herself to spit in the eye of the rule makers and to establish her own rules. She had taken Davis's observations to heart. What Montague's note alone had not convinced her to do, Davis's words added to it had. Now, as she rode bravely and proudly astride in Celeste's magnificent creation, she wondered how she could have gotten everything so very wrong.

The more she puzzled over it, the less sense it made. Gentlemen hailed Teweksbury and begged him to introduce them to her. Ladies, who only weeks ago had despised her, stood smiling as she passed them by. Here someone grinned; there someone waved. Teweksbury beamed at her as though the very sight of her pleased him immensely and he held her time and again in conversation, telling her what a fine horsewoman she was, asking if she had ever been to the Carey Farm in Ireland from whence Gaily Lad had come.

It's all turned about, Fleur thought dazedly. Teweksbury ought to have refused to accompany me from the first and Rotten Row should be empty of riders. All of them ought to have turned right back around in protest and refused to ride as long as I remained in the park. Gentlemen ought to be fleeing, not seeking introductions. And the ladies—but perhaps some of these ladies understand what I'm doing. Perhaps some of them wish to change the rules as much as Davis does.

"Still, if the rules are to be considered chiseled in stone," she asked herself, "and if it is truly the gentlemen who chiseled them to keep women under their thumbs, why—now while I am breaking at least two of the rules—do these same gentlemen appear to approve of me so highly?"

"Eh? What's that, m'dear?" asked Teweksbury, reaching over to give Gaily Lad's neck a fond pat. "Did you say something?"

"No, nothing. I was merely thinking what a sweet-goer

Gaily Lad is. I should not have guessed any horse could move so seductively at such a slow pace."

"Well, but he's extraordinary," Teweksbury replied. "And if I may be so bold as to say it, so are you, m'dear. Most extraordinary."

"What a kind thing to say, my lord," responded Fleur.

"Not at all. Not at all. You're a rare pleasure to be with, Lady Marston. Indeed, you are. I cannot tell you how much it pleases me to ride beside you."

It does? pondered Fleur, smiling sweetly at him. And to think that all these years you and your friends would not so much as acknowledge my existence.

Truly, it *was* puzzling. No matter how much she pondered the thing, Fleur could not seem to make a bit of sense out of it. Teweksbury and the others had chosen not to accept her among them because she had not one drop of aristocratic blood in her veins. And her husband had supported them in that decision. Rather than demanding they admit her into their ranks, Marston had derided her for her low birth right in front of them. No matter how many of the rules she had attempted to follow, no matter how hard she had tried to be worthy of her title of Lady, she had proved unacceptable to them all, and Marston had tucked her neatly away in Kent and gone on with his life in London without her.

And now I find that it makes no difference if one strives to follow the rules or not, Fleur thought. No difference at all. It's by breaking them that I've become acceptable. All that time, did I need only to be myself? Even down to preferring to ride astride? Well, it must be so for apparently now I'm a sensation.

Or am I merely a freak? she wondered then, the thought sobering her for a full minute. Does all this bowing and waving and conversing occur just so that these aristocrats can tell their friends and relations that they were actually present when the eccentric shipbuilder's daughter rode astride in Hyde Park? "That must be it," she murmured.

"They all wish to say they saw the freak show from the front row and participated in a small, insignificant fashion."

Just then, Gaily Lad tossed his head and snorted loudly. His feet danced in place as she pulled him to a halt to be introduced to another of Teweksbury's acquaintances. Fleur grinned the most delicious grin because of his dancing, though she was unaware of it. Such a horse he was. Proud, handsome, admirable, and delighted with all the attention he thought he so obviously deserved. How could she not grin at his prancing and posturing. "I am most pleased to make your acquaintance, Lord Steine," she said. "Certainly you may call at Marston House. We should be most happy to see you there."

I find I do not care one bit, she thought, as they moved forward again, whether I am a freak show or not. No, and I am not going to spend another moment puzzling over this sudden reversal of fate. By heaven, Lad and I are having the time of our lives and I am not going to worry anymore about yesterday, today or tomorrow. I vow I'm not.

As it did for everyone, tomorrow came for Fleur. And this particular day she expected to find herself at best, forgotten, at worst scorned. It mattered not. The ride yesterday had been well worth whatever suffering lay ahead. Regardless of what might be expected, she would do all in her power to remain cheerful. She found it not at all hard to do so. The light of laughter awoke and glowed all around her the very moment she viewed Davis's long, houndlike face.

"What is it, Davis?" she asked, as the abigail helped her to step into a blue and ivory striped walking dress. "You are beaming at me as though you've found the pot of gold at the end of the rainbow."

"Every one of the neighbors' abigails was talking about you this morning when I went out to breathe the air," Davis replied. "And oh, my lady, they were all so thrilled. There's not a woman in all of Cavendish Square has not heard what you did and how magnificent you looked and how exquisite you were."

"My goodness," smiled Fleur. "Magnificent and exquisite? Me? I think not, Davis. Timid and terrified would be more accurate perhaps. I was quaking in my boots."

"Well, perhaps you were, but no one took the least notice of it. And you *were* exquisite," Davis reiterated. "I saw you when you left this chamber. You were perfection."

"Yes, and luckily Gaily Lad was perfection as well—and *he* knew it! Oh, Davis, you should have seen what a perfect dandy he was, prancing and snorting and dancing about. He is the funniest, finest horse I have ever ridden. And such a poser. He has a pose for every step. You ought to have been there to see the two of us striking a blow for women's independence in our own small way. You would have laughed as much as I did."

Davis felt her heart flutter the merest bit as she closed the tabs at the back of Lady Marston's dress. She would very much like to have said, "I *was* there, my lady. I *did* see you. And I was so filled with pride that I came near to declaring right out loud that I was your abigail." But she could not. Oh, certainly not. Likely Wickens had his ear pressed against the door this very moment and that would be all he needed to hear. She would be discharged for some contrived reason before the day was out. Because an abigail had no business to be leaving the premises without it being her half-day off. And though he couldn't use that as an excuse, because her ladyship would never countenance her being fired for such a reason as wishing to see her own mistress's triumph, still Wickens would find some reason to get rid of her. He would contrive some horrible tale, relate it to Lord Marston, and she'd be gone. And that would put an awkward hitch in everything. A very awkward hitch, indeed.

Fleur left Davis behind, descended to the first floor and turned into the breakfast room to discover an enormous bouquet of red, pink and white roses decorating the center of the table. "How very lovely," she said. "Ally, who sent them to you?"

"Oh, they aren't mine, Mama. They're yours."

"Mine?"

"Um-hmmm," grinned Marston from the head of the table.

"From some gentlemen, Mama," offered Ally.

"Three gentlemen actually," Marston clarified, setting aside the morning *Times* and blinking innocently up at Fleur. "I thought you would like it if we put them all together. They're prettier that way, when the colors are mixed. You always planted the flowers in Kent so that no two colors the same grew side by side."

"I am amazed you ever noticed that, much less remembered," Fleur replied. "What three gentlemen? Are you going to tell me, or must I guess?"

"The pink are from Malcolm," smiled Althea.

"No, are they? Oh, Mal, how sweet of you."

"The white ones, Lord Hartshire sent. I've saved his note for you," Marston said. "And the red are from some gentleman by the name of Montague. Do you know a gentleman by the name of Montague, Mama? I don't. Ally doesn't either. I've saved his note for you as well."

Fleur sat down to a breakfast of toast with currant jelly and black tea. And though she attempted to keep up a conversation with Marston and Althea, she found herself thoroughly distracted by the sight of the roses. After attempting to ignore them for a full five minutes, she at last picked up the notes Marston had set beside her plate and read them. The first was from Lord Hartshire, a hurried scrawl on the back of his calling card. *To celebrate your triumph in Hyde Park and all your triumphs to come,* it said, and was signed simply *Hartshire.* The second was a folded sheet of paper, much the same sort of paper as she'd discovered beneath her pitcher yesterday morning. *Did you feel as free and joyful as you looked, my dear? I hope with all my heart that you did. Montague.*

He'd been there, watching her. Fleur's pulse raced. I must have seen him, she thought. I must have looked right at him. Perhaps I even spoke to him. But which one of the gentlemen could he have been? He is tall, I know. When he held me in his arms, the top of my head did not so much as touch the bottom of his chin, and I am not at all short. And he had to lean down a considerable distance to kiss me. It certainly felt as though he did. Oh dear, any of the taller gentlemen might be him—even—even—Lord Hartshire. No, not Lord Hartshire. He never left the music room nor appeared at Hatchards. And certainly if he had climbed the garden wall, I should have noticed it at once. And here are roses from Hartshire and from Montague. No, not Lord Hartshire.

"How odd that Lord Hartshire should send roses. I did not see him in the park yesterday," Fleur murmured, noting that both her stepchildren were staring at her. "I would have remembered had I seen him."

"Mal and I didn't see him either," replied Althea. "I think Val told him about it."

"Yes, I expect you're right," Fleur agreed with a nod. "Or perhaps some friend of his was there. It would be hard to miss seeing Lord Hartshire were he present, wouldn't it? Rather like riding along the Strand and missing Somerset House."

"Mama!" Marston exclaimed.

"Well, it would be much the same," Althea grinned. "I cannot imagine for one moment that Lord Hartshire could be overlooked, even in the most enormous crowd."

"You'd be surprised," Marston said so softly that neither of the ladies heard. He was remembering the tales of The Spectre that Conningford had so often related to him. "We'd all be surprised, I think."

"And since when, Ally," Fleur continued, "do you refer to Lord Conningford as Val?"

"Only for the past few days, Mama," Marston answered before his sister could. "There's nothing significant about it. We have all merely agreed to be friends."

"Oh? And yet, you don't call him Val, do you, Malcolm?"

"No, but Ally cannot go about calling him Connie. I should think that excessively odd, myself."

"And I would think it a good deal safer."

"Safer, Mama?" asked Althea, setting her empty cup aside and pushing her plate aside as well. "Why safer?"

"Because, dear heart, although you may think of yourself as Lord Conningford's friend, I am quite certain that he thinks of you as something else entirely."

"She has a point there," Marston agreed with a nod. "Connie's lost his heart to you, Ally."

"Never!" Althea exclaimed.

"Indeed, I believe he has, Ally," Fleur said thoughtfully. "And you would do well to consider that fact in all you do, too, because I heartily doubt that Lord Conningford has ever been in love with any young lady before now."

She glanced at Marston for confirmation of this particular fact and Marston nodded as he popped a grape into his mouth. "Just so, Mama. Never before."

"How would you know?" Ally demanded of her brother. "Do you think Val tells you everything?"

"Lord Conningford would have confided in your brother if he had ever been in love before, Ally," Fleur assured her. "They have always been the best of friends. And boys are forever speaking to each other about their lady loves. I don't mean to say you may not be friends with Lord Conningford, Althea. Or that, because he feels himself to be in love with you, you must overlook all other young gentlemen in his favor. Some young people fall in and out of love daily, you know. But such a shy young man as Lord Conningford does not give his heart lightly, I think. Be most careful that you don't return it to him broken in a million pieces, won't you?"

Hartshire folded his morning *Times* and set it aside. He rested his elbows on the table top, interlaced his fingers and rested his chin on the back of his hands. "So," he said, and waited.

Directly across from him, Conningford fiddled with his neckcloth, adjusted the set of his coat, tugged his pocket watch out, wound it, and tucked it away again.

"May I take it that what you've come to tell me is not something you particularly wish me to know?" asked Hartshire with a grin.

"No, it ain't that, Atticus."

"What is it then? Have some coffee, Val. Have a rasher of bacon, or some fruit."

"No, I can't. I m-mean, I ain't feeling just the thing."

"You're not? Were you out late last evening?"

"N-no. I was in. I was listening to Mama. All evening."

"Uh-oh. She heard about Lady Marston, eh?"

Val stared at him with the most pitiful wide blue eyes. "Didn't just hear about her. Saw her."

"Saw her? In Hyde Park?"

"Uh-huh. That's what started the whole thing."

"Blast! She's so upset that she kept you talking the entire evening? Blast and damn! I shall have to go and explain to her somehow."

"Explain?"

"Yes, about Lady Marston riding astride. I don't want your mother to be holding it against her, you know. I want them to like each other."

"I shouldn't worry about that, Atticus."

"No?"

"Mama is already determined to stand beside Lady Marston no matter what."

"She is? Well then, there's nothing to worry about, eh? I owe you many thanks, I expect, for calming your mama down and persuading her to accept Lady Marston's, ah, bit of impropriety."

Lord Conningford ran his fingers through his well-groomed curls, completely ending their hard-won symmetry. He stood partway up, located his handkerchief, sat down again and wiped a thin layer of perspiration from his brow.

Hartshire bit his lower lip to keep from chuckling. "I haven't seen you this nervous, Val, since you were called upon to explain to Lady Con how you came to be outside the house, tangled up in the fallen trellis at midnight, when you'd gone to your room to read three hours earlier."

"That was n-nothing compared to this."

"Compared to what? What is it, Val? I'm not going to bite you, you know. You can't have done anything so very terrible in just one day."

"No."

"No. So just open your gibbet and spill it out."

Conningford's lips parted; his mouth opened; "Teweksbury," tumbled out.

"Teweksbury?"

"Mama wishes me to—She told me I should—Oh, Jupiter, Atticus, she spent the entire evening telling me why I had to come here this morning and what I was to say and—and—I did come, but I cannot get the words to come out of my mouth."

"Just tell me, Val," grinned Hartshire, standing and going to fetch the coffee from the sideboard. He returned, poured them both a cup, set the pot on the table and resumed his seat. "I could put some brandy in it for you."

"N-no, I don't think so. I think my tongue is going to get twisted around itself enough without brandy. Because Mama says I'm to speak to you, you see, about your being in love with Lady Marston and Lord Teweksbury being in love with her as well."

"What?"

"Uh-huh. And—and—I think I should, too, because some-one has to do it, and I'm the only brother-in-law you have. And—well, the thing is, Atticus—I know you love Lady Marston. I could see it in your eyes the very first time I saw you with her. That's why Mama made certain to invite her to the musical evening, because I told her how your eyes fairly glowed at just the sight of the lady. And then, when Lady Marston came to the musical evening, and Mama saw for herself how it was with you—and then yesterday when she saw the look on Lord Teweksbury's face and you were nowhere around—Well, the thing of it is, Atticus, that you cannot let Teweksbury intimidate you."

"Let him intimidate me?"

"Yes. And you know you will. Mama and I both know you will. You let every gentleman in London stand in your way when it came to Miriam. You ain't one to put yourself forward at all. Especially when it comes to the ladies. And this time, you have got to put yourself forward, Atticus, be-cause Mama says Teweksbury is fairly caught already and likely as not, he'll propose to Lady Marston before the Sea-son ends. So I am to offer you my support and to say that since you want her, you had best make a push to get her before Teweksbury beats you to the punch."

Twelve

Dashfield handed his hat, gloves and cane to Wickens and then followed the first footman up the staircase and down the corridor to the summer drawing room where he was properly announced to the company gathered there, and went to bow before Lady Marston.

"We have met before," he said, taking her hand, "though I doubt you remember me. You knew my dearly departed Lydia, I believe."

"A bit," replied Fleur. "You are still in mourning for her, my lord?"

"Yes. I go out to quiet gatherings, of course, and to my club, but nothing more. Nothing more. It will be a year this summer and still I feel her absence greatly."

"It was a great tragedy for you," murmured Fleur, uneasily. All she really knew of this man was that he had known her husband and that his wife had taken her own life. She could not think what had brought him to her doorstep this day, but she welcomed him nonetheless and invited him to be seated. "You know Lord Teweksbury, I believe."

"Yes, indeed. Good day to you, Teweksbury."

"What the deuce is he doing here?" Marston grumbled, staring across the room as Dashfield made himself comfortable beside Lady Marston.

"I don't know, but we shall need to tell Lord Hartshire as

soon as possible," Ally responded in a whisper. "I cannot do anything at the moment but pay polite attention to my own callers, but you're free to run off whenever you like, Mal. Perhaps you ought to excuse yourself now and fetch Lord Hartshire to us. Yes, and fetch Val as well. It will not seem odd at all for Lord Hartshire to insert himself into the group around Mama. And you, I and Val can take turns observing if any of the servants come in contact with Lord Dashfield in any extraordinary way—whisper to him when the tea is served, or hand him something on the sly for instance or leave something on a table that he later picks up and puts in a pocket. If the three of us are watching, and Lord Hartshire hears everything Lord Dashfield says while he's with Mama, the man will not be able to slip anything past us."

Marston stared at her. "I doubt Dashfield will do or say anything at all extraordinary, Ally. Certainly none of the servants will. Why would he make use of Father's cane to send that message secretly and then come here in person to make contact with that very person and risk giving all away?"

"I don't know. Perhaps there's been a serious change in their plans—some alteration that must be relayed one to the other without delay. And he doesn't know, Mal, that we are on to him, you know. Lord Dashfield has not the vaguest idea that he's suspected of anything at all."

"Is something wrong?" asked Lady Julia, coming up to them. "You are both over here whispering to each other so intently. Has something dreadful happened?"

"Oh, no, nothing," Ally responded, turning to Julia with a wide smile. "Mal and I were merely discussing whether we ought to—to—"

"Get up some sort of game," finished Marston for her.

"Oh! What sort of game?"

"Spillikins," Marston offered at once, blurting out the first game that came to mind.

"Mal has never outgrown spillikins," Ally said, taking Lady Julia's arm and turning her back toward the group of young people who had gathered on the opposite side of the drawing room from their elders. "Go and see if can you find them, Mal," she called over her shoulder. "He is so childish sometimes," she added quietly to Julia. "Men are, you know. Apparently they can bear only so much conversation and then they are impatient to be actually doing something."

"Oh, I know," nodded Julia. "Even though they attempt not to let on, they always look so pained sitting about twiddling their thumbs. Even when they're determined to court someone, they don't want to do it by sitting about a drawing room, talking."

Hartshire, in his shirtsleeves, leaning on a rapier whose button-blunted tip rested on the floor of his drawing room, took one look at the expression on Marston's face and nodded. "Enough of fencing lessons for today, Will, m'lad," he said. "I have business to discuss with Lord Marston."

"But Papa, we have just got to the best part."

"Yes, I know."

"Yes, and I want to do it, too. I have practiced and practiced with Mr. Canton. Can't we do it just once? You won't mind, will you, Lord Marston, if we do it just once? It will only take a moment."

"Oh, you think so, do you?" asked Hartshire with a saucy gleam in his eye.

"Yes, because I have practiced so much that I'm excellent."

"All right. Once."

Marston stood looking on as Hartshire and Will in stocking feet, took their places on the hardwood floor. The carpet, he noted, had been judiciously rolled back and everything breakable removed from reach of the participants.

The two saluted each other. *"En garde,"* Hartshire said, and in a moment two foils were flashing in the sunlight streaming through the windows as Hartshire attacked and

Will parried. "Don't diddle around, Will," Hartshire said. "Marston has a vague, desperate look about him."

"He does?"

"Yes."

"Oh. Well, but I ain't going to look to see, Papa. That's what you want me to do, isn't it?"

Hartshire merely grinned in answer and began his attack afresh with a feint to Will's head.

Marston's eyes widened as Will unexpectedly counterattacked with a thrust feint and a time cut to his father's arm. *"Touché,"* Marston called.

"Just so," nodded Hartshire. *"Touché."*

Engaging again, Will renewed his attack. His blade slid over and to the inside of his father's and with a quick snap of thumb and wrist he flicked the foil from Hartshire's grip and sent it soaring across the room.

"I told you I was excellent at it," Will announced gleefully, resting the point of his weapon on the floor.

"Indeed," Hartshire grinned. "And we missed breaking the windows as well. Fetch my foil, eh, Will, and put them both away while I deal with Lord Marston?"

"Jupiter," murmured Marston, as the boy departed. "I should hate to meet him on a dueling ground some foggy morning."

Hartshire grinned, tugged two chairs away from the wall and offered one to Marston. "No fear of that. He's merely ten, Marston. You'll be a doddering old man by the time he's old enough to call you out. Now, what is it?" he asked, pulling off his gloves and slapping them down on a table. "Something amiss?"

"Dashfield is paying Mama a morning call even as we speak."

"Oh?"

"Yes, and he looks as if he means to stay longer than the requisite fifteen minutes, too. Ally thought you ought to come right over—you and Connie. She thinks something unexpected may have happened concerning their plans and that Dashfield will attempt to pass on a message to whomever it is he contacts in Marston House."

"Ally thinks that, does she?"

"Um-hmmm."

"It could not possibly be that Dashfield has simply decided to pay a call on your stepmother and acknowledge her existence?"

"No, why would he?"

"Oh, I don't know. Possibly he finds her attractive."

"Dashfield? Jupiter, I hope not! Can you come?"

Hartshire nodded as he tugged on a boot. "Be there as soon as I can. Don't wait for me. Go on and fetch Val. I'll meet the two of you in Cavendish Square."

He was better than his word, already standing before Marston House by the time Marston and Conningford arrived. "How does he do that?" asked Marston, as he dismounted and handed his horse's reins to a waiting groom.

"Do what?"

"When I left him, he was in his shirtsleeves, pulling on his boots, and here he is waiting for us and looking a proper dandy."

"I wish you will tell him that," sighed Conningford, giving his mount into the groom's keeping as well.

"Tell him what?"

"That he looks a proper dandy. He thinks he don't, you know. Thinks the very sight of him frightens little children."

"He don't!"

"Yes, he does."

"He does what?" asked Hartshire.

"Nothing," Conningford replied. "We were just discussing a friend of ours."

They entered without so much as a knock. Marston tossed his hat at the startled footman on duty, laid his gloves on the hall table and started for the stairs. "Oh, damnation!" he exclaimed as he reached the third step. "The spillikins!"

"The what?" asked Conningford, close on Marston's heels.

"Told Lady Julia I was going off to look for spillikins to play. Forgot all about them."

"Do you know where they are?" asked Hartshire, handing his hat to the footman and straightening his neckcloth before the looking glass.

"Yes, they're in the linen closet."

"Let this footman fetch them for you then. We'll wait here until he returns. Then we'll all go up together, eh? Val, come and wait in the parlor. We may wait in the front parlor, Marston?"

"Of course. James, on the top shelf in the linen closet is a hat box with a black cover. Fetch it down to me, will you?"

"But there is no one else to man the door at the moment, my lord," the footman replied.

"Never mind, James. If someone comes, I'll open the door myself. The spillikins are a good deal more important at the moment."

Marston and Conningford bounded back down the stairs, as the footman hurried up them.

"Interesting," murmured Hartshire, staring after the man.

"What's interesting about that particular footman, Atticus?" asked Conningford innocently.

"Nothing," Hartshire replied. "The thing that's interesting is in that enormous vase beside the table there, but I could hardly call your attention to it and stand here and stare at it with a footman lingering about."

"What?" asked both the young men at once, going to look into the vase where Marston and visiting gentlemen generally stowed their canes.

"Well, I'll be deviled!" Marston exclaimed, lifting his father's malacca cane from the vase, and then lifting out its twin as well. "They're exactly the same."

"Not exactly," offered Hartshire. "The eyes are reversed."

"They are," Conningford said, amazed.

"Do you know which is yours, Marston?" Hartshire asked.

"I—I—Well, no, not actually. I mean, one eye is a ruby and the other an emerald and the sapphire is in the right place on both of them. I never took note which eye was— Let me think—I think Papa's cane had the ruby on the left and the emerald on the right."

"Val, watch the stairs for the footman. Try that one and see if it opens, Marston."

"Yes, it does. And here is the swordstick. There's no message inside."

"Now try the other cane."

"This one opens the same way, and has the same sort of swordstick. How the devil is one to know—"

"Is there a message stuck down in that one?"

"Yes! By Jove, Hartshire, there is!"

"I can hear the footman returning," hissed Conningford from the staircase.

"Quick, hand me the message and put the canes back in the vase," Hartshire whispered holding out his hand. He quickly stuffed the rolled paper into the inside pocket of his coat. Now what the deuce is this? he wondered as his fingertips brushed against something oddly soft and warm. But he hadn't the time to check on it just then and so he ignored it as the footman reappeared.

Fleur was incredibly pleased to see Hartshire enter along with Malcolm and Lord Conningford. She smiled at him most graciously and he grinned the most disarming grin back.

"Look what I discovered along with the spillikins," announced Marston with what Althea considered to be obviously forced joviality. "You do all know Connie and Lord Hartshire?"

"Indeed. Good day to you. Your servant," replied a bevy of young voices, one tripping over the other. Hartshire nodded in their direction, gave Val a shove toward them and crossed the room to where Lady Marston sat with Lady Tate, Mrs. Haley, Teweksbury and Dashfield.

"That evens our numbers," observed Dashfield quietly.

"Afternoon, Hartshire," Teweksbury said, standing and offering Hartshire a hand. Dashfield did the same, his eyes alight with laughter. "I say, you are not pursuing one of these lovely ladies as well, are you, Hartshire?"

"What?"

"In pursuit of one of them? Teweksbury is, you know. Already planning to spend the rest of his days sitting right there beside Lady Marston on the settee. Not that I blame him, mind you. Might be thinking the same had I not just recently lost my Lydia."

Hartshire's gaze met Fleur's and then he bowed to all three of the ladies. "It's Val has come hunting," he said, "though he won't admit it. Lost his heart to the lovely Miss Avondale, I believe."

"Just as he should," replied Mrs. Haley. "I have just come along with Julia and Lady Tate for the drive," she added. "Haley and I have no more daughters to bring out, you know. No more fuss and bother with eligible young gentlemen spilling out of the drawing room and into the corridor. I was just telling Lady Marston how busy she will be after the ball."

"The ball?" queried Hartshire, lowering himself carefully into an ancient wing chair as he and the rest of the gentlemen sat. "What ball is this?"

"Why, my Grecian Ball, Lord Hartshire," piped up Lady Tate. "You have received an invitation, I'm certain. It is most likely sitting on your vestibule table this very moment. You will come, will you not?"

"Indeed. Honored," he replied. And then his hand went to his left breast most suddenly and he made the oddest noise.

"What is it?" Fleur asked. "My lord, are you ill?"

"Hartshire gazed across at her and gave her the oddest look. "N-no," he replied.

"Are you certain, Hartshire? You've gone a bit pale," Dashfield observed, just as Hartshire seized his claret morning coat by the left lapel and began to flap it back and forth.

"Oh, my goodness!" exclaimed Fleur, "you are ill! Lord Teweksbury there is brandy over on the sideboard. No, no, he doesn't like brandy. It gives him the headache."

"It gives him the headache?" Teweksbury asked, looking from one to the other of them with considerable suspicion. "How would you come to know that?"

"Oh, he told me so when first we met. I was ill myself and—Never mind, Lord Teweksbury. Tea! Tea will be arriving shortly. Perhaps a cup of tea, Lord Hartshire?"

Hartshire, sitting forward now in the chair, continued to flap the left side of his coat. He stared at Fleur with the most helpless expression on his face. The sudden paleness had departed his cheeks and now they were becoming suffused with red. "I think I had best—I had best—step outside and get some air."

"Oh, yes, what a good idea. Let me take your arm and we shall just go out on the drawing room balcony for a moment," said Fleur, rising and crossing to him. "Come right this way, my lord." And she took his arm the instant he rose, led him straight across the room, right through the middle of the game of spillikins and out through a charming set of French doors.

"Let me," gasped Hartshire. "Let me just lean back here against the bricks." And he tugged her with him to the side of the doors, against the house, out of everyone's line of vision.

"What is it? Lord Hartshire, what is it? Are you in pain? Would you like to go upstairs and lie down for a bit? Is there anything I can fetch for you? A physician? A surgeon?" Fleur's questions increased in anxiety as Hartshire leaned back against the bricks, releasing a great puff of breath. And then he was holding his morning coat away from him and reaching inside of it, breathing raggedly and making the strangest noises. For a moment Fleur was certain he was going to die, and she turned to run back into the room to beckon the gentlemen to come and carry him upstairs to one of the guest rooms at once.

"No, don't!" Hartshire managed.

"But my lord, you are likely ill unto death!"

"No, no, I'm simply trying not to—not to—No, do not you dare you little hellion—" he hissed. "I beg—your p-pardon, m'dear. I c-cannot help myself. I'm attempting not to fall down and roll about laughing, but it's hard not to do it when I'm being tickled to death."

"T-tickled to death?" Fleur's eyes widened considerably.

"No, don't look at me that way, Little Flower. I ain't gone mad, I promise you. It's—Do cease squirming about and let me get my hands on you!—It's Henry," he finished, lifting the little creature by the scruff of the neck from his inside pocket.

Fleur stared and then she started to giggle. She simply took a step back, looked Hartshire up and down as he stood there—a veritable giant holding a tiny dormouse up before him by the scruff of the neck—and the giggles took hold of her.

"Sshhhh, they'll all hear you," chuckled Hartshire, putting an arm around her and pulling her close to his chest to muffle her giggles. "They'll think we're doing something most unacceptable out here if even one of them hears."

"I c-can't help it," Fleur replied. "Never in all my d-days have I s-seen—Why do you h-have him in your coat pocket?"

"Because he wouldn't fit in my waistcoat pocket?"

"No, no, don't! I—Oh, Hartshire! You are incorrigible!"

"Not me. Henry. I was simply in a rush and grabbed any old coat and lo and behold, it was the one whose pocket Henry had chosen to sleep in. Just you wait until I get you home, you—you—villain," quipped Hartshire, allowing the dormouse to settle in the palm of his hand and petting it with his thumb while he kept his other arm around Fleur.

"What are you going to do? S-send him to bed without his d-dinner?"

"No. Fleur. Stop. You've got to stop giggling or Teweksbury will come out here and challenge me to a duel to defend your honor."

"Heaven forbid!" Fleur took a very deep breath, turned her back on Hartshire and the dormouse, strolled to the balcony rail, closed her eyes and thought very hard about not giggling. It didn't quite work. She burst into gales of laughter instead. Then she turned back and saw not only Lord Teweksbury, but every one of her guests, young and old, crowded together at the opening of the French doors.

"I expect he's not dying, eh?" observed Teweksbury with a slow drawl.

Her hand covering her mouth, Fleur shook her head.

"No, of course he ain't," said Conningford. "But where the deuce is he?"

"I'm here," Hartshire answered, stepping around to where he could be seen again, Henry sitting up attentively in his hand, whiskers wiggling.

"Oh, what a darling!" cried Julia, leaving Marston's side, pushing past Teweksbury and Val and going directly to Hartshire. "Mama, look! A dormouse!"

"I did wonder what got you to flapping your coat about like a madman, Hartshire," Dashfield said over tea.

"Yes, well, you'd be flapping yours as well if you had got a dormouse nibbling and scrabbling at you through your pocket. I would have taken him out, but I feared to frighten the ladies."

"Bah, as if we're afraid of dormice," protested Mrs. Haley good-naturedly. "When you've raised as many children as I have, you become accustomed to myriad little creatures scampering about the house. Once Thomas had a hedgehog as a pet. Now *that* I could not understand. Have you ever attempted to pet a hedgehog?"

"No, thank you," Teweksbury replied. "I shouldn't like to try that. So you see, Hartshire," he added, peering at Atticus over his teacup, "things might have been worse. You might have had a hedgehog in your pocket."

"Heaven forbid," murmured Hartshire, selecting a cherry tart for himself and gazing across the way to where the young people were conversing over their own tea as they passed a curious and happy Henry from one to the other of them for playing and petting. Hartshire was anxious to depart the drawing room but could not think how to go about it without raising a number of eyebrows because he had to take either Val or Marston with him. And then it dawned on him. Ally. It did seem a bit unreasonable, after his protesting her involvement with them in the matter of the cane so energetically, but she was the perfect answer. "I wonder, Lady Marston," he began, swallowing the last of the tart, "if I might have your permission to stroll with Miss Avondale in the garden for a bit."

Fleur looked up at once from the polite, but tentative conversation she was holding with Lady Tate. "Stroll in the garden?" she asked, a puzzled frown wrinkling her brow.

"Yes. With Miss Avondale. If she will do me the honor, of course. We will take her abigail with us to play propriety, eh?"

The look in Lady Marston's eyes gave him pause, but now was not the time to explain to her. Once tea had been dispensed with, Dashfield was not likely to remain. Hartshire was amazed, in fact, that the man had stayed as long as he had.

Fleur looked to Lady Tate, who brightened considerably for a moment as she was asked for her opinion and gave it freely. "Well, I do not see why not," Fleur replied at last.

It was most extraordinary, and Fleur could not help but wonder what business Hartshire had to be strolling with Althea in the garden, but then she thought she knew. She rang for a footman and sent the servant off in search of Davis, while Hartshire excused himself and crossed the drawing room to bow quite nicely before Althea and beg her to join him for a stroll.

A considerable number of young ears perked up to hear it and Conningford frowned at him something fierce. Hartshire noted the frown and glowered back. "No, don't offer to join us, Val," he said. "Or any of you rapscallions either," he added, looking about at Lady Julia and the rest of the beaux who had come to call on Althea or had followed in Julia's wake. "There's something of importance I wish to discuss with Miss Avondale and none of you is invited to join in."

"Well, of all things," whispered Julia as Davis stepped across the threshold and Hartshire, Ally and the abigail departed. "You don't think that Lord Hartshire has developed—an interest—in Ally?"

"Of course not," Conningford replied at once. "He's a good deal too old for Ally."

"Oh? Well, I don't know about that. He doesn't seem old at all to me. And he does have the most beautiful eyes."

"He what?" asked Marston, stunned to see a look rather like envy on Lady Julia's face.

"I said, Lord Marston, that he has the most beautiful eyes I have ever seen in a man or a woman. Eyes that see straight into your soul, I should think."

Hartshire glanced over his shoulder, determined that Davis was far enough to the rear to allow him to speak freely and reached into his coat pocket. "Oh, tarnation!" he groaned, as he pulled out the message from the cane. "That little beast Henry nibbled on it."

"On what? What is it? Is it the reason we've come to stroll in the garden?" queried Ally.

"Precisely. I could hardly ask your brother to accompany

me here, and though I could suggest to Val that we needed to be off, I didn't wish to actually leave, because I need to read this first and then we need to get it back into the right cane as soon as possible."

"Into the cane? There was another message in the cane?"

"Not exactly. This one came in another cane. One that matches your father's, except that the gems in the eyes are reversed. Oh, devil it," he grumbled, scanning the thick, black handwritten lines.

"What does it say?"

"That the person to whom it's addressed is to continue on as before. It warns him to be extra careful. And it says there's to be a special meeting, though our man ain't invited apparently. Says certain things have popped up and may need to be attended to before all is done."

"What certain things?"

"Doesn't say. Well, I expect the only way to find out is to attend the meeting."

Althea looked at him with worried eyes. "You cannot possibly. You would be recognized on the instant. Especially if Lord Dashfield is among them."

"No, no one will recognize me as long as it's to be held in a public house, which, apparently, it is." He rolled the message back into a tube thin enough to be slipped back into the malacca cane and offered it to Ally. "I was foolish to protest your becoming involved in this. I see now how helpful it can be to have a young lady as a compatriot. However," he added with a stern look, "I don't wish you to be putting yourself in any danger whatsoever, do you understand? Simply give this to your brother and tell him to return it to the proper cane as soon as humanly possible. And tell him to be certain that he puts it in the correct cane. We don't want them to suspect that we know messages are being passed and especially, we don't want them to discover that we know how they're doing it."

"No, of course not," Althea replied. "We would never be able to disrupt their nefarious plotting then."

"Just so," smiled Hartshire. "You're a veritable prize, Ally—beautiful, intelligent and able to keep secrets. If I were ten years younger, I'd be courting you myself."

"Would you?"

"Well, I would dream of courting you."

"But you would not?"

"I—No, I expect not."

Ally stopped in midstride, bringing him to a halt. She tucked the slightly chewed paper away into the pocket of her dress, released her hold on his arm and took both his hands into her own, forcing him to face her directly. "Atticus," she said. "May I call you Atticus as Val does? You are one of the sweetest, kindest, most honorable gentlemen I have ever had the privilege to meet. No, don't protest. Everything you say and do proclaims it, even down to the obvious respect and understanding you show for Mama."

"I—I—"

"And now you sound like Val," she smiled. "Please don't. I don't mean to frighten you, only to say the truth. There is no woman in the world—if she truly came to know you—who would not wish to be courted by you. Not one. I will tell you what Mama always says to me. 'Handsome is as handsome does, but a true and loving heart is not so easily gained'."

She gazed up into his eyes as though she would tell him more—a great deal more—but then she simply turned him about and began to stroll back toward the house. "I will get this into Malcolm's hands immediately and without the least fuss. You may depend on it."

Hartshire waited to take his leave of Marston House until Dashfield did so. He accompanied that gentleman down the staircase and fiddled with his hat and gloves, watching covertly while Marston lifted his cane from the vase. "Liked

Marston's, eh?" he asked, tilting his hat at a more rakish angle as he gazed at his reflection in the looking glass.

"Yes, indeed," nodded Dashfield. "Missed it once it was gone. Had a copy made."

"I'll wager it cost you more than a guinea, that one," Hartshire said, smiling companionably as Dashfield waited to have his curricle brought up. "It was kind of you to sell the boy his father's back. Been wanting to mention that to you. Admirable, in fact."

"Why, thank you, Hartshire. I was pleased to do it. I'm bound for White's. May I give you a lift somewhere?"

"No, no, I rode over. Radical won't like to be left behind in favor of a vehicle."

"Radical? Your horse is named Radical?"

"Um-hmmm."

"Why would you give him such a name as that?"

"Seemed to fit him. Fascinating animal, really. Has a head stuffed full of ideas all his own. Independent rascal."

"And you find radicals filled with ideas and independent as well?"

"Certainly do, Dashfield. Cannot like all their chalking of slogans on the walls. Messy that. But I can't say I ain't amazed at some of their pamphlets. Have valid points, most of them."

Hartshire could sense a distinct interest in himself rising inside of Dashfield.

"Best watch yourself," Dashfield murmured as his curricle and Radical entered the square. "Not the time, politically speaking, to be known to take an interest in radical ideas. Our Regent is so frightened by the mere thought of equal suffrage and the sharing of wealth that he's like to have you brought up on treason just for the name of your horse."

"Just so, Dashfield. You'll not tell Prinny the name of my horse, eh?"

"Not me," grinned Dashfield, chuckling as his vehicle halted at the curb and he climbed up to take the reins from one of Marston's grooms. "Fare you well, Hartshire. It's been a pleasure."

Hartshire stepped up into the saddle, took Radical's reins from the boy who had brought him around and tossed the lad a coin. "My thanks, scoundrel," he said, then patted his coat pocket to be certain a very sleepy Henry was still inside. He turned Rad's head toward home and rode off, deep in thought. But it wasn't Dashfield's almost certain involvement with the Spenceans that occupied his mind. No, not at all. It was Lady Marston. She had looked at him with such puzzlement and such astonishment when he'd asked to stroll with Ally through the garden that he'd wanted to explain to her on the spot why he wished to do so. He couldn't have done it, of course. Give the whole thing away and send Dashfield running from the house—or have Dashfield challenging him to a duel to defend his honor. But he'd wished to explain himself so badly.

Cannot bear to have her think I've taken an interest in Ally, he thought to himself. Must discover some way to relieve her of that worry. Only think the fear it must instill in her breast to think of having me for a son-in-law. He grinned at the thought. It certainly had disturbed Lady Con in the beginning, the thought of him as a son-in-law. Disturbed her so greatly that she had gone out specifically to purchase a chair he could not possibly destroy simply by sitting down in it.

Fleur held Teweksbury's interest the entire afternoon, he thought then. I ought to be overjoyed for her. Teweksbury is just the gentleman she deserves—honorable, loyal, and outstandingly handsome. And she will not hold it against him that he's horse mad. Likely enjoy accompanying him from one breeder to the other looking for the perfect animal. "Yes, I'll wager she would," he murmured. "She'd love to travel about and see the world now she has my beads to stave off the *mal de mer.*"

But I should like to be the one to take her, he thought. Not Teweksbury, me. And not to horse farms either. The places I would like to share with her! Places I've seen and places I've merely read about! I should like to take her to every one of them and watch those oh, so innocent eyes of hers fill up with wonder. Only think, he grinned to himself, how large and filled with surprise those eyes would grow to be introduced to Jung Kaow. And that old pirate would laugh aloud to see them so, too. If only I could make myself believe all the things Val said to me on behalf of his mama. Yes, and I should like to believe what Ally said this afternoon as well, about any woman who knew me well being willing to be courted by me. Only—only—I can't. I know what a freakish man I am. I would be a fool to believe any of what the two of them said. They are children merely.

Fleur sorted through the invitations that lay on the silver salver atop the cricket table beside her chair in the now empty drawing room, wondering what she ought to do with them. Which she ought to accept. To whom she ought to send her regrets. I will discuss them with Malcolm, she thought. He'll know which of these Ally would do best to attend.

The truth was, she could not keep her mind on them. Not right now. Not for the remainder of the day most likely. Her mind insisted, instead, on replaying for her the scene of Hartshire, nearly convulsed with laughter, on the balcony. The way he had held Henry up before her by the scruff of the neck, the very sight of the two of them setting her to giggling. The manner in which he'd placed his arm around her and held her against his chest to keep her giggles from being heard while everything he said caused her to giggle the more. The tenderness with which he'd held Henry in his palm, his thumb alone almost large enough to cover and pet the creature's entire back.

"The way he held me against his chest," she whispered, stopping with both hands in the air, both clutching invitations. "It felt so—familiar—as though he had held me just that way before." But that is perfectly ridiculous, she told herself. No one has ever held me so. Not even Montague. He held me facing away from his chest, not into it, when he kissed me. And then Fleur took a very deep breath. It's what I dreamed that night, she thought, surprised that she should suddenly remember. I dreamed of a gentleman holding me close like that, rocking me, speaking to me so very softly. Whispering that I was safe. And it felt like—just like—"And he called me Little Flower on the balcony," she said under her breath. "Hartshire called me Little Flower, which is exactly what Montague called me in his note."

She began again to sort through the invitations, pondering over whether Lord Hartshire and Montague could be one and the same and coming to the same conclusion she had before. Impossible. Not only would she recognize Lord Hartshire, his voice, his size, even in darkness, but he had been in Lady Conningford's music room and not at Hatchards. The confusing ache that had circled her heart when Lord Hartshire had sought her permission to stroll in the garden with Ally, flowed through her now.

"Honestly," she muttered to herself, "anyone would think I was falling in love with him. Not only do I wish to make him and Montague one, but I was jealous—jealous of Ally simply because he wished to discuss something with her in private."

Still, what could Lord Hartshire possibly have to discuss with Althea, if not to profess his admiration for her? Certainly an older gentleman might find Ally as alluring as a younger gentleman does. Even Lord Teweksbury admits that Althea is likely the prettiest girl to come out this Season. "Just the thing," he called her. "Just the thing." Why should Lord Hartshire not think her "just the thing" as well?

Fleur gave herself a little shake, set the cards down on the salver and rose to pace the drawing room. Besides, she thought, I have already lost my heart to someone. I have lost my heart to the mysterious Montague. What a fool I am!

First I marry a beast to please my father, and now I give my heart to a gentleman who has told me straight out that the love blossoming between us is hopeless.

But why is it hopeless? Why? Why will he hide always in the shadows so I cannot see who he is? Is Montague already a married man? No, he cannot be! Oh, please God, don't let him be a married man! Anything else we can overcome. If he is promised to another, he can speak his heart to her and surely she will release him. If he is poor, it makes no difference to me for I have enough to support us both. If he is lowly born, what cause have I, a mere shipbuilder's daughter, to despise him for that? Oh, no, I would not. Never. Certainly he must know that I would not. Perhaps he is deformed in some way. Perhaps he has lost an arm or a leg in this war we fight with Napoleon. But I would never refuse to love him because of that. Never.

And then she thought of the handsome, honorable, horse-mad Lord Teweksbury and smiled. "It would be nice to love and be loved by Lord Teweksbury, but I don't think it will ever actually happen. He and I are not at all alike, except that we both love horses. Whoever would have believed that I might turn a gentleman who despised me into a gentleman who worships me simply by delivering a magazine about horses into his hands?" she said, stopping in midpace to gaze out through the French doors. The memory of Hartshire, flapping his coat and reaching down into his pocket, lifting the dormouse out by the scruff of its neck as he struggled to keep from bursting into guffaws, flashed before her once again and caused a giggle to bubble out of her. "Oh, but I do love Hartshire," she whispered to the balcony. "I love him almost as much as I love Montague, but in such a very different way."

Thirteen

Mr. Little faced the horse with fear in his heart and a trembling hand. "Hold," he told it, his voice quavering. It took him four attempts to get his boot securely into the stirrup. He clung to the front of the saddle with hands sweating inside his gloves and tried to pull himself up onto the beast's back. Unfortunately the horse shifted impatiently and instead of swinging his leg over the animal's back as he had so often seen Lord Hartshire do, Little panicked; his hands slipped; he kneed the poor horse in the side and ended with his stomach in the saddle, his leg in the stirrup sticking straight out behind him and his head dangling much too close above the ground to be at all acceptable.

Hartshire bit his lip to keep from laughing and rushed at once to his butler's aid, as did the snickering groom.

"Let me get him free of the stirrup here, Gorely. Then you push him up from that side and I'll catch him before he hits the ground."

"Yes, m'lord," chuckled the groom. "Jus' what I were thinkin' meself."

Between them they got Little off the horse. Gorely fetched a mounting block and with both men to aid him, the butler settled himself uneasily atop the beast. "Harder than it looks, my lord," Little said, in hopes of saving face.

"A good deal harder," nodded Hartshire, more than willing to let him save face. "We forget, people like myself and Gorely, just how big horses are and how small are the saddles, don't we, Gorely?"

"Indeed we does, m'lord," said the groom at once, prompted to it by the speaking look in his lordship's eyes. "Bin doin' it so many years, we don't notice it no more a'tall."

"Just so," Hartshire said, pleased. "Come, Mr. Little. We are expected at Marston House within the hour. You've not forgotten what I told you about how to get the horse to move forward and how to make him stop?"

"No, m'lord. I wrote it down and have memorized every word of it."

"Did you? What a good idea, Little. We go this way," he added, as the horse beneath the butler turned in a hesitant circle. "Just point his head in this particular direction. You needn't worry about traffic or anything, Little. There are very few riders and vehicles about at this hour. All you need do is to keep a firm grip on the reins and stay in the saddle. We won't go faster than a trot, I promise."

"Why we must ride at all, I cannot comprehend, my lord," Little managed nervously as the horse stepped forward and he lurched awkwardly in the same direction. "Could you not merely walk with the lady in the park?"

"No, because how would we get to the park, Little? Lady Marston would not look kindly on tramping along blocks and blocks of dismal, dirty streets. No doubt, by the time we reached the park, she'd be in a foul mood and exhausted as well."

"Of course I should not expect her ladyship to walk to the park. We would drive in a carriage."

"We can't. I don't have my beads. I would be violently ill after the first corner."

"Well, you ought to get them back," frowned Little. "Had you got them back, we could be in a carriage right now."

"I'm afraid not. Because I gave them to Lady Marston,

you see. Did I take them back, I would do fine in the carriage, but she would be violently ill. Riding or walking is all that's open to us, Little, and walking is not in the least acceptable."

Little sighed but nodded, resigned to his fate. "Are you certain Lady Marston will bring her abigail, my lord? I mean, it is not the usual arrangement. A lady who goes riding with a gentleman is generally accompanied by a groom. Odd that she would bring her abigail on a ride."

"Yes, well, that's something I meant to tell you about, Little. I asked her specifically to bring her abigail instead."

"You did, my lord?"

"Um-hmmm. Told her you had gotten a glimpse of the woman and were languishing away because you couldn't think of a way to bring yourself to Davis's attention."

"What?"

"Said you had set your heart on meeting Davis, but couldn't think of one acceptable way to go about it. Explained that I intended to bring you on the ride and requested especially that she bring her abigail."

"Oh, my lord!" exclaimed Little in a voice filled with dread. "You cannot have done!"

"I know I cannot have done it, Little, but I did. I did ask Lady Marston not to say anything to Davis about it, though. About your having fallen in love with the gel at first sight. Lady Marston is a bit of a romantic, I think, because she made not the slightest quibble about bringing Davis instead of a groom. No, and she didn't protest my bringing you, either."

"But, my lord, you cannot wish me to actually court the abigail not even if she is, as you think, the very female that Robes and I saw following Mr. Wickens from The Nag's Head."

"I can't? Not even to save the Crown, Little? It seems such a small thing to do. And think of all the information you may gain from her."

"No. I would if I could, my lord, but I cannot."

"Why not?" asked Hartshire, reaching across to remove a piece of lint from the claret riding coat that he'd borrowed from Gorely. It did hang rather loosely around Little's shoulders, but otherwise it fit respectably. Gorely's riding breeches had proved a bit too tight, but it turned out that Val's groom had actually had a pair of breeches that fit Little and a pair of boots as well. "Why not, Little?" Hartshire asked again, his eyes aglow.

"Because—because—I have already given my heart to another, my lord."

"You? You, Little? And you did not say a word to me about it? Of all things!"

"Yes, well, I was going to tell you, my lord, when up jumped all this business about the radicals, and I—I thought it better that you deal with the radical problem first, my lord. That being the most important. I vow, I could not so much as pretend to court the abigail or my beloved would hack off my head with a butcher's knife."

Hartshire noticed that his butler was tilting progressively toward him in the saddle. He reached across and pushed Little upright. "Keep your nose over the horse's head, Little. That's the trick. Do you notice your nose going to one side or the other of his, you are likely on your way to losing your balance and you must readjust yourself. About this lady love of yours, Little. The one with the butcher's knife. You are thinking to marry her, I assume."

"Yes, my lord. Just so. And I expect I shall have to resign my position as your butler. I don't wish to do that, but 'tis most likely she'll not wish me to remain in my present position."

"And why is that?"

"Well, it is because—because—she is a gently bred lady, my lord," whispered Little hoarsely, forcing the words past his trembling lips.

"What? Not a housekeeper? Not a clerk in some shop?"

"No, my lord."

"Ah, a parson's daughter, eh, Little?"

The butler squirmed in the saddle and not merely because of the bouncing of the leather against the seat of his breeches. "No, she is not a parson's daughter. Higher than that."

"Higher? A governess, Little? Someone's poor relation? Inform me, if you please."

"She is—she is—the granddaughter of an earl, my-my-l-lord."

Hartshire noted the beads of perspiration popping out on his butler's brow and quite suddenly felt ashamed of himself. "And her name, I think, is Celeste, is it not, Little?"

"My lord!"

Hartshire recognized both the guilt and the accusation in the butler's gaze and shook his head. "I do beg your pardon, Little. Truly, I do. Celeste mentioned to me that she had lost her heart to a gentleman by the name of Arthur, you see. And I did remember your name to be Arthur. It took a bit for me to realize—I've grown so accustomed, you know, to calling you Little. You will not keep the name Little, now you've decided to marry my cousin, eh? You will go back to the name you were born with?"

"I should like to do so, my lord. All the uproar over Despard has died down by now. Twelve years ago it was."

"Twelve years? Already? How time does fly, Mr. Little."

"I—I—shall despise to part with you, my lord. Truly, I shall. You saved my life, you know, and I am not proud to repay you by turning about and marrying your cousin. But she is too much for me, my lord. She overwhelms me. I cannot bear the time I spend away from her."

"Which is most of the time."

"Well, it is at present," agreed Little. "But when Robes and I first came to London to open the house—"

"Don't tell me," interrupted Hartshire. "I don't want to know."

"But, my lord, you ought to know that I—that the awe-inspiring Celeste and I—"

"Please don't tell me, Little," Hartshire repeated. "I really, truly don't want to know. But I have been thinking, Little, and I think that once you meet Davis—if you should believe her to be the female who followed Mr. Wickens home—I do think it would be commendable of you to introduce her to Robes."

"But you already told Lady Marston, my lord, that I was the one who fell heels over head in love with her."

"Yes. Well. I shall simply say I misunderstood and you were loathe to tell me until after you discovered I had arranged this surprise. Indeed! That's the ticket, Little. If the abigail is the one, you must tell her straightaway that I made a dreadful mistake and that it is my valet who thinks so fondly of her, and that you will make arrangements to introduce the two of them."

"And if it is not the female from outside The Silver Swan, my lord? What then?"

"You will say the same and we will discover a way to introduce her to Robes regardless. It would not be at all gentlemanly to just abandon her and it's about time Robes had a bit of fun and a dance or two. *He* does not have a secret understanding with one of my female relatives, does he?"

"No, my lord," Little replied, relieved. "He has no secret understandings with anyone except you as far as I know."

Fleur grinned from ear to ear when she saw them turn into the square. When Hartshire had stopped by and begged a private word with her yesterday afternoon, she'd been afraid the gentle giant was going to ask her for her permission to propose marriage to Althea.

Well, he did ask to stroll with Ally in the garden only the afternoon before, she thought now, remembering. What was I to think? First a private conversation with Ally and then a private conversation with me.

Her fears on the subject he'd eliminated almost at once. "It's about my butler," he'd said. "Little is his name." And from that point on until now, she had wondered what sort of person this Mr. Little could be to persuade a peer of the realm to intercede for him with Davis. Not that Lord Hartshire had actually interceded at all with Davis. No, he'd come to her with the most outlandish plan of throwing the two together.

The truth is, I was so enthralled with the idea of Davis having an admirer from afar that I would have agreed to anything to see who he was and what he looked like, Fleur thought. And only look at him. He is quite the dandy. Though Lord Hartshire truly ought to have asked Mr. Little if he could ride, before he set the poor man up in that saddle. Thank goodness we shan't have to worry about Davis falling off. "Where did you learn to ride, Davis?" she asked abruptly. "You have been in service since you were very young, you said."

Davis, whose gaze was likewise fastened upon the approaching riders, responded at once. "It was Lady Blessing, my lady. Had me taught, she did, when I was serving in the scullery. Oh, I do remember it well. That horse was so tall and I was so small. I thought surely I would fall right off and die."

"She had a mere scullery maid taught to ride. But why?"

"Well, it were like this, my lady. Lady Blessing had an all-out fear of dying with no one about to keep her company. And she thought, in her mind, that the more servants who knew how to ride, the more people she could send for to gather about her when the time came. Taught every one of us to ride, the grooms did, except for Cook. Cook would not go near a horse and let it be known loud and clear. Whoever is that riding beside his lordship, my lady?"

"I believe it's his butler, Davis."

"His butler?"

"Yes. He did mention that, ah, he might bring his butler

with him. I do believe Mr. Little indicated to his lordship that he should like to learn to ride, and Lord Hartshire mentioned that Farley Field might be just the place to teach him."

"Oh! Oh!" Davis exclaimed abruptly. "He is drifting to the left! He will fall right off and break his skull! No, his lordship has got him, thank goodness! No, no, now he's dipping to the right!"

Fleur came near to giggling again as she watched Hartshire reach out and seize his butler's arm to tug him back into the middle of the saddle. Oh, poor Mr. Little, she thought. How lovelorn he must be to attempt to ride a horse when it is perfectly obvious that he has never been on one before in all his life. I do so hope Davis likes him. She has not the least idea that all he suffers is for her sake.

"Good day to you, Lady Marston, Davis," Hartshire greeted. "Pull back on the reins a bit harder, Little," he added, lurching to grab the back of his butler's coat before that gentleman went tumbling off over the horse's head. "Ready for our excursion, are you? Davis, if you should require any assistance—"

"No, she doesn't," Fleur interrupted in the most cheerful voice. "Davis learned to ride years ago, when she was a mere dab of a girl."

"Thank heaven for that," mumbled Hartshire *sotto voce*.

Fleur heard. "Shame on you," she whispered back.

"No, but I could just imagine attempting to keep both of them mounted. I would have to ride Rad without holding to the reins at all and keep one of them on each side of me. I ought to have thought a bit more about this, hadn't I?"

"It wouldn't have made a bit of difference, I think," Fleur responded, watching as Mr. Little introduced himself to Davis all the while wobbling as though he might well take a dive onto the cobbles. "You would have attempted the thing anyway, I believe."

"You do?"

"Yes. It's in your nature."

"What's in my nature?"

"Whimsicality, sentimentality and a joy in your fellow man. If you had to hold them both up by their collars to give your butler this opportunity to make Davis's acquaintance, I do believe you would."

Hartshire studied her seriously and then he grinned his utterly boyish grin. "You're correct," he agreed with a nod. "I would."

"They're gone," Ally called, peeking out from behind the curtains in the front parlor.

"We know. We were watching from the antechamber. I thought they'd never get under way," grinned Conningford, drifting into the room followed closely by Marston.

"Did you see Little?" asked Marston. "Poor man. I shouldn't like to spend this morning in his shoes."

"No, but I'll wager *he* would, because his shoes are at home. He's probably wishing he were in them right this very minute. Those boots he's wearing belong to my groom."

"It has something to do with the messages being passed back and forth, doesn't it?" asked Ally, flopping down into an armchair. "I can't think of one other reason for Lord Hartshire to take his butler riding with him else. No, or for him to request that Mama get Davis to accompany her. His lordship suspects it is Davis whom Lord Dashfield contacts."

"A woman?" Marston's eyebrows rose almost to his hairline. "What a thing to think, Ally. Why would Dashfield select a woman to be his contact in this house?"

"Why not?" asked Conningford. "Davis always strikes me as a competent, capable person whenever I get a glimpse of her. Reminds me of a hound, but that's neither here nor there."

"But she's a *woman,* Connie."

"So? Women can be as fanatical and zealous as men. Yes, and they can be fierce in defense of things, too. Atticus has had to thwart a number of plots in which women took part, and he says they are generally more dedicated and more fierce than men."

"Well, perhaps so, but Davis? She is so, so, quiet. One barely notices her when she is standing right in front of you."

"Yes, and that's just the thing that makes for an excellent spy, ain't it?" offered Conningford. "She's a good deal like Atticus then, able to be perfectly invisible while in plain sight."

"Somehow I still cannot imagine Lord Hartshire being invisible—ever," Ally murmured. "But back to Davis. I never did tell you, but there was a night that Mama and I saw her sneaking back into this house through the garden. It was very late at night, too. Had Mama not been standing at the window and noticed her coming in through the gate, why, no one at all would have known she had gone out. Abigails have a good deal of free time, you know. Well, they do, if they are good at their jobs and know just how to manage."

"That's probably so," Conningford agreed, sitting down on the footstool at Althea's feet. "I expect Atticus will find out this very day if Davis *is* the person Dashfield is passing messages to. Likely he'll discover it without Davis even knowing he has done so, too. But we haven't gathered at the moment to discuss Davis, you know. Marston, have you got it?"

"Yes, but I don't understand it at all," Marston replied, crossing to the mantel and taking a piece of paper from beneath the mantel clock. " 'The beheading block in wretched woe,' is what it said," he offered, reading from the paper.

Ally and Conningford stared up at him, puzzled, as he settled on the arm of Ally's chair.

"That's all you copied?" queried Conningford.

"Well, I didn't want to take the time to copy it all. Hartshire told Ally that I should get the message back in the cane as soon as possible. And I thought it a good idea to do so, too. So I just read it and then wrote this down. It has got to be the name of the meeting place. I could not make much sense of the message, but that this was the place where they planned to gather seemed obvious enough. I wrote down what must be the day and the time, as well." Marston gazed at the paper again. " 'On mighty moor at nine plus four,' " he read.

"Well, that will be one o'clock," Ally said without a second thought. "Yes, and one o'clock in the morning, too."

"Indeed," Conningford agreed. "Nine plus four will be thirteen, one hour past twelve, and there ain't a servant alive would be leaving the house at one o'clock of an afternoon."

"Just so," nodded Marston. "We're agreed on that, but what about the place?"

"Read it again, Mal," Ally said.

" 'The beheading block in wretched woe.' Makes not the least bit of sense. Rhyming cant, Hartshire called it. But what's the point of it? What rhymes with beheading? Or is it block that the name rhymes with? Or both? And wretched woe. Where the deuce is there a place rhymes with wretched woe?"

The three of them stared glumly into space. "Lord Hartshire seemed to know right where the gathering would be held," Ally said after a time. "Read the note right off and didn't puzzle over it a moment."

"I don't suppose he'll tell you, Connie, where the meeting is to be?" queried Marston hopefully.

"After the way he bellowed at me when he first discovered I had gotten involved with his Spencean Philanthropists? I don't think so. No. He would throttle each of us, one by one, if he so much as suspected that we mean to attend this particular gathering."

"The beheading block in wretched woe," mumbled Marston then. "The beheading block in wretched woe."

"Cut your hair before you go," grinned Ally.

"Bow your head and watch your toe," Conningford chuckled.

"Kill the cock and ride the bull," offered Marston, his frown fading.

"Cock!" Ally exclaimed at once. "The Cock! That certainly sounds like the name of a public house!"

Conningford nodded. "Any number of public houses with cock somewhere in their names."

"Yes," agreed Ally excitedly. "And a cock is beheaded for dinner—at least I think cocks are beheaded. Beheaded or strangled."

"A cock? We don't eat cocks," frowned Marston.

"Perhaps not, but the poor do," Conningford said knowledgeably. "They aren't particular, you know, where their meat comes from. They get little enough of it as it is."

"If we're right," said Ally excitedly. "If it is called The Cock, then I see how the rhyming cant works. Think for a moment, Val. Think of it. It not only rhymes. It tells something about the word it refers to."

"So wretched woe would be someplace sad and wretched?"

"Precisely. Well, perhaps not precisely. Perhaps it is merely wretched and rhymes with woe. But it will be one or the other or both."

"Wretched woe," Marston murmured. "Wretched woe. Well, it don't rhyme with St. Giles or Seven Dials, though both places are perfectly wretched."

"St. Giles and Seven Dials rhyme," Conningford pointed out helpfully.

"Yes, but it doesn't say either in the message, Val," Ally sighed. "It says, 'in wretched woe.' "

"I know. That rhymes as well."

"What?"

"Wretched woe and I know."

"Turkey guts," grumbled Marston. "There must be millions of words rhyme with woe."

"Yes, and I don't want to sit here listing them one by one," Althea sighed. "It will take us forever. What other places do we know to be perfectly wretched?"

"The docks, the alleys, the mews. All of the east end of London."

"Soho!" Conningford exclaimed. "Wretched woe is Soho!"

"Do you think so, Val?" asked Ally.

"Well, it's wretched all right. Read in the *Times* just the other day about a riot there and a Runner beaten to death with his own cudgel."

"Rotten place. Crawling with poor Irish and French émigrés," Marston nodded. "I think you've got it, Connie. So, they meet in Soho at The Cock at one o'clock in the morning. But what's mighty moor, then?"

"The day," offered Ally. "We don't know the day. Mighty moor—mighty moor—Thor! Thor was a god, he was mighty, and his name rhymes with moor." Ally grinned. "I rather like this way of saying things," she admitted gleefully. "Thor's day is Thursday, of course. What an ingenious code it is, this rhyming cant."

"I expect the message means tomorrow then. It don't specify a date."

"No, but it would make sense that it would be tomorrow," Conningford said, "because Atticus did say they wished to discuss something urgent, didn't he, Ally?"

"Yes. And if it's urgent, it won't be put off until next week or the week after."

They were sitting beneath an oak on a blanket Hartshire had brought with him and watching Little and Davis pick wildflowers. Farley Field was green with grass and empty but for the four of them. Fleur, enjoying the quiet of the early morning, absently fingered the scar on her cheek.

"It cannot still hurt," Hartshire said softly.

"What?"

"You're touching that bit of a scar. It cannot still hurt. The memories of how it came to be there are what cause you pain, I expect."

Fleur dropped her hand into her lap at once. Their gazes met. The silver that flecked his irises seemed to pulse and flicker. Fleur lost herself for a moment in the sheer beauty of his eyes. Perhaps I'm mistaken, she thought. Perhaps this is the man I truly love and not Montague at all. What if it is merely that Montague kissed me so secretly in the garden? So secretly and so tenderly. What if that is the only reason I think myself in love with him—the only reason I dream of Montague and not of Lord Hartshire?

"What happened?" Hartshire asked, reaching out and touching the horrid thing, caressing it gently with his thumb as his fingers played against her cheek. "Marston did this to you, did he not?"

Fleur nodded. "He did not intend to do it. Not precisely. He hit me and his signet ring—"

"He hit you with his fist?"

"Yes."

"Dastard! If he were alive, I would seek him out this minute and plant the tip of my foil in his heart."

"No."

"Yes. A wound for a wound. A scar for a scar. Though the wound I'd give him would not have time to heal in this world. I'm amazed you will so much as speak to any man."

Fleur, still lost in the beauty of his eyes, smiled. "I am a grown woman, my lord. I know all men are not alike, just as I know all women are not alike. I shan't fault you or Lord Teweksbury or—or—any other gentlemen—for what the brute I married did. But let us not discuss him any further. The very thought of him still makes me most uneasy. Tell me something instead."

"What?"

"Tell me how you came to know the inimitable Celeste."

Hartshire took his hand from her cheek, transferred his gaze from her to Little and Davis in the field and shook his head. Then he laughed what Fleur thought to be the saddest little laugh she had ever heard.

"Tell me," she said, placing her hand on his shoulder because in her heart she knew he required it there. "I will tell no one else. I give you my word on it."

"It is the oddest thing," he said in an almost whisper. "That I should—that you should be—I ain't proud of it, what happened."

"You're not?"

"No. There ought to have been a better way. A more civilized way. But I'm not the civilized sort, I expect. Only think what I just said of your husband. That I would have plunged my foil into his heart. It slips out of me, that."

"What? What slips out of you?"

"The evil giant," he replied, and laughed the sad laugh again. "The monster from the woods. The barbarian. Because did your husband stand before me now, God help me, I would kill the man and without a second thought. It is only afterward that I would have second thoughts."

"Well, but I should like to have killed him myself. Even now, sometimes, I wish I had."

"But you didn't."

"No."

"I did."

"What? What did you do?"

"I killed someone."

Fleur stared at his wide back, rubbed her hand back and forth across his broad shoulders, feeling the hard, thick bone and muscle of him even through his coat. "Who?" she asked after the longest time. "Who did you kill, Atticus? Had it something to do with Celeste?"

He nodded, his hands clasped in his lap, his eyes staring off over Farley's Field. "Celeste is my cousin," he said. "I love her. I have always loved her, since first I began to toddle about. She wasn't always as odd as she is today, you know. Once she was as young and innocent as Ally and pretty, too.

I always thought she'd missed out completely on the curse of the Howards. Never did grow an inch above five feet, never got giant ears either. But then—What she did get— What she did get—was Benjamin Drake."

"Benjamin Drake?"

"Sir Benjamin Drake. Rich as Croesus, handsome as a Greek god stepped down from Olympus, and as cruel and evil as the devil himself."

"Celeste? Celeste married a cruel and evil man? Oh, I cannot believe it. Was she forced to marry him?"

"No. She loved him at first. She wouldn't believe he *was* evil. Sometimes people don't, you know. They don't believe things they don't wish to believe, no matter how many friends tell them otherwise. But she discovered her mistake soon enough."

"He was cruel to her."

"Oh, more than cruel. So evil, so degraded, so without conscience that living with him, being his wife, drove her somewhat mad. She *is* somewhat mad. You've noticed, I expect."

"I like Celeste," Fleur whispered, moving closer beside him, the better to hear all he said. "She's the most remarkable person."

"Yes, she is," he agreed, a bit more loudly. "There ain't another like Celeste in all the world. Any other woman would have killed herself rather than face life with Drake once he doffed his mask of acceptability and became his true self."

"And this is the man you killed? This Sir Benjamin Drake?"

"The very man. I was seventeen. Came down from Oxford to surprise Celly. I was the one surprised. Found the house empty of servants and master and Celly alike. Door to the garden was standing open. Wretched night. Storming. Cold. Thought Drake to be in London. Imagined something had happened to Celly and the entire staff gone searching for her. Stepped out into the garden and saw him—saw the silhouette of him in a flash of lightning. He was searching through the bushes growing along the wall with a short sword raised above his head."

"Oh, my dearest God," whispered Fleur, shuddering. "He was not—He could not have been—Was he searching for Celeste?"

Hartshire nodded. "Searching for Celly. Going to kill her. Chop her head right off. At least, that's what she told me after it was all over. I ran out into the garden when I saw him. Began to search for Celly myself. Search for her and stay out of his sight at one and the same time. Found her, too. Thank God to this day that I found her. Huddled behind the fountain, getting ready to flee again to some safer place. Came up behind her. Took her in my arms. She screamed and spun away from me. I grabbed at her again, wanting her to stop screaming, you know. Wanting to make her see it was me and not that animal. Pummeled me black and blue before she came to her senses and realized who I was."

"Did he—did Sir Benjamin—hear her? Oh, he found you, didn't he, you and Celly. Oh, Atticus!"

"Found us. Just got Celly to see it was me when she screamed again and attempted to tug me aside. Right behind me Drake was, his short sword already descending. Caught me in the shoulder."

Fleur gasped. The sun had disappeared. Farley Field had faded. She was in that garden, the storm raging about her, a madman rising from out of the darkness amidst thunder and lightning, rising like a demon from hell, the sword above his head coming down, down, straight at—Montague!

Her heart ceased to beat, she thought, in that moment. Montague, in the garden, coming up behind her. Montague, hiding himself away. Hiding, always in darkness, in shadow. Montague—Hartshire—becoming one in her mind. "No, it can't be," she murmured. "Why? Why would he hide from me one day and not another? How could he ever be present and not be seen, not instantly recognized?"

"Turned and jammed my fist up under his chin," Hartshire continued, not having heard her speak. Lost in his own memories. "Set him reeling backward. Seized the sword from his hand and drove it through his black heart."

Fleur stared at him, though he continued to gaze out over the field. His was not a perfect profile, not perfectly beautiful that face, even studied from the side. But there was a tear in the corner of his eye. Fleur watched it, shimmering there, unwilling to fall. She braced herself against his strong shoulder, got to her knees, leaned around him and slowly, tenderly, kissed the tear away.

Hartshire, startled from his reverie, fairly jumped, his shoulder knocking Fleur on the chin. He reached out for her as she lurched away, reached out to keep her from falling. His arms went around her. He pulled her close. "Are you all right?" he asked urgently. "Fleur, my dearest Little Flower, can you hear me?"

"Ow," Fleur said, rubbing at her chin. "You are not only the largest gentleman I've ever met, Atticus, but quite the most solid."

"I am, am I not?" he said, attempting a grin, but failing badly at it. "I'm so sorry. I was so lost in it all. I have never told anyone about it but my uncle Pan and those who investigated the thing. And that was so soon afterward that I could not—I did not let myself get taken up by it. Words. All I told them—nothing but words. Forgive me," he added then. "I ought not have told you. Not so very much. Not in such a way."

"Yes, you ought," protested Fleur, ceasing to rub at her chin and quite comfortable inside the ring of his arms which he'd forgotten to take from around her. "You ought to have told me precisely what you did and precisely in the way you did. I'm glad you killed him, Atticus. You saved Celeste's life. You saved your own life."

"Yes, that's what the investigation concluded. It's why I was not hanged or transported."

"You believe now that Sir Benjamin wouldn't actually have murdered you, do you not?" Fleur whispered. "Well, you're wrong, Atticus. He would have chopped your head directly from your shoulders and then done the same to Celeste and most likely laughed while doing it, too. No wonder Celeste adores you. No wonder!"

No sooner had Fleur bid Lord Hartshire farewell and watched him and his butler ride off, than she hurried into the house and up the staircase to her chamber where she opened her jewelry box and took from it a small stack of calling cards she had saved. She dealt them out across her counterpane. Teweksbury's she set aside, and Panington's and Haley's, Lady Tate's and Julia's, Mrs. Haley's and Malcolm's and Conningford's. She smiled pensively as she found the note that Hartshire had sent with his roses and the one Montague had sent with his roses as well. Then she took the note Montague had sent concerning her ride in Hyde Park and carried all three to the window seat where the light was brightest.

"I knew it," she whispered as she studied the dark, bold writing on the two notes and the card. He has obviously attempted to disguise these he wrote as Montague, but so many of the letters are formed alike, she thought. Most certainly that dear man wrote them all. "All the while, deep inside I knew it," she whispered. "And yet, I cannot think how he managed to—Did he enter the library at the Conningford's after me then? Well, he must have done and I not even heard him. And when I went to wash my face and fix my hair, he hurried back to the music room. Yes, of course. And if we didn't see him at Hatchards, it's because he didn't wish us to see him. What a simpleton I am! But why? Why should he pretend to be someone else? Why hide from me in shadows? Unless—"

She heard a light scratching on her door. "Come in," she called, and turned to discover Davis on the threshold.

Davis's gaze darted to the cards strewn across the bed and then to the notes Lady Marston held in her hand. "I came to thank you, my lady, for the lovely morning."

"To thank me? But Davis, I simply added to your work by asking that you accompany me."

"No, my lady, you did not. Mr. Little told me."

"He told you?" Fleur felt the corners of her mouth tilt upward into a smile. "What did he tell you, Davis?"

"Why you asked me to accompany you. And it was very kind. Excessively kind. There are not many who would do such a thing for a servant, I assure you."

"It's Lord Hartshire whom you ought to thank. If his heart had not gone out to Mr. Little so much so as to arrange the entire outing with me, I should still know nothing about it. Do you like Mr. Little, Davis. Perhaps a bit?"

"Oh, yes, my lady," Davis declared, her hands clasped tightly before her. And then she smiled so widely that all her teeth showed and Fleur was somewhat startled by how white and sharp they looked. "But his lordship made a great mistake."

"He did?"

"Indeed. Mr. Little was not wasting away for lack of a means to meet me. Mr. Little is despondent because he has asked a woman to marry him and she's accepted."

Fleur's eyebrows shot up on the instant. "He's despondent because she agreed to marry him?"

"Yes, my lady. Apparently, she is of a higher station than he and though he wishes her to be his bride, she doesn't wish for him to be Lord Hartshire's butler any longer once she marries him."

"Then it was all for naught, Davis? Oh, I am so very sorry. It seemed so romantic, you know, when Lord Hartshire proposed it to me. Why did his butler not tell him at once that he was mistaken?"

"Because Lord Hartshire did not say why he wished Mr. Little to ride out with him until they turned into the square and Mr. Little did not like to disappoint his lordship then, seeing as it was an opportunity, so to speak, for Lord Hartshire to ride with you, my lady. But apparently all is not for naught," Davis added, stepping farther into the chamber. "Mr. Little did say that his friend, Mr. Robes, who is Lord Hartshire's valet, actually is somewhat withering away from lack of a means to make my acquaintance. Spied me strolling behind you and Miss Althea at one of the shops and fancied me right off, Mr. Robes did. At least, that's what Mr. Little told me."

"Oh, Davis!" Fleur set the three notes aside, crossed to her abigail and gave her a hug.

Davis stared at Lady Marston, flabbergasted, as Fleur stepped back a bit.

"Why do you look at me like that, Davis?"

"I—I—don't know, my lady. I expect because no one for whom I worked ever hugged me before."

"You are not offended by it? It is merely that I am so happy for you. Happy that you aren't without an admirer after all. Oh, surely, when his mistake is made clear to him, Lord Hartshire will see that his valet has the opportunity to meet you, just as he did for his butler. Although, if his valet does not ride any better than Mr. Little, Davis, I do not think we shall go about it in the same manner."

"No, my lady," replied Davis, almost giggling. "But you and his lordship will not need to become involved in it now, for Mr. Little has promised to introduce me to Mr. Robes himself. We have made arrangements to meet on my half-day off, my lady."

Fourteen

Little descended before the stable giving thanks. His seat hurt; his back hurt; his arms hurt. His legs hurt as well, but he'd survived the ride without a fall. Of course, a good deal of the thanks for that, he knew, belonged to Lord Hartshire who had not once abandoned him while he was on the horse. The earl's quick hands and strong arms had always been present to support his butler, to straighten him in the saddle, to show him what to do with the reins.

"You're certain, are you, Little?" asked Hartshire, giving Radical into Gorely's care.

"Quite, my lord. Definitely the female who followed after Wickens. She is to have her half-day off on Saturday, my lord, and I did tell her about your mistake and promise to introduce her to Mr. Robes on Saturday afternoon."

"Good. Good job, Little. You and Robes will not want to ride to Cavendish Square, eh?"

"Ah, no, my lord."

"I'll have John Coachman drive you, eh? In the barouche?"

"That would prove excellent, my lord."

"Done, then. I do thank you, Little, not merely for this morning, but for spying for me at The Swan in the first place." Hartshire frowned as he and his butler turned to stroll through the mews to Hartshire House.

"What is it, my lord?"

"Hmmm? Oh, nothing, Little. It is merely that I know I've seen this Davis woman somewhere before. Quite a while ago, I think. But no matter how I try, I cannot bring the occasion to mind. Uh-oh. Something tells me I'm bound back to the stable before I ever reach the house," he added, the frown departing at once as Will came running toward him, arms pinwheeling, boots clomping down the path.

"Papa! Papa! Mr. Canton was going to take me to ride on my pony, but now you are here, you can do it!" the boy exclaimed and at the end of his words, leaped full-tilt into Hartshire's waiting arms.

"Doesn't that pony have a name yet, Will?" asked Hartshire.

"They only just brought him this morning, Papa. Just barely an hour ago. But Mr. Canton and I were in the middle of the Orient and so Mr. Canton said I couldn't come down to see him until we were finished."

"Just so. Good for Mr. Canton. Morning, Canton."

"Good morning, my lord. Mr. Little. You need not climb back in the saddle if you don't wish to, my lord. I will be pleased to take Will riding."

"No, thank you, Canton. I'll take him. You could use a bit of time to yourself, I think."

"Yes, my lord, I certainly could. I've a number of things to catch up on."

"Just so. Off with you then. Will and I will be out of your hair for an hour at the least. Possibly more."

"More than an hour, Papa?"

"Possibly. It depends."

"On what?"

"On precisely what sort of pony we discover you've selected for yourself. Perhaps he'll be tired at the end of an hour."

"No, Papa, I don't think so. I picked him mostly because of how much he was frisking about in the paddock."

"Oh, my," groaned Hartshire dramatically. "Rad and I and two frisky frolickers! We may not get home until this time tomorrow."

No sooner did Lady Marston leave her chambers, than Davis appeared there once again. Her gaze darted about the room checking for Martha, but the upstairs maid was not to be seen. She closed the door softly behind her and walked directly to the pretty little jewelry box that sat on Fleur's chest of drawers. She opened the box and lifted out the stack of cards. Moving to stand before the windows, she sorted through them, one after the other. Is this all? she thought. What is there here to put such a puzzled look on her lady-ship's face? She paused when she reached Hartshire's card and read the message he'd scribbled on it. Nothing in that. He'd sent roses. Yes, she remembered. Her ladyship had been most surprised and pleased he had done so. She'd spoken to Davis about them the very day they'd arrived.

Beneath Hartshire's card was a handwritten note on plain paper. Odd, Davis thought. Gentlemen put their calling cards with the posies they send, not pieces of note paper. She scanned the message on this one as well and smiled a quiet smile when she reached the signature. "Montague," she whispered. "That's the name he gave her in the garden. He doesn't have any calling cards that say Montague on them? He was always thorough, The Spectre. Never one to ignore little things like that. Not when lives might be at stake."

He doesn't realize lives are at stake here, she thought. No one has summoned him up from the country to look into things then. All is just as it seems to be with him. He loves this lady and means to help her gain a footing in the ton and nothing more.

Then Davis peered down at the note on the very bottom of the stack. Her green eyes blinked in disbelief. Her mind spun. What day? What day was it she had stepped into this room, pulled back the curtains and discovered the first set of windows unlatched? It was the very day that Lady Marston had ridden astride in Hyde Park. The very morning of that very day! "I'll be deviled," Davis murmured. "It was him! Here I've been hiding behind that blessed tree every night since, and it was The Spectre broke into this house, no one else!"

Davis gathered the cards and notes together and replaced them in the jewelry box. Well, at least I shan't have to spend any more time looking out for our housebreaker, she thought with a relieved grin. What a magician he is, that one. Slips in and out, here and there, thither and yon without so much as an eye blinking to see him pass and not so much as a sound to wake her ladyship from slumber. Well, he couldn't have awakened her. She would never have allowed him access to her bedchamber had he waked her. Thrown him right out the window with her own hands, I should think, before she even realized who he was.

"Perhaps not tossed him from the window," Davis conceded, "but she would have raised the alarm and instantly, too. No matter whether she imagines she loves the man. She's a grown woman, not some green girl fresh from the country. Love him or not, she would have called out loudly had she discovered him entering through her bedchamber window."

Which thought filled Davis again with admiration for Hartshire. He was the perfect spy, The Spectre. All the tales she had heard of him since first they'd come across one another had been as true as true could be. "But he doesn't know," she whispered as she turned to leave the room. "He hasn't the least idea what is going forward in this house. It is merely coincidence that he appears here and now, just as I thought, and his lacking cards with Montague written on them is proof of it, too." For some reason, that thought made Davis feel a good deal better.

* * *

Late that afternoon, just as it came on to six o'clock, dark clouds rolled in from the west and a stiff breeze began to blow through the backstreets and the alleyways of London. By eight, the fog, which had struggled to flutter across the city for hours, had been sheared and tattered. By ten, torrents of rain had come and washed what remained of the fog away.

"Not a fit night out for man nor beast, my lord," observed Robes, pulling the curtain aside to glance down into the square just as the clock was striking eleven. "Looks to have settled in for the night. It will likely not end until well into tomorrow morning."

"Nevertheless, I must go out in it, Robes. If I'm lucky, I will discover precisely what we need to know about Dashfield's connection with Spence and his boys. Won't know who his contact is in Marston House, though. Note instructed that particular person not to come. I'm hoping beyond all measure that Davis is not what we think her to be, Robes. Lady Marston is partial to Davis. You can see that without so much as asking. However, a good deal of what we know so far does point to Davis. Mr. Little did tell you about Davis, eh? I mean, about introducing you to her on Saturday afternoon?"

"Yes, my lord."

"You don't mind, Robes?"

"Oh, no, my lord. I am pleased to do it."

"And you'll be very careful."

"Extremely careful. That I will."

"Because you don't have to do it, Robes. I don't demand it of you. I am quite satisfied, you know, to have you remain merely my valet. Truly, I am, Robes."

"I have been thinking on it since our night at The Swan, my lord," Robes offered, crossing to where Hartshire sat and helping him to tug off his boots. "And I do remember all the trouble you took to save Mr. Little and me from that dastardly Despard. Why, that villain might have got us hanged had you not stepped in and explained to us what the man truly intended."

"Yes, well, but I was very late at doing it or your names would not have been mentioned in connection with the dastard. Ever. You were both so useful to him, working in the royal household as you did. You provided him with all the little tidbits he wished to know."

"Indeed we did," Robes said, nodding sadly. "Indeed we did."

"Yes, which was why I was so certain that you and Little were dedicated to his cause. I vow, Robes, if you hadn't confided in me how Despard intended to foil The Spectre's plot against King George and how you and Little were bound to help him do it, I would have gone right on believing you both to be true members of his band of cutthroats. I ought to have done better by you, Robes. By you and Little both."

"Still, my lord, if you had not promised the King, on your honor, to make us disappear, we might well be in the colonies now, doing gawd knows what. King George was that angry."

"Wished to hang the two of you, Robes. Didn't care in the least that you had been tricked into the thing. Wished to hang you regardless. That's how angry he was."

Robes inhaled raggedly as he crossed to the side of the armoire and knelt down to open a rather large chest. "You did never tell us that. I am thankful you didn't tell us that, my lord. I would have died on the spot."

"Well, but Robes, to discover that two of his ushers—two lowly servants who did nothing but serve his servants—had actually managed to learn enough about his doings to provide useful information to a man who planned to assassinate him made him extremely uneasy. He could not think whether the two of you were that adept at gathering information or his servants were that openmouthed about his private life."

"We were that good at gathering information," said Robes with a bit of pride.

"Yes. I know. And I told His Majesty so, too. And I did

explain the mixup, but he wouldn't have you around any longer and—and—"

"And what, my lord?"

"And I would have you around, Robes. I wished to have you around. So I made it possible for you and Mr. Little to disappear without actually leaving London at all. Still, you needn't get back into the business of collecting information if you'd rather not. Because I've been thinking about it all day, and I *do* know this Davis woman from somewhere. I have seen those darting green eyes and that carroty hair before. As much as I hope for Lady Marston's sake that Davis is not a radical, she may very well be. She used to work for Lady Dashfield, Robes. Lady Marston told me as much this very morning. And Lady Dashfield, if you recall, is presently dead."

From where Hartshire stood, Robes looked as if the sea chest were in the process of swallowing him whole. The valet halted in the midst of digging, brought his top half from out the trunk and gazed over his shoulder at his lordship. "Davis is familiar to you? Then most certainly I will go to be introduced to her on Saturday afternoon. And I will discover all there is to be known of her before I'm done. I must. I do not like to think of Mr. Wickens in danger, my lord, but most certainly any threat to Lady Marston must be prevented."

"Any threat to her must be thwarted at the instant we discover it, Robes. Those will do," Hartshire added, as Robes tossed a pair of old buckskin breeches onto the floor and dived back into the chest.

"I wish you weren't going," sighed the valet, his voice echoing strangely. "Not tonight. I have got the most uneasy feeling about tonight, my lord."

"Well, but I can hardly not go, Robes. If I'm to discover what all the fuss is about, I can't do it by spending this particular Thursday night at home."

"But it's such a dreadful night, my lord," the valet's voice echoed back at him from inside the chest. "I cannot find it."

"What?"

"That filthy old shirt. I stuffed it in here and now I cannot find it. Oh, here it is. On the very bottom under your boots, of all things! Well, but that's all the better. Now it looks as if you've slept in it for nights on end."

"Toss it to me. And the catskin vest."

By the time Hartshire was dressed he looked a good deal more like a thief or a pickpocket than an earl.

"Devil it, Robes," he muttered. "I look the part and smell the part, too. I do hope I don't expire from the odor. These things have grown positively rank. Gawd, the rest of my clothes don't smell like this, do they?"

"No, my lord. That's why we keep these clothes in the sea chest and the rest of your things elsewhere."

"Of course. I know that. My mind is off in some distant place, I expect. Cannot think why I should even ask such a foolish question."

Hartshire, with Robes's help, pulled on his scuffed, down-at-heel boots, placed a raggedy cap on his head and paused a moment to listen to the thunder explode. "Hit something that time, the lightning did," he murmured. "Close."

Robes nodded. "You'll be careful, my lord? It is not only your Spencean Philanthropists I mean you to be careful of, but the night and the very storm itself."

"Have you gone completely mad?" growled Marston softly. "No, you cannot. Certainly not."

"But Malcolm," Ally protested, as the two stood before the hearth in the front parlor.

"Do not 'but Malcolm' me, little sister. You will stay right here *inside* this establishment where you belong. Of all things, wishing to dress like a boy and wander about London at night and in the midst of a storm, too."

"I am not frightened of London or storms," pouted Althea so alluringly that had Conningford been present to see those lips pursed just so, his ears would have turned a brilliant scarlet and he would have begun to stutter on the spot. Her perfectly delicious pout, however, had not the least effect on her brother.

"If you are truly not frightened, Ally, that only goes to prove what an innocent you are."

"I am not an innocent. You and Val would be right with me. I would be quite safe."

"You *are* an innocent if you think that, Ally. What if we should be attacked by thieves and they take us down? We could neither of us protect you then. It ain't a *bad* thing to be innocent," he added as his sister frowned. "There's a great deal to be said for innocence. You ought not make such a face as that because I call you so. At any rate, you ain't accompanying us so give it up and go to bed. Mama has already retired and I'm off in a moment or two. It will take Connie and me a bit of time to shed our respectable clothes and don the others. Ain't easy changing gear in a dark, cold, smelly stable. Not fun, either. Lucky thing we are accustomed to doing it or there's no telling what we would look like once we reemerged."

"Have neither one of you heard of a lantern?" Althea asked.

"Of course we have, but to light a lantern would signal to the grooms that we're there, Ally. They sleep above the stables at Conningford's. We've got to dress in the dark and be astoundingly quiet about it, too. Once all Connie did was drop one of his spurs and three grooms came galloping down from the loft on the instant to see what was going on."

"And what did you tell them?"

"Nothing. Hid. Waited and held our breath until we were certain they'd departed." Marston placed a hand on each of his sister's shoulders and gazed caringly into her eyes. "Please don't pout, Ally," he said softly. "I know you're brave, and likely you could do it, just as you say, but I could not bear it if I allowed you to place yourself in danger and something happened to you. And Connie would be devastated. Mama is right about that. Connie is completely besotted with you."

Althea hung her head. "But there must be something I can do," she whispered.

"There is," Marston replied, giving her a supportive hug. "I have just thought of it."

"What?"

"Well, there is someone in this house who receives these messages, no? But why? Why is that person in this house? I mean, it ain't as though this house is staffed by old family retainers. I only just hired them all. There's not one servant here who ever worked here before. So whoever it is took a position here for a purpose."

"Perhaps it has something to do with Papa."

"I don't know. It would make sense, the two canes and passing messages back and forth if Papa were still alive and he and Dashfield doing it. It would even make sense to have a servant know of it and able to help them. I wouldn't put it past Papa to be involved in something evil and nefarious. But he's been dead for more than a year. No, some one of the servants insinuated himself or herself into this house for a specific reason. And since we know Dashfield is involved in it, then it would make sense that it's either Davis or Wickens. They both worked in the Dashfield household. But then, would Dashfield be so obvious about it? Sending someone from his own household into ours? Perhaps it's someone we've not even considered. Of course none of that truly matters—The real question is why. Why is the person here at all?"

Ally nodded. "It is puzzling now that you mention it. I have not once thought about it."

"No, and neither has anyone else. I don't expect even Hartshire has given it the least consideration. But it is certainly something that ought to be considered, and something you could do that would help us enormously." He gave her another hug and a peck on the cheek. "I'm counting on you, m'dear, to figure it out," he said, as he left her. "If anyone can do it, Ally, you're the one."

Althea slumped down into the chair before the hearth and stared into the small coal fire flickering there. "It's nothing but a hum," she muttered. "Something Mal thought up on the spur of the moment just to make me feel better. Men! They think they are the only ones able to succeed at anything the least bit exciting. All we women are allowed to do is to play the pianoforte, paint pictures and simper up at males from time to time with flirty eyes. I'm amazed Mal has given me permission to think."

"I should not be amazed at that. You've a marvelous mind," came a voice from the opposite side of the pocket doors that separated the front parlor from the library beyond. "A much better mind than Malcolm's, as a matter of fact."

"Mama?" Ally jumped up from her chair as Fleur slid the pocket doors farther apart and stepped into the room.

"My, but you do look guilty," Fleur observed. "What a shame that Malcolm can't be here to look guilty with you. I was merely searching about for something to read when quite out of nowhere your voices came filtering in to me."

"Mama, you listened at the door!"

"Indeed I did. Shameful of me, but I could not resist. And he was perfectly correct, you know. There is no earthly reason why you should be allowed to dress up like a boy and accompany him and Lord Conningford anywhere. Ever."

"But you don't in the least understand, Mama."

"No, and I'm particularly upset with myself because I don't. Obviously something sinister has been swirling through the air all around me and I have not so much as caught a hint of it. Where has my mind been to miss it all?"

"You've been concerned with any number of things, Mama. And besides, we've been attempting to keep this secret from you. Even Lord Hartshire would not have you involved in it."

"Lord Hartshire is involved as well?"

"Oh, yes, Mama. He is the most amazing gentleman!"

"So I have come to believe. But I begin to believe as well, that he is more amazing than any of us know. Be kind enough, Ally, to accompany me to my bedchamber where we will not be overheard, accidentally or otherwise. I wish to know all that's going on, and you're going to tell me. Then, we will both put our minds to it and see can we not come up with some way other than traipsing off into the night dressed as lads to deal with the situation."

Hartshire, all six foot five, two hundred and fifty pounds of him, was fairly blown into The Cock by a great gust of wind. Soaked to the skin, his cap limp and soggy, his dark curls pasted to his forehead, he tumbled through the door and stumbled his way to a chair at the table farthest from the glare of the fire. There he slumped down with his elbows on the table and his chin resting on his fists. "A pint o' ale and a wee bit o' the gin, m'dearie," he told the barmaid who appeared before him, clinking a small stack of coins down on the table. " 'Tis a miserable night. I does find m'self in need of a bit o' warmin'."

"Ought ta sit ye closer ta the fire," suggested the buxom barmaid. "There ain't but a few o' the lads 'ere tanight, an' they be in a mood ta welcome strangers."

"Naw. It ain't me outsides does require warmin' but m'insides. Be a good girl an' fetch me m'pint an' m'gin. I be fine right here, I do."

From the shadows Hartshire studied The Cock's patrons surreptitiously. His gaze never lingered on one or another of them for more than two seconds at a time for fear of attracting attention to himself. Ain't a one of them the least bit familiar to me, he thought. Spence himself ain't here, thank God. I doubt Thomas Spence would overlook my face even after all these years. Must be a doddering old gent by now,

Thomas Spence. Unlikely he'll make an appearance. Well, but there's no telling. Best to hang back here and keep silent. It's early hours yet.

It was a good quarter hour before the door to The Cock opened again. This time the storm blew in a man Hartshire did recognize. Alfred Plummer? Hartshire's eyes widened in disbelief as the man sloshed his way to a place close to the hearth and slouched down around a table already occupied by two other men. He greeted them with considerable familiarity, then doffed his hat, shaking rainwater onto the dirty floor.

Hartshire moved uneasily in his chair. He lowered his gaze then raised it again, afraid to stare boldly at the man but unable not to do it. Devil it, Hartshire thought. Devil it, it can't be him! Plummer's dead. Been dead for five years. Hartshire tilted his chair back against the wall, planted his boot heels on the table top and took a long drink of his ale. The brim of his cap sagged low on his brow as he peered again, over the rim of his pint, at that table near the fire.

Not dead, Hartshire thought. Alfred Plummer's not dead. His mind reeled at the thought of it. If I had a pistol with me, I'd shoot that blackguard through the heart right now, right where he sits. Damnation!

Hartshire had made only one official trip to London since he'd married Miriam. That trip had occurred five years ago and Alfred Plummer had been the cause of it. Alfred Plummer, who'd not once threatened the Crown, not once spoken against the government or the King or any of the royal family, but whose very existence had caused the briefly recovered George III to summon Hartshire before him and demand that The Spectre turn his considerable talents to capturing the vile monster who had broken into the house of Viscount Armington and slaughtered that man, his wife, child and three servants with a hammer. From there, the fiend had broken into three more homes in that same square and murdered all he found asleep within. In that one night, Alfred

Plummer had slaughtered twenty-two people—men, women and children, peers and servants alike. But Alfred Plummer had burned to death in the fire that had taken Drury Lane to the ground that cold February night. Hartshire and the little band of Bow Street Runners who had gone inside after the man had barely escaped with their own lives. Surely the monster had died in the blaze. There had not been sight or sound of him since. And yet, just as surely, here he sat before the hearth in The Cock.

Hartshire sat struggling silently to keep from walking over there and strangling the man with his own two hands. He downed one pint after another and watched his stack of coins diminish as his presence slowly faded into the rear of everyone's mind but the barmaid's. A few more men entered The Cock within that hour but not one of them did more than spare the men before the hearth or The Spectre a passing glance. Only Plummer, as the barmaid delivered him a second pint, thought to ask about the stranger slouched at the far table.

"Aye, he don't be one o' the reg'lars, but he done been sittin' in that there corner ferever, Lovey," Lulu answered with a sweet smile. "Come atrippin' in 'ere hours ago. Ain't set on botherin' nobody, he ain't. Just a drinkin' of 'is troubles away. Be workin' on his fifth pint, he be. Like as not he'll be passin' out afore long an' Ollie'll be forced ta prod 'im out inta the street when we closes up."

As if in confirmation of this, Hartshire slumped even lower in his seat as the tavern door opened once again. He scowled as two more men blew in on the wind. He muttered under his breath behind his tankard. "Take a horsewhip to the both of 'em!"

I told Val in no uncertain terms that he was to leave off dogging about after these people, he thought, frowning. And I made that perfectly clear to Marston as well. How the deuce did they discover where and when this bit of a gathering was to be held? I didn't tell them. He watched them very closely

as they seated themselves at a table near the three men gathered before the fire and sent Lulu off to fetch them drinks.
A spark of pride lit Hartshire's eyes. They look exceeding
fine, he thought, forgetting his anger for a moment. Even I
wouldn't guess them to be gentlemen, did I not know it for
a fact. Look like they came straight off the docks.

With their backs to the one man they'd recognized from
other meetings—the man Hartshire knew as Alfred Plummer
and they as Sterling—Conningford and Marston began what
might pass anywhere for a drunken conversation between
themselves. Their voices rose; their voices lowered; they
mumbled and muttered; and when Lulu brought them tankards, they set to work downing the ale with great enthusiasm.
Hartshire scanned the faces of the men at the table behind
the lads, read in them at first a certain cautiousness, then
curiosity, then acceptance. None of them appeared inclined
to consider the two thoroughly drunken young men a threat.
Then Dashfield entered The Cock and the game began in
earnest.

"Think hard, Mama. There must be some place in this
house that Papa could have hidden something away. Somewhere safe where no one would think to look for it."

Fleur sat on the window seat in her bedchamber and stared
out at the storm. "There are any number of places he might
have hidden things, Ally. It would help a great deal if we
had some idea of what we were looking for. Is it something
of great value? Is it large or small?"

"I don't know. We don't even know if there is anything.
We are merely guessing that there is."

"Guessing correctly, I think. There must be something,"
Fleur replied, allowing the curtain to close over the darkness,
the rain, the lightning and thunder. "If all you've told me is
true, then there must be a particular reason for this spy of
Lord Dashfield's to reside at Marston House. And the most

logical conclusion is that he's come to find something that your father hid away. Something that was in his possession when he died. Something Lord Dashfield, at least, knew him to have and now means to have for himself. We are assuming that Lord Dashfield is well aware that he carries the messages in his cane, are we not? We're assuming he isn't some innocent dupe."

"Not an innocent dupe, Mama. He knows. He went out of his way to see that Malcolm remembered Papa's cane and got it back without the least trouble and then he strolled in here as bold as you please and deposited a matching cane in our stand."

"Your father and Lord Dashfield were involved in something despicable together then."

"Do you think so, Mama?"

"Oh, yes. I cannot think that twin canes came into being on the spur of the moment. Likely he and Lord Dashfield passed messages back and forth to each other that way for quite a while. Only think, Ally, how easy it would be. They both go to White's for instance, set their canes aside, and when they leave, each of them picks up the other's cane. *Voilà!* Whatever the message, it is passed on, one to the other, without so much as a word splitting the air between them."

"Yes, I see it now. It would prove most convenient, especially if they didn't wish anyone to know that they were more than nodding acquaintances."

"Just so. And if this thing your papa has hidden away is something small but was truly valuable to him, I know where it will be, Ally."

"You do?"

"Um-hmmm." Fleur rose from the window seat and began to pace the floor. "Is that not the nicest little bed?" she asked, smiling at Ally, who had settled down upon it while they were pondering together.

"Yes, Mama, but we are discussing—"

"I know perfectly well what we're discussing. I haven't

grown so old that my thoughts disappear from my mind once they've spilled out into the conversation. I am merely wondering, Ally, whether we ought to go and discover this mysterious thing your papa has hidden away ourselves or wait until the gentlemen can come with us."

"Mama!"

"Well, I know you wish us to do it all on our own and boast of it to Malcolm and Lord Conningford, but the more I learn of Lord Hartshire, the more I think it would be best to wait until he's here with us before we go after it. If anything should happen to us, Ally—"

"Happen to us? What could happen to us? Is it not in this house, Mama, the hiding place you're thinking of?"

"Oh, yes. In this house. But so is the person who seeks it. And we have not the least idea who it may be. We might be followed and attacked and the prize taken from us, Ally. Did not you say that Lord Hartshire warned you this person who has come to work for us under false colors might prove dangerous?"

Althea thought for a moment, considering. "I will tell you precisely what I think, Mama," she said at last. "Even though we believe the note told him not to do it, I think whoever it is has sneaked out of this house and gone off to this meeting tonight—The very meeting that Malcolm and Val have gone to."

"Oh, no!"

"Oh no what, Mama?"

"Ally, think. Whoever it is will see them there and know we're privy to their secrets."

"No," Althea said after some consideration. "I expect Lord Dashfield will be there as well, but Malcolm and Val will be in disguise, both of them, so it won't matter."

"And they will be wearing masks?" asked Fleur with merely a twinge of sarcasm.

"No, but you know how it is, Mama. When you meet someone you don't expect to meet in a place they don't belong, even though they're not disguised, you don't truly recognize them until they say something to you. And from what Malcolm and Val say, their disguises make them look precisely like they belong in a place like The Cock in Soho. And I *know* Malcolm and Val will not let on who they truly are. Not for the world."

"Well, then," sighed Fleur, "I expect we had best go and fetch whatever it is your father's hidden away and see for ourselves why someone would consider it so valuable that they'd risk taking a position here under false pretenses to find it."

Everything would have gone quite nicely at The Cock if Marston had not gasped at precisely the point he had.

"Still ain't found nothing," Dashfield had said quietly to the three men gathered around him near the hearth.

"Ye called me 'ere ta tell me that?" the man Hartshire knew as Plummer had grumbled.

"No, I called you here to tell you that Lady Marston has taken up residence at Marston House for the Season."

"Oooo, I am shudderin' in m'boots, I am," Plummer had sneered. "Lookit me, Donny. I'm ashakin' an' ashudderin'."

"You ought to be," Dashfield had hissed, "because she ain't the timid, cringing little know-nothing Marston led us to believe. She's a bright one and brave as she can stare. Does she come upon papers referring to you, Sterling, which include your new name and direction, I remind you, she'll run straight to Bow Street with them and you'll be seized within the hour. She knows you by your real name. She was not in London when you did the deed, but she read about it in the newspapers and she remembers your name as clear as anything. I know. We held a brief conversation about you, she and I, the other afternoon. There's not many were old enough to read the papers who don't remember your name to this very day."

"If she's smart like you say, she'll attempt ta blackmail us, just like that husband o' hers."

"No, she won't," Dashfield had replied. "Not her. She'll turn you in as quick as quick can. And that'll not only put an end to you, my dear fellow, but it'll put an end to a number of us as well. Marston boasted he'd a list of names and proof of who it was saved you and harbored you for the past five years. There's a number of Thomas Spence's followers among them, myself included. Does she discover those papers before Charlie does, you're a dead man, old chap, and the rest of us one step closer to the gallows."

"Well, I'll jist kill 'er then," Plummer had grumbled. "Won't waste no time arrangin' no proper accident like fer Marston. No, nor attempt ta make it look like she done it 'erself either. I'll jist take me over there tanight an' bash 'er head in with my little hammer. Aye, an' ever'one else's head what 'appens ta be there as well, 'cept Charlie's."

And right at that point Marston, who had his back to the lot of them and had been pretending to be listening to the drunken mutterings of Conningford, had gasped.

"What the devil!" exclaimed one of the men, rising from his seat. He was tall and lean with cool grey eyes and hair the color of muddy river water, and as he rose, a knife seemingly leaped into his hand. He was across the table and seizing Marston's collar before either Marston or Conningford had time to move.

"They bein't drunk! They was alistenin'!" thundered Plummer, sending his chair flying halfway across the room as he gained his feet and grabbed for Conningford.

Every other man in the public house looked up. "A brawl!" several of them shouted enthusiastically.

"B'thunder it be a bit o' a waltz like!" cried a deep voice. This was accompanied instantly by the table in the far corner crashing to the floor and a large body soaring through the air at Dashfield, Plummer and the other two. "I'll 'ave me a bit o' that," exclaimed Hartshire, delivering the man with the knife an upper cut likely to kill a cow and sending him bouncing back over the table from whence he'd come. "An' a slice 'er this, too," Hartshire continued, lifting Plummer straight up into the air and tossing him in the wake of the other villain.

In that moment every man in the tavern joined in the mad dance that consisted of a fist thrown here, a chair clumping down across someone's shoulders there. In and out, over and under the chairs and tables of The Cock, everyone who was sober enough to stand took advantage of the God-given opportunity to vent their frustration. Hartshire laughed like a drunken madman and sang a bit of a ditty here and a bit of a ditty there as bone crunched against bone and tankards flew at unprotected heads. Conningford grabbed a chair leg, took aim and bounced the thing off Dashfield's skull, sending him senseless to the floor. Lulu screeched and scurried to save what glasses and tankards she could from destruction while the barman stood with a stout club in hand before his shelves, determined to defend his crockery and his bottles and kegs to the last. Marston landed a glancing blow to one fellow's jaw and followed that with three swift jabs to the chap's stomach. In an attempt to get back to Plummer and drag that particular villain out into the street and all the way to Bow Street and the Runners, Hartshire broke at least two noses and tossed four flailing bodies aside. But he tripped over the unmoving Dashfield on the floor, and though he rose hastily, Plummer was already on the run, disappearing out the door and into the street.

Conningford turned with fists at the ready as a heavy hand caught at his shoulder. "Val, go!" hissed Hartshire. "Follow that man who just dodged out of here. Don't let him out of your sight!"

"Atticus?" Conningford asked, astonished.

"Go! Go, Val! Don't let him get away from you! Yell for the Charlies if you must, but get him!"

And then Hartshire dived back into the midst of the brawl

and dragged a puffing, furious Marston out by the arm and shoved that gentleman ahead of him out the door. Conningford disappeared around a corner into an alley just as Marston and Hartshire reached the street. "Go home, Marston," Hartshire yelled as he turned on his heel and started after Val. "Go home at once!" his voice roared over the thunder. "He'll kill her! That blasted madman will kill Fleur as soon as he can reach Cavendish Square if Val and I cannot catch him! Go home to her now!"

Fifteen

Fleur led Althea behind the butler's pantry into what decades of Marstons had grandly called 'the wine cellar' though it was little more than a small room in which five racks capable of holding, at best, twenty bottles of wine apiece, stood. With lamp in hand she made her way to the rear of the last rack and began to count her way through the bottles.

"A bottle?" Althea queried in disbelief. "Papa kept his secret things in a bottle?"

"No," Fleur replied with a grin. "He didn't keep *them* in a bottle. Come to think of it, I doubt your father ever told Malcolm about the safe. I had best do so. No telling but that Malcolm will wish to make use of it someday. Had your papa's will not been kept safely at his solicitor's, I would have remembered at once about the safe. We would have been forced to go looking in it for the will then. But since we had no need—ah, here it is." Fleur slipped a bottle of port from the rack and handed it to Althea. "Your father was not fond of port. I expect that's why he always used a port bottle. We shall need to take it to the kitchen, Ally, draw the cork, and pour out the wine."

"Pour out the wine?"

"Uh-hmmm. Thank goodness it's so very late and all the servants abed. Especially Wickens and Cook. They would have an apoplexy to see us pouring perfectly good wine out into the sink. Did you note the time, Ally? Surely Malcolm must come home soon."

"It was near a half past one, Mama, when we left your chamber."

"Was it? As late as that? Great heavens, this is certainly not a night meant for sleeping, is it? Why must the gentlemen always do things so late in the evening? We shall likely be awake until dawn waiting for your brother to return home. Nevertheless, we will have something, at least, to keep us occupied."

They left the wine cellar, closing the door tightly behind them, and carried the bottle to one of the kitchen sinks. Ally drew the cork, inexpertly, bit by crumbling bit, and then poured the wine from the bottle. It came galunking out in great gulps accompanied at the last by a brass key.

"That's what we're looking for, Ally. We'll clean it up and dry it off and open the safe."

"What safe? Where is it?"

"Under the servants' staircase."

Ally's jaw dropped.

"I never understood it either," chuckled Fleur. "Seemed a perfectly senseless place to put a safe to me, but nevertheless, that's where it lies. Bring the lamp. We'll need it."

Fleur crossed the kitchen to the green baize door behind which stood the servants' staircase. She walked to the little closet beneath the stairs, opened the door and stepped inside pushing her way through oilskin coats, tromping over gardeners' boots and outdoor shoes, to the very back. There, she loosed a piece of paneling and set it on the floor.

"Hold the lamp a bit higher, Ally. I cannot see the keyhole properly. Yes, much better." Fleur inserted the key into the safe, turned it and pulled open the heavy metal door. She reached inside and pulled out a jewelry case. Reached inside again, and this time brought out a carved wooden box, its top inlaid with ivory and onyx squares. Both of these she handed to Ally. "Can you manage them and the lamp?" she asked.

"Yes, Mama."

"Good, because there are any number of loose papers in here as well and one more rather large box." Fleur placed the last of the safe's contents on the closet floor, closed the safe door and replaced the section of paneling. Then she took her share of the load and she and Althea struggled though the hanging slickers and over the boots and shoes back out into the hallway.

"Oh!" gasped Ally, almost dropping all she carried as she walked straight into a solid form.

"What?" Fleur asked, stumbling into Ally's back.

"I do beg your pardon, miss, madam," droned Wickens in a positively sepulchral voice as he reached out to steady Ally. "Is there something I can do to be of assistance?"

Amidst crackling lightning and great booms of thunder they darted down the alley, Plummer far ahead, Conningford next, and Hartshire gaining on the both of them. Rain blown by the wind hissed straight into their faces, blinding them for five or ten seconds at a time. Their boots slipped, slid, skidded across the cobbles, threatening to send them plummeting to the pavement.

"Right!" roared Hartshire over the thunder. "He turned to the right, Val!"

Conningford reached the corner and skidded around it to the right, his heels trowled grooves through the rainwater, the soles of his boots flew out from under him, he leaned forward, pinwheeling his arms in an attempt keep his balance and then thwacked down, cracking his chin mightily against the paving stones.

Hartshire, rounding the corner just as Conningford fell, gazed up the alleyway they'd entered hoping for a glimpse of Plummer. He could see the running man nowhere.

"Blast!" he shouted, kneeling down beside his brother-in-law. "Val? Val?"

Conningford rolled over and gazed up at him. Blood mixed with water flowed down the young man's chin. "I'm fine, Atticus," he gasped breathlessly as the rain assaulted him. "Go on. Catch him. I'm fine."

"Can't catch him, Val. Lost him. Gone to ground in one of these warehouses I should think. Can you sit up, m'lad?"

"Of course I can. I ain't a cripple. Ow! Ouch!"

"Not yet, you're not," murmured Hartshire. "Easy does it, Val. You don't want to fall back down."

"I ain't going to fall back down, Atticus. I'm just sore is all. Who is it we're chasing? Was it the one called Sterling? Ought we not go to try the doors on those warehouses? Perhaps the one he ducked into don't lock and we'll find him that way."

"Well, at least your jaw's not broken."

"What does that mean?"

"It means you're talking well enough. Lose any teeth did you?"

Conningford paused for a moment, felt around inside his mouth with his tongue and then shook his head. "All there as far as I can tell." And then he spit a bit of blood out into the rushing rainwater in the gutter. "Bit m'lip though. How come it's light here?"

"Because there's a fire burning down the way. Here, put an arm around my shoulder, Val. We'll head down there and get warm a bit."

"But Sterling—Was it Sterling?—The warehouses—"

"Hush. I'm not going in any pitch black warehouses after Alfred Plummer and neither are you. I value life a bit more than that. Besides, Val, it's not at all likely we'd find him. Just as I thought," he added as they approached the fire leaping and sizzling away on the threshold of one of the buildings. "May we join you?" Hartshire asked the four men gathered around it.

"Don't see why not," answered one of them, and then his eyes widened considerably. "Yer Majesty! What ye doin' down 'ere? And in sich weather as this? An' dressed like that."

"Tom Landy," Hartshire nodded. "Fancy meeting you here. This'll be Etram's glue factory, no?"

"Aye, that it be," replied another of the men. "Ye be lookin' fer work though, ye be out o' luck."

"No, not looking for work."

"He do talk funny, don't 'e," observed a third man. "Talks like a reg'lar swell."

"Aye, he do," agreed Tom Landy. "But I knows 'im an' he be all right, this 'un."

"Thank you, Tom," grinned Hartshire, having remembered his appearance only after he'd spoken to the men. "I'm getting old, I think. Little things slip my mind."

"Like the way ye be dressed."

"Just so. You didn't happen to see a man pass by here a few minutes ago, eh? Running like the devil was at his heels?"

"Nope. Didn't seen no one. Does ye be lookin' fer 'im special."

Hartshire nodded.

"He is a—a—" managed Conningford, and then he ceased to speak, puzzled. "You didn't say why I was to chase after him in particular, Atticus."

"Because he's a fiend, Val. A monster."

"What monster?" asked the fourth man with interest.

"Alfred Plummer."

A general muttering welcomed the mention of this name and the four men gathered around the fire began to peer over their shoulders into the alley. "I thought he done burned ta cinders five whole years ago," murmured Tom Landy.

"So did we all, Tom. So did we all, but it ain't the case. He's alive and we chased him this far and then lost him."

"Who's Alfred Plummer?" asked Conningford. "Why does everyone know that name but me?"

"You know it, Val," Hartshire assured him. "You just don't remember as clearly as some of us. You were young then, and just beginning to lark about Town. Probably not paying any attention to the newspapers. Tom, if I leave this fellow with you, can you find a hackney cab, stick him inside and send him home for me?"

"No, Atticus!" Conningford protested.

"Yes, Val. To Hartshire House is where I mean to send you. You must pound on the front door until you wake Little, eh?"

"But, Atticus."

"I can't stand here and argue, Val. For all we know, Plummer has gone out a window and into another street and is even now heading toward Marston House."

"God no!"

"I hope not. I pray not. But I can't take the chance that he isn't, Val. Marston is on his way home as we speak. I'm bound for there now. You must go to Little and say to him that Albert Plummer ain't dead. That I have seen him with my own eyes and that he threatens Lady Marston's life. You will do this for me, won't you, Val?" he asked, taking a number of coins from his pocket and handing them to Landy. "For the hackney cab, Tom, and a few for yourself and your friends, eh? We appreciate your letting us share the warmth of your fire for a bit." And then Hartshire was transferring Val's arm to Tom Landy's shoulder. "He's a bit dizzy I expect, Tom. Gave his chin a solid whack. Likely as not broke a bone or two, though he don't feel it yet. Be careful with him, will you?" And then Hartshire was off, not running, but walking with deadly determination through the remainder of the alley and out into the adjoining street where he stopped to peer about him, squinting through the rain. Then he nodded and loped off to his left as lightning split the skies above him and the thunder roared.

* * *

"I do beg your pardon, madam," said Wickens again, gazing at the abruptly pale faces before him in the lamplight. "I was on the stairs and heard noises, so I came to see who it could be. Is there some way in which I may be of assistance?"

"No. No thank you, Wickens," Fleur replied on a long, drawn-out breath. "Oh, but you frightened me to death. I had no idea you were still up and about."

"I am waiting up for the master, my lady."

"You are? Well, I expect you might help us a bit then, Wickens, now I think on it. Perhaps you could carry some of these things into the library for us. If you will take these three boxes, Miss Avondale and I will manage what's left."

"Yes, my lady," the butler responded with a bow. "I shall be pleased to do it."

Davis watched in silence from the firstfloor landing as the three of them exited through the green baize door. When she was certain they had had time enough to move through the kitchen and into the main corridor, she came softly down the stairs and stepped into the kitchen herself. This she crossed as quietly as any human being possibly could, peeked around the door frame into the corridor, discovered no one in sight and made her way along it, past the library and into the front parlor. Carefully she parted the pocket doors the space of a cat's whisker and stood behind them, listening.

"You're quite certain there is nothing more I can do, madam?" Wickens asked. "I do not mind at all to remain if you think you might require my assistance."

"No, we're perfectly all right now, Wickens. Thank you. You may go," responded Fleur. "I am quite certain Lord Marston will wish to go through these things later, so we'll not return them to the back of the closet tonight."

"Just so, madam. Good evening to you then."

Althea, without the least subtlety, followed Wickens out

into the corridor where he made as if to go toward the front staircase, then, noticing her on the library threshold, turned about and walked off in the opposite direction where he disappeared into the kitchen. "Curious old cat," Ally giggled, as she went to join Fleur at the library table. "I vow, he was thinking to sneak into the front parlor and spy on us from beyond the pocket doors."

"Ally, for shame. Wickens has never given us the least reason to suspect him of any such failings."

"No, that's true. But didn't you notice, Mama, the glint in his eyes as he set these boxes on the table for us?"

"I took more notice of how large he truly is. Noticed it directly when we stepped out of that closet and into him."

"Oh, I did too! I have never thought of Wickens as particularly large, but he did give me such a start, and I did take immediate note of how much taller and stronger than me he appeared to be. Of course, that's nothing at all, because almost everyone is taller than me and all the men, I should think, are stronger. Oh, Mama, look!" Althea ceased her chattering as Fleur opened the jewelry case. "Are they all Papa's?"

"They were. Now they belong to Malcolm. I cannot think how I came to forget about them," mused Fleur, lifting a number of jeweled stickpins, a silver snuff box, and a set of matching diamond studs from the case and setting them out on the table. "Now, this is yours," she said. "How does it come to be in here? Never mind. It was mine when I was a young lady and you are to have it." She held up a gold locket with a tiny diamond embedded in the center of it for Althea's inspection. Then she opened it and smiled and showed it to Ally.

"Oh, Mama, a miniature!"

"Very miniature," Fleur agreed. "It's a painting of my mother. She would have loved you. I know it. Take it, dearest. It will bring you good fortune."

"It didn't bring you very good fortune. You married Papa,"

mumbled Althea, accepting the locket on its delicate filigree chain.

"That only happened after I took it off. Though I don't remember ever having given it to your papa. Well, never mind. I must have done. To keep it safe, I expect. Now, whatever did he keep in here?" Fleur lifted the lid on the carved wooden box. "I have never so much as seen this box before. Of all things!" she exclaimed, taking a small, leather-bound book into her hands and opening it. "It's a diary, Althea. I never once imagined that your father kept a diary, did you?"

"Never," Althea replied, fastening the locket around her neck as she gazed at the book her mama held. "Did Papa always write in as fine a hand as that?"

"No," murmured Fleur, beginning to flip hastily through the pages. "No, he didn't. This is not your father's at all. It's written by a woman. Perhaps it's your mother's, Althea. Yes, see here, she signs it. Lila. This is yours as well."

"I don't wish to have it, thank you."

"Althea."

"I don't wish to have anything of hers."

"You will put it away somewhere then. Perhaps there'll come a time when you'll be glad to have it, to learn more about her. Perhaps the excuse for her behavior toward you and Malcolm can be found in these pages. Take it, do, my dear. Someday, you will want to know what she was like. I know you will. Not today or tomorrow, perhaps, but someday."

Althea took the diary reluctantly and stared down at its open pages. Then she blinked in disbelief. "Mama?"

"What dearest?" asked Fleur in the midst of opening the largest of the boxes.

"It's not signed Lila, Mama. It's signed Lydia."

"No." Fleur peered at the signature over Althea's shoulder. "Such a scribble! But I am almost positive it is—L-i-l—"

"No, Mama, not L-i-l, but L-y-d. See here where the ink has splotched. It is L-y-d-i-a."

"Lydia?" said Fleur in puzzlement. "Why would your father have a diary belonging to some woman named Lydia? Perhaps it's your grandmother's then."

"My grandmother on Papa's side was named Henrietta and on my mother's side, Prudence."

"Oh." Fleur's cheeks reddened considerably and she held out her hand to take the diary back from Ally.

"You know whose it is!" Ally exclaimed, reading the thoughts apparent on Fleur's face.

"No. I only think—I mean—Well, it could belong, Ally, to your papa's—mistress."

"Mistress? Papa had a mistress on top of everything else?"

"Well, I don't know that to be a fact, but, it does seem the most likely thing. Though why he should have his mistress's diary I cannot think. Unless it's filled with love letters to him or somesuch. Give it to me, Ally. I will put it away again."

The largest of the boxes contained a ledger for the very year that the elder Marston had died, a map of the City of London with a number of circles inked in upon it, and one ruby earbob. Fleur set the box aside and began to look through the loose papers.

"Whatever it is they want, Mama, it must be among those papers because there's nothing else here of any importance. Give me some of them. Perhaps if we read them carefully . . ."

Fleur divided the pile in half and they both sat down at the library table and began to read.

"It must be here," Althea murmured again. "Certainly whoever this villain is cannot have come to abide with us in search of a mistress's diary or an old ledger or one ruby earbob."

"No, I don't think so either," Fleur replied, studying the second of the papers she had taken to read. "We must hope the answer lies somewhere in one of these piles."

* * *

Marston sat, soggy and scowling, in a hackney cab as it trundled along the slick cobbles in the direction of Cavendish Square. He had the greatest urge to poke his head up through the hatch and insist that the driver urge the horse to a faster pace, but he knew it couldn't be done. In such a storm as this, dressed as he was, he'd been lucky enough to find a cab to hire. The driver certainly wasn't going to risk his horse or their necks by urging the animal into so much as a gallop, not for one of the Great Unwashed, at least.

I could run home faster, Marston thought. Except I should probably get lost along the way. Or slip and fall and kill myself. Why did we not so much as notice Hartshire? he wondered then. Did not even think it him when he came flying out of that corner into the fight. Jupiter! To think he was there all the time and even Connie and I didn't take note of him. But I thank God he was there. I do.

A particularly bright bit of lightning streaked across the sky and for a moment Marston thought it was coming straight at him. Straight for his heart. Might as well strike me dead, he thought, and Ally too, if I am not in time to save Mama. But I will be in time. I must be. "Kill Mama," he groaned. "How dare they even speak of it. What has she ever done to them? To anyone? Well, I should like to see them try while I'm there to protect her. They'll be the dead ones. Just see if they ain't!"

But how did Hartshire know? he wondered. He cannot have heard what they said from where he was sitting. No. Impossible. I barely heard what they said. And yet, he said that Sterling fellow would kill her if Connie and he didn't catch him. How could he know that when he couldn't possibly have heard a word?

"He knows the fiend!" Marston exclaimed. "Hartshire knows the man from some other place, some other time. Knows him well enough to believe him capable of murder!

But why Mama? Why would he conclude the fiend intended to kill Mama?"

Don't matter, he thought then. Don't matter a bit how he knows. I believe him. He's The Spectre after all. He knows things. There's something purely mystical about him! Well, I'll get Papa's dueling pistols from the chest the moment I get home, load them, wake Wickens and give him one. Yes, that's the ticket. Wickens can guard the rear door while I guard the front. We'll keep our eyes and ears peeled. Shoot anyone who attempts to break in. Won't ask any questions, either. Just shoot and be done with it. Don't matter if it's the fellow Hartshire and Connie are chasing or one of the others who was there tonight or Dashfield or a perfect stranger. Man's got a right to protect his home and his family. Got a responsibility to do it. And by George, I will do it, too.

Davis knew Wickens would not remain absent for long. She had been hurrying to hide herself behind the parlor curtains when he left the library, but then she'd heard his muffled steps go off toward the backstairs. Thank goodness! She'd been given a bit more time at least. But he'd be coming soon. He wouldn't be able to resist peering in at the ladies through the crack in the pocket doors. Even now he must be longing to stand where she stood, peeking in and listening to every word uttered. Well, but there was a way to thwart him at that. Davis sneaked silently out of the front parlor, crossed the vestibule and climbed up to the fourth stair of the main staircase. Then she came down the stairs stomping her feet loudly and humming. She spun around the newel post, loped past the front parlor and turned in at the library door. "Good evening, my lady," she said.

Fleur and Althea were not, of course, surprised to see her. She had made quite enough noise to alert them to her approach. "I thought you were gone to bed hours ago, my lady," she said. "I was that surprised when I heard Mr. Wickens in the stairwell and went to see who it could be, and he informed me that you and Miss Avondale had forsaken your beds for the library."

"Yes, well, Miss Avondale and I found sleep impossible, Davis, with the storm and all."

"Ain't it a proper one, my lady? Keeping me awake as well. And since I am yet awake, I thought to myself that perhaps you and Miss Avondale might like a nice cup of tea. My goodness, but it's chilly in this library tonight. The storm most likely. Makes everything so very damp. Shall I put more coals on the fire for you, my lady?"

Lady Marston gazed steadily at Davis and then she glanced at Althea. "Do you know, Althea, Davis is right. It is chilly and dismal in here. Why don't we take these things up to my chamber and continue to sort through them there?"

"I should be pleased to help you with them, my lady," Davis offered, stepping toward the table to gather up the boxes.

"Thank you, Davis. And we should like some tea, shouldn't we, Ally, once we're settled in my chamber?"

"Just so, my lady," smiled Davis. "A cup of tea and a cheery fire will while away the hours as this storm pounds on. That it will."

Once Davis had got them settled in Lady Marston's chamber she hurried down to the kitchen, put the water on to boil and fretted away the minutes pacing the kitchen floor. She knew perfectly well that what she'd helped the ladies carry up the stairs had come from somewhere at the rear of the little closet under the servants' staircase because she'd been standing within three feet of Wickens, hidden in the little nook on the landing just above him as he'd stood watching and listening to the ladies. Nervously she found a tray, the teapot and cups and then began to prepare a bit of this and that for the ladies to nibble on as she paced back and forth across the kitchen floor. When at last the water boiled and all had been assembled, she made her way up the backstairs, down the corridor and into Lady Marston's chamber. She set the tea before them, curtsied and left the room, closing the door tightly behind her. And then she crept into Miss Avondale's chamber across the way, closed the door until merely a sliver of space remained to peer through, and put her eye to it, determined to remain there until the ladies discovered what needed to be discovered if it took them until tomorrow at noon.

Hartshire stalked through the storm like a god gone mad. His long legs carried him swiftly along the pavement, across the cobbles, down black alleyways, under flickering street-lamps. Whenever he remembered a more direct route that led toward Cavendish Square, he took it—through stables, gardens, over walls and hedges. Lightning threatened, hit a tree limb in one garden a mere second after Hartshire passed beneath it. Then, it shattered a column on a building as he hurried by, but he took no notice of its random strikes. Nor did he notice the rain, the cold, the wind any longer. His thoughts were for Fleur and for Fleur alone. He had to get to her quickly. Plummer was a madman. He'd taken it into his head to kill Lady Marston in those few seconds before the brawl had broken out, and he would do it. He would do it as soon as he possibly could. It was a race now between Plummer and Hartshire to see who could reach Marston House first.

He'll not get to her, Hartshire told himself again and again. Marston will be at home before either of us arrives. Val will pound Little awake even as Plummer and I are slogging our way through the gutters. By the time either of us reaches her, she will be surrounded by people determined to protect her.

But he doubted it. The more he attempted to convince himself Fleur would be well protected, the more he doubted it. Marston would take a hackney and the horse would slip on the wet cobbles, going down in the traces, delaying the boy just the number of minutes necessary for him to beat Plummer to the house. Tom Landy and his friends would take the coins he'd given them and traipse off to some tavern to warm their insides, abandoning Val in the alley. Little would not be pounded awake. No one would appear on the Marston doorstep except Alfred Plummer who would be let into the establishment by whoever it was there that did Dashfield's bidding.

Hartshire's pulse thundered in his ears and lightning sparked before his eyes, deafening him, blinding him as he rushed on. And deep in his breast, his heart cried out in staccato beats—"for Fleur—for Fleur—for Fleur—for Fleur."

"Oh, Heavenly Father!" Fleur stood straight up from the chair in which she'd settled.

"What? Mama, what is it? What've you found? Mama, you're reading the diary!"

"There was nothing in those papers, Ally. I could not read through them another time. There was nothing there because it's here. It's all right here. Oh, my dearest God, I cannot believe what I've just read!"

"What, Mama?" Ally was beside her, taking the diary into her own hands. Fleur did not so much as seem to notice. She walked to the window, pulled the curtains aside and stared out into the night. "He's out there. He's out there waiting to kill again and your father—your father and Lord Dashfield and a list of names barely half a page long—are all that hold him in check. And your father's dead, so the chain that holds him has been weakened by that one link. Who's to say how strong the others are? We must tell someone. We must tell someone now, Ally!"

"Is it this man she writes about here on the third page that you're speaking of, Mama? This Alfred Plummer person? But she says nothing about his killing anyone. She merely writes that Lord Dashfield and Papa have taken him out to Lord Dashfield's estate in Devon. And that was—why that was five years ago, Mama. Look. The date on the entry is—"

"I know what the date on the entry is, Ally."

"Indeed, madam, merely a week after Drury Lane burned to the ground."

"Wickens! Wickens! How—where—what are you doing in this chamber? You were not summoned!" Fleur exclaimed, her hands beginning to tremble as she turned to see the butler step across the threshold, a pistol in his hand and a quiet smile on his face.

"I will have that book, Miss Avondale," he said softly, extending his hand toward Ally. "It does, after all, belong to my employer."

"To your employer?" asked Ally innocently. "To my brother do you mean?"

"No, my dear, to Lord Dashfield. He sent me here to locate it and bring it back to him. It is all he has, you know, to remember his dear departed lady by. Give it to me."

"Well, it seems very odd to me that my papa should have Lady Dashfield's diary in his safe. Doesn't that seem odd to you, Mama?"

"Very odd indeed," managed Fleur. "And odder still that you should be standing before us with a pistol, Wickens."

"I did not like to bring the pistol, but I thought it best. Had you been so good as to simply leave that diary on the library table and come back up to bed, my lady, I would not be pointing this thing at you now. All of it could have been handled much more pleasantly."

"You mean you would have slipped into the library, purloined Lady Dashfield's diary and disappeared into the night, do you not, Wickens?"

"Just so," nodded the butler. "Exactly so. But now you know, my lady, about Alfred Plummer, and you have seen the list of names, and there is not much I can do but take the diary to Lord Dashfield and the two of you as well."

"So, you don't intend to shoot us here in my chamber?"

"Hardly, my lady. This pistol fires only one ball. Once I fired it, what would I do with whichever of you is left alive, eh? I expect I should have to resort to strangling her with a curtain cord. No, no, much too messy and it would take a good deal of time as well. And likely the rest of the staff would be aroused and I should have to invent some story about a housebreaker and then go running about attempting to find the nonexistent man. Much too involved, I say. You, Miss Avondale, will hand me that diary now. And then you will both accompany me down the stairs and out into the night. Dashfield House is not so very far from here. In Hanover Square merely."

"Give him the diary, Ally," said Fleur, her voice trembling as much as her hands.

"But Mama—"

"Do as I say. Hand it to him nicely so as not to frighten him into shooting you."

"Frighten me? As if that child could frighten me," scoffed Wickens, reaching out to accept the diary from Ally's outstretched hand. And just as he touched the end of it, Ally bit her lip, hard, to keep from gasping. Fleur seized the ledger that lay on the window seat before her and tossed the enormous book his way as a heavy silver candlestick cracked down against the back of Wickens's skull.

"Oh, Davis! I thought I would gasp aloud at the last and give you away!" Ally cried.

"Are you all right, miss? My lady? I couldn't come any quicker for fear the floorboards would squeak and call his attention to me."

"He is not dead, Davis?" asked Fleur, kneeling down beside the man.

"No, m'lady. But he will be soon enough. Hanged he'll be, can we prove it was him killed Lady Dashfield. And hanged he'll be even if we can't," she added on an after-thought, "for we can prove, you know, that he intended to kill the both of you."

With a swish of her skirts, Fleur rose again and went to the window. "I expect it would be best to tie him up until Malcolm returns," she said, freeing the curtain of its cords and tossing them to Ally and Davis who proceeded to bind Wickens tightly. "Then we'll take him to Bow Street and tell the people there about—about—Alfred Plummer. Oh! Thank goodness!"

"What Mama?"

"A hackney cab pulling up before the house. Ally, run down quickly and tell your brother to have the cab wait, then bring him to us at once."

Ally dashed from the room and down the staircase as fast as her feet would carry her, not noticing at all that merely one lamp stood lit on each of the landings nor worrying that she might trip on the stairs. She reached the front door just as it opened.

"I knew you were a veritable treasure from the first evening you walked into my chamber, Davis," Fleur said, as soon as Ally had departed. "But you aren't an abigail, are you? Not really?"

"No, my lady. I am—I work for—Bow Street."

"I see. And you merely pretended to be my abigail because—?"

"Well, because Wickens came here, my lady, and we could none of us think why, but we thought it best to see that nothing happened here like what happened to Lady Dash-field."

"But you were with Lady Dashfield and could not protect her."

"No, but only because we hadn't the least idea that she was in any danger. I was merely sent to follow her about because she was forever involving herself with groups of radicals, you know. Her husband wields a good deal of power. Should he have been convinced to join her at her meetings, well . . ."

"It was Dashfield corrupted Lydia, I fear. The story is in her diary, though I haven't read it all. But it's likely Dashfield corrupted Lydia and my husband somehow took advantage of them both."

Davis nodded. "And Alfred Plummer is not dead," she added on a whisper. "Not dead at all. Had I known—had I known even but a few weeks ago—I would have—"

"What? What would you have done?" asked Fleur.

"I would have told The Spectre of it the very day he helped me down from the coach before Madame Celeste's."

"The Spectre. Lord Hartshire, you mean?"

"Aye, madam. For years and years they called him The Spectre. He was the finest protector any Royal Family ever had. Heard everything, went everywhere, was never took note of by anyone until he'd grasped their intentions and foiled their plots and even then they did never know who it was had done the thing."

"What the devil?" growled Marston, stomping into the room, streaming rainwater behind him. "Ally, it's Wickens."

"Yes, Wickens," Althea answered, rushing to Fleur's side and taking her Mama's cold hands into her own. "He held a pistol on us, Mal, and threatened to kill us. If Davis had not come in when she did, we might not even be here to speak your name."

"Yes, but it's Wickens."

"You were expecting it to be one of the other servants, Malcolm?" asked Fleur.

"No. That is to say—it's Wickens who was working for Dashfield, is that it?"

"Yes, Mal. Has the rain made your brain shrink?" cried Ally impatiently. "Mama and I found what he was searching for and—"

"Hush, Ally. What is it, Malcolm? Who did you expect?"

"A fellow called Sterling. At least, that's the name Connie

and I know him by. He rushed out of The Cock and Hartshire and Connie went charging after him. Hartshire sent me here to protect you. He said—he said—if he and Connie didn't catch up with the fellow, Sterling would come here and kill you this very night, Mama. But it ain't going to happen. I tell you that right now. I am not about to let it happen."

"Perhaps we should all go to the Bow Street Office," Fleur suggested, glancing significantly at Davis. "Is the hackney large enough to take us all, Mal?"

"Indeed. A big old thing."

Davis nodded. "You, my lady, Miss Avondale, Lord Marston and I must put Wickens into it and then the three of you will take him straight to Bow Street. I'll take this pistol and—"

"You'll what?" interrupted Marston, astounded.

"I will take this pistol of Wickens's in hand, my lord, and await this—Mr. Sterling's?—arrival."

"You, Davis?"

"Davis works for Bow Street, Malcolm," Fleur explained.

"Bow Street don't hire women."

"I beg to differ with you, my lord, but they hired me. Pay me reasonably well, too," murmured Davis. "Once we get him down to the cab, you will take this villain and your mother and sister to the Office at once and I'll stay and watch over your servants."

"But he ain't interested in the servants. He is after Mama."

"If this Sterling is the man I believe him to be, he will kill everyone in this house should he be presented with the opportunity. You said Lord Hartshire is in pursuit of him?"

"Y-yes."

"I expect it's Alfred Plummer, my lady," Davis acknowledged the question on Fleur's face.

"But Davis, you cannot—" Fleur began.

"If Lord Hartshire is in pursuit of him, my lady," Davis replied confidently, "and he knows Plummer is bound for this house, then Lord Hartshire will be with me shortly and

London will see the end of Alfred Plummer. It will merely be easier for us if there is no fear of his discovering you or Miss Avondale anywhere around."

"I see," Fleur replied. "We would be more hindrance than help. But ought we not to arouse the servants and send them somewhere else just in case? Across the square perhaps, to Lord Browning's."

"An excellent idea, my lady. I will do just that as soon as I help his lordship bundle Mr. Wickens down the staircase and out to the cab."

Sixteen

Between them, with Fleur and Althea manning the doors, Marston and Davis bundled Wickens down the main staircase, tipped and turned him most inconsiderately through the front door and carried him to the waiting cab. Marston climbed inside and arranged the butler as best he could on one of the seats while Davis, pistol in hand, stood watch, and Fleur and Ally dashed from the house through the gusty downpour and climbed into the cab themselves. "He's bound securely, my lord," Davis said then, leaning in a window. "Even if he should regain his senses before you get to Bow Street, I doubt he'll be able to give you any trouble. Go directly to John Stafford and say that Jenny Day sends him this prisoner. Say that he's the Mr. Wickens we spoke of and that I have considerable evidence to see him hanged. And then you must tell him that Alfred Plummer is alive and well and that I am awaiting Plummer's arrival at Marston House."

"Did you hear, Mama?" Marston said. "Do precisely as Davis just said. But you must remember to call her Jenny Day, I think," and with that he opened the door and stepped down onto the cobbles.

"Mal!" cried Althea in surprise as he exited the coach.

"My lord!" protested Davis. "You ought to go with them."

"Malcolm, what do you think you're doing?" asked Fleur.

"I'm staying here with Davis, ah, Miss Day, Mama. Two

of us on guard are better than one, and four of us, once Hartshire and Connie arrive, cannot fail to catch this Alfred Plummer."

Fleur nodded. He was correct, of course. "And you will help to get the servants from out the house as well, will you not, Mal? I shan't like to think of them in any danger."

"Yes, Mama, first thing. In fact, I'm off to pound on Browning's door this instant. You," Marston called up to the hackney driver, "take them directly to the Bow Street Office, and safely too. And don't stop for anyone, no matter what. There's a desperate criminal somewhere about in this storm. You wouldn't want to be attacked by him and your coach taken, eh?"

His collar pulled snugly up to his chin, the brim of his tall hat tilted low over his brow as the rain continued to assault him, the driver nodded and gave his horse the office to start. Marston glanced after the vehicle for a moment as it departed, then sprinted directly across the square to raise someone at Lord Browning's residence. As soon as he'd reached the Brownings' front door, Davis turned and hurried back toward Marston House. Neither of them noticed that the hack steadily increased its speed, nor that it halted abruptly just as it reached the far end of the square. Neither Davis nor Marston so much as glanced in the hackney's direction until Althea screamed.

Marston dropped Browning's knocker on the instant, stared down to the end of the square. Althea screamed again and her brother charged off toward the cab. Davis, who'd already entered Marston House, spun about on her heel, pistol in hand, and ran as fast as she could toward the hackney as well. What the devil happened? she thought. What brought the thing to a halt? What can the girl be screaming about? Surely Wickens ain't got loose from his bonds.

Inside the coach Althea screamed once more as the driver, snickering, swung down from the top of the coach, kicked open the door and attempted to get himself inside. His boots touched Fleur's knee, then her calf as he lowered himself into the vehicle. Scrambling over Wickens's inert body, Fleur shoved open the door on the opposite side of the coach. Instantly she seized Ally's arm and tugged the girl from the vehicle in her wake, both of them slipping down onto the cobbles because the coach steps were up, forcing them to leap a good three feet from the hackney to the ground. Almost in a panic now, they scrambled to their feet. Their skirts, sodden with rainwater and muck, tangled around their legs as they tried to escape the madman who, in his hurry to leap after them, knocked the unaware Wickens right out of the cab.

Rain sizzled down around the ladies. Wind whistled past their ears as Fleur looked back over her shoulder and saw the man only an arm's length behind them. He was just extending his arm, just beginning to reach out for them with one hand as he raised a hammer to the skies with the other. "Oh dear God, help us!" Fleur cried. And then she grabbed Ally by the shoulders and gave her a tremendous shove that sent the girl slipping, sliding, skidding across the cobbles ahead of her. "Run, Ally," Fleur shouted. "Directly to that house. Run!" And then Fleur trembled to a halt, spun toward the driver and bending low, prepared to launch herself at the man's knees, hoping that with the help of the slippery cobbles, she would be strong enough to knock his feet out from under him, to keep him from reaching Althea, to give Ally time to raise someone in the house who would take her safely inside with them. Preferably someone with a large pistol.

Before she could make the attempt to fell the dastard, however, the most enormous shadow came flashing at her from the side. Lightning flared and died. Flared once more and was gone. Thunder shuddered through the skies but the shadow came on, in darkness, across darkness, through darkness. Flying, she thought. Flying. Not so much as touching the ground. And in that very moment a strong arm pushed Fleur, tumbling her to the cobbles, away from the driver. She heard the driver grunt loudly, saw the shadow sweep the fellow up and carry him a good five feet beyond her. And then both shadow and madman crashed to the street.

As though in the midst of a nightmare, Fleur heard Ally screaming, heard her pounding on the nearest door, heard bits of Malcolm shouting, heard a pistol fire, but it seemed so far away, so very far away as she sat in the wet, staring horrified into the fitfully illuminated night. They rolled on the cobbles beyond her, the shadow and the madman, twisted together, entwined, unable to loose themselves one from the other as they battled.

Dazedly, with the greatest care, Fleur gained her feet. "Atticus!" she thought she heard herself scream, but it was merely a whisper. "Atticus." And then both men gained their footing. Hartshire stumbled a bit, his arms windmilling, attempting to snatch back some semblance of balance as the madman raised the hammer that seemed nailed to his hand high into the air over Hartshire's head and lightning flashed above them both.

Little protested against it as he struggled into his oilskin coat. He shouted as he tugged his hat down tightly on his head. He went so far as to bellow, scaring himself nearly to death with the great voice that boomed from between his unexpecting lips. But none of it did a bit of good. Conningford would not remain at Hartshire House to be tended to. As Little stepped out into the storm, Conningford stepped out beside him. Mr. Robes ran toward them leading an excited Radical. "I have sent Gorely off to Bow Street," Robes shouted over the storm. "Ain't room enough in the hack, what with Mr. Landy and his friend, so I'll ride. Go on, Mr. Little. Go on, my lord. Hurry!"

Ride? Little stared at his friend in wonder. Robes knew how to ride? And he was going to ride Radical?

"You can't," Conningford voiced Little's unspoken opinion. "You'll break your neck. I'll take Rad."

"Not as woozy as you are, lordship," Robes replied. "You'll take the hack or you'll remain here, which you ought to do anyway." And without listening to another word, the little valet swung up into the saddle and turned Radical in the direction of Cavendish Square.

"Well, I'll be deviled," growled Conningford, just as astounded to see Robes do it as Little was. And then the both of them darted to the hackney that had carried Conningford to Hartshire House. Landy and another man pulled them safely inside. The driver, with whip and whistle gave his horse the office to start and urged it to the fastest possible speed it could safely manage on such a night as this one.

"Don't ye be aworryin' 'bout any of 'em, Mr. Little," said Tom Landy, reaching across to give the butler's knee a supportive pat. "We ain't goin' ta let nothin' happen ta 'Is Grace nor 'is friends, we ain't. Is we, Nate?"

"No, we ain't," replied the other man. "Not at the hands of no Alfred Plummer, we ain't. Send him ta Hades wif these two bare mitts of mine I will, does I git me a chance at him."

"But who is he?" Conningford asked, staring out the coach window, willing the vehicle to mover faster, something at the scruff of his neck and the base of his belly telling him that Atticus was in grave danger, graver danger than any one of them realized. "Who is this Alfred Plummer? Am I the only one not heard of the man?"

The three older men informed him, with a good deal of cursing and swearing, precisely who Plummer was. Landy related the madman's atrocities. Little provided Hartshire's role in discovering the man's identity and told of the wild chase that had ensued. And Nate added, to Conningford's dismay, that his own fourteen-year-old daughter had been one of the servants slaughtered that night. A scullery maid, she'd been, in one of the great houses. Murdered as she slept on the kitchen settle.

* * *

Robes and Radical rounded the corner into Cavendish Square just as Fleur dodged behind Plummer's back and sprang upward. With her hands extended as high above her head as she could manage to get them, she was hoping against hope that she could seize the hammer and wrench it from Plummer's grasp. She took not the least note of the approaching horse and rider, nor the shouts echoing toward her on the wind from Davis, from Marston, from Althea and Lord Edgerton's butler who had come to answer Ally's pounding at his door. Fleur heard nothing at all, saw nothing at all but Hartshire, weaponless and winded, attempting to ward off a fatal blow. She did not so much as hear Hartshire himself shout at the sight of her. She simply launched herself at the villain, laced the fingers of her hands around his rain-slippery wrist and leaned backward, falling, dragging Plummer's arm backward and the man down with her. The hammer flew out into the middle of the square behind them. Fleur crashed to the cobbles, cracking her head against them. Plummer landed heavily atop her.

In the blink of an eye Hartshire was over them, tugging Plummer up by the lapels of his coat, spinning him away from Fleur, releasing his hold with one hand and landing punch after punch after punch to the man's stomach, his ribs, his breast bone, his jaw. "Get her away!" Hartshire bellowed above the storm as he pummeled the man. "Get her away!"

They all heard his bellow and each of them understood. Fleur lay barely conscious behind the hackney. Did the petrified horse in the traces suddenly back up, the vehicle would back up as well and crush her beneath a wheel. Did Plummer, in the midst of the struggle, somehow force Hartshire to the right and back, the men themselves could easily trample Fleur to death. They each of them, each one of the onlookers, understood and all rushed forward, but it was Robes and Radical who reached Lady Marston first. The little valet fairly dived from the saddle and seized the groggy Fleur by the shoulders, urging her up, taking most of her weight upon himself. And then Radical was stepping around them, between them and the hackney and the battle. And as Robes and Fleur stumbled in the direction of the opposite gutter, Marston slid to a halt and hauled them both out of the street to the comparative safety of the verge.

"Let me go," Fleur gasped weakly. "Mal, let me go. We must help him. We must—" And then Fleur looked out from the circle of her stepson's arms and saw Hartshire land a final blow that sent Plummer, senseless at last, to the cobbles. In an instant Radical was moving again, placing himself directly over Plummer as Hartshire reached out to the horse to steady himself.

In a moment more, Davis came running up to the earl, and Althea and Edgerton's butler in robe and slippers all came running up to him through the wind and the rain and the darkness. And Robes came running as well. Hartshire struggled for a deep breath and shook the rainwater from his head. His old, wretchedly worn cap had disappeared long ago. His clothes were dripping, torn and spattered with the muck of innumerable streets, yards, gardens. "Day," he said gasping, as Davis bent down and with Robes's and Edgerton's butler's help tugged Plummer from between Radical's legs. "My gawd, but you're Jenny Day, ain't you?"

Davis looked up at him and smiled. Her teeth shone white and sharp in the fading night, the approaching dawn.

Hartshire turned, walked behind Rad's back, puffing, attempting to stop his haggard breathing and breathe regularly again. He halted, wearily, a few feet from where Fleur and Marston stood on the verge.

"Let me go, Mal," Fleur whispered hoarsely. "Let me go to him." And then she was running, stumbling, flying toward Hartshire with her arms out, tears mixing with the rainwater on her cheeks, his name falling from her lips. In one moment more she was wrapped in the circle of his arms. As she looked up at him, his head lowered and his lips, cold and wet with rain, touched hers, gently, tentatively, breathlessly, then with a hunger, a passion, a need that stirred her very soul.

The kiss went on and on. Thunder, lightning, rain, the people milling about, the arrival of the hackney containing Mr. Little and Conningford, Landy and Nate, all failed to make one tiny impression on Fleur's mind. Hartshire, his arms around her, his lips hungry, insistent upon hers, the sound of their hearts beating together in erratic rhythm as love for the giant swelled up inside of her and overflowed, these things claimed her and would allow nothing else to interfere with them. When at last their lips parted, he pressed her against his chest and rested his chin on the top of her head. "Gawd, how I love you," he said hoarsely, his voice distorted by the raggedness of his breathing. "You cannot conceive of how much I love you."

He swept her into his arms and carried her up the street to Marston House, carried her inside and up the staircase, along the second floor corridor all the way to her bedchamber. There, Fleur still clinging to him, her head nestled between his jaw and his shoulder, he paused and gazed around. Then he set her down on the edge of the little sleigh bed, went to the hearth, knelt and put more coals on the dwindling fire.

Fleur sat on the edge of the mattress, her feet dangling, her slippers dripping rainwater onto the carpet, staring at him. Just staring at him. Drinking in the very sight of him. He was the finest, most beautiful man she'd ever known. There was nothing about him that did not fill her heart with love. "What are you doing?" she managed to say around the lump of desire that had risen all the way into her throat.

"Replenishing your fire," he replied, not looking at her. "You will die of the ague if you don't get out of those wet clothes and into a warm bed."

"I should like to get into a warm bed," Fleur murmured wistfully.

"Yes, I should think so. As soon as Jenny comes, she'll

help you to doff those clothes and dry yourself off. You'll feel a deal better then."

"I feel remarkably fine at the moment," Fleur whispered.

He turned from the fire and peered at her over his shoulder. "You do?"

"Oh, yes, Atticus. Remarkably fine."

"Too much excitement," he said softly. "Not come back to earth yet, but you will soon."

"Yes. Soon. Can you not unfasten my gown for me, yourself, Atticus? I do not require Davis if you will but undo the tabs."

He stood and she abandoned the bed. She put her arms as far around him as they would go and attempted to burrow into his chest just as she had long since burrowed into his heart. His large hands touched her back, fumbled awkwardly with the first of the tabs on her dress. Undid it. Fumbled with the next.

"Mama! Mama! Are you all right? All of Bow Street is in our drawing room, I think!" shouted Althea, bursting into the room. "Oh," she said much more quietly as her gaze fell on the two of them before the fire. "Oh, dear. I am—I should—I did not intend to—"

"Help your mama into her nightrail and into her bed, will you not, Ally?" Hartshire said, grinning his most disarming grin. "She need not deal with Bow Street tonight. She's had quite enough excitement for one evening."

Ally came near to dying on the spot. His grin enchanted her, but his eyes were not smiling at all. Those eyes as dark as the midnight sky, silver specks sprinkled across them like stars, were smoldering with passion, like banked coals. They blazed from the inside out.

"Well, to begin with, Davis and another fellow found the real driver dead in the strip between your house and Denbigh's. Plummer must have sneaked up on the man while he was waiting for you at the curb, Marston. At any rate, the dastard knocked the driver in the head with that hammer of his, wrapped himself in the man's coat and hat and hoped you wouldn't notice the difference." Conningford had come visiting at Marston House to provide them with the news from Bow Street.

"And I didn't either," sighed Marston. "What a great clunch I am. I looked right at him and I didn't notice anything different about him at all. Davis found the real driver, you said, Connie?"

"Um-hmmm. Except her name ain't Davis. It's Jenny Day. And five years ago this Plummer fellow dragged her off the street and inside a burning Drury Lane to keep Atticus and the Runners at bay," Conningford said with decided authority. He sat on the chintz-covered settee, his arm across the back of it, very near Ally's shoulders. The afternoon sun peeked spastically out from thinning storm clouds and in through the windows behind them.

Directly opposite, Marston sat grinning and fiddling with his father's cane. "I expect The Spectre saved her, Jenny Day, in his own inimitable fashion, eh?"

"Just so. Saved her, but lost Plummer in the smoke and fire. Had to carry Jenny from the place and let Alfred Plummer go. Still, there were people gathered all around the building. No one saw Plummer escape it. That's why they all thought him dead and gone."

"How did he escape, Val?" Ally asked, touching the sticking plaster on Conningford's chin with one gentle finger and then tracing the bruise along his jaw with a long, tender stroke.

"Don't know. The Runners asked, but Plummer won't say. Won't say anything. And all anyone knows about what truly happened that night and for the next few years is what's written down in Lady Dashfield's diary. Apparently your father and Dashfield found the fellow in some gutter and once they figured out who he was, they set about nursing him back to health. Planned to use him and his considerable talent with a hammer to their own advantage when the time for the great and violent revolution against the government came. 'Course, it didn't come. But that ain't the thing. The thing I'm saying is, it was Atticus made Jenny Day want to be a Runner. She's the first female ever that Bow Street pays on a regular basis to go about snooping into things."

"Amazing," breathed Ally with such hopeful seductiveness that it set her brother to laughing softly.

"Is your mama—all right?" Conningford asked then. "I mean to say, Miss Day told everyone how Lady Marston fought to save Ally and Atticus, you know. Said she'd never seen such a courageous and stubborn woman in all her days. Said she thought your mama the finest lady in all of England. Even said she wouldn't mind in the least to give up her job with Bow Street and continue on as Lady Marston's abigail if Lady Marston would have her."

"Well, she had best come here and tell *me* that," said Fleur as she entered the room, smiling at the speed with which Conningford's arm disappeared from the back of the settee and reappeared at his side as he clasped his wandering hands together in his lap. "I *will* have her, you know," Fleur continued. "She's a genuine prize, our Miss Day."

"Yes, Robes thinks so, too," nodded Conningford.

"Robes? Hartshire's valet?" Marston queried, leaning forward in his chair. "The little man who came charging to the rescue on Radical?"

"Just so. Pestered Atticus and Mr. Little all morning long wishing to know everything about her. Been severely smitten with her, Atticus says."

"I wonder if Miss Day is smitten with him as well?" Marston pondered. "Robes did look a bit like a knight in shining armor riding in on Rad like that, especially as dark as it was. Rather a wonderful sight, actually."

"You were all wonderful last night," Fleur said, gazing from one to the other of the young people. "Each one of you. I don't expect you discovered, Val, if Malcolm and Ally's papa—what Malcolm and Ally's papa—had to do with any of this?" she asked hesitantly. "I didn't have the opportunity to read much of Lady Dashfield's diary, but I did see Marston's name there and—"

"Atticus will tell you, ma'am."

"He will?"

"Yes, ma'am. He told me I was to button my lip on the subject until he could explain it to you himself. Oh! I almost forgot! He asked me to ask you if you were still planning to attend the Haleys' ball on Tuesday. You are, are you not? Everything will have died down by Tuesday, I should think. And even if it hasn't, the old gossips will not be saying anything evil about any of us. Most likely they will only find themselves speculating on how we came to discover Plummer and capture him. Nothing more."

"You're attempting to say most kindly that I likely will not see Lord Hartshire again until Tuesday, are you not, Val?" asked Fleur quietly. "But he does wish to see me then?"

"Just so."

"He is not ill or injured that he stays away?"

"Not at all. Merely called upon by Bow Street and Prinny, too, to help round up a number of the radicals and put an end to their nonsense for a time. Do you remember in that very first note we found, Marston, how they were thinking to cause a veritable riot at Vauxhall?"

"A riot? At Vauxhall Gardens?" asked Fleur, perfectly astounded.

"Oh, yes, ma'am. Hoping to learn when the Prince Regent planned on showing Vauxhall to the Tzar and his sister, they were. Laying plans to stir things up considerably that particular night. 'Course, they never did find out which night it would be. And it won't happen now. Not when they know The Spectre is back in London and he's already brought down Dashfield and captured Plummer. They wouldn't dare attempt a riot at Vauxhall now. Stuck a considerably large stick between the spokes of their wheels last night, we did."

"I have wondered," murmured Fleur, leaning against the edge of the fireplace surround, her fingers playing across the front of her rose silk gown. "Why did Lord Hartshire name that remarkable horse of his Radical if all he did for years and years was fight against them—radicals, I mean?"

"Well, because he admires a considerable lot of them," Val replied at once.

"Surely you jest," Marston said.

"No, I don't jest. Atticus don't like their ideas about violent revolution and overthrow of the government. Not at all. But he *is* somewhat partial to the idea of equal suffrage for all men and bettering the lot of the working man and child labor laws—well, any number of things. And he does have a place in his heart for Thomas Spence."

"Thomas Spence? But Hartshire absolutely forbid us to associate with any of Spence's followers ever again!" Marston exclaimed.

"Uh-huh. But he went off this afternoon to help the Runners round up a number of the radicals, as I said, and I heard him say that if they so much as knocked on Thomas Spence's door he would pummel whoever did it into next Sunday. Said Spence was a sick old man now and he'd suffered more than enough for his ideals, some of which Parliament actually ought to consider. Going to make a speech in Lords, Atticus is, before he goes back home, suggesting they consider one and another of the radicals' points."

"Well, of all things," Ally said. "He is against them and for them all at one and the same time."

"It's because he has a curious sort of mind," Conningford smiled. "A very curious sort of mind."

"Why do you smile such a smile as that, Val?" Fleur asked, smiling herself at the sight of it.

"Only because I've remembered something. Atticus plans to—to—do something downright exceptional at the Haleys' ball, and I cannot for one moment believe that anyone else would so much as think of it, much less do the thing."

"What?" asked three very interested people all at once.

"I can't tell. I promised I would not. Gave m'word."

"Are you all finished with working now, Papa?" Will asked, touching the bruises on his father's face one by one with a small finger as he sat comfortably beside Hartshire on the sofa that evening.

"All finished as far as I know, m'boy. Ow! Will, don't wiggle and bounce quite so much, eh? I'm sore in a good many more places than you know about."

"Mr. Robes says as how you are one big bruise from the top of your head to the bottoms of your feet," grinned the boy.

"Well, not quite. But close, I'm sure."

"Was Uncle Val brave last night, Papa? As brave as you?"

"As brave as any man in England."

"And he did a fine job of it, too, didn't he? An excellent job of it."

"He most certainly did."

"I knew he would. And Mr. Little and Mr. Robes were brave as well, huh?"

"Will?" asked Hartshire suspiciously. "Just how much do you know about what happened last night? I thought you were fast asleep when Mr. Little and Mr. Robes left this house."

"I was, Papa. I did not so much as hear Uncle Val an' the men come pounding on our door."

"You didn't?"

"Uh-uh."

"Well then, how do you know that they did, you rascal?"

"Because this very afternoon while you were gone, Mr. Little told Mr. Canton all about everything that happened and I was listening."

"Where were you listening?"

"I was peeking through the schoolroom door and listening."

"Will!" Hartshire exclaimed somewhere between a groan and a giggle. "That's called eavesdropping and it ain't acceptable. Not at all."

"I know you are always saying that, Papa," Will acknowledged brightly, his small hand supportively patting one velvet shoulder of Hartshire's coat, "but sometimes peeking and listening is just the thing. It proved just exactly the best thing for Lady Marston's abigail to do last night. She saved Lady Marston's life, Mr. Little said. And she did it by listening and peeking through a slit in a door."

"Yes, Will," Hartshire protested softly, his eyes brilliant with laughter, "but that was an exceptionally awkward situation and Davis was forced to do it."

"This was an exceptional awkward situation and I was forced to do it, too, Papa."

"Oh?"

"Uh-huh. Because no one would tell me anything at all about what happened. I asked and asked all morning long and all anyone would say was that you and Uncle Val were working last night and caused a tremendous hubbub somewhere."

"I see," Hartshire replied. "Perhaps no one told you anything more because they didn't want you to know."

"I did think of that," Will replied with a grave nod of his blond head.

"You did, eh?"

"Yes, Papa. And then I thought of you. And when you are doing your work and people don't want you to know things, you go and find them out anyway."

"Will—"

"You do, Papa. And I could not think of any other way that you could do it than what Davis done. So, I expect if it is all right for you and Davis both—"

"Will, I do *not* listen at doors and peek in at people. I never have done."

"Then how do you find out all the things that you must to be an excellent protector of the King?"

Hartshire felt the back of his neck grow warm. He grinned and kissed the tip of Will's nose.

"I don't want a kiss, Papa. I want to *know.*"

"It's a special trick, you scoundrel. I don't have to hear what people say. As long as I can see their lips when they speak, I know what they're saying."

"Uh-uh."

"Yes, Will, it's the truth. Your grandfather taught me to do it years and years ago."

Will smiled up at him enthusiastically. "Really and truly?"

"Really and truly."

"When are you going to teach me how to do it, Papa?"

"Oh, Will," Hartshire sighed. "I don't think—that is to say—Some day, Will. When you're old enough. Can you wait until I decide that you're old enough?"

"Um-hmmm. Are we going home soon, Papa?" Will asked then, scooting around on the sofa so he could stick his heels up over it, while he hung his head down toward the carpeting.

"I expect so. In a week or two."

"Oh."

"Will," chuckled Hartshire, "what the devil are you doing down there?"

"Staring up at the ceiling. It's fun, Papa, being upside down. You ought to try it."

"No, I don't think so."

"When you went to Marston House last night, Papa, did you say 'good day' to Lady Marston?"

"Did I what?" asked Hartshire, puzzled, putting a strong hand on his son's knee to keep him from slipping whop-bang down onto the floor.

"After you got done spying on the radicals and chasing all about in the rain and beating that villain to a merest shadow of his former self and rescuing Lady Marston, did you say 'good day' to her?"

"Ah, well, in a manner of speaking, yes, I expect I did, Will. Said 'good day' and more."

"Let go, Papa," ordered the boy, wiggling from Hartshire's grasp and slithering onto the floor, then jumping up and dashing into the schoolroom. In a matter of moments, he came skipping back and plopped down cross-legged at Hartshire's feet. "That's two," he announced. "I am marking them down."

"Two what? Marking what down, Will?"

"You know, Papa. Them."

"Them what?" asked a voice from the opposite doorway.

"Celeste!" Will was up and running to her before she could so much as step into the room. "Were you listening at the door?"

"Oh, good gracious, no," Celeste replied at once, her faded blue eyes coming alive with laughter. "People ought not listen at doors. It's not the proper thing at all."

"I know it ain't," announced Will, escorting her into his room by holding her hand and skipping along beside her. "And Papa has got a better way of finding things out than even that. And he's going to teach me when I'm old enough."

"Ah, you will regret that, Hartshire," Celeste laughed up at the earl as he stood before her and offered her his seat.

"No, no, I will just sit down here on the edge of the settle, Hartshire," she demurred.

"Me, too," announced Will.

"For a moment you will, and then you'll run all the way down to the kitchen and ask Cook to send us up some tea, won't you, my little budgie?" Celeste said, tugging at his ear.

"Yes, Celeste. I'll run down now if you are 'specially thirsty."

"I am quite as thirsty as I have ever been. Off with you then, Prince Charming. Tramp out through the schoolroom, if you please, because I have brought your papa a visitor and we must speak with him about something *private.*"

Will nodded and went charging out through the schoolroom door, just as she'd asked of him. "He is as tall as I am, Hartshire. Have you noticed? Grown an inch at least since Christmas."

"An inch? No. You're mistaken, Celly. He ain't grown nearly at all."

"Such a face, Hartshire. I was teasing merely. You needn't worry about Will growing to be as large as you. You ought not worry about your having grown to be as large as you are, either."

"Why ought I not?"

"Because you're the perfect size."

"The perfect size for what, Celly," asked Hartshire, leery.

"For a hero. I know you have been a hero again."

"And you've come to congratulate me, eh?"

"Of course not. I've come for something far more important than that. Arthur, do come in. He's not going to bite you. He already knows."

"Arthur? Little? Is it you? Why are you standing out there in the corridor?"

"Because he's a bit jumpy," offered Celeste. "Just a bit. Ah, there you are, Arthur." Celeste rose and went to stand beside him, holding onto his arm with both hands, her lemon yellow reticule dangling freely, knocking against his elbow.

"Don't say you've come to give me notice, Little," Hartshire pleaded quietly. "Please don't say that. Not until I have got Will back to Wilderhart Hall and this place closed up again. I couldn't bear to have anyone else in charge until then."

"Pooh!" Celeste said. "As if such a thing would occur to him. To abandon you before everything was settled properly."

"No, my lord. I would never dream of it," agreed Little, running a finger around the inside of a collar that he found quite tight. "I have come up here today because, well, because I wish to ask for Celeste's hand in marriage."

"You do? I thought you had already asked her and she'd said yes."

"But I have not asked you, my lord. And you are her closest living relative—well, besides her uncle Panington, of course, but that gentleman frightens the living daylights out of me."

Hartshire plopped back down on the sofa and fought to keep from roaring with laughter. "I—I—know what you mean, Little. Never know what Uncle Pan is going to s-say. Yes, Little, you may have her. With my blessings, too. I've no doubt at all that you will treat her with the kindness and respect that she deserves."

"No, my lord, you need never doubt I will."

"Just so. And Celly, will you treat our Mr. Little with the kindness and respect he deserves?"

"I expect I will, Hartshire. Most of the time. He is going to be Arthur Thoroughgood again, you know. You must grow accustomed to that."

"I will. I will grow accustomed to it. You ain't going to force him to live over that dreadful shop, are you, Celly?"

"No. We have talked it over hundreds of times and we talked it over again just before we came up here. And we have decided to move to the country."

"You have?" Hartshire smiled up at them both. "Truly, Celly? You are willing to leave London? Where in the country?"

"In K-Kent, my lord," Little offered quietly.

"Kent? Might I hope you will look for a place close to Wilderhart Hall then? Close enough so Will and I might ride over and pay you a call from time to time?"

"Very close to Wilderhart, my lord," whispered Little.

"You mean to say that you have already located the house? When in Hades did you find time to do that, Little, I mean, Mr. Thoroughgood? By Jove, but you are the most efficient manager! Where is the place? What's it called? Do I know it? Well, I must know it if it's very close to the Hall."

"You know it well, Hartshire," Celeste said, squeezing Little's arm with all her might. "You think his eyes are sparkling now, Arthur. Just you wait a moment more. It's called Awful Elms."

Hartshire's jaw dropped but he fixed it back in place almost immediately. "Awful Elms? You mean to say that you're planning on moving into my grandmother's little cottage? The one on *my* estate, Celly? The one just a hop, skip and jump from the home wood?"

"I told you he would be overjoyed, Arthur. Didn't I tell you? He is positively beaming."

"Yes, well, but what—why—" Hartshire stuttered ineffectually as Little's eyes began to actually twinkle at him.

"It's because of all that occurred last evening, my lord," Little declared quietly. "I felt it my duty, my lord, to inform Celeste of the danger in which you'd placed yourself—again. And to relate to her the near disastrous ending to the affair. And I did point out to her, my lord, that you are a father with a young son. Someone must look after you and be there to support you until Will is old enough to keep you out of trouble on his own, my lord."

"What Arthur's trying to say, Hartshire, is that he's finally convinced me what a particular handful you are. I already know you're a nodcock. He wasn't forced to convince me of that. So I've agreed to let him go on being your butler for as long as he thinks you need him, but he must have a good deal of time off, I warn you, if you are willing to accept this arrangement, and he must definitely come home to me at night—unless, of course, you are out being a hero and suddenly require his services for one evening."

"I accept!" bellowed Hartshire, bouncing up from the sofa and crossing to shake Mr. Little's hand heartily. Then he stooped to place a kiss on Celeste's cheek. "By Jove, I should be a complete fool not to accept such a fine arrangement!"

Seventeen

It was Friday evening before Jenny Day appeared again at Marston House. Without the least ceremony, she came loping into the drawing room after dinner, nodded to Althea and smiled a wide smile at Fleur. "His lordship has gone out, has he?"

"Indeed," Fleur replied. "Gone to one of his clubs. Did you wish especially to speak with Malcolm, Miss Day? I can't imagine why James didn't tell you he was out."

"Because James and I did not meet, my lady. I came in through the kitchen door and up the backstairs as I was used to do before—before—last evening, my lady."

"Oh! Well, but you need not come around to the back any longer, Miss Day. Surely, a member of the Bow Street Office—"

"Yes, that's just what I wish to speak with you about, my lady."

"I did speak with a Mr. Donaldson from your office this afternoon. We all of us did. I don't believe there's anything more I can tell you about—"

"I don't think Miss Day has come about Wickens or Lady Dashfield's diary or anything, Mama," Althea offered from her chair beside the cricket table. She set her embroidery stand to the side. "Won't you sit down, Miss Day? We have a great deal for which to thank you."

"Oh! Oh! Yes!" Fleur exclaimed. "I am so very sorry! I annot think where my mind has gone. Do sit down, Miss ʼay. I have not so much as set eyes on you since last evening nd now, to forget to thank you for saving us from Mr. Wick-ns! I am so very embarrassed."

"You've nothing to be embarrassed about, my lady. You ad a very exceptional night last night. Any other woman ʼight well be prostrate and sniffing at her smelling salts ʼery minute or two for the next seven days."

"No, really?" grinned Fleur.

"I expect that's one of the reasons I've come." Miss Day at down on the edge of a chair directly across from Fleur nd smiled her sharp-toothed smile. It flashed so quickly cross the woman's face that Fleur was not altogether certain ʼe had actually seen it.

"There's something I truly wish to speak with you about, ʼy lady. Two things, actually."

"Are they private things?" Althea asked. "Should you like ʼe to leave, Miss Day? No, you need not answer that. There ʼ a volume in which I am particularly interested that has ʼone missing recently. I think I shall go search for it."

"She's a lovely young lady," Miss Day observed as Althea ʼeparted, "and a very intelligent one as well."

"Yes," Fleur agreed. Her fingers played nervously with ʼe corded trim on the arm of the settee. "You are here for ʼwo reasons, Miss Day?"

"I wish you will not call me, Miss Day, in such a tone, ʼy lady. I am still the very same person I was yesterday fternoon and the day before and the day before that."

"Oh, no, you're not. Then you were my abigail, now you're representative of Bow Street."

"True," nodded Miss Day. "And precisely the problem. I ʼon't wish to be a representative of Bow Street any longer, ʼy lady."

"You don't?"

"No, my lady. I came here to ask if you would conside allowing me to remain as your abigail."

"Oh, Jenny, I would love it! But why? Why would you wis to do such a thing? There must be such an enormous differ ence between being Miss Day of the Bow Street Runners an just plain Davis, Lady Marston's abigail. Of course, yo would be Day not Davis," Fleur added, somewhat flustered

"I should like it a good deal more if I could be Jenny, Lad Marston's abigail *and* her friend. If it were possible. I hav never known such a thing to be possible as friendship betwee a lady and her maid, but you're so different from the ladies was used to serving before my entire life was changed by th dreadful Alfred Plummer. And I admire you so very muc And I—I don't know," Miss Day sighed. "I can't explain I just wish to remain with you in some capacity. It need n be as an abigail and a friend. Merely your abigail would su fice. I will just think of you as a friend. No one else nee know. I expect it would be considered quite unacceptable fo an abigail and her lady to actually be friends."

"And who cares what other people think of us? I used t do so, Jenny, but I'm coming to learn that it's not importan at all to live up to the expectations of others. I'm coming t know that it's a great deal better to be true to our own selve and our own expectations. And my own self positively want your own self with me. From now on, you'll be Jenny, m abigail *and* my friend, and neither of us will give a fig fo what anyone else thinks of the arrangement."

Miss Day's sharp-toothed smile did not just flicker acros her face this time. It appeared and grew and remained. " cannot believe I had the audacity to ask such a thing," sh said. "And now I'm so glad that I did! I'll get back to m work at once."

"You said there were *two* things you wished to discus with me, Jenny."

"Yes, well, I—I dread to mention the other, for it isn't a all my business, but I—I thought you should know, my lady.

"Know what?"

"That Montague and Lord Hartshire are one and the same."

"Jenny! How on earth do you come to know about Montague?"

"Well, well, I have b-been watching Wickens, you know, and at the same time, s-standing guard over you, my lady. And one evening I went to report to Mr. Stafford what was occurring on Mr. Wickens's part, because we thought, you know, that he had killed Lady Dashfield. At any rate, I came back to discover you wandering in the garden. Well, I couldn't just stroll into the house right past you, so I hid behind the privy and I saw him come over the garden wall, my lady. Lord Hartshire, I mean. Montague, he called himself."

"Jenny!"

"Well, I could not help but see and hear you. At the time was a—a—spy—of sorts, you know. But that's not the thing. The thing is, he is so in love with you, my lady. Mr. Robes and I spoke of it this morning at Bow Street. You will remember Mr. Robes—"

"Indeed," Fleur nodded. "I do indeed remember Mr. Robes. He is Lord Hartshire's valet who is to come and be introduced to you tomorrow on your half-day."

"Except that we have already met, my lady, for he was the very gentleman who came riding up on Lord Hartshire's horse and pulled you from behind the hackney cab. Oh, but he was wonderful!"

Fleur's eyes lit with considerable interest. "He was?"

"Oh, yes! But that's neither here nor there at the moment. No, what is more important is what Mr. Robes told me about Lord Hartshire, my lady. I do think you ought to know."

On Saturday afternoon, Teweksbury came and took Fleur riding in the park. She chose to ride sidesaddle this time and

he found her delightful regardless. So delightful, in fact, tha
he followed her into the house after their ride and propose

"Me?" Fleur asked in amazement as he knelt down o
one knee before her in the drawing room. "You wish t
marry me, my lord?"

"Yes, indeed. I know that I don't deserve you. I canno
help but remember how badly I treated you when first yo
appeared on Marston's arm—and when you returned t
Town, too. But I hope I have learned a considerable lesso
from it. For now that I've overcome my—my—damnabl
pride—I find you are the most intelligent, fascinating woma
I have ever met. No, don't protest. It's true. You don't realiz
the sort of women I've been pressed into courting since
first came of age. All of them simpering little featherhead
who don't know the first thing about horses."

"Oh, Lord Teweksbury, George, surely I'm not the onl
woman in England who loves horses and knows a thing c
two about them. You have simply not been looking abou
you with the correct attitude."

"Perhaps. But I find I have lost my heart to you, Lad
Marston, Fleur, and I would be honored if you would con
sider spending the rest of your life with me as my wife."

"I am honored, my lord, to think that you have come t
like me to such an extent, but I cannot."

"You cannot?" Lord Teweksbury's face seemed to crum
ple into despair right there before Fleur's eyes. "I have spo
ken too soon, is that it?" he asked. "You don't believe as ye
that I have changed my ways, that my nose has actually low
ered into a proper position, I mean. I vow it has, Fleur.
have changed and I'll prove it to you over and over. Only-
only say that in time, Fleur, I may ask you to marry m
again. Merely say that there is a hope you will change you
mind."

"You are such a dear man," Fleur murmured as he ros
from his knee and sat beside her on the chintz couch in th
morning room. She took his hands into hers and smiled u

t him. "Truly, my lord—George—if my heart were free, I vould be severely tempted to accept your charming offer. But I cannot. My heart already belongs to another."

"It does?"

"Yes, but you must not look so very sad, my dear, because will tell you a great secret that will make the remainder of our life truly happy."

"Without you in my life, I shall never be happy again."

"Oh, what a bouncer! Of course you will, because you're going to find a young lady who will share all of your dearest desires. She'll love horses just as much as you do and most ikely wish to travel with you to each and every breeder you can name."

"Never. There cannot be two of you in all the world."

"And that's the very secret I was going to tell. There are any number of women like me in the world. You must simply ook in the right places—which you haven't been doing. Not at all. I happen to know, for instance, that there is a Miss Snyder-Joylnes currently in search of a hero to whom she may lose her heart completely, and she is extremely fond of horses."

"Miss Snyder-Joylnes? But she's been on the marriage market for years."

"Merely two. But in those two years, you have never once looked her way, have you?"

"Well, no. She's a mere miss after all and I'm—I'm—"

"Yes?"

"A marquess. I'm doing it again, aren't I?"

"Yes. But you can't help yourself, I think. You were born o think in terms of titles and class. What you must learn to do, my dearest George, is to think in terms of individuals. Miss Snyder-Joylnes may be merely the daughter of a baronet, but I think you ought to take time to truly get to know her. You don't so much as realize that her mother despairs of her because the poor girl cannot find a gentleman she loves as much as her horse—which horse, by the way, happens to be a filly from Kelly Farm. You need but speak to her a bit, George. To get to know her a little and perhaps you will find her equally as admirable as you find me. And if not her, then another young lady, someone you come to see as the person she truly is and not as just another eligible connection."

Why could it not have been Atticus kneeling there before me? Fleur thought after dinner that evening as she draped a shawl around her shoulders and wandered out into the garden. Why does he hide away from me now, after all we've been through together? Oh, I know what Robes told Jenny about his thinking himself freakish and most unappealing to women, and I do understand how that could make him come to me in the shadows, to speak to me of love without so much as allowing me to see his face. But certainly he cannot believe that I find him unappealing *now*. Did I not go so far as to brazenly offer myself to him in my chamber that night? He cannot help but know that I love him now. And yet, he does not so much as come to visit me. He sends me a message by way of his brother-in-law that he will meet me at the Haleys' ball. Why? Why? I know he loves me. I know he does. Did he not prove it with such violent passion on Thursday night? Or was I dreaming? Is he truly a spectre—a spectre of my own making?

Fleur longed for him—so much so that she actually wished Ally had not stepped into her chamber that night when Atticus had been so sweetly and ineptly attempting to undo the tabs of her dress. Oh, I must be mad, she thought. To wish such a thing as that. What would he have thought of me had I given myself to him in such a way? Surely he would have doubted my honor, thought me no better than any woman who would sell herself on the street. My boldness offended him and embarrassed him no end, that's what it is. That's why he doesn't come. "He most likely thinks me no better than a lady of the evening."

"Who thinks that?" queried a voice from somewhere in the shadows.

Fleur's heart began to pound with excitement. She spun around in a circle looking for him. "Where are you? Come out at once!"

"No, not yet. I can hear you just fine from here. I want to know who thinks you are no better than a lady of the evening."

"Why?"

"So I can approach him and request the opportunity to put a pistol ball through his despicable heart."

"Oh! Oh, no!" Thoroughly appalled at herself, Fleur nonetheless giggled.

"Ho! You think it amusing, my lady, for one gentleman to kill another?"

"I d-do not. I only th-think it humorous for you to wish to challenge yourself to a duel."

"Me? You were referring to me? But why on earth would I think you no better than a lady of the evening? Have you lost your mind?"

"No. But I am going to lose my temper if you don't come out from wherever you're hiding and stand before me this minute!" Fleur declared.

"Yes, of course you're going to lose your temper. As soon as you cease giggling, I imagine."

"Atticus!"

"Atticus?"

"Yes, *Atticus*. I know perfectly well it's you."

"You cannot. How can you? You're merely guessing. Next you will call me Teweksbury."

"No, I will not. I know it's you, Atticus. I have known it since the day we went to Farley Field."

"And how did you reach such a conclusion, may I ask?"

"I came home and studied the handwriting on your card and on Montague's notes."

"Hah! Any number of gentlemen write alike."

"And yesterday," Fleur said, her ears at last having located him in the shadows, though her eyes still could not. "Yesterday Miss Jenny Day came and confessed to me that she had overheard our entire conversation in this garden while hiding behind the privy. She saw you come over the wall, my dear, and recognized you on the instant. Now do come here to me at once, because there is something I must discuss with you."

"Overheard," he muttered, as the bushes rustled around him. "Hiding behind the privy. Must be related to Will."

Fleur saw him at once as he stepped out of the shadow of the wall and onto the path. Her ears had not misled her. She went to him, meeting him in the very middle of the garden. "Oh, you can be so very aggravating!" she exclaimed, standing on tiptoe to put her arms around his neck. She drew him down to her and kissed him mightily. Then she released him and stomped on his toe. "Now I know what Celeste meant. It is the principle of the thing! You are the most aggravating man and I should be furious with you, but I cannot be!"

Hartshire did not respond. He stood perfectly silent, staring down at her.

"Atticus, what? Why are you looking at me in such a way? Oh, dear, I've hurt your feelings. I did never intend—"

"No, you've not even hurt my toe. I—I—You knew the gentleman who came out of the shadows would be me and you still—What is it you wish to discuss with me?"

"Well, first of all, I should like to know what you're doing here? You couldn't possibly have known that I would wander out into this garden tonight."

"No. I came, ah, on the possibility. I came last night, too, but you didn't stick one toe out here last night. I waited forever and there was no you. So, I thought, possibly tonight—"

Fleur took his hands into hers. "Would it not have been easier, Atticus, to simply knock on the front door and ask to come inside?"

"Yes, but then I would necessarily have been me. There would not have been the least likelihood of my being Montague."

"And what difference would that have made?"

"Well—well—you could have come to love Montague if you hadn't discovered that he and I are one. He ain't some freakish, ugly giant, like me, you know. He's handsome and sophisticated. A regular dandy. He's a good deal more like Tewexbury. At least, he could have been."

"No, he could not. He could not be at all like George."

"You call Tewexbury George now? I—am I to—to wish you happy then?"

"I hope you will wish me happy, Atticus, but not because I have agreed to marry George, for I have not. I sent him on his way only this afternoon. Pointed him in the direction of someone else. A young woman Lady Tate spoke to me about."

"Tewexbury proposed to you and you turned him down? Oh, gawd, I hope you didn't turn him down because of Montague. No, no, you knew I was Montague by then, did you not?"

"I turned him down because my heart belongs to someone else, Atticus."

"It does?"

"Yes, Atticus. It belongs to you."

"No, it can't."

"It can't?" Fleur dropped his hands and placed her own on her hips. "I should like to know why not."

"I mean to say, Fleur, that you—well, you feel an—an obligation of sorts to me. I was stupid not to realize it at first. My only excuse is that I was so overwhelmed by all that happened Thursday night. I ought not to have blurted out that I loved you the way I did. What else could you do after that, after that and the manner in which I kissed you and swept you up and carried you to your bedchamber but—but—Especially when I was bruised and bleeding and wet to the bone. I practically forced you to have pity on me. I almost forced you to give yourself to me on the spot, without so much as realizing I did so. Gad, but I am glad Ally walked in. I don't know that I would have come to my senses else."

"Atticus Charles Howard," Fleur said quietly. "I love you. You. Not some shadow of a Montague. Not George, Lord Tewecksbury. And I don't love you because I am so stupid as to think I'm obliged to, or because I pity you. What is there to pity in you? You're honorable, courageous, intriguing, faithful and kind. You kiss splendidly, too. And when your arms encircle me, when they do, I feel so very, very safe and secure and loved. And if you say one thing about your size—or the size of your ears, which Robes was kind enough to warn Jenny to warn me about, because he knows how you fix your thoughts on them, and most unfairly, too—I will scream so loud that everyone in Cavendish Square will hear me and come running and discover us alone together in this garden. And then, Atticus, you will be obliged by your honor to marry me."

Hartshire smiled. A slow, soft, sad smile in the moonlight. "No need to scream," he whispered, taking her into his arms. "I love you, Fleur. Until tonight I thought my heart would break for loving you and believing I should never have you. To be your friend and nothing more—I could hardly bear the thought of that, but I was willing to settle for it. It's a good deal better than not to be near you at all."

"Nodcock," whispered Fleur, stretching to place a kiss on his chin.

"Will you marry me, Fleur?"

"Without a doubt."

"No matter what?"

"No matter what? What is that supposed to mean? Is it an ominous sort of warning?"

"Exactly. I'm bringing someone to the Haleys' ball to meet you Tuesday night and he's most unacceptable. I may become a regular social outcast the moment I step through the Haleys' door. Will you still marry me?"

Fleur pulled him down to her. "All I can think is that then there will be two social outcasts in the same family," she whispered. And then their lips met, their hearts thrummed with happiness and above them the stars, like comets, streaked through the night sky.

Hartshire gazed down at his son with a considerable mixture of love and anxiety. Well, but Will was fast asleep. No need to worry about explaining things to him at the moment. Besides, the boy liked Fleur. At least he had liked her the one time they'd paid her a visit. "Good night, scoundrel," Hartshire whispered, and placed a kiss on Will's brow.

"Papa?" The clear blue eyes popped open.

"Will? I thought you were asleep. I couldn't possibly have awakened you with such a kiss as that."

"I have been waiting up for you, Papa," Will announced, bouncing up in the bed.

"You have?" Hartshire set the lamp he held on the table and lowered himself to the edge of the mattress. "Why? Has something happened?"

"Yes, Papa! He's here!" the boy replied in a hushed shriek, scrambling out from under the covers and dancing atop the bed. "He's here! He's here! He's here!"

"Shhhhh. You'll wake the entire house. Do get back under the covers and cease bouncing around, Will. Did Mr. Little put him in one of the guest rooms?"

"Uh-huh. In the blue room. To remind him of the sea," whispered Will loudly, burrowing back under the bedclothes. "But Mr. Canton don't like him, Papa."

"Oh. Well, he's not the sort of man people do like straight-away, Will. It takes time to get to know him."

"I don't think Mr. Canton wants to know him. I think they are going to become sworn enemies."

"Never. Mr. Canton ain't French, after all. The French are Chollie's enemies this year."

"Are you certain-sure that Mr. Canton ain't French?"

"Positive. It's merely that Mr. Canton has never met anyone quite like Chollie before. They'll turn out to be the very best of friends in a few days, Will. I promise you."

"You do?"

"Um-hmmm."

"On your honor, Papa? 'Cause I don't want Mr. Canton to leave and I don't want Chollie to leave either."

"Well, but, Chollie's only come for a visit. I doubt he'll stay with us very long."

"I wish he would stay forever."

"I don't."

"You don't?"

"No, because if he stayed forever, we should never get anything useful done, you and I. We'd be forever traipsing around behind him hoping he would tell us another story and another and another. Now go to sleep, rascal. It's very late and I'm tired." Hartshire stood and set about tucking in the bedclothes. He yawned mightily as he did and Will yawned mightily back making them both grin.

"Where were you, Papa?" Will asked.

"I went to visit someone."

"Who?"

"Never mind, Will. Go to sleep."

"Is it a secret?"

"No, it's not a secret. I went to visit Lady Marston."

"Oh. Did you say 'good day' to her?"

"Yes, Will. Now what're you doing?"

"I'm getting out of bed to go mark it down, Papa."

"I just tucked you in."

"But I've got to mark it down or I'll lose count."

"Count of what, Will? No, you stay in that bed. Tell me where your paper is and I'll mark it down when I leave."

"It's in the schoolroom, Papa. It's a piece of your writing paper and it has two marks on it. This will be the third."

"Yes, but what is it you're counting, scoundrel?"

" 'Good days,' Papa."

" 'Good days'?"

"You know. You said 'good day' ninety times to Mama before you married her. That's what you said. So I am keeping count of the number of 'good days' you say to Lady Marston. And when there are ninety of them, you have got to marry her."

Hartshire studied his son intently as the boy wiggled beneath the counterpane. "I cannot marry her until I say it ninety times?"

"Well, that's what you said, Papa."

"Do you like Lady Marston, Will?"

"Exceedingly. An' I wish we didn't have to wait for you to say 'good day' a whole ninety times, Papa, because you are excessively slow at it. If it was me, I should have 'good dayed' her at least thirty times, by now, not just three."

Celeste came, laughing, into Marston House on Tuesday afternoon with a parcel under her arm. "A present for you, my little flower," she announced as she entered the drawing room and discovered Fleur alone. "Miss Avondale has gone off to drive in the park with Conningford, has she?"

"How did you know, Celeste? Come in. Sit down. James, we will have some tea, if you please."

"Yes, madam," the first footman replied and departed for the lower regions.

"Our little Valerian is so in love with that girl that he cannot keep her name from his tongue. No matter where one meets him or what one says, it is always 'Ally did' and 'Ally said' and 'Ally thinks' that tumbles out of Val's mouth."

"Well, don't tell him I said so, Celeste, but I do think Ally is falling in love with him as well. I know she is, though she'll protest against it with every other word. She thinks him absolutely heroic now, you know, with his poor battered chin. I actually caught her batting her eyelashes at the poor boy. She has never done such a thing as that before in he life. What sort of a present?" Fleur added, studying the pack age Celeste had set on the floor beside her chair.

"A gown. I made it for Hartshire."

"For Hartshire?" Fleur giggled.

"Oh, my, not for him to wear! For you to wear for him."

"He asked you to make me a special gown?" Fleu frowned.

"No, no, he knows nothing of it. It is my idea. He ha confided in me that you will marry him. You will not regre marrying Hartshire, I assure you. But this gown—this gown is the most beautiful gown I have ever thought to create an it will make Hartshire's heart come bubbling right out hi nose!"

"Oh no! I don't think I'd like to see that, Celeste."

"No, no, perhaps not. But you will like to see the aw that will fill those marvelous eyes of his once he sees yo in this gown. He will likely be forced to run for a specia license and marry you before the night is out, so filled witl desire will he be. Of course, he will be forced to fight any number of other men to get to you, but he will. Hartshire will fight anyone he must to get to you, I am certain of it."

Celeste reached down, picked up the package, set it or her lap and began to unwrap it. The gown that emerged wa: the very color of Hartshire's eyes. Silk so blue as to be nearly black with shots of silver shimmering through it and to ac company it, an underdress of a stunning silver material Fleu had never seen before in her life.

"It's like his eyes, no?" laughed Celeste. "Hartshire wil not realize, of course. Of all the things he sees about him self—all of which he detests—he does never take note o his very beautiful eyes. But these colors. Oh, how he loves these colors. I made a pelisse for his sweet Miriam once jus these colors, and Hartshire kept her outside for hours and hours merely so that she would not take it off. This dress my little flower, is stitched with the splendor of the stars in the midnight sky, with a universe of hopes and dreams, with the shadow and the ecstasy. I've stitched into it everything that our Hartshire is made of."

Fleur stood alone on the Haleys' balcony staring out at the little faery lights that winked below in the garden. She took a deep breath and then she laughed. "To think, I'm hiding from people because they *wish* to speak to me," she said softly to herself. "What a wonder it is for one's reputation to be called a heroine in the London newspapers."

Of course, I'm no such thing, she thought. I did nothing that any other woman wouldn't do for those she loved. It is merely that the situation arose where I had the unfortunate opportunity to have to do it.

When in heaven's name does he think to arrive? she wondered then. Mr. and Mrs. Haley have deserted the welcome line. I've danced five sets and Althea seven and still Atticus is nowhere to be seen. If he doesn't arrive soon, I shan't have a chance to dance with him at all. And I should so like to dance with him!

"Mama! Mama! Come inside at once," Ally called, stepping out onto the balcony. "Lord Hartshire has arrived and you will not believe who he's brought with him. I cannot believe it and I have been staring at the man for a full five minutes!"

"Staring at a man for a full five minutes? Ally, who on earth?" Fleur crossed the balcony and stepped back into the ballroom to discover that the music had ceased to play and a great circle of people had gathered in the middle of the floor.

"He's in the very center of this crowd, Mama. All of them are."

"All of whom, Ally?" asked Fleur standing on tiptoe in an attempt to see over the people in front of her but finding herself very unsuccessful at it.

"Lord Hartshire, Lord Teweksbury, Val, Malcolm, even the Prince Regent. The Prince Regent came to Mrs. Haley's ball. Can you believe it, Mama? Mrs. Haley is utterly ecstatic. She was so ecstatic at first, in fact, that she didn't even notice *him*. Though how she could not, I don't know, because I noticed him the very moment he stuck his nose in at the door."

And then the crowd began to move and both Fleur and Ally had to dodge quickly back to keep from getting stepped on.

The orchestra began to play again; the merrily buzzing crowd parted and there at the very center of the dance floor stood Hartshire, the Prince Regent and the most extraordinary man Fleur had ever seen.

Hartshire looked up to see her standing at the end of what seemed a wide path bordered with people instead of flowers, and his eyes glowed so deeply, so fully, that Fleur could see the change in them from where she stood. He took a step in her direction, paused, took another, paused again.

"So that be the bit of a gel has won yer scurvy heart, eh, laddie?" The voice absolutely boomed out and around the ballroom, setting any number of people to laughing. "Aye, but she be a prize, that one!" And then the man came walking straight toward Fleur and Ally. "Interduce me, Hartshire," he demanded as he halted before them.

He was a short, muscular man with black mustachios that curled upward on each side of his nose almost out to his ears. He had a round face with slanted eyes as deep and brown as newly plowed soil and his head was as devoid of hair as a duck egg. He was dressed in wide gold pantaloons tied at the ankles, gold heelless slippers, a collarless scarlet shirt of the finest silk with a gold silk scarf tied negligently around his neck. And atop the shirt, in the most quizzical manner, he sported what looked to be a puce riding coat belonging to Hartshire who just then came walking up with the Prince Regent.

Hartshire's gaze lingered for an eternity on the vision Fleur presented in Celeste's magnificent creation. He licked his lips slowly, caught his lower lip between his teeth, made a soft hissing sound. And then he groaned and doubled over as a very muscular arm whopped him across the stomach. "I said interduce me, Hartshire, and interduce Prinny, too. Can't leave Prinny out."

Hartshire's eyes filled with laughter as he straightened. "Lady Marston, Miss Avondale, may I present Captain Jung Kaow, at the moment of the British privateers. And of course, our Prince Regent."

Both gentlemen bowed. The Prince took Ally's hand and placed a kiss on the back of it. Jung Kaow did the same for Fleur, except he did not let go of her hand, instead he began to walk back across the dance floor toward the balcony. Fleur gazed in puzzlement at Hartshire. He merely smiled and nodded, so she allowed the man to lead her from the room. Well, but what else was she to do? Fight him off in the midst of a ballroom filled with people? Out they went. Out onto the dark balcony where the faery lights twinkled in the garden below. Then he turned, put one hand on each of her shoulders and leaned down to stare into her eyes.

"Aye, they be as sweet an' innercent as he says. Has the damndest luck, that lad!"

"Wh-what?" stuttered Fleur.

"An' ye be wearin' m'beads!" exclaimed Kaow. "Well, shiver me timbers if that ain't a sight, them moldy old beads atop sich temptin' silk gloves."

"You're Hartshire's pirate!" gasped Fleur.

Jung Kaow roared into laughter. "Hartshire's pirate, be I? Should like ta see the day I belong to sich as Hartshire!"

"No, I didn't mean you belonged to him precisely."

"I know what ye meant, m'pretty. I only be a teasin' of ye a bit. My but that boy do love ye. Here he comes a stompin' m' way already. Begone, Hartshire! Ain't no one summoned ye."

"One more look at Fleur like the one I just saw and you be the one who's gone, Chollie. Right over that railing."

"Ye think ye kin, do ye?"

"Can and will."

"Atticus!"

"No, no, m'dear, he be only funnin' with me, yer Atticu I have comed ta meet ye an' ta bring ye somethin'." Kao reached into a pocket which was obviously somewhere his voluminous pantaloons and brought out a small bundl This he carefully unwrapped to display the most beautiful painted glass beads on the palm of his hand. "I has brougl ye these, m'lady, on Hartshire's behalf. Take them old thing offa 'er, Hartshire. Ought ta be ashamed of y'self givin' ' sich worn old beads."

"Oh, no!" Fleur protested. "No, these are the beads l first gave me when I was ill. And they have kept me fro the illness ever since. I would not dream to part with them!

"Ain't goin' ta part with 'em, m'gel. Goin' ta give 'em Hartshire ta wear fer ye, whilst ye display these lovel gems."

"But—but—I would rather have these."

"You can't have those," grinned Hartshire, taking ther gently from her, one wrist at a time, and replacing them wi the ones from Kaow's palm. "I asked Chollie to have thes made especially for you."

"Yes, but, Atticus, these are the very first gift you eve gave me."

"Um-hmmm, and you may keep them forever, but I'm th one who'll be wearing them, else we shall have to take ou wedding trip without a coach."

"Our wedding trip?"

"Didn't think about that, did you? But once we're marrie we shall have to take a trip to somewhere or we shan't hav a moment alone, Fleur, not with Will and Marston and All and Val and quite possibly, from what I've seen tonight, Lad

...lia, always underfoot. Speaking of which—Chollie, I thank ...ou, but at the moment you are definitely underfoot."

...Kaow chuckled, tickled Fleur under the chin, for which ...artshire swatted him, and left them alone.

"You look positively ravishing in that gown. Did I tell you ...at?" Hartshire asked, leading her to the rail to gaze out ...ver the gardens, wrapping his arms around her from behind ...d resting his chin on her head. "I don't know how it can ...e possible, Fleur, but every time I see you, I love you more. ...have promised to tell you something tonight."

"About Marston. About his involvement in all of that ...readful mess."

"Just so. You will not care, Fleur. I promise you will not, ...ecause you will forget all about Marston in a moment or ...vo."

"Tell me, Atticus. If there is something I can do to repair ...ny hurtful things he may have done—"

"Marston and Dashfield were compatriots of a sort. They ...aved Alfred Plummer's life, hoping to use him and Thomas ...pence's followers to gain significant power in Lords. But ...en Lady Dashfield and your husband became lovers."

"He—Marston—loved her?"

"Well, I expect as much as he knew how to love. And ...hen Dashfield discovered the two of them together, he ...reatened to kill Lydia."

"Oh no!"

"Well, Marston would not have that. He took Lydia's diary ...nd hid it away. He put with it a map of all the meeting ...laces used by the Spenceans in London, and he wrote a list ...f names of radical leaders. Then he blackmailed Dashfield ...nd the others. Threatened to reveal Plummer's existence and ...ll the rest. They killed him, Fleur. Alfred Plummer himself ...hoved Marston into the way of that team."

"Oh, Hartshire. I never imagined, never once, that—"

"Months later, Lady Dashfield discovered what they'd ...one and she, being a bit birdwitted, declared to Dashfield's

face that she was going to go directly to Bow Street and sp
everything she knew."

"Who—who killed her?"

"Dashfield. In a rage. And with poor Jenny Day right
the house spying for the Runners but not able to prove
thing, and not knowing herself but what Wickens had kill
the lady and not Dashfield at all. Well, then you and Al
decided to come to London. Malcolm opened the house a
hired servants, and Dashfield sent Wickens directly to yo
door. The rest, of course, you know."

"Yes," murmured Fleur. "The rest I know."

"And now," whispered Hartshire in her ear, "I'm goi
to help you to forget it all." He turned her about, lifted h
to a seat on the balcony rail and kissed her with comple
abandon for a full two minutes. Then he paused to catch h
breath, grinned down at her like a regular gudgeon and sai
"Good day, Lady Marston. Good day, Lady Marston. Goo
day, Lady Marston." Then he kissed her again until both
them ran out of breath, recovered himself and said, "Goo
day, Lady Marston. Good day, Lady Marston. Good da
Lady Marston."

"Atticus, whatever are you *doing?*" Fleur giggled.

"I'm saying good day to you, my lady. And I'm going
say it to you at least eighty-one more times before the nig
is out!"